Buried Heart

A **COURT OF FIVES** NOVEL

KATE ELLIOTT

LITTLE, BROWN AND COMPANY
New York · Boston

Little, Brown and Company
Hachette Book Group
1290 Avenue of the Americas, New York, NY 10104
Visit us at lb-teens.com

First Edition: July 2017

Little, Brown and Company is a division of Hachette Book Group, Inc. The Little, Brown name and logo are trademarks of Hachette Book Group, Inc.

The publisher is not responsible for websites (or their content) that are not owned by the publisher.

Library of Congress Cataloging-in-Publication Data
Names: Elliott, Kate, 1958– author.
Title: Buried heart : a Court of Fives novel / Kate Elliott.
Description: First edition. | New York : Little, Brown and Company, 2017. | Summary: "Jessamy is at the crux of a revolution forged by the Commoner class hoping to overthrow their longtime Patron overlords, but when enemies from foreign lands attack the kingdom, she must find a way to defend their home and all the people she loves, Efean and Saroese alike"— Provided by publisher.
Identifiers: LCCN 2016049233| ISBN 9780316344418 (hardcover) | ISBN 9780316344401 (ebook) | ISBN 9780316344449 (library edition ebook)
Subjects: | CYAC: Social classes—Fiction. | Sisters—Fiction. | Revolutions—Fiction. | Racially mixed people—Fiction. | Fantasy.
Classification: LCC PZ7.1.E45 Bur 2017 | DDC [Fic]—dc23
LC record available at https://lccn.loc.gov/2016049233

ISBNs: 978-0-316-34441-8 (hardcover), 978-0-316-34440-1 (ebook)

Printed in the United States of America

LSC-C

10 9 8 7 6 5 4 3 2 1

Tandi
Sea

Fire Sea

Oyia

Marsh Shore

WEST SARO

Saryenia

Maldine

Gem
Gardens

Reed Shore

Heyeng

SARO-
UROK

EFEA

Sand
Desert

EAST
SARO

Eastern Reach

Pellucidar
Lake

Rift Sea

n

N
S

The
Great Eye

Sand Desert

Akheres
Oasis

Bone
Escarpment

Crags
Fort

Pellucidar
Lake

Port
Selene

Green River

Eastern Reach

Seperens

RIFT SEA

EAST SARO

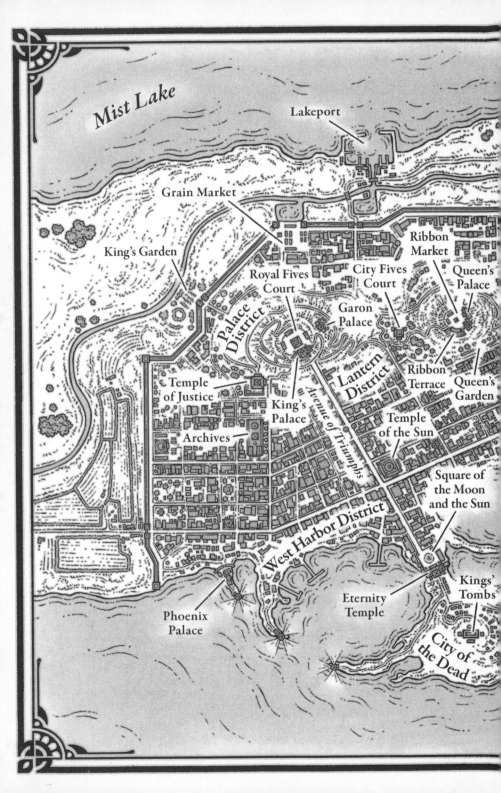

Warrens

Scorpion
Fountain

Capt. Esladas's
House

Avenue of the Soldier

East Harbor District

N

S

SARYENIA

Fire Sea

ᴍS

1

I stand poised on the shore of Mist Lake like an adversary gathering focus before a Fives trial. South across the waters, too far away to see from here, lies the city of Saryenia, from which we just escaped. A rhythmic sound drifts out of the dawn haze that obscures the horizon: the drums of a fast-moving war galley.

"Do you hear that?" I say. "The new king is already hunting us."

The boat I arrived in rocks wildly as its two occupants—Lord Kalliarkos and the poet Ro-emnu—jump out onto land and scramble up to either side of me. Kal takes my hand, the touch of his skin a promise against mine, and gives me a smile that makes my heart leap. Ro glances over, gaze flicking down to our entwined fingers, and looks away with a frown.

"We've got to get you out of sight," I say to Kal, reluctantly shaking loose from his grip. "And get my mother to safety where your uncle can never find her."

My mother has already disembarked. We are the last people out of the flotilla of now-empty rowboats in which our party fled the murderous new king. Surrounded by local Efean villagers, Mother is speaking to them with such an appearance of calm dignity that no one would ever guess how desperate our circumstances are. As the three of us run over, the villagers leave her and race past us to the shore, carrying baskets and fishing nets. They shove the boats back out onto the water.

"Are they abandoning us?" I ask as we rush up to Mother.

"Not at all, Jessamy. They are risking their lives to aid us."

"By fishing?"

Ro breaks in with his usual needling. "The sight of Efeans hard at work to enrich Patron treasuries always lulls our Saroese masters."

"By placing their own bodies between us and the soldiers," Mother goes on. "It isn't only military men wielding swords who defend the land and act with courage."

I look back again, viewing the scene on the lake with new eyes. "That's very brave, especially since they're unarmed."

"Doma Kiya, we need to get moving to the shelter of the trees," says Kal to Mother, offering her a polite bow with hand pressed to heart.

Although his words and tone are courteous, Mother's usually gentle expression stiffens into a stony-eyed mask. "I can see that for myself, my lord," she snaps.

Kal is taken aback by her hostility, and so am I.

Irritation and impatience clip off my tongue. "He's helping us!"

Kal looks from my mother to me and, still with his courteous voice, says, "I'll scout ahead to make sure my uncle isn't lying in wait in the trees to capture you."

He races away while we follow at a brisk walk. Mother holds my infant brother, Wenru, while, beside her, my friend and former Fives stablemate Mis carries Wenru's twin sister, Safarenwe. All the other Efeans have either gone out onto the lake or have left to escort the wagons conveying the fugitive Patrons of Garon Palace, who own this estate and its surrounding villages.

"Maybe the soldiers will pass by," I say with another anxious look toward the lake. The shape of a mast coalesces in the mist. Oars beat the water in unison as the warship speeds toward us.

"Seeing only dull Commoner fishermen and farmers, not bold conspirators who just rescued the new king's rivals from certain death," murmurs Ro.

"Don't speak of such matters in front of Lord Kalliarkos, Ro-emnu," says Mother, with a warning glance at me.

"Kal won't—"

"Enough, Jessamy. Keep moving." Her tone scalds.

Kal waves an all clear from the edge of the orchard and ducks out of sight before the war galley can get close enough to spot his Saroese features and clothing. The fig and pomegranate trees aren't particularly tall but they are bushy enough to conceal us. As the others push forward on a wagon track through the trees, I pause to look back one last time.

While most of the rowboats have dispersed out onto the water, six have made a rough circle with a large net between them, blocking the approach to the shoreline where we landed. But the galley cuts straight through the little flotilla. Two of the boats flip, and the others rock wildly as their occupants struggle to keep them from overturning. Oars slap the heads of people in the water to jeers from the oarsmen. Arrows streak out from the deck. Most splash harmlessly into the water but one strikes a hapless swimmer in the back. The armed men crowded on the deck shout excitedly and laugh as the victim's head sinks beneath the surface. It's a game to them.

The drumbeat ceases. The galley plows through a stand of reeds with a rattle of noise before dragging to a stop in the shallows exactly where we just disembarked.

A man steps up to the rail of the ship.

It is the new king himself, once Prince General Nikonos and now the man who murdered his older brother and innocent young nephew so he could seize the throne of Efea. From this distance I can't fully distinguish his face although I know he resembles Kal in having regal features and a golden-brown complexion; they're cousins, after all.

Nikonos calls out in the voice of a man used to shouting over the din of battle. "The Garon estate lies beyond the trees! The man who brings the corpse of Lord Kalliarkos or Lord Gargaron to me I will raise to become a lord! As for the rest of the Garon household and any who shelter them, show no mercy to traitors!"

I sprint after the others. Thorns from the pomegranate branches scrape my arms. Mother has been jogging along at the rear but she slows to a halt, puffing as she struggles to catch her breath. The others stop too, Mis supporting Mother with a hand under her elbow.

I charge up. "It's Nikonos himself. Right on our heels."

"Honored Lady, I'll take the baby to lighten your burden," says Ro.

To my consternation—because I should have asked first—Mother hands Wenru over to the poet. After a moment of disgruntled squirming, my infant brother settles into Ro's arms with an expression of unbabyish disgust.

The sounds of snapping branches and men cursing at thorns chase us onward as the soldiers push through the trees. We emerge at a run from the orchard and hurry through grain fields toward the stately roofs and walls of the main compound, built for the Saroese stewards who supervise the estate with its rich fields, groves, and fishing. A path lined by trees leads to the northeast, toward an Efean village.

"Shouldn't we head toward the village?" I whisper urgently.

"My grandmother always keeps an escape plan in reserve," says Kal. "There's a merchant galley hidden in a backwater river channel beyond the northern fields for just such an emergency as this. She and the rest of the household should already be boarding it."

"In other words," remarks Ro, because he just can't stop himself, "you Saroese nobles expect at any moment to be murdered by your own relatives."

Kal touches my arm as a warning not to bother answering. "This way," he says in a tone like an echo of my military father, a reminder that Kal fought a campaign in the desert and commanded a squad of spider scouts.

We splash through a shallow irrigation canal and race across another stretch of fields.

"Do you visit here often?" I ask in a low voice, sticking beside him.

"Twice a year with my grandmother. When I was a boy I would play on the hidden ship and pretend I was a sailor on the high seas."

I grin at this innocent memory. Without breaking stride, he bumps a shoulder against mine, just a tap. Despite the danger we're in, it's exhilarating to keep pace together, feet hitting the ground in perfect time.

Mudbrick reservoirs rise at the end of cultivated land and the beginning of marshier ground where bushy-headed papyrus sways over our heads. Fresh wagon tracks in the earth mark where the Garon fugitives passed only moments ago, so it's with shock that we emerge onto the bank of a backwater river channel to find the dock empty.

The merchant galley is gone.

Except for an embroidered blue silk shawl fluttering in the branches of a sycamore, there's no trace of the Garon household; of Kal's grandmother, Princess Berenise; his sister, Lady Menoë; his uncle Lord Gargaron; nor any of the fifty relatives and retainers who escaped with us out of Saryenia. Nothing except three village rowboats bumping against the pilings with neatly folded fishing nets inside, and the two abandoned wagons.

"How could they have left without me?" says Kal, a hand on his neck like he's trying to stem the bleeding from having his throat cut.

We stare, all too stunned to ask the same question. Safarenwe gives a fussing cry, and Mother takes her from Mis, soothing her with kisses. Wenru remains uncannily silent in Ro's arms.

Mis points back the way we came. "Look!"

We turn. Shock tightens to a new stab of fear. Threads of smoke rise in the distance. They thicken to columns and then boil up into fierce black clouds.

Nikonos's soldiers are burning the estate.

2

The tops of papyrus start thrashing: soldiers following our trail.

"I found fresh wagon tracks!" a man shouts in Saroese.

Kal and I instantly scan our surroundings. The channel has been dredged along the steeper bank to give enough draft for a galley to dock, while the other bank is a shallow marshland choked with reeds. We glance at each other with a flash of shared understanding.

"I can swim underwater to hide in the reeds," he says.

I nod. "We'll pretend to fish in the boats."

He doesn't protest that we'll become targets while he hides. We both know this is the only way. I grab his wrist and, even with my mother right there, give him a quick kiss as a promise.

If his gaze slides to meet Ro's in challenge, it happens so

fast I am sure I have mistaken it. But then Ro says, as if in retort, "Don't you fear crocodiles, Kal?"

"The ones on two feet are sure to kill me, so I'll take my chances."

He slips into the water, vanishing without sound or splash. I run to the end of the dock and yank the shawl out of the branches so our pursuers won't guess that Patron women have passed by here. By the time I race back, Mis and Ro, with Safarenwe, are already rowing away as Mother, holding Wenru, waits for me.

We push off. Mother gives Wenru to me and takes the oars. She handles them with an adeptness that surprises me until I remember she grew up in a rustic village far from sophisticated Saryenia. Wenru clutches at my vest like he's afraid I'm going to toss him overboard. A pair of ducks flutters up noisily from deep within the reeds. I can't see Kal from here but he must have surfaced and startled them. The thrashing in the papyrus comes closer as men shout, having heard the quacking. Ahead of us, Ro and Mis glide behind a thick stand of reeds. We're too far behind to have a hope of concealing ourselves.

Mother stops rowing and takes up a net as five soldiers burst into view and stamp out onto the dock. She flips out the net, which flares like a flower blooming, strikes the water, and sinks. The movement draws their attention.

"Hey, Sergeant! Let's catch some Efean delicacies for our supper," calls one, his accent that of a man from overseas, not a locally born Patron.

I hate the way they stare at us as if they are hungry and we are food. If only I could slam my oar into their ugly faces.

Mother whispers, "By no sign show you can understand them."

Wenru stirs, stout infant legs shoving against my chest as he twists around to look their way. He sucks in a breath, prelude to a scream.

In Saroese I snap, "You should be ashamed of yourself, you little rat."

Our gazes lock. His face is as brown as my own, and his eyes so black they are shadows dropped into his heart. A flicker of irritation passes across his face, and I'm once again sure that an unknown self resides in my dead brother's body.

I lower my voice to a whisper that brushes his perfect little ear. "I know you aren't what you seem, but to Saroese soldiers you look like an ordinary Efean baby. They will throw you into the river to drown. If you betray my mother, I will pin you to the dirt and let the vultures eat you alive."

Mother is staring at me, eyes wide. But the net twitches, distracting her, and she briskly hauls in two fish.

From out of sight a man calls, "Here's mule tracks, Sergeant! Someone went this way with animals, maybe the ones used to haul the wagons."

"You two!" The sergeant points to the man who was just insulting us and his nearest companion. "Bring in those women for questioning."

"But Sergeant, they say the rivers here are infested with monsters that eat people."

"Use the boat. You others, follow me."

He and two other soldiers hurry off on a track that leads behind the crowds of willow and sycamore shading the opposite bank. The two remaining soldiers, arguing with each other in the tone of very nervous men, climb into the boat.

"Switch with me." I thrust Wenru into Mother's arms, the boat rocking as we change places. "I need my hands free."

"What do you intend?"

"I don't know yet."

I row as Mother uses the shawl to sling Wenru to her hip. I'm not as skilled, so the oars skip over the water a couple of times. The soldiers gain on us. We skim past a clump of reeds into a backwater overhung by trees, where Mis and Ro have paused to wait for us.

I gesture at them to keep rowing upriver. Something large in the water passes beneath us and rocks the hull of our boat. I'm so startled I yelp out loud. Beyond the reeds, the soldiers shout in excitement; they think I'm scared of them, and that's true too.

A hand emerges from the water to tap the side of our boat, then Kal's head emerges. He gulps air.

I murmur, "Two soldiers in a boat behind us. No one else in sight. They're scared of crocodiles."

"Distract them." He dives.

I turn the boat and start back the way we came.

"Jessamy, we should follow Ro-emnu and Missenshe, not expose ourselves like this for some reckless plan."

"Father trained him. Kal knows what he's doing."

The soldiers have come up so fast it takes only three strokes for us to skim past their bow.

"Good Goat!" One laughs. "The luscious fruit drops into our laps."

Reaching for our boat, they don't notice Kal launch out of the water on their boat's other side. He grabs the gunwale with both hands and uses his weight to tip them.

Alone he can't overturn it, but I shout, in Saroese, "Crocodile!"

Their panic and flailing does the rest. The boat goes over with a huge splash. One man goes under and never comes back up, while his comrade churns the murky water with his arms, struggling to keep afloat in his stiff leather armor. I slam an oar down, clip the side of his head, then slam it down again, stunning him momentarily.

He goes under, dragged down as if by a mauling crocodile. Thrashing disturbs the water. Bubbles fleck the surface, staining it red. I balance in the boat, an oar in my hand, ready to strike. I'm breathing so hard I can't catch my breath.

A head breaks the surface: Kal, alive, expression grim and yet satisfied. A body bobs up briefly, then rolls over to flash the dead man's slack face before the heavy leather armor drags him under. Kal grabs the gunwale of our boat and tosses his sword in. The blade gleams, already washed clean by the river water. He dives under twice more, retrieving the soldiers' swords, then mires their boat in the reeds so it can't be seen from the shore.

"May the blessings of the Mother of All give mercy to the living and the dead," Mother whispers.

She and I throw our weight to the opposite side as Kal hauls himself up and over the gunwale, flopping gracelessly atop the now-tangled net. He's dressed in the clothes of a laborer, and the cloth of his keldi—the knee-length skirt Efean men wear—is plastered to his muscular thighs. I glance away, only to find Mother examining me with a frown.

As we drift out from under the overhanging branches of a giant sycamore, Kal straightens up. The stark sunlight gilds his face, making him look like a hero on the stage despite his dripping-wet clothes and bedraggled hair. His grave expression fixes on me, but there's a wild light in his eyes that unsettles me and yet also sets my heart pounding.

Hoarsely he says, "Ask me again when we're safe, Jes."

My cheeks flush as if I've been burned. He said those same words when we escaped Garon Palace with his uncle, when we caught a moment alone in a secret passage to kiss in a way I have never kissed anyone before.

Was that only last night?

Mother taps my arm as if she's angry. With *me*. "Jessamy! We must get out of here. The others will come looking for their comrades."

Irritated by her unrelenting hostility to Kal, I start rowing after Mis and Ro, who are now out of sight around a bend in the channel. Smoke billows up in the distance, accompanied by shouts from the searching soldiers. A bird whistle pulls my head around.

"There," says Mother.

Ro is waving at us from partway up a tree. I maneuver the boat in beneath branches. We rustle through bulrushes and bump up against the other boat, which is tied to a post in a hidden inlet. Three Efean sentries armed with sickles help us out onto the bank, paying particular attention to Mother, whom they address as Honored Lady. Kal greets each by name, and it's clear they know who he is from his occasional visits to the estate and aren't surprised that he recognizes them.

Ro tests the heft of the captured swords. "How did you get these?"

"The crocodiles took their tax," I say, hoping to get Kal to smile, but his grim expression doesn't lighten.

Ro makes a fist of his hand and bumps the side of Kal's fist in a gesture Efean men make with each other. "Well done."

The unexpected mark of respect startles a grin out of Kal after all.

"Thank you for saving our lives, Lord Kalliarkos," I say with a meaningful glance at Mother.

"Your quick thinking served us well, my lord," says Mother, finally sounding more like the gracious, accommodating woman I grew up with than like this angry, mistrustful person I don't recognize.

"My thanks, Honored Lady," says Kal cautiously.

But she's not done. "We must also thank the honored poet, Ro-emnu, for arranging our passage out of Saryenia. It was astoundingly well managed, especially with so many people to transport in secrecy."

"My thanks, Honored Lady," Ro murmurs with downcast eyes, and spoils the pretense of humility with a sidelong look at me, making sure I've heard my mother praise him.

Kal says, "I hope you know how indebted Garon Palace is to you, Ro."

"I do know."

An awkward silence follows.

I catch Mis's eye, and she comes to the rescue by handing over one of the bundles she's carrying. "Here's your Fives gear, Jes. Darios grabbed it when they evacuated Garon Stable. Now what? We can't hide here."

"That's right," I agree. "Nikonos isn't going to give up searching. Is there a plan?"

One of the sentries says, "We were sent by General Inarsis to look for the honored lady and bring her to shelter."

Instead of waiting for Kal's order, which he normally would give as one of the Patron masters of the estate, all five Efeans look to Mother, who nods agreement. If Kal is offended at being bypassed he gives no sign of it. We leave one of the swords with the two sentries remaining on guard at the inlet. The third leads us along a concealed path through a tangle of overgrown vegetation. Of course, despite our frantic situation,

Mother has brought the two fish in a basket, just as if we are returning home with our night's supper to a happy family.

I blink back tears, remembering the days when we four sisters would sit in the courtyard at dusk as Mother embroidered: Amaya writing poetry and practicing speeches from plays, Bettany muttering about injustice and hypocrisy while her sisters ignored her, me counting the moments until I could escape to run the Fives, and Maraya studying for the Archives exam she hoped to take one day.

"Where are Maraya and Polodos?" I ask in Efean, with a glance at Wenru. He's looking around as if he's trying to figure out where we are and where we are going.

"They stayed in Saryenia at the Least-Hill Inn. That way they can listen to the gossip of foreign soldiers and pass on intelligence."

"As spies? That's dangerous."

"We are all fugitives now, Jessamy. We are in danger no matter where we are. Anyway, you said Bettany and Amaya are on their way to the city by ship."

"Yes." I'm not yet ready to break her heart by telling her what really happened with Bettany.

"So Maraya will be there to shelter them when they arrive." She pauses, then goes on sternly. "Was calling your baby brother a little rat your idea of a jest? Because I am not laughing."

Nothing is worse than Mother's disapproval but I don't know how to explain my suspicions or whether she'll believe me.

"Don't think I didn't notice that you spoke to Wenru in Saroese rather than Efean. I've raised enough children to know his behavior is unusual and even at moments disconcerting."

We plod along, her expectant silence as she waits for my reply like a hand tugging insistently on my arm. What if I don't warn her that her infant son is actually dead, and whoever resides in his body has a chance to betray her because she's not on her guard? To protect her, I have to try.

So I say, in Saroese, "There's a huge poisonous snake about to drop out of the trees right onto your heads."

Wenru's head snaps back in fear, but Mother has heard the lie in my voice. Her gaze stays on the baby and his slow confusion as he realizes what I've just done. He tucks his head down as if he wishes he could turn into a turtle with a shell to hide in, and then says, "Ba ba ba" in the most unbabylike voice.

Mother stares at him as if he has turned into a snake. In Efean she says, "Jessamy, what is going on?"

Our guide raises a hand for silence. Concealed by a stand of trees, we look across well-kept gardens to an empty Efean village.

The guide murmurs, "Move fast and keep your heads down."

We dash along a wagon track that takes us into the center of the village, where stands a simple Fives court. I hear soldiers speaking Saroese, their voices far too close, and I gesture toward the gate into Pillars, thinking we can hide in the maze. But a burly, threatening man steps out from behind that very gate, sword drawn, to halt us in our tracks.

3

"Kiya! I was afraid we'd lost you." The man facing us presses a hand to his heart. The intensity of his gaze on my mother disturbs me.

"Inarsis! There you are at last," Mother gasps in evident relief.

He glances toward the rising voices of foreign soldiers entering the village. "Follow me."

We head in the opposite direction, trotting past a row of granaries toward the northern edge of the village. Inarsis opens a closed gate, and we slip into a walled garden that encloses a tiled pool and neat herb and flower beds. Months ago I bathed here with my Fives trainer Tana and my stablemates Mis and Dusty, amid a friendly gathering of Efean villagers. Now an Efean woman emerges from a stand of lush rhododendrons, carrying a staff as a weapon.

Scowling, she addresses Inarsis in Efean, a language Kal does not understand. "Him too, General? All of *them* were meant to go on the ship."

"He fell behind." Inarsis looks at me as if it's my fault.

The woman looks at me too. She says, "Ah, I see," and steps aside.

Behind the thick screen of bushes, a brick-lined tunnel plunges under the wall. We climb down into an underground storage pit crammed with children, elders, and sealed jars of oil and baskets of grain.

"Hidden from the Garon tax collectors," says Kal.

At the sound of his voice, every head turns. People stare at him. Tension thickens the air, and blades glint as they brace to attack.

"Is that you, Doma Henta?" With his perfect highborn manners, Kal bows over the hand of an elderly woman as if she is an exalted Patron lady. Of course he's speaking Saroese, which most Efeans can understand. "I see you are keeping a share of your crops out of the hands of the Garon treasury, just as we hide a portion of our harvest from the royal tax collectors."

I hear a few chuckles, and people lower their knives.

"Come along." Inarsis has the same habit of command as Father, honed on the battlefield. The only Commoner ever to be granted the rank of general in the Royal Army, he has served Garon Palace for years, a loyal servant of Kal's royal grandmother, Princess Berenise.

I make sure to fall in behind Kal, keeping a hand on his back. The cloth of his vest is still wet, but the heat off his skin seeps through to warm my palm. When we pause for Inarsis to speak to sentries guarding an opening to another underground storage chamber, Kal slips an arm around my shoulders and pulls me close. He's on edge, practically bouncing on his toes. The darkness gives us a freedom we've never had out under the sun. I take the chance to touch my lips to his. He tightens his arm around me and returns the kiss. The heat of our connection burns every other thought out of my head, but he pulls away with what seems like shocking abruptness as Inarsis moves on. Yet he doesn't let go of my hand.

He speaks into the darkness. "General Inarsis, can we fight them? We have a chance to ambush Nikonos and kill him."

"I thought you did not want to be king," says Ro from behind us, his tone as stinging as the scrapes the pomegranate thorns have left on my skin.

"Of course I don't."

"Of course he doesn't! Hasn't he said so often enough?" It makes me so angry that both Mother and Ro act suspicious of him when he's done nothing but help us. "I saw Nikonos murder Prince Temnos. His own innocent nephew. A child! We can't let a man like that rule."

Ignoring me, Inarsis says coolly, "My lord, we can't take the chance of attacking Nikonos. His soldiers have the armor and weapons that we lack."

"But his soldiers are spread out, searching in smaller

groups, so they're vulnerable," I object. "Nikonos won't expect an attack from Efeans. It might work."

Kal squeezes my hand.

"I did not ask your opinion about military matters, Spider." By Inarsis's curt tone, I can tell I have offended him. Worse, Mother does not defend me. Her silence is its own rebuke.

We hurry forward until we enter an ancient vault lined with stone. There's a crack in the roof where a vine's tendril has grown down, giving just enough light to see. Mis takes Wenru from Mother and sits on an old stone bench with a baby on each leg.

Inarsis gestures, indicating the abandoned space. "My lord, my best advice is to conceal you here until we're sure all the soldiers have moved on. Then I will personally escort you by a different route upriver to meet your people at Furnace Gate, where I have agreed to rendezvous with them."

When I glance at Kal, he nods as if he already guesses what I mean to say. That's all the encouragement I need. "The soldiers searching for us wore hawk badges. That means they are from East Saro. Why would Nikonos bring in a detachment of foreign soldiers to occupy Saryenia when, now that he has made himself king, he has a Royal Army that is the equal of any in the world?"

Inarsis answers me. "Because the Royal Army is currently in the Eastern Reach with General Esladas. They are fighting off an invading army from East Saro that marches with allies from the kingdoms of Saro-Urok and West Saro."

"Exactly. My father thinks King Kliatemnos is still in

power. It could be weeks before the news reaches him that the king is dead. In fact, Nikonos must be counting on Father's ignorance. He knows the Royal Army is loyal to my father, not to him. And of course he knows that Father is now married to a woman who has a rival claim to the throne."

We all look at Mother, then wince and look away. But Mother long ago mastered the ability to conceal her true feelings behind a bland curtain. "You are suggesting, Jessamy, that Nikonos must suspect the Royal Army will support Lord Kalliarkos and Lady Menoë's claim to the throne instead of his."

"It doesn't matter," says Inarsis. "The Royal Army is stuck at Port Selene fighting a rearguard action against the invaders, who have superior numbers."

"Yes, but if any commander can win under those circumstances, it will be my father. So if I were Nikonos, I would march east as fast as I could with a cohort of East Saroese soldiers disguised as members of the Royal Army. General Esladas will welcome him, thinking he's come with needed reinforcements. Then Nikonos will execute Father for treason and take over the Royal Army."

"Jes is right," says Kal. "Keeping control of the Royal Army with General Esladas in command is our only chance to defeat Nikonos. We have to reach the general first."

"Even traveling at courier speed it will take twelve days or more to reach Port Selene," objects Inarsis, but I know how to measure the adversaries I'm running against. I can see his resolve crumbling.

So can Kal. "If you can arrange to escort me upriver to reunite with my family, then you can surely arrange for Jes and me to ride east."

"Jessamy is not going," says Mother.

"I'm going. Father will listen to me."

"The scenario you have described is real, and your father will listen to you, it's true." Mother's lovely features and gracious, accommodating manner make people believe her to be compliant and passive, but nothing could be further from the truth. "But you can't go. Lord Gargaron knows you rescued me."

"Was the rude kiss-off gesture really necessary when we reached the shore?" Ro laughs. He's leaned against the wall right where the sunlight illuminates his face so we can all see how handsome he is. "An ordinary person would savor such a victory in private, but only you—*only you*—would make sure to rub it raw right in a powerful Patron lord's angry face."

"He'd already seen Mother. Anyway, he deserved it. I beat him at his own game."

Mother isn't amused or appreciative. "He'll be furious and won't rest until he finds a way to punish you. So you cannot have anything to do with anyone in the Garon household ever again."

I'm so dumbfounded by her unfair words that I can't speak. Bad enough to forbid me to associate with Kal, but how can she demand I never again see my father just because he's now married to Kal's sister?

She goes on as if she doesn't even realize what she's just said. "The safest course is for you and me to return to Saryenia, because none of the Garon nobles dare set foot in the royal city while Nikonos rules. Lord Kalliarkos should do as Inarsis suggests and travel north to his people."

"No! I won't go with you to the inn."

"*No?*" says Inarsis. "Is that how you speak to your honored mother?"

"You're not my kinsman to scold me, Honored Sir."

"Jessamy! Apologize to Inarsis at once."

"My apologies, Honored Sir." My tone is grudging. I'm so angry. "But I'm going to find Father, with Kal."

I look at Kal expectantly, but before he can agree, Mother strikes for her target like an arrow loosed.

"Lord Kalliarkos, my daughter is not an ornament to gild a Patron lord and to show him as more broad-minded than others of his rank. Nor is she a badge of defiance with which he can prove himself to kinsmen who have ruled him for so many years. She is not a toy for you to play with and then discard."

A flush darkens Kal's cheeks.

Inarsis whistles.

Mis looks embarrassed, while Ro looks shocked—and delighted.

I'm stunned. Father has made it clear that he sees the attention of a lord like Kalliarkos as a danger but also as a distinction, even an accolade. It never occurred to me that Mother would see it as an insult.

"Doma Kiya, I have nothing but the highest respect for your daughter." Kal's fingers twitch when he is thinking really hard, as if he's driving a carriage pulled by high-strung horses, alert to the slightest nuance. This is what makes him good with people. "She's never been afraid to defeat me on the Fives court even though another might have chosen to let me win merely because of who I am. Furthermore, without Jes's determination, you and your children and servants would be dead in an oracle's tomb."

"That is true," she concedes without the slightest softening.

Kal can look as pleasantly unassuming as my mother as he circles in for victory. "Look at it with my eyes, Doma. Even a highborn lord, heir to two thrones, can marvel at a girl who will let nothing stop her."

He smiles winningly. Her flat stare doesn't thaw.

"Kiya." Inarsis steps forward. "I think it's a good idea."

"You're not Jessamy's mother!" she retorts with more belligerence than I ever thought she had in her.

Inarsis raises both hands, palms out, in appeasement. "Yet she's not wrong. A quick victory for Nikonos will hurt us all." He nods at her in a conspiratorial way I can't like. How deep runs the plot that's clearly at work among the Efeans? Does my own mother not trust me enough to share what she knows?

Curling her hands into fists, she says, "Very well. Give us a moment alone."

The three men go over to cluster around Mis and the babies, far enough away to give us the illusion of privacy if we speak softly.

I'm still angry but that doesn't mean I'm going to let her

walk into an ambush. In a low voice I hastily say, "Wenru isn't what he seems. It's as if there's a different self in his body. You need to be careful."

"I am aware there is something unusual about Wenru. But I can handle a baby." She raises a hand to seal my attention. "Your situation concerns me far more. Now listen to me, Jessamy."

My name on Mother's lips can sound as praise, as resolve, as encouragement, as love. But right now her tone takes a steep dive, like she's plunging in for a kill.

"Lord Kalliarkos may believe he can treat you with the same consideration he would show a Saroese woman of his own rank—"

"Mother!"

"—but this is not their land. They build their palaces and temples atop what once were our cities and holy places. They trample our dignity beneath their feet. They live on what they steal from us, our hearts, and even the sparks of our lives."

"If that's what you think, then I wonder you could ever have fallen in love with Father."

She takes my tone not as sarcasm but as a question. "I was young and naïve. I mistook a handsome smile for something it wasn't. No Saroese man can ever treat an Efean woman with the respect an Efean man will show her."

"So is that what all this conniving with General Inarsis is about?" I lash back. "Are you going to marry him, since he's a good Efean man?"

She actually laughs. I know I can never ask her to forgive Father, but this dismissiveness infuriates me.

"That's what you want for me, isn't it?" I go on. "A nice Efean life with a nice Efean boy like Ro, who, I should mention, seems to have a girlfriend in every tavern."

"The honored poet Ro-emnu has behaved toward me as would a dutiful nephew over the last few months. He made my life easier during a difficult time."

Her championing of Ro goads me over the edge.

"It's like you want me to pretend I'm not half-Saroese. Like you want me to forget I have a Saroese father and to act like I've never been anything but Efean. Well, I won't, because no matter what you wish, people will still throw names at me. I'm proud of who I am. I will make my own choices. And Kal and I will not end up with broken promises, not like you and Father!"

The instant I say those final words I'm horrified at how petty they are. I press a hand to my mouth but it's too late. The memory of the day Father abandoned the life they had built together twists a shadow in her eyes.

"I'm sorry," I whisper through my fingers as tears well up. "That was an awful thing to say."

Yet my harsh words finally soften her. She never takes her solemn gaze from me, nor would I dare insult her by looking away.

"You're right to scold me, Jessamy. You and your sisters *are* half-Saroese, and you shouldn't be ashamed of it, and no one should ask you to repudiate any part of yourself, not even me. Especially not me. But please listen. For your father and me to fall in love and try to build a life together was unusual but not unheard of. No one really cares if a lowborn Patron man cohabits with a Commoner woman, even if they aren't allowed to marry under the law. But Lord Kalliarkos has a claim to the throne. The moment you become his lover, you will be marked for death, not by Efeans, not by the ordinary Saroese who live and work in Efea, but by Garon Palace, his own noble household. Do you understand me, Jessamy? Do you?"

I can't say no. I won't say yes.

So I say nothing.

She wipes away a tear and then embraces me, her strength and affection the shelter I've known all my life. "Come back to me, my fierce Jessamy. Don't get lost in a false dream."

She can't disguise the fear in her voice: She's not sure if my loyalties lie with her or with Father. With Efea or with Efea's Saroese rulers. The truth is, for all my bold words, I'm not sure either.

4

A wiry Efean man named Khamu guides us northeast, inland away from Mist Lake. We stride along farmers' paths that wind past fields, ponds, and uncultivated land. It's a hot day, the blue sky like polished lapis. Normally people do not travel long distances with the sun blasting overhead, but we have to warn my father and get Kal to the safety of the army.

For most of the weary, sweaty day, we circle wide around every village, avoiding people no matter who they are. We dare not speak, communicating by army hand signals. So when Khamu abruptly signals "down," we drop right where we are on a path cutting through a palm grove interspersed with pomegranate trees. I've been given an iron-bladed hoeing stick so I can pretend to be a farmer if we run into soldiers, but it's the knife General Inarsis gave me before we left that I grip tightly as we wait.

A hand grabs my sandaled foot. I look back. Mis tips her head in a question, and I shrug. Behind her, Ro has unsheathed the sword we took from the soldiers Kal killed.

Kal is crouched beside the trunk of a palm, sword held ready. It's so hot he's stripped off his vest, wearing only his keldi and a bundle slung over his back. I'm briefly distracted by shoulders honed by all the climbing he used to do when he still ran the Fives, but then he raises a hand to cup his ear in the signal for "listen" and all my senses focus on the threat.

A splash sounds from a nearby pond. Footsteps pat a rhythm on the ground. Someone is coming up behind us.

We scramble to get out of sight, shielded by leaves. I peer through a gap as three barefoot Efean youths amble into sight, carrying baskets heaped with dates and pomegranates. Khamu calls in the manner of a dove, three times, and the youths halt.

"If you are honorable travelers, you are welcome to ask for hospitality from our dame council," says one in a high, light voice. They giggle nervously and race away, vanishing around a bend in the path.

Khamu stands. "I think we're far enough that we can safely enter a village now. We'll see if we can get mounts here."

Mis takes the lead, with Ro falling into step behind her and Khamu taking up the rear guard.

I fall back to walk beside Kal.

"I like the dress the dames gave you to wear. It looks good

on you." His intimate grin makes me smile. "But you and Mis can't ride in dresses."

"I have my Fives gear."

"Fives trousers are too lightweight and they're seamed for agility, not for riding. You'll be chafed and blistered in half a morning. If we really can get horses here, I have a spare pair of reinforced cavalry trousers. They'll fit you."

He pats the strap of the bag he's carrying. The thought of wearing his clothes makes me blush a little.

"No Patron trousers for me to change into instead of this keldi?" Ro asks over his shoulder.

"They didn't invite you into the conversation, Honored Poet," says Mis. "Keep your thoughts on the words you're going to have to say to persuade the dame council to help us."

Either Kal has gotten too much sun today or he's blushing too. I take his hand, astonished by how easy it is, how I could never have imagined that one day this would be an ordinary act. Not that it feels ordinary.

He murmurs, "We have no parents or relatives looking over our shoulders, Jes."

"I know. Not until we reach the Royal Army."

"You two! Give me silence," Mis calls back as if Kal is not a Saroese prince who could have her executed for disrespect. "There's a specific protocol we need to follow when we enter a village as strangers."

A post supporting a lantern marks the edge of the village. As strangers, we aren't invited up onto the boardwalks linking the houses, so we walk on the main wagon track into the central square.

Villagers have gathered, alerted by the youths. Children jiggle in excitement at the sight of newcomers, but the adults stare with skeptical expressions. About half of them carry weapons. No one says a word. I'm nervous and Kal keeps his head bowed, but Ro looks around with an easy smile although of course he doesn't speak.

Three old women appear. Mis steps forward to address them in Efean.

"Honored Dames, my name is Missenshe, daughter of Hametwe, daughter of Rihanwe the perfume maker, of Saryenia. On behalf of the honored poet Ro-emnu and his entourage, I request shelter."

They smile on Ro like benevolent aunties. "Welcome, Honored Poet. Your name is known to us. How may we assist you?"

He uses the flourishes of an actor: a swept arm, a lift of the eyebrows. "I come to you as a fugitive, carried in the sheltering arms of the Mother of All. I arrive with my companions. Missenshe you have met. The honored sir Khamu acts as our guide."

He then settles a hand on Kal's shoulder exactly as an actor playing a master marks his faithful servant for the audience to see. "This is my groom and loyal bodyguard, Kallos."

Everyone looks at the strange sight of a rather grimy Saroese youth dressed in a workingman's keldi.

"*Kallos?*" Kal mutters under his breath, recognizing only the Saroese name out of all the Efean words Ro said.

"Kalliarkos is a prince's name and would give you away in an instant, but both lowborn and highborn men may be called Kallos," I reply softly. I don't know whether to laugh at Kal's disconcerted expression or to punch Ro for finding this exact way to aid Kal by making him stand in Ro's shade.

Ro goes on in Efean. "I have fled the city of Saryenia lest I be arrested, for the Saroese king cannot abide a poet of my particular magnificence casting aspersions on his history. We barely escaped with our lives. Your hospitality nourishes us at a moment in our journey when we might falter, and we thank you. For our part, we will not let your generosity go unanswered. Of course I will declaim for you from my most recent play, the one the Saroese king himself banned."

The villagers eat up this prospect, and in truth I'm curious too, not that I'll ever let Ro know that. But he's not done as he finally steps away from Kal.

"But that isn't all we have to offer," he says, gesturing to me. "This adversary won her first Novice trial at the King's Court and became a Challenger on the strength of it. She saved the Royal Army of Efea from defeat by escaping an ambush and bringing a warning to the Royal Army's commander. You'll not defeat her easily when she takes on all comers!"

"What?" I say.

"Perhaps her fame has reached you here already. This, my friends, is Spider."

"Spider!" Whispers buzz through the crowd as they stare at me in delight. A voice pipes up in the refrain: *"She'll fight for Efea, and win!"*

"Yes, my friends." Ro gestures with his hands as if to beckon them closer to hear a momentous secret, and since he is speaking in Efean, the words stay a secret from Kal. "The tomb spider, the herald of that which has reached the end of its time on earth, does indeed fight for Efea and Efeans."

In answer, several of the villagers call out the phrase he's coined: "Efea will rise!"

It feels as if everyone knows their part in a play except me, but I'm given no chance to demand Ro explain what he's up to because he is immediately invited to bathe away the dirt of travel and swaggers off, surrounded by admirers.

"Is every girl in this village determined to be the one to charm Ro?" I say to Mis.

"I thought you didn't like him, Jes."

"I have complicated opinions about the poet." But he's not the person I'm worried about. When Khamu takes Kal with him to the pastures to discuss borrowing mounts for the next stage of the journey, Mis catches me before I can follow.

"You have to run now that Ro has volunteered you. It's an honor to the village."

"Will Kal be all right?"

"Khamu will watch over him. Anyway, no one here cares about Kal now that Ro has declared him an ordinary laborer.

But you running a trial is a big deal. It's part of the exchange of hospitality."

After I wash my hands and face and drink down a bowl of broth, I dig my Fives gear out of my bundle and change. Three adversaries are waiting for me beside the Fives court: a stocky older man named Ofru, a gangly boy about my age called Kenwis, and a sleek, strong, and very pretty young woman who goes by the name Precious.

"Precious?" I can't hide my surprise.

She shades her eyes to look in the direction in which Ro went. "It's actually Itet, but everyone's called me Precious since I was born because I was the first girl after my mother gave birth to five boys. Do you think the poet is going to come back to watch us?"

Mis and I share a look.

"I'm sure that is his intention," I answer with a steadfastly straight face.

"Then I'll run," she says magnanimously as Mis stifles a giggle.

Ofru leads us through a warm-up menageries, the long sequence of movements that trains our bodies in the patterns we need to run the Fives. He uses a form of menageries closer to the one I learned at Anise's stable than to the one our trainers Darios and Tana followed at Garon Stable. I slip into the flow of my early training as easily as a fish sliding back into water.

We finish and draw for starting positions. Precious preens as Ro is seated on the guest porch in a sling-back chair in the company of the dames and honored elders. Young people serve them drinks.

The poet's life in Efea is a burden, clearly.

I look around for Kal but don't see him amid the gathering crowd. I'm surprised by how many wish me good fortune. That just makes me more determined to win.

The village court is sturdy but simple. Pillars has movable canvas walls. Trees is a series of posts that can be fitted into different post holes. Traps has ropes, beams, and nets that can be shifted around to create variety. Rivers is a set of tilting planks dusted with sand. My competitors are good, but my serious training gives me the edge. I want to offer them the best thrills I can, so I throw in a few flips and twists. The crowd is cheering, "Spider! Spider!" as I reach the fourth platform in the lead, only to find myself staring over an entirely unfamiliar configuration that looks nothing like spinning Rings.

Long afternoon shadows patch the central area, where a wide spiral path encircles a tall scaffolding: the village victory tower. The spiral path has four pebbled strands, each a color representing one of the four outer obstacles: blue, green, red, and brown. There's no trick or turn here that I can see, just a choice, so I take the blue spiral. My feet crunch on the tiny rocks. The spiral's curve gets tighter and tighter.

The victory tower is taller than I realized because it is set into a large well with sheer stone sides. It's hard to tell how far down it goes because there's water below but depths don't intimidate me. I jump from the pit's edge to grab a ladder set within the scaffolding. I'm well ahead by now, yet as I climb the crowd begins laughing.

I discover why they're amused when I reach the top with its superb view of the flat terrain now mostly hidden by dusk.

There is no victor's ribbon.

Confused, I feel the jar of the tower as another body leaps onto the ladder. Ofru gives me a jaunty wave and clambers down.

Down.

It's so easy a trick that I overlooked it entirely. I can't help but shake my head, half laughing and half-disgusted with myself.

A bell rings out of the depths. The villagers cheer the victor.

Of course I climb down, because I have to see. The enclosed space smells of dirt and secrets. Ofru is seated on a ladder rung, feet dangling just above the water. Beside him a handbell hangs from a hook on the tower's scaffolding. He's holding a brass cup.

"I didn't expect this," I say, perching beside him.

It's too dim to see his expression but I hear the grin in his tone. "You ran that trial well, Honored Niece, but you were looking for the wrong landmark."

"Why a bell in a cistern instead of a victor's ribbon on a tower?"

"The Fives court represents the land of Efea. Water is the blood of the land. The bell represents the pulse of the Mother of All's heart."

"Do you ever run a trial so you win by climbing up?"

"A victory tower is the Saroese custom, not ours. We use ours as a watchtower, to keep an eye out for people we need to hide from. But to win a trial, you must climb down to ring the bell. It's traditional for the victor to pour well water over their head."

He dips the cup into the water and pours a few drops out onto his hair, then generously offers the cup to me. "You try it, Adversary. You earned the right."

Here in the depths, there's an uncanny whisper, maybe just the slow voice of the still water or maybe the five souls of the earth trying to speak to me. When I tip the cup over my head, I pour too much, a big splash, and Ofru laughs in a friendly way. But the cool water sliding down my face feels like a blessing, not a mistake. For an instant I feel that the land of Efea has whispered a secret in a language I don't understand.

He hangs the cup back up beside the bell and we climb out.

Kenwis and Precious are waiting. Kenwis enthusiastically gives me the kiss-off sign as a show of respect. I flash him the sign back as a courtesy, and he bounces in excitement as he starts asking me questions about my practice regimen. He breaks off when Ro saunters up with a flock of admirers behind.

"Spider!" Ro pulls my attention away from Kenwis. "I would say you ran well, except I can't because you made the wrong choice."

"I don't think you're talking about the trial," I jab back.

"But if you know so much about the Fives, why did you tell me that it isn't an Efean game, that the Saroese brought it to Efea?"

"Because that's the truth."

"But my father never heard of the Fives until he came to Efea. The game doesn't exist in old Saro. And if it's not Efean at all, then why is there a Fives court in the middle of every Efean village I've ever been in? Why does this village run the Fives with a slightly different set of rules and traditions, ones that make sense for Efeans but not for Saroese?"

"When did you start caring so much about Efean customs, schemer?"

"I'm half-Efean, you know, not just half-Saroese. Anyway, I intend to figure it out to prove you wrong."

He laughs, but when I glance past him to see if Kal has appeared yet, he draws Precious into conversation as if he wants me to notice him paying attention to another girl.

Mis comes up, accompanied by several girls our age who are eager to congratulate me. "If we hurry, there will be time to bathe before supper. With me, I mean, not the one you wish you could wash with."

I laugh. "I'm so filthy and sweaty I'll bathe even with you. But shouldn't we get on our way after that? With a few lanterns and the moon, we can ride at least part of the night. We have to get to my father as quickly as possible."

Mis looks at me with something like disappointment on her face. "We can't leave before Ro gives the dames the poetry we've promised. You know that. Now come on."

The bathing pool lies on the outskirts of the village, a walled compound that also encloses an herb and flower garden.

Our new friends peer at me excitedly. "The honored poet is so charming and handsome. Are you in love with him?"

"He's got the cry of a peacock, that's for certain. Loud enough that all the peahens are sure to hear him."

Of course they want to hear more about him as we wash in tubs and rinse with a swim in the outdoor pool. Yet I don't mind the gossipy chatter, even if I have to detail every least thing I know about Ro-emnu. Washing amid a flock of friendly girls reminds me of how much I miss my sisters. It makes me think of Bettany and how she left us, a grief as harsh now as the day she betrayed me and Amaya. Despite everything, I hope she is safe because I know that is what Mother would want for her, even if I can't forgive her.

I put up my hair, and when I pull my sheath gown back on I look like the other girls except that I, of course, will never look entirely Efean with my Saroese eyes.

Afterward we troop back to the central square. The open space in front of the guest porch has filled up with villagers seated on mats. Lamps burn around us like stars fallen to earth. Father told me once that when he first came to Saryenia, Efea dazzled him because of its light. Where he had grown up, night meant you were trapped inside as darkness stalked the streets. Only the wealthy could afford lamp oil and candles. But in Efea every village and household presses its own lamp oil from sesame seeds and castor beans. Markets, festivals, and entertainments thrive in the cool of night after a hot day.

A table laden with food awaits us. We fold flatbread around a spicy mash of gingered fish and leeks, and tear off chunks of bread to spoon up delicious bites of a lentil-tamarind-and-date stew, finishing off this repast with sweet slices of melon. I almost feel it's wrong to savor it, knowing Nikonos is surely already on the road, getting closer and closer to Father while I linger over a meal.

And yet it tastes so good.

Kal is seated behind Khamu on the porch. He has bathed and is wearing a clean keldi and laced-up linen jacket like all the village men. "Kallos" is invisible in a way Kalliarkos can never be, except for his lighter coloring and short, straight black hair. For that matter, I've not been called a mule even once in this village. For the first time in our lives, we are just two young people in a crowd.

I stay standing until Kal sees me amid the other girls.

Our gazes lock.

"Spider!" Ro lifts a mug of palm wine in my direction as a salute. He wears his jacket gaping open to show off his manly chest. "Now that you're here, Adversary, I can begin."

All at once I realize there's a way to be sure no one will have any possible interest in me for quite a long time. All I have to do is force Ro to change the order of his presentation.

Since everyone is looking at me, I flash the kiss-off sign in Ofru's direction.

"Well run, Adversary," I call out to cheers. "Not many people can defeat me."

To my delight, a few people shout, "Sing us the song of Spider. How she saved the desert frontier from invaders."

Ro's frown flashes. I'm pretty sure he meant to sing my song as the final part of his performance, meaning I would have to sit through his entire recitation of his play in order to be here when he called at the end. However, he shifts stance quickly, and I can't help but feel flattered by the way he singles me out with his compelling gaze. His robust voice can fill a theater, and when he sings the story of how Spider became a spider scout, his resonant singing penetrates to my bones.

The general's valiant daughter will fight for Efea,
She'll fight for Efea, and win!

How clever he is to turn my impulsive dash in service of my Patron father and Patron master into a story that speaks to Efeans and their desire for the freedom they lost so long ago. He's an instigator, sowing indignation in fertile soil. He's made me part of the story, a symbol for people to admire.

When he finishes, the villagers salute me with their cups. I open my arms in the gesture I use on the Fives court, as if I'm throwing my spider threads to the winds. Then I grab a cup of tea off the table and retreat to sit at the very back of the group of girls.

Mis settles down beside me. "You have a reckless look in your eye. Is that buckwheat tea you're drinking?"

I don't have time to answer because Ro raises his arms in a poet's welcome. Flames hiss around him, lamps hung to frame him in light, a poet ordained by the Mother of All to speak only truth lest he be struck down for dishonesty and lose his gift. He begins, his golden voice pouring over us like sunlight, although his words burn. It's impossible not to get wrapped up in the story as he tells it.

> *How fortunate was Prince Kliatemnos, who fled Saro to make*
>   *a new home here!*
> *Was he not worthy, honest, forthright, brave, and true?*

His audience hisses their displeasure.

> *Beloved of the gods, they called him, because he came through*
>   *that fire,*
> *The fire that was the war of greed that tore apart his home,*
> *And safely washed up on the clean and peaceful shores of rich*
>   *Efea.*
> *So the story goes. Their priests and poets tell it again and again.*
> *So the Saroese histories tell us, that Efeans welcomed*
>   *Kliatemnos as savior,*
> *Deposed their own ruling council and Custodian and Protector*
>   *and priests*
> *In favor of the better, wiser, nobler man—*

"All lies!" the villagers shout, and I find my lips forming the angry refrain with them.

> *A man who soon proclaimed himself King Kliatemnos in the*
>   *foreign way*

And set his wise and noble sister as Serenissima beside him
To guide his warlike hand in the gentler methods of peace and
    plenty.
Saviors both! For our own good—that's how they speak—for
    our own good
Their priests tore down the ancient temples to the Mother
And built their own atop them as if it were a form of cleansing.
They buried us stone by stone and lie by lie and heart by heart.

He's alight with conviction, blazing with a fierce need to convince every Efean he meets that it is time to act, that *Efea will rise.* I lean forward, caught up in the emotion.

Across the gap, Kal's gaze meets mine. Ro's fiery criticisms don't disturb or inflame him because he can't understand Efean, although he must recognize the names Kliatemnos and Serenissima—his Saroese ancestors. In fact, he seems to have something entirely else on his mind. He lifts an eyebrow as a question.

There's no one here looking over our shoulders, no one who can tell us what to do.

I tip my head to the left, indicating the darkness beyond the well-lit square.

He dips his chin in agreement and glances over his shoulder, seeking a path off the porch.

Mis whispers, "Jes, don't do anything you can't take back. Remember, he's a prince—"

"Not here he isn't. He's a mere groom, no higher placed than me."

I should be a courteous guest and a prudent young woman. It's what my father would tell me to do.

I should sit right here with everyone else and admire the poet's stirring and rebellious rendition of the horrific crimes of Queen Serenissima the Third, called "the Benevolent." It's what my mother would want me to do.

I should. But there's no chance that I will.

5

I slide to the edge of the crowd, ease back to sit on my heels, and carefully rise to my feet. Gently I place my sandals on the dirt one careful step at a time as I move backward into the night.

So fast I have no warning, dizziness washes over me. Slowly I breathe through the calming cycle Anise taught me as a fledgling. Slowly the night steadies around me.

A footstep scrapes softly around the back of the guesthouse I'm leaning against.

"Jes?" My name is a sigh on his lips.

My breathing stutters again, all erratic, my pulse leaping like a gazelle.

I have never been so nervous in my life. Every wrong thing that could happen spins through my mind like Rings so off-kilter they crash into each other and shudder to a halt. My deepest fears surface: What if I'm clumsy and make a fool of myself? What if he decides I'm not attractive enough?

His feet scuff the earth. I still can't see him around the corner but I feel the heat of him an arm's length from me. He coughs, chuckles awkwardly, and shifts his feet.

"Jes, not that I like to admit this to anyone, even to you, but if we don't go now, I'm going to lose my nerve."

My fingers creep around the corner of the house. His hand brushes my knuckles. We both jolt back. I giggle, and I never giggle, not even with my sisters.

To reach the victory tower you have to jump across the gap that scares you most.

I step around the corner and grab hold of his arm.

"I know a place," I say, so out of breath I can barely speak those four simple words, just as he says at the exact same moment, "The garden by the bathing pool."

Holding hands, we walk briskly down the lane that leads to the walled garden and pool. I can't speak, and Kal doesn't say a word but I feel his breathing like it is my own. His fingers tangle in mine. The linen of the borrowed jacket he's wearing brushes repeatedly against my bare arm.

Efeans love their lamps. The pair hanging on either side of the garden gate are molded of ceramic with slices cut out before the soft clay was fired. Petals of light bloom over us.

The gate isn't quite closed; it's been left a handbreadth ajar, as if the garden is inviting us in.

Kal drops his gaze, lashes hiding his eyes. His embarrassment is the most ridiculous thing in the world and yet somehow it makes me see him as a precious shard of heaven that has unexpectedly dropped into my lap.

I'm biting my lower lip. Who knew this would be so hard?

He takes in a breath for resolve and squeezes my hand. "Are you sure, Jes?"

"Of course I'm sure. It's not like we're ever really going to be safe. I don't want to wait for something that may never come. Are *you* sure?"

"Of course I'm sure. But there's one thing...." He shifts his feet, scratches his forehead, and flashes an awkward grin. "I feel like an administrator in the king's palace, tidying up the books. Eager lovers never say things like this in the plays."

"Things like what?"

He turns serious. "However free we feel right now, my situation means it would be dangerous for you if you got pregnant."

"Don't worry. I'm drinking buckwheat tea. It's what Efean women do to make sure that doesn't happen. I have no intention of interrupting my Fives career."

"Only someone who doesn't truly know you would ask you to do that," he says with a laugh so genuine and sweet that I can't imagine another boy who would have found that funny.

His laughter gives me the courage to push the gate open with a foot. We dash inside, and he pulls it shut behind us. In the gloom beyond lie trellises and bowers wreathed in vines and shielded by shrubs.

Yet now that we are here, we stand motionless, two adversaries at a loss for how to take the next step. I keep thinking there is a better move or a best move but there isn't. There is him, and there is me, and we get to make our own choice, no matter what the people around us say, no matter if our reasons aren't perfect. Maybe it's partly that I'm a rebellion for him, while he's the highborn boy who should have been out of my reach. We don't always have the right reasons for what we do and what we want.

"I can hear you thinking," he says, laughter still in his voice. "Jes, sometimes you just have to let yourself fall."

"All right." I turn so we stand face-to-face, so our bodies touch all along their length. I lean my cheek against his, and he trembles all over. My lips brush his skin, tasting his eagerness and his yearning. "I'm falling."

⸎

Much later and much sweatier, I sprawl across a wide bench beneath a bower roof of blooming jasmine. Kal sits cross-legged beside me, a hand resting on my knee. I spider-walk my fingers up his spine.

"I could come to like that as much as running the Fives," I say.

"My thanks for the compliment. I think."

It's strange to feel so purely light I might float up to the stars and eat them, one by one, like sweet hot candy. "We would need to practice more to get really good at it."

He leans against me. "We would need to practice a great deal. Many, many trial runs."

I start giggling and I can't stop. Who is this giddy person I have become? I don't even recognize her and I don't care.

"Teach me Efean."

"What?" The words jolt me.

"Teach me Efean. General Inarsis taught me the basic courtesies for addressing people, like Honored Sir and Honored Lady and Honored Dame. I know the numbers and names for food, things like that. But without an interpreter, I can't talk to Efeans who don't speak Saroese. I want to be able to ask questions and hear answers without another voice standing between mine and theirs."

"Why do you want to talk to Efeans?" I ask cautiously.

"I would like to be able to understand what Ro is saying without worrying that the people who are translating aren't telling me everything."

This is not the conversation I was hoping to have. I'm not the only one who can't stop turning Rings in my head.

"Jes, you and I both know Ro isn't helping me because he wants me to become king. At best he knows we have to drive Nikonos's foreign allies out of Efea lest the invaders decide to take the land for themselves."

I'm not ready for the world to intrude. In the distance Ro is still declaiming; it's a really long play. And I have a better idea than I ever did before of how to distract Kal.

"Very well. I will teach you Efean, although I warn you it

is a much more formal and sophisticated language than Saroese, which Efeans consider blunt and crude."

"Is that so?" He grins.

"So, taking pity on you, I'll start with something easy, like body parts." I touch each one as I name them in Efean. "Eyes. Nose. Mouth."

"I see where this is going."

"Chin. Throat. Chest..."

He touches a finger to my lips to silence me.

The crickets have stopped buzzing.

Someone is coming.

I yank my dress on. He fumbles to wrap his keldi and tug on his jacket.

Thus we are sitting primly side by side an arm's length apart on the bench when a lamp shines into view and Mis appears, flanked by several local girls. Fortunately the night covers my flaming blush as the girls grin hugely and look Kal over with more interest than they did before, especially now that the jacket is gaping open to display his attractive chest. He tries to discreetly straighten his keldi, which he's tied on askew. With an extreme effort, I do not lean over to lace up his jacket.

I await a lecture, courtesy of some bug my mother has put in Mis's ear, but when she speaks, the words come out almost apologetic.

"A runner came in from a village west of here. Soldiers showed up there, searching for fugitives. Mules are being saddled as I speak."

51

"Mules?" I ask. "Not horses?"

Mis sighs with a glance toward Kal, and says in Efean, "The law forbids Efean villagers from owning horses."

"Oh. I didn't know."

She switches back to Saroese. "Kal, these girls will take you to your riding gear to change. I brought your extra gear for Jessamy."

Kal gives me a secret smile before departing.

"Any other Patron lord would have me whipped for switching to Efean so he can't understand me," Mis adds when the others are out of earshot. She plucks at the fabric draping my shoulder. "By the way, your dress is on backward."

I slap a hand over my face, but what can I do? Despite the seriousness of our situation, we both start laughing.

Yet as I change, more sheepish than I thought I would be at slipping on Kal's riding trousers, I ask her quietly, "I know why we need an Efean woman to introduce us at every village, but why did you volunteer to help us reach my father? You could be killed if Nikonos gets to us first."

A half moon casts the garden into a mass of stark shadows and pale contrasts. She picks up my dress and folds it neatly as she replies.

"When I saw Dusty taken away at Crags Fort, I swore to the Mother of All that I would learn to fight. Maybe I'll never see Dusty again, maybe he's dead, or cursed to a life of slavery in a land far from here. But I will not stand by while there is a hope we Efeans can take back what should belong to us."

She pauses, as if wondering if she's let her passionate anger reveal too much to me, the girl with the Saroese father.

"Don't worry, Mis. I've figured out what's going on. I just don't see how Ro's ragtag Efean rebellion can defeat well-trained and professionally equipped Saroese armies. I'm sorry. I just don't see it."

"Of course you don't." I can tell she's disappointed in me, and it stings.

"That doesn't mean things can't change. I can convince Father and Kal that we need to do things differently."

"Do you really believe that?"

"They aren't monsters just because they are Saroese," I mutter, wishing I did not sound sullen and defensive.

She turns my hand over, palm up, and presses a finger to the middle, the Efean gesture for truth-telling. They believe the smoky eye of our shadow-soul peers out through the palm. "No person is a monster until their actions make them so."

"And Nikonos really is a monster. None of our fine dreams of change will matter if he and Queen Serenissima win this trial. If he reaches Father before we do, all Efea will be crushed."

6

"Yes."

A hand touches my knee, and I startle awake, swaying. I'm tied to the saddle of a mule, and it is Kal, riding beside me, who has woken me. His smile bursts like a sun in my heart. He kisses one of his fingers and touches it to my leg. I copy the gesture, one we've developed in the last five days of grueling travel.

The sun hasn't quite risen, and cocks are crowing as we ride into a village. Women haul water and grind grain to get a start on a new day. I wonder if my mother grew up in a village like this, if she carried pails of water from the village well to her mother's house and slapped away mosquitoes and breathed in the musk of animal manure and the smoke of hearth fires.

After Mis and Ro make our greetings, Kal and Khamu take the mules away, accompanied by local villagers.

"Why are you traveling with one of the foreign monsters?" one of the dames asks Mis.

A spike of anger makes my head want to blow off. "The man was born here just like you and me, Honored Lady."

"They are poisoned flowers never meant to grow in Efean soil. You see what one did to me when I was no older than you are now, child." A scar starts along her jaw and winds a thick seam across the edge of her lips to end in a mass of scar tissue at the bridge of her nose.

"I'm sorry. That is a truly terrible thing. But they aren't all like that."

She studies me, the complex blend of my height, my hair, my complexion. My eyes. "And the man who sired a mule like you? Has he kept faith with your honored mother?"

Humiliated, I look away.

She discards me by turning her attention back to Ro. "Honored Poet, why do you travel with a Saroese man when you know their hearts are filled with stolen blood?"

Poets cannot lie.

He looks at me, and they all follow suit as if he has spoken aloud that he can't tell them the whole truth while I'm here to listen. Suddenly I am not Efean enough for them. It wasn't like this in the villages closer to Saryenia, the ones who saw more Saroese. Dusty grew up out here in the east, on the fringe of the desert, and I see why he left as soon as he could.

"I'll go to the stable with the rest of the mules." My voice is stiff. I stalk off quite rudely although I can't bring myself to care how I appear to people who have already decided to dislike me. Anyway, now I worry about hostility Kal might be facing.

When I get to the village stables I hear a buzz of agitated conversation. Khamu and Kal are watering and brushing the mules, surrounded by locals who are giving our guide what appears to be a stream of information. Khamu pauses frequently to pat Kal on the shoulder and refers to him multiple times as honored nephew.

"The soldiers came from the south, from the coast," one of the men is saying. "Took half of our grain stores and left us only with a piece of papyrus that their captain claimed the royal treasury will make good on if we bring it to the palace in Saryenia. As if people like us would ever have time to travel that far, much less be admitted into the palace when we got there!"

I hurry over. "What badge were the soldiers wearing, Honored Sir?"

Kal's gaze flashes up. He's surprised to see me here and nods to show me he's all right, guessing I'm worried about him.

The elder answers politely, "The royal sea-phoenix, Honored Niece."

Father would never loot Efean villages, and he's in Port Selene, isn't he? It must be Nikonos's East Saroese allies, disguised as local troops. If so, that means they've gotten ahead of us.

"How far away is the Royal Road from here, Honored Sir?" I ask, because we have stuck to an inland path in the hope of avoiding any more of Nikonos's soldiers. Now we need the quickest route, despite the risk.

The old man measures the rising sun. "A person can make it to the coast by midday."

Khamu gestures. "Jes, why don't you and my honored nephew go take a quick wash? There'll be porridge waiting on the guest porch."

I nod my thanks. In the last five days, Khamu has quietly facilitated every stolen moment of privacy Kal and I have managed. The bathing garden is empty this time of day, and it welcomes us as a fragrant bower full of promise. But we can't linger, no matter how much we want to. Not after I've explained what I heard. I'm ready to charge back to the others but he takes my hand, kisses my palm. Kisses me. He presses his forehead against mine.

"Jes," he whispers, as if he fears the gods might hear, "what if we just left?"

"What do you mean?"

"You and me. We could sneak south to one of the harbor towns, get work on a ship, and sail away. Vanish forever. We could make a life where no one can find us."

"What about my father? Nikonos will kill him if we don't reach him first."

"We could write a letter and send it with Mis."

"His command staff will never let an Efean girl through to see him. It has to be us. You know that."

He breaks away, paces a circle around me, and returns. "Once I declare myself, I can't step away, not ever. I don't want to be king. I don't want to fight over who has the most power, the most gold—"

"We can't leave Efea in the hands of Nikonos and Serenissima. You can't want that!"

He sinks down on a bench and rests his head on a hand as if he's so weary. And why wouldn't he be? "No. I don't want that."

"And your uncle Gargaron. If you're not there to counterbalance him, to push against him, what will happen then? He doesn't even consider me a person, Kal. How will he treat Efeans if he holds the reins of power? What if he goes after my mother? What if he decides my father is a threat? He'll kill the very people who can make things right."

He pinches the bridge of his nose, shakes himself, and stands with a heavy exhalation, as if he's bracing himself to race as hard as he can through a Fives trial.

"No, you're right, Jes. I can't escape this. It was too late the day I was born."

I have no answer. The precious solitude that has sheltered us during our overland journey has burned down in an instant's firestorm, leaving us standing in ashes.

We walk in silence to the guesthouse as dread grows in my heart. Khamu and Mis are eating porridge while Ro regales the dame council and the elders with a passionate speech. The instant he sees us coming, he stops speaking.

Kal pauses politely at the bottom of the steps so everyone will notice he has arrived, but he doesn't wait for an invitation to approach. He climbs up to the porch and offers a series of *Honored Dame*s and *Honored Sir*s to the assembled elders before turning to Khamu.

"We need to turn south at once. Khamu, you grew up near here. Is there a way we can approach the Royal Road without being seen, to make sure it's safe before we risk using it?"

"Yes, my lord. I know a path that only locals dare take."

"Very well." Again he addresses the elders, who are staring at him as at a branch that has revealed itself to be a snake. "My thanks for your hospitality. I promise you, whatever has been requisitioned or stolen from your village will be repaid. For now, we need the loan of fresh mounts."

Ro stands. "So. How quickly you abandon your performance as a humble groom, Lord Kalliarkos."

Ro is taller and bigger but Kal doesn't give way. He doesn't know how to give way; he's a prince of the realm.

"A massive foreign army has broken through the frontier on the Eastern Reach. Nikonos is in league with them. There can be nothing more important than stopping this threat."

"I won't deny it, but if you don't mind my saying so, *my lord*, I don't see any difference between these latest Saroese invaders and your ancestors."

"I think you and I know the situation is more complex now." In the last few months, serving in an army chased by defeats, Kal has undergone a fierce test, like metal in a forge, and been hammered into a harder person. "I am Efean born. I am not my ancestors."

"Of course you aren't, *my lord*." Ro opens a hand, palm up, as a question. "Yet if you and Garon Palace do overthrow our new child-murdering king and his complicit sister-queen instead of being slaughtered yourselves, what then? Will you and your sister, Lady Menoë, rule as king and queen justly and wisely over your fawningly grateful subjects, Patron and Commoner both? As your ancestors have done for a hundred years?"

"The danger to Efea isn't from me. It's from Nikonos's weakness. I'm sure his East Saroese allies intend to overthrow him once they make sure my sister and I are gone and they can make Efea a province of East Saro. Is that what you want?"

"I want justice."

Then they both look at me, like they are waiting for me to agree with one or the other.

Irritation spikes through me. I'm not the victor's ribbon in the victory tower, waiting to be claimed.

I'm the adversary.

"You two are both missing the obvious. At the moment we are fugitives and Nikonos is king. He will have all of us executed if he catches us. So we need to reach my father before Nikonos does. Right now."

"The general's valiant daughter has no time for nonsense," Ro remarks in Efean to the council, who are trying to sort out the new dynamics at play as Kal asserts himself. No one laughs. Nothing about this is amusing.

We gulp down a thick porridge and set out again on fresh mules, accompanied by ten villagers. They carry field and carpentry tools as if they are weapons, but all I can think of is how quickly they will be cut down by armored soldiers wielding swords, spears, and arrows.

As we head south, Kal taps my knee. "Jes, promise me you'll run if there's trouble, not charge straight into it."

"I never charge into trouble unless I've considered all my options and decided it's the only choice."

His lips tug up. "It was worth a try."

Sun bakes the dusty ground until it shimmers like an oven. Soon the terrain starts to drop in ragged tiers toward the narrow coastal plain. A dark strip running parallel to the coast must be the Royal Road. I'm sure I see ships out on the distant water but the late-afternoon haze makes it hard to tell. We halt at the edge of the last, steepest drop, hand the mules back to the villagers, and bid them farewell before descending a slope into a mucky depression, a diseased-looking marsh that spreads east and west as far as I can see.

My soft leather boots are soon grimy with muck, but it isn't true mud that sticks and clumps but rather a slippery sheen that reeks. Tears stream from my eyes and my nostrils itch from the stench of oozing petroleum seeps. In front of me Mis sneezes twice, then murmurs a prayer for the safety of her shadow, since sneezing can dislodge the shadow-soul. But when I check, hers is still stuck to her, rippling across the islets of plug grass we use as stepping-stones.

An antelope caught in the mire is far gone in decay. Insects who drowned trying to feast on its viscera float in an oily sheen, eddying up against its whitening skull.

Palms and sycamores mark a village ahead. All I can think about is the chance to pour a bucket of cold water over my head.

I hustle after Mis through empty lanes and into the center square—where we run straight into a crowd of villagers facing down a column of soldiers wearing the royal sea-phoenix.

I spin desperately to warn away Kal, but he has already halted out of sight. The soldiers mark Mis and me as grubby Commoner girls, nothing of interest. The sergeant is laboriously attempting to inform the village men that he will pay for supplies and that the villagers need to flee immediately . . . but he doesn't speak Efean and they don't speak Saroese.

Are these Nikonos's men?

A crow suddenly appears. It circles us and lands on a nearby roof to study our faces with keen interest.

"Do you recognize that crow?" I murmur to Mis.

"Why would I recognize a crow?"

"At Crags Fort, with the spider scouts. Don't you remember the priest who'd had his eyes put out and saw through the eyes of his crows? My father has spider scouts with his army, and each squad has a crow priest."

"I'm more worried about these soldiers right here, Jes."

But I have a feeling, just as I do on the Fives court, that this is an opening I can take. I extend an arm and the crow flaps down to land on my wrist, feet tightening on my skin. It bobs once, then flies off. That decides me. I step forward.

"Sergeant, may I help? I speak both Saroese and Efean."

My proper Saroese speech startles him. His kit is filthy, his face bristling with a stubbly beard, and he looks as exhausted as I feel, but he nods as if my presence is a relief. "Thank the gods. Can you tell these people we don't want grain? I've been sent to collect oil and naphtha."

"You're with the Royal Army, under the command of General Esladas?"

Instead of indicating his sea-phoenix tabard, he taps a fire-bird badge sewn to the cloth. "Proud to be so."

"I thought you were dug in at Port Selene, holding the eastern approach into Efea."

"The enemy's army is too large. We had to retreat."

Father is marching straight toward Nikonos.

More curtly than I intend, I say, "You must take us to him."

He waves a dismissive hand. "My job is to get these supplies and warn the villagers that they need to clear out before the enemy comes pillaging. Now either help me by translating or get out of my way."

I don't waste time arguing with him. I call, "Kal! It's safe to come out."

Kal strides into view. Where a prince walks, every gaze must follow.

"Sergeant." He acknowledges the man with a nod but walks past the troops and places himself before the guesthouse porch, where he invites Mis to join him.

She throws a glance at me, rolls her eyes with a smile. For all that Mis has her own goals, she likes Kal and I think she even respects him.

After she introduces him, Kal offers a proper greeting to the dames of the village with the painstaking diction I've taught him. The women are happy to get paid directly rather than make a journey to Port Selene with their oil and naphtha, a trip that is now impossible anyway.

In the square, Ro has worked his way into a crowd, meeting their gazes, touching the arms of those young men and women with grievance writ large in their discontented expressions. He speaks with so much intensity, and anyway I'm curious about the discussions they hide from me, so I move toward him to hear better.

"We are quiet dogs biding in the shadows while the lions fight. When they have wounded each other and lie bleeding, then we become wolves. Those who can, follow me. Our war has begun at last."

His words wrap around my heart but I stay just outside the group, not moving too close.

As people start loading casks and vessels onto the wagons the soldiers have brought, Kal takes a formal leave of the dames and returns to the soldiers.

"Sergeant?"

"Leukos, Your Highness."

"Sergeant Leukos, I must reach General Esladas at once. There's an enemy force west of here as well as the invaders on your tail. The Royal Army is at risk of being caught between two hammers."

"Yes, indeed, my lord. That's urgent news! Agas! Klidas! You'll personally escort Lord Captain Kalliarkos to the general."

Two soldiers not much older than I hustle over. They check out Mis and me, dwelling too long on our figures.

Ro pushes his way out of the crowd, headed for me. He halts as Agas and Klidas step into his path to prevent him from getting too close to an exalted lord captain. Mis notices their interference with an angry shrug that reminds me what an ordinary part of life it is for her and Ro to have to get out of the way and not protest. But of course Kal can walk right past them. Maybe he thinks Ro is anxious to say good-bye to *him*.

"You and Khamu have done your part and brought me to the Royal Army," he says to Ro. In Efean he adds, "My thanks to you, brother."

They tap fists.

"Wherever it is you mean to go," Kal continues, "please warn the villagers to hide. The East Saro and Saro-Urok troops will burn and pillage, as we've seen."

"It's habitual with the Saroese," agrees Ro.

Kal has about a hundred smiles, each conveying a different emotion. This time he glances at the ground as if to give himself an instant's privacy as he decides how to respond, then back up to meet Ro's sardonic stare. A wry smile softens his lips but his eyes give a harder message. "Change can happen. I believe that."

"You always do believe that you mean what you say. I like you for it, but I know better than to trust in Saroese promises."

"I'll keep my promise to you. You'll see."

"That I will."

Kal nods and walks away to make his farewell to Khamu.

In Efean, Ro says, "Jessamy. You don't have to go with him. Their fight isn't your fight."

"Of course it's my fight. It's Efea's fight."

"If he dies, you'll be taken down with him. If he wins, you'll lose him anyway." His deep voice snaps with emotions too complex to untangle. "You don't belong to them, Jessamy. You belong with us."

He touches my shoulder as if he wants to embrace me, then winces and pulls his clenched hand to his chest. Whether by accident or design, he has just copied the fist-to-heart theatrical gesture of a person heart-stricken by a hopeless love.

My tongue has turned to brick.

Kal waits beside Agas and Klidas. He sees us talking but does not interfere.

I meet the poet's gaze with all the clarity I can muster. "We can't risk being conquered by the East Saroese with Nikonos as their puppet king. You don't have an army or weapons, Ro-emnu."

"I have the truth, Spider. I just hope it's not too late for you when you finally realize it."

I don't bid him farewell; I'm too angry.

Yet as I walk away he says, "If you are ever in trouble, I pledge on my five souls that I will aid you."

I don't look back.

7

We set out at a brisk walk along a wide path rutted with wagon tracks.

"What promise did you make to Ro?" I ask Kal.

"That it's time to allow Efeans back into the army, as my grandfather did. For one thing, men like Inarsis don't take well to proving their worth and then having it stripped from them. For another, we are warring against kingdoms who have bigger armies than we do. There are far more Commoners than Patrons in Efea. We could easily double or triple our army in size if we allowed Efeans to become soldiers."

This is exactly what I've hoped for, the bridge between one part of my life and the other.

He adds, "Working together, can you and I convince your father that it's a feasible idea?"

"Oh! So that's why you wanted me to accompany you on this journey."

He's such a flirt with his eyes. "Yes, that's the only reason."

"I knew it."

Mis coughs, and I look around to see Agas and Klidas watching us with frowns that skate close to hostility.

I say to them, "Any chance we can move faster, or do we need to stay walking for you soldiers to keep up with us?"

My crisp, fluent Saroese and blunt manner confuse them.

"We can run!" they protest, forgetting to be angry that I've challenged them.

I settle into an easy jog, the best we can manage in our exhausted state. A crow passes over us, winging its way south. I'm sure it's the same one. We pass several more hollows of stinking, tarry ground, then climb a slope to a low rise. Ahead lies the sea. The high embankment of the Royal Road runs parallel to the shore. King Kliatemnos the Second had the road built to ease the way for Efea's army when he began fighting border skirmishes on the Eastern Reach against his cousin kings of East Saro, Saro-Urok, and West Saro. The wars among the four kingdoms have never ended, only paused and started up again in a cycle that goes around and around.

Now a huge line of soldiers and wagons rumbles west along the road and out of my sight. Every unit flies the sea-phoenix banner: this is the Royal Army in retreat, marching toward what they believe is the safety of Saryenia's walls.

The silhouettes of spider scouts flash as the light of the setting sun glints off their brass carapaces.

The baggage train moves slowest and thus at the rear. The wagons are almost past us, and if we don't hurry they'll leave us behind. Far to the east movement trembles on the road, difficult to discern as the light fades: there marches the enemy, hard on Father's heels.

"Let's go!" I say impatiently.

"Mules don't give orders." Klidas slaps me.

The blow really hurts. Tears stream.

A staff slams Klidas in the chest and whirls around to catch him behind the knees and flip him to the ground. Kal steps in, bracing the tip of his staff on the soldier's chest.

"No honorable man uses that word. Nor does he strike women. Do you understand me?"

"Y-yes, my lord." He's heaving, sides shaking from pain. Agas stares wide-eyed.

Kal removes the staff and nods at me.

"Let's go," I repeat. We head out with no further protests.

Outriders wave us through. We climb the embankment up onto the road and race after the last group of wagons grinding along, three heavy catapults being pulled by eight mules apiece. The road crosses a steep-sided gully, where water flows in the rainy season. Efeans wielding pickaxes and shovels are digging a trench through the road here so the enemy won't be able to cross without time-consuming repair work. The noise of iron hammering rock rings a cacophony around us.

Mis shrieks, "It's Dusty!"

She bolts. I run after her, losing Kal in the confusion. The laborers swing their pickaxes with zeal, as if they are imagining the surface of the road as the faces of men they hate. Dusty is barefoot, clad only in a grimy keldi. Whip scars run cruel tracks across his back.

A Saroese sergeant holding a spear blocks our path.

"Girls! If you're here to work, haul rock and pile it on the road as a barrier. Otherwise get out of the way."

For once Mis does not obediently step back but charges forward.

"Dusty. Dusty!"

His back still to her, he brings the pickax down with a blow that cracks the surface. He hasn't heard her.

"*Dusty!*" she shouts.

He hesitates, then turns.

I wince, and Mis presses a hand over her mouth.

His right eye is seamed shut with a mass of fresh scar tissue, like a clumsy seamstress tried to sew shut his eye socket. His good eye passes right over us, then tracks back. He shakes his head, tapping his right ear as if to clear it.

"You're dead. I'm seeing things." He shifts the pickax to ready it for another blow.

Mis grasps his arm. "No, we're alive, Dusty. How did you get here?"

Dusty's thinness makes him look fragile but an intensity burns in his ruined face that scares me. "The doctor and those mercenaries gave me to the East Saroese as a slave. At the battle by Port Selene, General Esladas sent skirmishers to burn the enemy baggage train. A bunch of us prisoners took the chance to run after them when they returned to the Royal Army, and they took us on as laborers. I don't know how you survived but I thank the Mother of All that you both did. You have to get out of here. If the enemy captures you…" He touches his ruined eye, then pushes Mis roughly away. "Go! We're trenching the road to slow them down."

A horn blasts, calling the alert.

The wagons keep rolling but the rearguard infantry turns to face back the way they've come. A rumbling sound resolves into skirmishers wearing the hawk tabards of East Saro, racing out of the gloom to attack the laborers working on the trench. The shadows make their numbers seem enormous, like swarming locusts.

I'm too stunned to run.

"Brace! Pull!"

A loud racheting noise clacks behind me.

"Fly!"

With thumps, the three catapults let fly. Pots spin overhead. A few arc harmlessly to the side of the road but the rest slam down amid the enemy. Ceramic shatters.

Shouts of laughter spread among the East Saroese soldiers at this ineffective blow.

Then a scream. Followed by an outbreak of cries and shrieks.

Dusty heaves up his pickax and slams it down. "Scorpions," he shouts with a wild laugh as he and the other laborers really start pounding.

The catapults are being ratcheted back with a *clank clank clank* for another volley. Arrows fly as our soldiers shoot at will into the confused and frantic enemy.

Mis shakes me. "Go on, Jes! I'm not leaving without Dusty."

"I can't leave you here, Mis! You heard what he said. You saw what the enemy did to him."

"Do you think Efeans don't risk that every day, where the Saroese rule? Maybe your father treated his servants fairly, but there's no law to protect us against abuse. Can't you understand? Your father's rank and Kal's attention don't make you Saroese, Jes. In their eyes you'll always be Efean, like me."

"No. I reject that. I'm not one or the other—"

She cuts me off by hugging me, hard. "I know you have to make your own journey. And I have to make mine. Be safe, Jes."

With a kiss to my cheek, she pushes me away and runs back to the laborers, where she starts hauling rock.

"Mis!" I shout after her, but the catapults thump, drowning out my voice. Scorpion-laden ceramic bombs fly to scatter amid the enemy.

"Jes!" It's Kal, looking for me. I've imperiled him by hanging behind.

It makes me sick to leave, knowing I may never see them again, but I do.

ᕫᕤᕥᕡᕠ

Kal commandeers horses from a passing cavalry regiment. As we gallop forward, weary soldiers glance up.

"Lord Captain Kalliarkos! The hero of Pellucidar Lake has returned to us!"

A ragged cheer flows down the impossibly long column of soldiers.

When I was younger, the Royal Army at full strength marched out of Saryenia to fight a war in a foreign land. The king and queen declared it a festival day. We girls with Mother were allowed to wait amid the crowds on the Avenue of the Soldier to watch them go, since Father marched with them in his first campaign as a captain. It took all morning and into the afternoon for the army to pass through West Gate, a long, hungry, hot day for four young girls and their anxious mother. Amaya started crying because her favorite doll got stepped on, Bettany threw up from the dust, and Maraya blithely named off all the regimental banners as they passed, which made me jealous because I had secretly been trying to learn them so Father would praise me when he got home.

It's the same mass of numbers here. For all that the Royal Army is understrength and weakened, the ranks seem endless, moving relentlessly and in silence but for necessary commands and the sounds of feet, hooves, and wheels in constant motion. As twilight descends, lamps get lit until the road becomes like a stream of spark-bugs. We ride forward and forward as in a dream that won't end.

But at last a cluster of banners marks the command company, a mix of infantry and cavalry guarding the general's carriage. A company of spider scouts clanks along on either side, a gleaming wall of brass and articulated limbs.

A captain cuts across our path. He's wearing the firebird badge that marks him as an adjutant under Father's direct command.

"Halt! We are under orders to observe strict order-of-march discipline…." In any other circumstances I would laugh at his double take. "Lord Captain Kalliarkos! My lord, I did not expect to see you." He hesitates, then acknowledges me with a nod.

"Captain Helias, I must see General Esladas at once."

"Did you not arrive with your cousin, my lord? We just received a messenger from Prince General Nikonos that he and you have made a forced march from Saryenia with new troops and arms with which to defeat our enemy."

It's no victory to know I was right about Nikonos's plan. What if we're too late? As impatient as I am, I have to remain silent as Kal speaks.

"Captain! This is an ambush, not an alliance. Nikonos has murdered his brother and nephew and proclaimed himself king beside Queen Serenissima. He has done so with the assistance of our enemies from East Saro. Do you understand what I've just said?"

The captain's eyes widen, but he immediately salutes with a tap to his shoulder. "What is your command, my lord?"

"Send messengers to every unit. We must be ready to fight because we are out of room to run on either side. Hand out weapons to all Efean drivers, grooms, and laborers."

"To Efeans? Only the general can give such a command."

"I am a royal prince, Captain. Do it."

"Yes, my lord." But he frowns and glances at me.

I ignore him. I've already looked ahead to a group of horsemen with a familiar figure among them, not in the general's carriage as we thought he would be. My father has a stiff seat on his horse, nothing like Kal's effortless grace or the easy seats of the officers accompanying him, highborn men who grew up learning how to ride.

"Father!" I shout, because I can't restrain my fear any longer, spurring my horse to reach him.

Father's expression becomes a mask made cold and grim by our arrival.

"My lord, this is an unexpected meeting," he says to Kalliarkos. His gaze flicks to me and he gives a dip of his chin to show he will speak to me later. "I just received word from one of the crow priests that a man fitting your description was sighted moving this way. Given that the message we just received from Prince Nikonos claims you are with him, your presence here cannot signal good news."

"You are riding into an ambush," I blurt out.

"Explain."

Kal describes the situation in crisp strokes. All emotion vanishes from Father's face except an uncanny twist of brightness I can't explain, like a banked fire compressed until its glow becomes the fiercest light of all. He's absorbing, he's thinking, he's calculating.

Yet we keep riding forward toward disaster.

We reach the very front of the army, the vanguard with its proud sea-phoenix banner parting the night like a ship's prow. Here march Father's most decorated veterans, the men he brought with him from his old command, the only soldiers allowed to wear a firebird badge. Spider scouts stump along, split into a squad on either side of the infantry. By their markings, I recognize them as the company Kal commanded in the desert.

Flashes of light reveal lanterns in the distance, a large group approaching from the west.

"Nikonos is almost on us," I whisper harshly. "Father, we have to turn back."

"No. We are now caught between two enemy forces that are working together." Father lays open the problem in the same analytical manner that I chart a path through Rings in my head before I throw myself into the obstacle. He speaks loud enough so all can hear. "Nikonos will come himself out of fear I won't believe a surrogate. He knows it's possible Lord Gargaron will have sent someone to warn me, so he'll have tried to move quickly without a full army. I'm going to gamble that Nikonos has a smaller force than ours. That makes him weaker than the army behind us."

His pause falls like the silence after a bolt of lightning, waiting for the thunder to crash. Every man there hangs on his next utterance, as if he is the only lamp in a room where darkness kills. They all know that without Father's brilliance the Royal Army would already have been destroyed.

"So we will punch."

"Punch?" I mutter.

A few of the captains exchange surprised glances, but no one interrupts as he goes on.

"I am the bait. I will meet Prince Nikonos in the formal way, with only four adjutants, as if I did not suspect."

"Father, he'll kill you!"

He gives no sign he's heard me. "My presence will lull him into a false sense of security. A squad of spider scouts will accompany me, which is my privilege as general. Meanwhile, Lord Captain Kalliarkos will command a troop of cavalry to swing around and attack their force from the rear. My lord, if you can capture or kill Nikonos, all the better."

"What about me?" I demand.

"Jessamy, you will stay with the command unit under the supervision of Steward Haredas."

No! I want to shout as Father continues to give orders. All I can see in my mind's eye is Prince Temnos awash in his own blood, dead on the floor by Nikonos's sword because I ignorantly led him to his death. I will not stand aside while my beloved father walks into range of the man who slaughtered a child with as little emotion as that with which he might have swatted a fly.

So I make my own plan.

8

~~~~~

My plan is simplicity itself: as Haredas escorts me toward the command company, I allow a column of advancing cavalry to split me away from him.

"I will meet you there!" I shout as the inexorable flow separates us.

My mind teases apart noises and sights and smells to pinpoint the information I need: the location of the nearest spider scouts. At the edge of the road I dismount and shove the reins into the hands of a surprised infantryman. Then, with Inarsis's long knife bumping against my thigh, I set off at a run.

The last scout in line is always the lowest in rank. I cut in front of its heavy legs. With a thunk, the scout slams the spider to a halt and tilts the carapace forward. He's shielded front and back, only his eyes and nose visible, making him seem like a monstrous blend of spider and man, a creature out of legend.

"Get out of my way!" he shouts.

"By order of General Esladas and Lord Captain Kalliarkos, I order you to relinquish your spider to me. You're to report to Steward Haredas in the command unit for a new assignment."

"Who are you?"

"I'm the general's valiant daughter. Spider. I'm part of the plan."

Names and reputation work a potent magic. He doesn't dare risk defying the connections I have invoked, so he obeys.

I climb into the straps and tighten my hands on the levers that control the huge brass creature. Energy buzzes against my palms, the presence of the spark that gives the spider a kind of life.

"Walk with me, comrade," I whisper to the dead man whose essence powers this spider. Acknowledging him matters, even though he is long past being able to hear me.

My arms and legs fall back into the flow of handling the eight limbs and the pivoting carapace. Spider scouts can outpace a running man, and although a galloping horse will pass a spider in a short race, in the end a spider's uncanny endurance will leave a blown horse in the dust. I quicken my steps to catch up to the end of the line. My legs thud down like deadly hammers. Men calm their horses as I pass.

The spider scouts form up in front of Father and clank out in front of the infantry vanguard like a spear thrown in advance of the line. Ahead, pinpricks of light grow until I see they are lanterns hanging from the heads of pikes. They illuminate the shields forming the vanguard of Nikonos's group. Each shield is marked with the white sea-phoenix of the king's royal household but I am sure they are East Saroese troops in disguise.

A horn blasts three times. The men in the front rank slam the lower rims of their shields onto the ground, a wall bristling with pikes that horses won't charge. It spans the entire road, blocking our path.

We spiders clank to a halt a stone's toss from the shields. Father and his four adjutants approach. In the line facing us, two shields lift away, and five horsemen ride through the gap to meet him.

The man in front wears a helmet with a gold prince's circlet worked into the iron to mark his exalted rank. Of course there's no hint of the king's diadem. His officers are likewise wearing full armor and helmets. The night makes it hard to distinguish their faces because only their eyes are visible.

Father rides forward with his helmet tucked under his arm, head uncovered as a sign of subservience.

"Well met, General Esladas!" a voice rings out commandingly. I recognize Nikonos's rich, silky tone, and how false it sounds when he isn't spewing sarcasm and disdain. "The gods have providentially brought about our meeting at this very convenient time and place."

"Well met, Prince Nikonos. What reinforcements do you bring?"

My gaze catches on the slightest of movements: two shields part to create a narrow gap. Bodies shift position behind it, and I'm suddenly sure I see the curve of a bow. This is it. This is the ambush.

I lever back my forward limbs. My spider rears up like it is clawing at the starry heavens as I wildly cast one of my javelins toward Nikonos. Of course it goes wide but it's only a distraction.

"Ambush!" I scream.

Father ducks instinctively. An arrow sings through the air right where his head just was. A second arrow slams into his horse's withers. His officers push their mounts forward to place themselves in the line of fire between him and the enemy, and he lets them do it. He falls back, is hit in the leg, slides off his wounded horse.

With the same motion, I lower my carapace and charge. I can't look back or I'll die. Adjutants screen Nikonos with their own bodies and several go down in a flurry of arrows. I can't find a way around their thrashing horses as he flees.

Another spider punches through a shield with its lance arm, scattering men. Arrows pepper my brass skin as I slam down a leg atop more shields, its weight crumpling metal. All I can think of is my father sliding off the horse with an arrow in his flesh.

Braced on six legs, I punch with my two forelegs, over and over, breaking down the shield wall until the soldiers give way and fall back.

Behind us, a horn calls twice, pauses, calls four times, pauses, calls twice.

It takes me a moment to realize the other spiders are pulling back from the half-broken line. Why? *Why?* The enemy is giving way because we are metal and they are flesh.

I want to punch and punch but Nikonos has vanished into the roiling mass of his troops and I remember that Father has a plan.

I swing around, using my left foreleg like a scythe to cut a path out of the fray. Soldiers scatter, scuttling out of reach like crabs. My carapace swings over a corpse all bloody and crushed until, fully turned around, I stump after the other spiders. We flee like dogs retreating with tails between their legs as projectiles slam harmlessly into our brass backs.

Jeers rise from Nikonos's troops as they mock our flight.

But I know what is coming.

"Brace! Pull!"

A loud ratcheting noise clacks.

"Fly!"

Sealed ceramic pots sail over me and crash to the ground, shattering amid the enemy. There is a momentary silence, then more laughter from Nikonos's allies.

No scorpions here.

Flights of burning arrows streak out from our ranks. They set alight the naphtha splashed through the East Saroese pretenders.

A second volley launches and splatters, followed by a second flight of burning arrows. The fire spreads in stubborn, fierce flames.

Men scream and scramble. We spiders swivel back to the

attack. We become a moving wall of blades and claws, brass flashing, legs thumping down in a shuddering rhythm, the fire no menace to our metal. There isn't enough naphtha to burn for long but the damage to their cohesion is done.

Arrows and javelins slam my carapace, shaking me in my harness. A soldier backpedals in front of me, trying to get out of my way as I raise my forelegs. My memory flashes to a day long ago in the Ribbon Market when a spider's leg crushed a tiny child in front of its mother.

I can't think. I mustn't think. I must keep pushing forward and not think about what it means, how in war we use weapons to cut the spark of life out of bodies. We steal sparks to win battles. We are all in the business of killing to stay on top.

A horn cries in bursts. A noise rises like the rumble of waves beating on a rocky shoreline. My father's firebird veterans race across the last dying naphtha flames, past our brass legs.

Their punch shatters the weakening enemy line. Weapons rise and fall, clash and crunch. Lanterns crack and break and fall, transforming into a pulse of shadows as men keep fighting although they can barely see.

I follow the other spiders off the edge of the road and barely keep to my eight feet as I race down the slope. Something warm, wet, and salty slides from my forehead into my eyes, running around the curve of my nose. I don't hurt anywhere. I don't feel injured. Yet I swallow blood. I'm so thirsty.

Up on the road soldiers die or surrender. I am numb to the cries and screams of messy, ugly dying. I have to be numb.

Stars blaze in pinprick thickets overhead. The moon advances into the west as our beacon. The Royal Army plunges into the night in pursuit of Nikonos and his fleeing allies.

Instead of giving up the road we have claimed it.

I clank alone against the tide, stumping east as the Royal Army marches west past me. By the time I come up alongside the banners of the command company, I'm shaking with exhaustion and my head throbs.

I jerk my spider to a halt, unlatch the shield, and hang there, half in and half out of the carapace. Soldiers scramble down the bank as I drop to the ground. My legs give out, and I collapse to my hands and knees. Blood drips onto my left hand.

"Jessamy?" Steward Haredas's voice cuts through the haze. "Good Goat! Are you wounded?"

At home the steward would never have touched one of Captain Esladas's daughters. Now he hoists me and force-marches me up the steep embankment. The general's carriage rolls at a walking pace with shutters open and my father inside. My lips move in a soundless thanks to all the gods that he is alive. Naturally he is leaning out the window, flinging commands like spears. Messengers appear and vanish, bringing him news, racing away to deliver new orders.

When I'm unceremoniously shoved into the still-moving carriage and slam down onto the bench opposite him, all I can think to say is "It's not my blood."

He's seated with his injured leg stuck straight out in front, his boot resting on the bench beside me. A man wearing the coiled serpent badge of the physicians' guild is holding aside the skirted plates of his armored coat so they don't jostle the arrow sticking out of his thigh.

"By the creases and smudges on your riding gear, I see you have spent some time in a spider. Which I do not recall giving you permission to do."

He beckons with a hand for me to come close enough that he can brush his fingers along the injury. My hair is still tied back although the scarf is working loose.

"Turn your head," he orders so curtly I cringe. He is really angry with me. But he probes the wound with a touch as gentle as Mother's.

To the doctor he says, "What do you think? It feels like a graze, not a deep wound. There's a lot of blood."

The doctor considers me with the dispassionate gaze of a person who has seen much suffering and death. He does not remove his hands from Father's armor, however, and his feet are braced on the floor so he can absorb every shake and rattle of the carriage without allowing the armored coat to jostle the protruding arrow.

"Scalp wounds bleed a great deal. A salve of honey and alfalfa should set it to rights."

"Have you this salve in your pouch?"

"Yes, General, and if you would be so kind as to allow me to stop the carriage as I have requested ten times now, I can treat her wound as well as get this arrow out of your leg before more damage is done."

Father ignores the doctor's sarcasm. He signals to a captain trotting alongside the window. "Take your squad to the rear. Cover the road with naphtha and wait, in hiding, until the enemy's vanguard arrives. Then set it alight. That will slow them down."

"Yes, General." The captain taps his chest twice, the salute we girls learned when we were tiny. Father replies with the same salute, and the captain rides off.

"But Father, how can a few men sent back to enemy lines like that not get cut down as they try to run away afterward?"

"Quiet, Jessamy!" This stern look is the one that made me fear I could never win his approval, but I see the shadow in it now. How many men has he sacrificed in this way in his years in command?

"General, I need to get this arrow out," repeats the doctor.

Father rests an arm on the window's edge, leaning out. "Any news of Prince Kalliarkos?" he calls to someone I can't see.

A male voice answers, out of my view. "By last report his troop was chasing the royal carriage."

"Very good." He calls out to the driver to halt, then settles back with a sigh. "Very well, Doctor."

"Thank the gods, stubborn goat," the doctor mutters.

We slow to a stop.

"Give me the salve," says Father. He unties my scarf. On one side the fabric is soaked through with what must be my blood. Carefully he uses the doctor's tiny trowel to press salve along the cut. At first the mixture feels oddly cool and then it stings so brutally that I'm dizzied by the pain and shut my eyes. My memory flashes to an image of a dead man crushed on the ground, and I open my eyes because I can't bear to think of how I mauled through soldiers and kept walking.

Father takes the scarf out of my hands and does a creditable job of tying it around my hair, bloody patches and all. "As well I allowed your mother to teach me how to deal with you girls' hair," he murmurs so low he probably doesn't even mean me to hear. The words carve misery straight into my heart. It's a battle not to burst into sobs, but I manage to focus the agony into the burning gash.

He grasps my right hand between his. "Go ahead, Doctor."

I tense, ready for anything. He fixes his gaze on a target spot behind my head as the doctor works the arrow loose from the flesh. His grip crushes my fingers, his lips pressed together until they lose all color. Sweat drips down his face.

"Ah!" The doctor gives a satisfied gasp. The arrow clatters onto the floor. After smearing salve over the wound, the doctor gives it two neat stitches and binds it with a cloth. "Not as bad as it could have been, General. You're fortunate."

Slowly Father unclenches his fingers. My hand aches, and I shake it to get the blood flowing. He gestures out the window to a waiting adjutant.

"Bring a horse."

"General!" objects the doctor.

"Father! You shouldn't be riding."

A soldier leads a horse up. Father tests his weight on the wounded leg. He winces at first touch, then nods crisply when the leg doesn't buckle. Finally he turns back to me.

"If we don't capture and kill Nikonos now, we'll lose our best chance to defeat him cleanly. I know it was you in the spider who warned me. But now you will stay in this carriage. Not because I believe you are incapable but because adversaries work alone while soldiers work in concert. Do not cause trouble for me by trying some new reckless stunt. You aren't trained for this."

"Yes, Father."

An officer cups laced fingers under Father's boot to lift him to the saddle. He mounts clumsily for all that, with a grimace of pain he would not normally show in front of me. I grip the windowsill, staring after him with my heart twisted into knots and my head stinging, blood gone sticky on my lips as he rides into the night.

I want to leap out of the carriage and race after him but strength also lies in knowing when to wait. Anyway, I'm so exhausted, dragged down by my vision of the crushed soldier, that when I brace my body into a corner of the carriage, its jostling and jolting shakes me into sleep.

☾⟋⟍⟍☾

I wake when the carriage halts. I'm alone, the doctor gone, the shutters closed. The stuffy air makes me sneeze, and the sneeze makes my head flare with pain. Just as I put my hand on the latch to look outside, the door opens. I jerk back in surprise, but it's Kal who leaps up into the carriage. His face is smeared with grime, his hair looks crusted by sand, his hands are several shades darker from layers of dirt, and I could gaze at him forever.

He examines me with a frown, then carefully touches my head. "There's blood on your scarf."

"Just a cut on my scalp." I lean across him and shut the door. "I'm fine, Kal."

What's fine is the way his mouth feels when I kiss him. What's fine is the pressure of his knee against my thigh. What's fine is the stroke of his thumb across my palm.

He breaks off, sets me back on the bench, and sits opposite, careful not to touch me.

"Kal..."

"We're not alone anymore. Everyone is watching me."

His tone is gentle but it still hurts, even as I know he's right. "What happened to Nikonos?"

"We won the battle and took possession of the royal carriage, but Nikonos escaped. His East Saroese allies were able to signal to a war galley that was shadowing them offshore. He got away on the ship." He rubs his eyes wearily. "He abandoned most of his troops."

"He abandoned the people who fought and died for him? No wonder the soldiers of the Royal Army have the good sense to prefer my father, and you."

His bleak expression lightens as his smile melts into me. I take hold of his hand, and he gives up the pretense of formality and slides across to the bench next to me, bringing his mouth to mine.

The door opens.

"My lord Kalliarkos." There stands my father, with his impeccable timing, catching us doing the thing he adamantly warned me never, ever to do with a highborn Patron lord.

9

Kal squeezes my fingers in reassurance and only then releases me and steps down from the carriage. He does not blush as he nods at Father. Why should he? Father may be a general, but Kalliarkos is the prince.

"My lord, the army awaits you." Disapproval sharpens Father's diction.

Kal presses his lips together, glances at me, then says, "Doma Jessamy will accompany me."

"My lord, these soldiers have maintained exceptional discipline under extreme circumstances. Your presence gives them courage for the final and most dangerous phase of our fight. Don't let this get in the way; it will be seen as a sign of poor judgment and weakness on your part."

Only then do I realize how many people are within view of the carriage and its open door, how many saw that the prince who means to be our next king woke the sleeping girl in the carriage and must suspect he gave her a kiss that should never belong to her. They don't want a mule mascot to fight alongside. They want a noble Patron king to fight for.

"I'll stay with you, Father."

Kal's gaze meets mine accusingly.

"You just said essentially the same thing in the carriage," I say to him in a low voice.

His frown deepens. "Very well."

He walks away, officers falling in beside him. A resplendent carriage flying the crowned sea-phoenix banner of the royal palace has been drawn up to take pride of place in the command company. The carriage also flies the personal banner of Nikonos and, to my surprise, they leave it flying.

Officers wearing the livery of the royal guards kneel before Kal and offer their swords, hilts toward him, as if expecting him to drive the blades into their bodies. They are commanders of the troops whom Nikonos abandoned. Kal speaks words I can't hear; their weapons are taken away by the soldiers surrounding them. I press a hand over my mouth, short of breath, but they are allowed to live, to offer their allegiance to a new prince.

A splendid brown gelding is led forward. An officer ties a magnificent hip-length cloak of gold silk over Kal's grimy riding clothes. Purple ribbons attached to the cape's shoulders flutter in the wind. He swings onto the horse and a golden-handled whip is handed up to him. From this elevation he gives a triumphal wave and a crisp salute to the watching men.

A wild cheer roars, carried out along the ranks. His gaze touches mine across the distance that separates us.

The heat seems suddenly overwhelming. My vision blurs.

"Move back from the window, Jessamy." An unfamiliar vulnerability trembles in Father's tone.

An adjutant helps him in beside me. The frowning doctor hops in after and begins fussing over his leg as horns blare and the carriage rolls. Father massages his forehead, in more pain than I had guessed, but when he lowers the hand his gaze is clear. "Tell me what happened to Bettany."

"To Bettany?"

"Do not pretend you do not understand me. When we were at Port Selene together, both you and Amaya slid around the topic of your sister as if around a scorpion on the path."

I fold my hands on my lap and bow my head.

"If you are frightened to confide in me, Jessamy, then I have not been a good father. Bettany and I have had our troubles, but I love her just as I do all you girls. Please do not leave me wondering."

The plea sounds so odd coming from his lips that it chases past all my defenses. So I tell him the story of how Amaya and I concocted a plan to search for our sister among the workers on the far-flung Garon estates, and how our journey brought us to Akheres Oasis.

"Bettany couldn't forgive you or Mother. When she was taken to the mines with the other household servants it was a foreign doctor named Agalar who protected them. He took her on as an assistant and promised to train her as a healer. But it turned out he was a mercenary working with the East Saroese. She did try to warn us at first, without giving away the ambush at Crags Fort, but in the end she betrayed us in favor of him. I don't know where she is now. I don't expect to ever see her again. I'm not sure I want to."

He sits in silence for so long that I wonder if I should comfort him, but I don't know how.

Finally he shifts, a twist of pain parting his lips. "It should have been me who protected her."

He looks so weary I feel shame using his regret against him, but I do it anyway. "Father, I left two fellow adversaries at the rear of the army, digging a trench to slow down the East Saroese. I need to go back and see if they're all right. You wouldn't want me to abandon my comrades."

He winces. "Your desire to look for your friends is commendable. Steward Haredas will escort you with a squad of twelve."

"I—"

"We are not discussing this, Jessamy. Besides being my daughter, you now have a relationship with the king that must and will change how people treat you."

"Yes, Father. I was about to say I understand your concern."

His rare smile flashes, and it warms me.

When Steward Haredas appears, I am handed over.

The rising sun bathes the royal banners with its brilliant light. A wind off the sea unfurls them like triumph. Around us, men sing a hymn to the Sun of Justice, and the roll of their voices thunders through me and makes tears come to my eyes. Isn't this what justice looks like? The murderer Nikonos forced to flee and the Royal Army under its proper leader, a prince who will be a just and wise king as soon as he has driven the invaders from the land?

And yet Kal will have to fight his way into a city still ruled by his cousin Serenissima, knowing a huge East Saroese army dogs our heels and Nikonos is still alive.

"Doma Jessamy, please stay with me this time." Steward Haredas has the look of a man who wants to be anywhere but at the duty he's just been assigned.

"Yes, Domon."

"Now that your father is the general in command of the Royal Army, you must call me 'steward,' Doma. To call me 'domon' is to suggest I outrank you, which I do not."

My surprise must register on my face.

He adds, "Despite your irregular birth, you are the general's daughter. His position must never be called into question, so therefore you must never be seen to be a lesser person than those who serve him."

"Even though I am a mule."

"The general has always made it clear he will not tolerate any use of that word among his household."

The weary soldiers stride with renewed determination as the news filters back along their seemingly endless column that Lord Prince Captain Kalliarkos has won a victory and now leads the Royal Army. The sun is halfway up the sky before Haredas and I reach the last wagons and the rearmost unit. I shade my eyes into the glare. The road stretches eastward through flat countryside. Smoke twists in columns behind us, marking the destructive path of our enemy through the once-peaceful Efean countryside as they burn villages close to the road. Only the brutal speed of chasing us prevents them from doing far worse.

Two bodies lie at the base of the embankment. One twitches, and I'm aghast that a wounded man has been tossed away to die, but then a fox emerges from beneath the fabric of his tabard with a glistening moist organ in its mouth.

Hastily I swing my horse around to pace the captain overseeing the rear guard.

"Captain, where are the Efean laborers?"

He stares at me as if I am a crocodile abruptly capable of speech, then looks at Steward Haredas for help.

"Doma Jessamy is looking for two Commoners who were back here with the trenching crew," says Haredas.

"Cursed Commoners." The captain spits on the ground. "We distributed weapons to them, as we were ordered to do, even though I knew nothing good would come of it. They abandoned us just as if we hadn't rescued them from the enemy. And stole the weapons we lent them. Lazy thieves! That's gratitude for you."

"None of them stayed behind?"

I'm going to find a way to fight for Efea, Mis told me. *For Efeans. Not for them.*

96

Here I am, riding with *them*. Allied with *them*.

A wild desire bursts in my heart: to take my horse and ride inland, to find Mis and Dusty, to vanish into the heart of Efea alongside people who will accept me as I am. But I can't leave Father now, and I won't abandon Kal. I have to see this through to its end because there's no other way to make sure Nikonos and Serenissima and their foreign allies do not destroy Efea.

Yet an unquiet voice tugs at my loyalties. What if I'm wrong?

⌇

Two days later, not long after dawn, we march into view of the sycamores marking the turnout to Falcon Villa, where Father married Lady Menoë. The command company with its carriages pulls out for fresh horses. I can't help but think of Kal driving me here in a race to get Father's help to free Mother and the others from the oracle's tomb.

"We will reach Saryenia by midday." Father sips at a flask, looking out the open window of the carriage at the army marching past, still in disciplined ranks.

"Are we going to set a siege? Won't that just trap us between the queen inside the city and the East Saroese army marching up behind us?"

"We are going to bluff." He has ruthlessly kept me beside him, acting as my constant chaperone. I have seen Kal twice, and always with Father in attendance so we have been allowed only to greet each other from a polite distance. "We are taking a dangerous chance. Once we enter the city, if fighting breaks out you must melt away into the population of Commoners."

"No."

He blinks. "What did you say?"

"I want to stay with you, Father."

He takes a much longer draft of the wine in his flask. His face is flushed, and maybe that is a tear in his eye. "Very well. But you will stay in this carriage."

"Yes, Father."

We roll on past grain fields, lush orchards, and prosperous villages. Efeans pushing carts and driving wagons are streaming away from their homes, some hurrying for the walls of Saryenia while most head north into the interior.

We pass the regimental encampments, now empty. The Royal Road's night-lanterns hang at intervals, unlit because it is day, and beside each lantern hangs a cage. No new prisoners have been hung out to die in recent months; the old prisoners are dead, rotting away under the sun, skin turning to leather and viscera decaying until there is nothing left but bone.

I think of the horses left behind, the stragglers, the skirmishers, the captain sent to light an oily fire; he knew his task was to create havoc and cause damage, not to survive.

I brace myself for what I fear is coming as the walls of Saryenia rise out of the west. Always in my youth those walls meant security. Now I see only the promise of death. How can Kal possibly win his way through a city occupied by foreign soldiers and a queen who wants to kill him?

We pass companies of soldiers who have halted at the side of the road to allow the command company to move forward to the vanguard. They cheer as the royal carriage and the general's carriage pass. For people watching from the city walls, it will appear that the conquering hero, Nikonos, has returned, flying his banner and the king's flag of Efea, bringing General Esladas with him as prisoner or as an ally.

That is our bluff. Let them see what they expect to see.

Even so, Father's ability to march calmly into a potential disaster amazes me. The walls loom so high I have to tilt back my head to see the battlements.

Horns blare from the tops of the walls. Will they close the gates? Do they guess the ruse? Has Nikonos arrived here before us?

The horns blare again, singing out the fanfare that rouses the city when its king or queen returns in triumph.

Unmolested, we cross the plank causeway across the canal that rings the city and pass under the triple gates. I brace myself, waiting for boiling oil or hot sand to be poured down on us, but no attack mars our entry. Nikonos's banner carries us past the gate and the guards. Kal cannot be seen behind the royal carriage's closed shutters.

"Shut the window on your side, Jessamy." Father does not close the shutter on his side but draws a gauzy curtain across, making it hard to see him. When I don't immediately obey, he reaches across me and latches the shutter.

Our procession rumbles down the Avenue of the Soldier.

Squads of enemy soldiers on patrol line up at intervals to salute in the East Saroese manner, a bow with hands braced together. They are paler than the local Saroese, and many are burned red from too much sun.

Beyond them, I glimpse local people staring with wary interest, although they keep a wide berth from the foreign soldiers and do not cheer the arrival of Nikonos and his banner. It seems the populace does not trust their new king and his foreign allies, but they are caught by the majesty of the procession, our tattered remnants marching with dogged pride. It is only after the royal carriage has moved on that I hear people shout out greetings as they see familiar faces in the Royal Army.

We reach the Square of the Moon and the Sun and make a wide turn onto the Avenue of Triumphs, which leads to the king's palace. How strange that I am part of a royal victory procession like the one Amaya and Mother and I watched the day Father sat in glory as a newly promoted general, the last day we were a happy family all together.

The words come out as if I have no rein on them. Hoarsely I say, "Mother was so proud of you that day. She wept to see you given pride of place in your own general's carriage. How could you have abandoned her, Father?"

He doesn't look toward me but I hear his words, murmured for himself and not for me. "I will make it up to her. She'll understand."

"How can she understand you just leaving her when you

didn't even know she was safe? How could you bear to do it, if you truly loved her?"

His fingers tighten on the hilt of his sword, not aggressively but with suppressed tension. He won't answer, and he refuses to look at me.

I don't have the courage to ask again.

I ride with the victorious army he commands. That is answer enough.

The gates of the king's palace open before the combined force of the royal carriage, the royal sea-phoenix banner, and Prince Nikonos's personal banner of gold and purple, all of which taken together fool the guards into thinking that Nikonos sits inside. This has to work. If they realize it's Kal, they'll cut him down without mercy.

I still have the knife Inarsis gave me. Heart racing, I set it across my lap, ready to fight if we're discovered. Putting Kal on the throne is the only way to defeat the invaders. I'm sure of it. I'm sure.

The outer courtyard fills up with our infantry units. Officers come to the curtain where, hidden behind the gauze, Father gives a stream of orders in a low voice.

"Make sure all approaches to the palace are under our control. Secure the grounds. Search every chamber and storehouse. Imprison all East Saroese soldiers who surrender, and kill those who resist. Restrict the palace guards to their barracks until we can determine their loyalty. We remain on high alert."

Our soldiers race up stairs to the guard walks, spreading out to take over the palace.

The royal carriage passes through a second gate into an inner courtyard. Here courtiers sit on benches beneath the shade of trees, waiting for permission to enter the king's audience chamber. As the royal carriage halts, these courtiers leap to their feet and press fists to hearts, each wishing to be seen as first to greet the returning king. Officials wearing the gray silk of the royal stewards push open a third gate. Accompanied by a complement of Father's veteran troops and Kalliarkos's personal guards, the royal carriage passes through.

The gate shuts before we can follow.

"Father, what if the palace officials attack him?"

"Quiet."

No screams and no clash of arms reach my ears although I am certain the palace officials, confronted with Kalliarkos, will react with immediate and drastic measures. He's armed. He'll defend himself, but we have to reach him before he's overwhelmed. From farther away, in the other precincts of the palace compound, a flare of sound from a confrontation bursts like a flock of birds taking wing, then calms.

Father gets out of his carriage and limps to the gate. I'm right at his heels. Courtiers murmur, staring at Father and at me. Always at me. One of the stewards steps out of line to block my path. The purple stripes on his sleeves indicate that somewhere in his past he can boast of a palace forebear.

His haughty gaze flicks over Father's stained tabard and

dusty boots. "Without a letter of entry marked with the royal seal, you may not enter. And this...creature may not pass under the gate that admits the elect to the king's audience hall. It should not be walking within these walls at all."

Father still carries the captain's whip he earned years ago. He presses its tip against the man's chest and shoves him hard enough that the steward stumbles back.

"Open the gate."

But a palace official with palace antecedents is not easily cowed, not even by my father. "No. There is protocol to follow, something a lowborn man like you cannot understand."

I've already eyed the wall and the trees. "It's all right," I say. "I don't need to pass *under* the gate."

I launch myself into the friendly canopy of a persimmon, a tree favored by the royal family. The branches sway alarmingly as I climb. One cracks under my weight as I leap but I'm able to grab the top of the wall and roll onto a walkway. A surprised guardsman runs up, sword drawn. I vault past him and scramble down the stairs. There's yet another courtyard inside, paved in marble and lined by pillars, where the royal carriage has come to rest. It's abandoned; the area has emptied, not a soldier or official in sight except the man on the wallwalk who is now being yelled at by my father from the other side.

Where is Kal?

I drag the gate open and Father enters. In his wake a flood of firebird soldiers move in so fast that I'm pressed back against the wall, caught there as they fill the courtyard. Father hammers on the magnificent dark wood of the two-story-high double doors to the audience hall. There's no answer.

He corrals the haughty steward and demands, "Is there another entrance?"

A hollow knocking sound from inside the hall makes us all jump.

The doors swing open to reveal palace stewards in gray silk. Father beckons to me to follow but he doesn't wait. With his loyal soldiers at his back, he strides into the massive audience hall, larger by itself than the entire compound I grew up in. The murals painted onto its walls depict the perilous sea voyage of the first Kliatemnos, the fleet's miraculous survival in a fierce storm, when the shadow of a sea-phoenix kept his ships afloat, and the glorious shores of Efea where he made landfall and gained a crown. The sea-phoenix diadem is painted on his noble brow in gold leaf. Real jewels are embedded as his eyes, and his sister and queen, Serenissima the First, glitters, for her figure is constructed of tiny tiles rather than painted. The effect makes her seem to leap out from the mural like she is doubly alive, a woman with two sparks.

Our footfalls thunder on the marble floor because we are so many. Father walks in front, his limp quite noticeable, providing an easy target for the palace guards stationed on either side of the hall, swords and spears held ready at their sides. More palace officials cluster at the far end of the hall, whispering as they take their ordained places. It all happens so fast.

The king's throne sits on a dais, framed by a vast carved

lintel that captures the throne as if within a picture's frame. The seat has a simple base with a back that flares outward in the shape of sea-phoenix wings, enfolding and embracing the ornately cushioned chair like white foam rising off the water.

A man already sits on the throne.

At first I think it is Nikonos, that he has arrived on a swift war galley before us and we have walked into his trap.

But it is Kal who surveys the men sinking to one knee to surrender their loyalty and lives to him. I'm so surprised that I forget to kneel. Across the distance he sees me standing. His expression isn't triumphant. Instead he wears a mask of grim resignation.

King of Efea. The destiny he never wanted.

I helped him win this trial. He climbed the victory tower, and now he can never let go of the victor's ribbon until he is dead.

10

⟨≈≈≈⟩

Kal makes a stirring and fortunately brief speech to the Royal Army.

"Your courage…hard fought…sacrifices not in vain… We have prevailed here but more battles await us.…Our enemy must be vanquished and Efea set free of foreign boots.…"

He might as well be speaking gibberish.

Servants fan the warm air to keep it moving. Watching their seemingly tireless arms, I cannot help but think of the boy I saw murdered to keep Prince Temnos alive. The son of a lord named Perikos, he'd been brought into the palace to be a loyal companion to the prince. When I think of that nameless youth, I'm not sorry King Kliatemnos was murdered for his part in the child's death. And yet when I think of Temnos, I know we did the right thing in driving Nikonos away. Kalliarkos and Father can make something better. They can.

They have to.

After Kal finishes and the obligatory cheers die down, palace officials form a phalanx of silk and escort him out a bright red door set into the back wall. I want to follow, but the palace is a Fives court with new rules, ones no one has bothered to explain to me, and for once I'm too intimidated to move.

A squad of veterans under the command of Captain Helias sets up a tight guard at the red door. Once they've secured the entrance the captain cuts across the hall to where I'm standing at the back.

"King Kalliarkos commanded me to make sure you are safe, Doma."

He offers a smile, then blushes as if he's been caught trying to filch a cake that belongs to someone else. He's a nice-looking young man who has been nothing but punctiliously polite. I want to break out laughing because he's exactly the sort of promising young highborn captain Amaya once chattered incessantly about snaring. But I'm afraid anything I say or do might reflect poorly on Kal, might make me a liability to his moments-old claim to the throne.

Father appears, shedding dust and disapproval. "Captain, I will take charge of my daughter. Your responsibility is to guard the king."

The captain salutes. "Yes, General."

Father ushers me through the red door into a part of the palace I would never in a hundred years have dreamed I would see. A path bisects a lovely garden, its twin pools lush with lotus flowers. Gray-robed stewards and palace guards in gold tabards watch me like they wish they could pluck me from where I've fallen amid the blossoms and toss me out with the rubbish. Whispers catch at the edge of my hearing, making me flush at such demeaning comments.

"...shameful...embarrassing..."

"The general dangling his daughter like ripe fruit before a hungry boy..."

Father halts, and they cease whispering at once. Nevertheless he takes his time memorizing the features of each official who has dared to gossip in his presence.

At the far end of the garden, Kal has halted on the steps leading up to a luxurious audience pavilion for noble visitors. A splendid couch embroidered with a sea-phoenix stands above the rest, placed on a dais.

"I will take reports here," he says to the officials who have arrayed themselves on the steps to block his ascent.

A senior steward bows. "Your Gracious Majesty. Of course you must first wish to bathe after your arduous journey. I will assign attendants to oversee your ablutions in the private residence." He gestures toward a gate on the other side of the garden. "Once you are clean and properly attired, you will be fit to preside over any immediate administrative duties."

Kal's voice is clipped with annoyance. "We must secure the palace and clear the city of all East Saroese soldiers before I can consider a bath and proper attire."

"But Your Gracious Majesty—"

"No."

I would laugh at his blunt tone but there is nothing to laugh about. Palace officials make their lives serving the king and queen. Did these men greet Nikonos with the same obsequious flattery with which they flutter about Kal? Are they just putting on a show for him, waiting to betray him the moment his back is turned?

He glances toward me. I lift my chin, and he breaks away from the officials and walks over.

"General Esladas, what do you recommend? I never thought we would get this far. It happened so fast."

"The palace should fall under our control quickly, Your Gracious Majesty. It will take longer to be sure we have the city under our full jurisdiction."

"I have no concern about the military aspect of our enterprise, not with you in command, General. I meant, how should we direct these officials who are so determined to cage my every step in protocol?"

"As far as I can see, the palace stewards are like dogs fighting over scraps. One to polish the king's boots and another to adjust his sleeves. I would never allow so many useless hangers-on in any army I command. But your understanding of palace politics far exceeds mine, Your Gracious Majesty."

"Before, I never had to give the orders or worry that I would make a mistake in protocol that would open me up to derision and insubordination." Kal glances at the waiting officials, then at me again. But now that we are here, I have no idea how to proceed, no way to help him, no thought at all. I've run into a trap I don't know how to get out of.

"If I may make a suggestion, Your Gracious Majesty. I was raised at court." Captain Helias salutes, fist to heart.

"I wish you would."

"Allow the royal officials to feel useful and not to feel threatened. Let them go about their routine, as they are trained to do in exacting detail. But do not be ruled by their whims if they go against your wishes, lest you be seen as weak. Meanwhile, assign a trusted officer to interview each official separately over the next few days. Those who criticize their comrades in hope of gaining your favor can be eased aside into positions where they do not wait directly upon Your Gracious Majesty."

I break in, still thinking of the surprised look on Temnos's face when his uncle stabbed him, the moment when the shock of his mother's betrayal hadn't started to hurt yet. "I would not put it past Queen Serenissima to have insinuated knife-carrying men among the officials, willing to murder anyone she points to."

"Jessamy!" Father's tone is cutting. "I did not give you permission to speak."

"The doma is not incorrect." The captain has the highborn ability to speak in a perfectly modulated tone but the tension in his shoulders makes him seem annoyed. "Nikonos ruled as king for less than ten days. He was never popular. He's still a threat with the East Saroese army, of course. But here in the palaces it is Queen Serenissima of whom Your Gracious Majesty must beware. Besides ruling the queen's palace, she will have loyal servants and spies insinuated into every corner of the king's palace."

Kal nods with a resigned glance toward the officials, who are waiting with prim disapproval for him to summon them. "So to begin with, I must confront Serenissima."

"Not yet, Your Gracious Majesty," says Helias. "It is imperative you meet Queen Serenissima on your terms, not hers. Make her wait and wonder. Furthermore, do not summon her until you can show yourself before her in kingly splendor."

"Very well. I will take a bath. I will ask—"

"Command," I murmur, with a glance at Father.

"I will *command* the royal stewards to assign to you, General Esladas, a suite of rooms next to mine until matters are more settled."

Kal carefully does not look at me as, with a kingly nod, he leaves us and walks to the stewards, but everyone has seen whose advice he values most.

Father bids Captain Helias stay behind. "You and your company will guard his person at all times, day and night. Secure the royal kitchen. Let no food or drink touch his lips that has not been sampled in front of you by the head cook."

"Yes, General. I had understood that to be my duty."

"You may go."

Captain Helias taps his chest twice, to signal obedience, and Father answers in the same way.

Yet the instant the captain is out of earshot, Father is the same strict disciplinarian I've always known. "Do not again speak to the king until I give you permission. We will discuss your relationship with him later." He keeps his voice low as a stout man dressed in steward gray glides up.

"General Esladas, I am Junior Royal Steward Sarnon." He punctuates his speech with so many bows they begin to seem disrespectful. "His Gracious Majesty has given me the honor of escorting you to your new apartments and arranging for a bath and refreshment."

"Jessamy, come with me and do not stray."

Sarnon gives a visible start at my inclusion. "My orders—"

"Are to settle me securely. Find women attendants who can help my daughter bathe." Sarnon glances toward an older steward for orders, and the older man signals with hand signs I can't interpret. "This way, General."

The bustling streets of Saryenia and the obstacles of a Fives court seem like child's play compared to the maze of the palace, with gardens nested inside gardens, corridors lined with paper lanterns trailing ribbons in every color, statues of poets and playwrights flanking doors like literary guards congealed into stone. Accompanied by Father's entourage of officers and military stewards, we are shown into a suite of rooms so magnificent I can't help but think they must belong to the king, until Sarnon informs Father these are the apartments that belonged to Prince Nikonos, back before he made his play for the throne.

Haredas takes over as Father's traveling chest is brought in and a clean uniform unwrapped from a layer of protective cloth. I sit on a stool as Father vanishes with the doctor and an aide into another part of the suite. Haredas does not allow the scarcely concealed sneers of the royal stewards to deter him from clearing jewel-encrusted ink pots and a lacquered writing board off a desk and setting out Father's writing board, ink, and pens, all crafted out of ordinary materials that can withstand the rigors of a campaign.

Two soldiers wearing different regimental badges appear to give reports and have to wait. They work very hard not to look at me while the royal stewards, also relegated to waiting, stare at me and whisper. I wish I could be anywhere but here. No wonder Kal tried to convince me that we should run away together. He understood what awaited us. And yet to abandon Efea would mean to abandon my beloved mother, my sisters, everyone I care for, and I can't do it.

At last Father returns, freshly bathed. The two soldiers report that the palace has been secured. Father gives a new string of orders, directing a brisk roundup of the East Saroese troops in the city, then sits down and begins writing the daily report he has kept all his life.

A stir at the door startles us. A trio of women enter. They wear calf-length orange jackets over pale yellow sheath dresses. The eldest wears her age-whitened hair in a plain braid but the two younger ones are highborn women with beaded and beribboned hair in the most fashionable style. The instant these two get their first glimpse of Father they look surprised, then exchange glances hot with unspoken words.

Father rises politely, his steely gaze more intimidating than any weapon.

The youngest speaks to Sarnon, who speaks to Haredas, who tells Father that the chamber ladies, the king's own attendants, have come in response to his request.

The youngest simpers, "General, I am Lady Volua. Please know that my companion Lady Galaia and I can provide any service you need."

His frown kills her ingratiating smile. "Very well. Please assist my daughter Jessamy with bathing and an appropriate change of clothes."

All this time the women have been too busy ogling my father to see me seated against the wall. But they notice me when I stand.

"Junior Steward Sarnon, we are royal attendants, not stable hands." Lady Volua taps her nose as if to object to the smell.

Father tenses with outrage, but when his glare merely makes her smirk, I break in because I am not about to let them think they intimidate me.

"It's all right, Father. I can manage on my own."

"She speaks Saroese, and so well!" exclaims the shorter one, Galaia.

"Yes, I don't only bray." I'm so much taller and bigger than they are, with my mother's height and my brawny shoulders honed in the Fives, that Volua and Galaia take a hasty step back as if to get out of the way of my kick.

Father shakes his head and I can't tell whether he's about to correct me for my rude manners or is suppressing a rude comment of his own. I don't want him to get into trouble, so I nod respectfully at the older woman, hoping she'll be more cooperative.

"Perhaps you can assist me, Doma."

She nods in reply, looking as if she'd like to express her opinion of the other two ladies but age has given her the wisdom to remain silent. I want to like her, but I know better. She might be an asp in disguise.

She shows me through a curtained sleeping chamber and onto a shaded portico overlooking a private bathing courtyard tiled with jade. Three walls form a long mural depicting a royal garden party with a queen presiding over the festivities. The depictions of food and drink flowing out of a gigantic double-horned cornucopia are created with actual pearls and jewels. Its casual splendor takes me aback.

The attendant clears her throat.

"I am Jessamy, Doma," I say in my most courteous voice, and I'm embarrassed when she doesn't even bother to reply or give her own name.

In formal silence she helps me remove my clothing. The ties and clasps are clogged with dirt and grit; the scarf wrapped over my hair is stiff with dried blood. Unlike the other women with their sneers and pretended surprise, she makes no comment as she sets each disgustingly filthy item into a large brass basin beside my father's discarded gear. Once I am naked she hands me a shift, then goes inside some kind of steward's cupboard full of vials and unguents and soaps.

I pull on the shift, woven of a sheer cotton that leaves little to the imagination, but I'm still glad of even this much covering when the other two ladies hurry onto the portico, all smiles and graciousness.

"There you are. Larissa is just collecting a few things for your bath. If you'll come with us, we will take you."

Do they intend to escort me to the actual stables? Doma Larissa has not looked away from the shelves and her silence makes me feel I have no choice but to go. The last thing I want is to make my father look bad.

"Are you sure I'm not supposed to bathe in this courtyard?" I ask.

"That pool is for swimming and cooling off and entertainment. You don't *wash* there."

We pass through a gate onto another portico that overlooks the most splendid garden I have ever seen, saturated with the intense colors of flowering vines and shrubs. The fragrance alone is staggering, like pots of incense. My companions hurry me along a winding path. I hate the way they urge me along, like they don't want me to get my feet under me, like they want me to stumble. They cover their mouths, trying not to laugh, as we emerge onto a polished marble pavement surrounding two bathing pools and an awning furnished with painted screens and embroidered couches. The larger pool is rectangular, tiled in a blue lapis so incandescent it hurts my eyes. In the small pool Kalliarkos reclines at his ease, eyes closed as water is poured over his head by one of a squad of eager attendants, all male.

He's freshly shaved, and his hair has been clipped. Rose petals float around him. Seeing him is like seeing a dream of what I've always been told is most desirable in the world.

I know instantly that I am not supposed to be here.

Lady Volua lifts her chin with a gloating smirk. "Your Gracious Majesty, we have brought you a special gift lightly wrapped. I confess the girl has picked up some mud along the way, and I fear not even the strongest soap will scrub off *all* the dirt."

Kal opens his eyes.

His double take would be funny if everyone weren't looking thunderously disapproving. My own furious blush doesn't amuse me at all. Should I run back the way we came? Or refuse to budge, to show I can't be bullied?

Of course at that very moment Captain Helias strides into view, escorting in several high-ranking palace stewards for some manner of royal consultation. When he sees me he stops dead. Lady Volua's glee turns positively radiant as the officials take in the full degrading glory of the scene. All my proud defiance dissolves under the scrutiny of so many censorious eyes. I wish I could sink into the ground and vanish.

Kal looks angrier than I have ever seen him, as if rage has stolen his voice.

Brisk footfalls interrupt our tableau. Larissa enters, carrying a tray, which she sets down on a table beside the pool. Without a word, she whisks a clean towel off the table, snaps it out, and holds it open to conceal Kal from the rest of us as he gratefully stands and allows her to wrap it around him. She then sweeps off her orange calf-length jacket and settles it over my shoulders as an extra layer of modesty.

"Out!" Kal's curt command stirs them to immediate obedience. All the attendants and officials hurry away into the garden. "Except you, Doma Larissa. If you please."

The old woman nods, and only now, because she's no longer wearing the jacket over her sheath underdress, do I realize she wears an ill-wisher's beads around her neck!

Every well-to-do Patron family keeps an ill-wisher to guard its children, for such a woman can cast the evil eye onto any person who tries to harm her charges. They carry in their bodies the bad fortune that marred their own lives, which is why people fear even to touch them. When Father gained his captaincy he informed Mother that we would now need to employ an ill-wisher, and Mother retorted that the Patron custom of cutting out the tongue of any newly widowed woman who had never borne a child was grotesque and hateful. But she agreed to employ such a woman, Taberta, because it meant she could offer a haven to a person who would otherwise be scorned and mistreated.

"Jes, it's all right. Doma Larissa is no danger to you. She was my ill-wisher. Mine and Menoë's."

Kal's sweet smile burns through the air, and the old woman offers a proud bow in acknowledgment. Honor shines in her face. What she thinks of me I cannot know but that she cares for him is apparent in the wordless exchange that passes between them.

"I didn't know you had an ill-wisher," I say awkwardly, still flushed.

"When I was little, she acted as our nurse because Grandmother did not trust anyone, so I can assure you no harm will come to you if you allow her to help you bathe, not even if she touches you." He worries at his lower lip, glances coyly at the marble paving, and looks up. "Unless you would like me to help you bathe."

Doma Larissa gives a negative slice of her hand through the air.

"Perhaps not," he adds obediently, and I wish my cheeks weren't burning, but they are, and I can't help but meet his gaze and remember everything that has passed between us.

We smile at each other as if we two are alone.

Leaves rustle in the garden and whispers float on the air.

A king is never alone. Not really.

With an emphatic gesture, Doma Larissa indicates the screened awning and the royal clothing neatly folded atop a table inside.

"Yes, yes, just like when I was five and you dressed me," says Kal with a rueful glance that makes me stifle a laugh.

He steps under the awning. The wet towel is plastered to his form in a way that interests me more than the beautiful garden scenery, that reminds me of the sweetness we have shared, the trust that binds our hearts. But a squad of attendants swarms out of the garden like a disturbance of cockroaches to dress and settle him in a waiting sedan chair and carry him off through the garden into the king's chambers, where I am not invited to follow.

My giddiness vanishes, burned away by the thought of so many invisible knives.

Doma Larissa picks up the tray and escorts me back the way we came.

"So I was always meant to bathe in the other courtyard?" I ask, desperate to figure out how to negotiate this endless succession of traps.

She nods. Two guardsmen have arrived to stand duty at the gate between the compounds; they let us through without a word. Now that I get a better look at the original private courtyard, I see there is a separate area for washing before you get in the pool, with a stone bench, a drain, and a cloth screen if you wish for privacy.

Doma Larissa hums a pretty melody as she pours jasmine-scented water over my grimy skin, soaking me repeatedly as I sigh with pleasure. Her fingers gently tease apart my matted hair. The cut barely hurts as she uses a small brush to gently clean away dried blood, then washes my entire body with a brisk energy I haven't felt since I was a little child and Mother would scrub us down.

She dresses me in silk undergarments, a finely woven sheath dress, and a calf-length jacket of pale yellow. However costly the fabric, this is the garb of a servant, not of a highborn doma or noble-born lady. I want to refuse the clothing but I don't have anything else clean to wear.

This whole place reeks of rottenness. I don't want to leave Kal and Father, and I don't want to stay here to face off with the likes of Volua and Galaia every day. I've walked myself into a blind trap where I can't go forward while the path behind me has closed off.

When I offer to help her carry the basin holding my dirty garments, she refuses with a gesture and hauls it herself to the portico. I wait in the sun. A soft click brings my head around. One of the tile-encrusted cornucopias shifts, develops a seam, and starts to open.

It's a secret gate.

I dash for Larissa. Her back is to me, so I yank on her sleeve. When she turns, I point, then pull us behind a pillar.

An armed man dressed in the tabard of the queen's guard steps through and surveys the pool and courtyard as would a scout. He speaks to someone behind him, and six men carry a curtained litter in through the narrow gate and set it down. A harried-looking attendant holds aside the heavy curtain and assists the woman sitting hidden within to climb out. She has come in such furtive haste that she appears more like a clandestine lover than a proud highborn woman. She isn't wearing the queen's diadem, but what gives her away is her striking resemblance to statues of her mother, Serenissima the Fourth, with her round face and slightly bulging eyes.

Her expression seems gentle, even timid, but I know Queen Serenissima the Fifth for what she really is: a conspirator and murderer who colluded in the death of her brother Kliatemnos and her only child, Temnos, so she could hold on to power.

Now she has come for Kal.

11

I **desperately want to** be the one to warn Kal but Larissa won't be able to make Father understand the urgency.

"Go warn the king," I whisper.

Her path to the gate into the king's garden is shielded by a hedge so she can scurry away while I'm still trapped. If I try to go to the doors that lead into Father's suite, they'll see me. But cowering behind a pillar is not the only way to hide. I'm dressed in servants' garb, and even though Efeans never work in the palace, I only need the queen and her attendants to hesitate for an instant.

I grab the basin and, bracing it against my hip, stride along the portico to Father's suite just as if I were an ordinary servant about her ordinary tasks. I make it to the doors before I hear a concerned exclamation followed by a demand to hush.

Steward Haredas has just set a tray of food and drink down on the desk in front of Father. "Personally sampled by the head cook so it is safe," he remarks with a dry smile, a legacy of years of trust built up between the two men.

"Father! The queen just entered the courtyard through a secret door—"

He's on his feet and moving so fast that I barely have time to set down the basin and hurry after him onto the portico. Serenissima is already speaking in a rush as a new group of figures enter the sunlit courtyard from the king's garden.

"Nikonos! I was so frightened for you! Thank goodness you have returned in triumph."

The light of *triumph* dies in her face as she takes in Kal with his coterie of officers and crowd of exalted officials. He wears an ankle-length keldi of soft purple and a sleeveless vest. Of course he looks the very image of a handsome prince in a play. Maybe it would be more truthful to say that actors playing handsome princes strive to look like him.

The new king speaks no word. He waits. Not one of the senior palace officials who surround him moves toward the queen or makes any effort to acknowledge her. The silence settles, grows heavy, and becomes oppressive.

At last, slowly, as if she can barely find the energy to act, she presses a hand to her chest. "Kalliarkos. You have surprised me."

"Yes, I must suppose I have."

Her gaze darts around the courtyard now filled with men. It pauses on Junior Palace Steward Sarnon, who gives the slightest shake of his head. Father whispers in an adjutant's ear and I'm absolutely sure Sarnon will be expelled from service in the king's palace before the day is over.

Oblivious to this byplay, Serenissima takes several tottering steps forward. Officers shift inward, ready to fling themselves in front of Kal, but she drops to her knees in supplication.

"Oh, thank the gods, my dearest cousin Kalliarkos. I prayed and prayed to be rescued from my brother's brutal attentions—"

"Which brother?" he interposes. A twitch has started up at the corner of his right eye.

"Why, Nikonos, of course! Everyone knew he was a brute. He murdered my darling son...my gentle Temnos...." She sobs gustily.

My hands close into fists.

The queen heaves a tremulous sigh. "That innocent boy, fresh as the morning dew, ripped from my loving arms and killed before my wounded, weeping heart."

"Isn't that a line from a play?" Kal remarks lightly, and because he is correct, the most nervous of the officials laugh.

An expression of such contempt ripples across her face that I recoil. "How dare you mock my grief? What was I supposed to do when Nikonos arrived so unexpectedly in the city accompanied by foreign troops? The instant Kliatemnos and our son lay dead in their own blood at my feet, Nikonos made sure to strip away all my allies. Then he told me I had to agree

124

to bear his child. What would you have had me do, Kalliarkos?" Her sobs are thick with thwarted rage.

"What would you have *me* do now, Cousin?"

An attendant glides forward to dry her hands and pat her cheeks dry. With fresh confidence, she straightens.

"Marry me. We shall reign as king and queen together."

His expression goes blank.

I'm choked with disgust, which is a good thing, because otherwise I would scream.

"You have chafed for years in Garon Palace under the rule of your grandmother and Lord Gargaron." Her voice gains strength. She's sure of her ground. "Why would you wish to rule as king knowing your grandmother favors your sister while meanwhile your uncle pulls your strings and treats you as his puppet? I would not treat you so."

"An interesting offer. And should we marry, how would you treat me?"

"As an equal."

"What of my sister, Menoë?"

"Menoë! That naïve girl? She fancies herself a courageous lioness, but she is nothing more than a squealing pig."

Father stiffens at this mocking disrespect for his new wife, and I feel his reaction as an insult to Mother even though a tiny part of me is also angry on Menoë's behalf, knowing what she suffered at Nikonos's hands.

Kalliarkos laughs so sharply it hurts because he looks as

contemptuous as Nikonos ever did, and contempt sits horribly on his usually open and good-natured face.

"What of the East Saroese soldiers who occupy the city, Cousin?" he asks.

"I am not a fool, although everyone treats me as one. I have cunningly misled their general by requesting he barrack his troops in the Grain Market so they do not inflame an anxious population. All the off-duty soldiers can be sealed inside the warehouses and burned to death with a single command."

I must flinch, because Father nudges me, and it is only then I realize he hasn't left my side although by rights he should be standing next to the king.

"'Burned to death with a single command'!" Kal's tone is flat. "Ah. Well. Wise thinking on your part, Cousin."

"Of course it is! Efea's rich harbors and envied trade are due to my administration, not the king's! These rude foreign men treat me as if I am a decorative flower rather than a queen just because they keep their women ignorant and stupid."

Kal paces toward her. Just as I think she means to grasp his feet and beg for mercy, she draws herself up instead. For all that I hate her for what she did to her innocent son, I admire her for meeting her fate with dignity.

Kal extends a hand. "You have convinced me, Serenissima. I do not wish to live under my uncle's heel. We shall proceed now to the temple."

"We cannot marry today. I am not even dressed for a public appearance. I came here in haste only because of the unexpected nature of your arrival, because I thought you were…"

Because I thought you were Nikonos.

"…I thought you were in need of advice appropriate to the king. My people can tend to all your needs, Kalliarkos. As can I."

Father's hand clamps down on my forearm before I realize I've taken a step forward, meaning to slap her. Kal has enough discipline not to look toward me even though half his officials do. I have never heard anything so grotesque and disgusting. I'm shaking with anger.

The twitch appears again beside Kal's right eye. "Speed is of the essence, my dear cousin. An enemy army advances on Saryenia even as we speak. Our situation must be settled before they arrive."

He gestures a command. His adherents outnumber hers so her attendants must acquiesce. They help her back into the litter. With soldiers a fence on every side, she is carried in procession through the garden and into the forecourt where the carriages await. Kalliarkos does not get into the king's carriage. Instead he grabs a soldier's tabard and, pulling it on to hide his royal garb, takes a place amid the guard surrounding the queen's litter. He must mean to walk all the way down to the temple so as not to be a target. He can't win if he's struck down by a lucky shot by an East Saroese soldier or one of Nikonos's last loyal men.

Wearing this humble raiment, he crosses to us.

"Jessamy must not accompany us," he says, and to my surprise, Father defies him.

"Your Gracious Majesty, my daughter is not leaving my side. I am sure you understand why I cannot allow her to remain unguarded in the palace."

My once sweet, cheerful Kal looks held together by a thread of calm so frayed it is close to unraveling. A new hardness lurks behind his eyes. "No, you are correct, General. Keep her close to you."

"You're not really going to marry her?" I say in an outraged whisper.

But Kal has already turned his back on me and walks away. Father steers me to the general's carriage, now hitched to fresh horses. Once we are inside, he shifts like a man who will never again find a comfortable seat.

"Father! He's not really going to—"

"Of course not. But everyone has now seen the overly familiar way in which you address him. So listen carefully, Jessamy. The risks and pleasures you two took as adversaries, even as captain and Challenger, were reckless and improper—"

"We didn't know he was going to become king!"

"That is immaterial. It looks as if you and I have colluded with Garon Palace in every respect. The risk of you being poisoned or knifed by courtiers envious of our new position is now exceedingly high. Do you understand me? *Do you?*"

Father has imagined my death and what it would mean to him. How I hate this. And of course I now recall that Mother warned me about the exact same thing, that being with Kal would mark me for death at the hands of Kal's own household.

We leave the palace and descend the Avenue of Triumphs in a mockery of a procession.

More people have come out to line the street, but their calm is a thin shell over a seething underbelly of anger at the sight of their hated queen. Muttering sweeps through the crowd like fire through dry grass, only to die away. Like embers, the people only need stirring, and a bit of fuel, to explode into new flame. I push aside the traveling curtains to try to catch a glimpse of Kal, to make sure he is safe, but I can't spot him among the soldiers.

Father pulls me back inside just as I hear someone shout, "There's the mule our new master rides!"

No matter how I gasp, I can't get enough air.

"Jessamy." Father grasps my chin and turns my face so I have to look at him. I am so humiliated I pull away, and he immediately releases me.

"This is what you warned us against, isn't it? That your daughters had to behave as proper Patron girls and never be spoken of in a way that would insult you."

"I was strict because it was the only way I could protect you and your sisters. I don't care about insults directed at me. It is what you and they might have to endure that concerns me."

I wipe tears from my face with the back of a hand.

"You're a brave girl, Jessamy. I'm proud of you even when I disapprove of some of your actions. You're not unlike me when

I was your age." A pensive smile softens his face, and it calls an answering smile from me because his approval is my sun.

"Father, I don't know what to do."

"As with all battles, one must be careful not to strike too soon. The king must first win the support of the population. Once we drive the East Saroese out of Efea, the courtiers will fall in line. If Kalliarkos proves a strong and competent king, then he may take his pleasures where he wishes. Citizens who cheered on an adversary named Spider will make a story of the king and the Challenger, if they see it as a success, as a tale that ends well."

"That's not what I meant. None of this seems right to me. The palace. Kal becoming king. I was so sure it was right for Efea."

"It has happened very quickly, hasn't it? Perhaps you will be safer if I take you to your mother for now."

Fear and hope crowd my thoughts until they skitter every which way. "Do you know where Mother is? Has she communicated with you?"

"Polodos keeps me informed."

"Polodos! Does Maraya know?"

"I do not inquire."

"What if Mother refuses to see you?"

His gaze rifles through memories I don't share, through regrets I can't begin to fathom.

In silence we proceed through the Square of the Moon and the Sun, and I finally realize we are going to the City of the Dead. I honestly can't figure out what Kal intends to do and I'm starting to get nervous.

130

Eternity Temple, dedicated to Lord Judge Inkos, runs along one side of the square. All other Saroese temples, even the other Inkos temples, open into spacious sanctuaries where images of the gods are placed on pedestals and adorned with flowers and ribbons, but not this one. It is a high and windowless wall—a fortress, really—that separates the living city of Saryenia from the City of the Dead, where oracles are entombed alive.

All movement in and out is controlled by the temple wardens at a single entrance called Eternity Gate, a long, dim passage through the thick wall. The priest-wardens claim they safeguard the sanctity of the holy oracles and the hallowed dead but I know what else Eternity Gate guards: the ruins of an old Efean complex buried beneath Saroese dead.

I have walked the dark length of Eternity Gate to take offerings to oracles. I crossed under Eternity Gate while in the funeral procession for Lord Ottonor, the man Gargaron murdered to take control of my father's military prowess. With the help of the great General Esladas, Gargaron launched a personal campaign to put his nephew and niece on the throne.

And now half of that plan is complete.

But this time our procession does not move all the way along the passage and into the City of the Dead. Instead it turns aside halfway, still within the wide temple wall. We cross through an interior gate that normally opens only for the holy priests who serve Lord Judge Inkos. Beyond the gate lies an elongated courtyard where they keep their offices and sleep apart from the world of the living.

"Jessamy," Father murmurs. "According to law, no Commoner may enter this sanctuary. If the priests see you, you'll be convicted of blasphemy and put to death. And I would be executed too, for allowing you in. Do you understand?"

"Yes."

The moment we come to a stop, Father steps down from the carriage, positioning his body to block the door. I peek carefully through the curtain.

The courtyard is no wider than the Royal Road, a garden running between high walls like a canyon. A center lane of greenery eases the eye: harsh red poppies, cheerful daisies, and cornflowers like scraps of sky brightening the dreary confines of earth.

At our unexpected entrance priests scurry out of rooms and the High Priest appears. He is an older man, pale from lack of sun, lips cocked down in haughty disapproval. Is this the man whom Gargaron bribed to allow my pregnant Efean mother and half-Efean sisters to be buried with an oracle in Ottonor's tomb? To admit Efeans into an Inkos sanctuary is blasphemy, but to entomb a pregnant woman is an even worse crime against the gods because she might give birth to a boy, and boys are valuable.

The High Priest's confidence falters as he approaches an unbending Kalliarkos. The two men stare each other down in a battle over precedence.

"Why are you here, my lord?" he asks, clearly not yet aware that Kal is king.

132

"You may address me as Your Gracious Majesty," Kal snaps with uncharacteristic testiness.

When he gestures for the queen's litter to be carried into the courtyard, the High Priest steps back with a look of distressed confusion and then genuine fear.

I'm confused too. What does Kal mean to do with Serenissima here? It's long been the tradition in Efea for highborn Patron lords to donate an excess daughter's life to Eternity Temple. Always it is described as a humane way to get rid of a girl they can't afford to raise and then expensively marry off. Always it is explained as being more merciful than the custom in the old Saro kingdoms where unwanted girls are exposed as infants and left to die.

Girls chosen to become oracles and their attendants are spoken of as honored, even though it's such a troubling fate to be bricked up alive in a tomb that people usually feel afraid of oracles. But the rest of the girls and women—perhaps one or two hundred at any given time—live quiet, orderly lives in an inner sanctuary untroubled by the clamor and distress of ordinary life. Their innocence is like incense to the gods, who therefore shower divine favor upon Efea.

But suddenly I wonder if the truth is a different story, just as Ro warned me.

The long courtyard terminates in a closed and barred gate. The queen's litter is set down here.

Tied curtains flap apart, and the queen stumbles out, staring wildly around.

133

"This is not Hayiyin's temple, where marriages are solemnized."

"It is not Hayiyin's temple," Kalliarkos agrees.

She falls to her knees as a supplicant. "You've brought me to Eternity Temple. I pray you, Cousin. Do not condemn me to the inner sanctuary. If you mean to kill me, be merciful and cut my throat instead."

"I won't kill you because I refuse to be like you and Nikonos. I do not presume to act in judgment in the place of Lord Seon, the Sun of Justice. You will be safely held here until such time as a trial can be convened. Then I will present my case to the population, to inform them that you and Nikonos invited our enemies to invade Efea."

"Do not punish me in this way. Heavenly gods, I pray you, Kalliarkos."

She flings herself full length onto the ground at his feet. The distress on her face is not feigned. Dread chokes me because I'm sure something horrible is about to happen.

Kal's tone remains set and unyielding. "It is a holy temple, Cousin, where girls and women devote their souls to prayer. A place of strict justice and rigid piety, it's true, but it isn't as if a woman who was once queen will be chosen as an oracle, if that's what you fear."

"I will do anything...anything...just don't lock me up in there, I beg you." Grabbing Kal's sandaled feet, Serenissima kisses them repeatedly, a beggar groveling for a scrap of pity. "I beg you, Kalliarkos. Hideous things happen in there."

"You will be protected by these walls and holy priests, Cousin. I am being merciful by safeguarding you here in the temple instead of letting you be torn to pieces by an angry mob."

But what if you're mistaken? What does Serenissima know that you don't? I want to scream the words at him but Father softly taps a knuckle against the wood to remind me to stay still and silent, to not protest, to do nothing about the ugly scene unfolding before us.

Kal looks like a man contemplating a nest of dead, rotting adders he has to eat for his supper. He gestures toward the gate as if he can't trust himself to speak.

After a glance at all the armed men, the High Priest kneels before him. "As you command, Your Gracious Majesty."

Thus is Serenissima's fate sealed.

Priests lift away a bar and swing open the inner gate. What I see is worse than I expected: a gloomy passageway into windowless darkness, nothing but stone walls and iron doors where girls are raised in night and solitude as if they have committed some atrocious crime, when all they have done is be born to Patron families who don't cherish them. The very air breathes of despair and misery. It's so dark.

"Please, Kalliarkos. Please show mercy to me. Don't make me go in there. Please."

Serenissima shudders with uncontrollable sobs of genuine terror. I hate her, of course I hate her. She callously handed her son over to be slaughtered. Yet even I am appalled. Even this is too much for me. Doesn't Kal see how wrong it is?

135

"Father, can't you stop this?"

"Quiet." Father surveys the battlefield and its grim debris. "He's showing her more mercy than she showed Menoë or her own son. The court will call him weak for imprisoning her instead of killing her outright, but once he defeats the invaders they'll acclaim him as just and wise."

"You heard what she said. Terrible things happen in there. Can't you see it? Can't you feel it? Don't you understand?"

"It's a holy temple." He can't see because his whole life he's been told that the tombs are a sacred place, that the men running them are pious and just, that they would never harm the revered women dedicated to the inner sanctuary. "She's play-acting, anything for a chance to stab Kalliarkos in the back. She'll be safe here until he has time to put her on trial before the Sun of Justice. Be patient."

Kal stands in profile to me. I study the features I've come to know so intimately now turned into a cold, merciless mask. This is the lesson he has learned from Gargaron, from Nikonos, and from the dead king. From my own beloved father, the general who kept the Royal Army together to bring him to the royal city as victor. My father, who at this moment is blocking anyone from seeing me while keeping me silent.

Kal learned these lessons from all of them, and from Serenissima. He told me himself. The king sits atop a mountain of treasure. His army, and his actions, defend not the country but his power, which he'll do anything—*anything*—to keep.

Tears stream down my face. It's not that I'm weeping but that I am sick to be watching this unfold. He tried to get away, he asked me to escape with him, but I convinced him it was his duty to come here, because I thought this was the only way to save Efea.

I wanted to believe the people I loved would be better and stronger, that they wouldn't succumb to the same justifications that allowed a holy priest to brick my mother into a tomb. I wanted to believe that Father wouldn't be trapped by it. That Kal wouldn't be forced to act as monstrously as the people who came before him, the ones who built this edifice stone by stone. I wanted to believe that the father I respect and the boy I love could recognize what is staring them in the face.

Watching Kal's expression turn from one of distaste to one of self-loathing as he forces himself to witness Serenissima be dragged screaming and struggling into the passage, I finally have to admit I have run this trial utterly wrong. The path I chose doesn't lead to a victory tower. Or at least, not to a victory I can live with.

12

~~~~~~

Father and I arrive at the Least-Hill Inn late in the afternoon. He's arranged for us to change out of palace garb and into our cleaned clothing from the march, and his firebird soldiers have found a less conspicuous carriage in which he can travel into the city. Another man would have waited for the business of unseating one set of rulers and installing a new pair to be completed before taking such a chance, but not Father, not when he hasn't seen my mother since the day he abandoned her.

"Let me go in first," I say, sure he will refuse.

He doesn't reply. He is fussing with his hair, as short as it is, and smoothing out the fabric of his clothing so it isn't mussed. I have never seen him act like a nervous youth going courting, but I take advantage of his hesitation and jump down to the street.

The door of the humble inn has gotten a paint job. Instead

of having flaking, faded brown paint, it glistens with a depiction of a lush sycamore tree hung with goats' horns like tiny cornucopias. I walk in to find the common room already half full of people off work for the day, a mix of foreign sailors and local Saryenians, Saroese and Efean, mingling as they laugh and chat. The floor has been set with new tiles. The walls have a fresh coat of whitewash enlivened by flowering trees that have been painted on either side of tripod lamps standing against the walls.

Polodos is serving a tray of drinks to a group of sailors, while a girl I recognize as Ro's sister pours ale from a pitcher into the waiting cups of a trio of Efean men. When she worked for my family, her hair was shorn to the scalp to prevent lice but now it is growing out. She actually smiles at the men. She never smiled once that I saw in the year she worked for us, not that I ever bothered looking.

She sees me. Her smile flattens to a frown. People turn to look as I stride through the room.

"Doma…" Polodos looks alarmed. "How are you come here?"

A tip of my head alerts him that someone is about to enter behind me. Then I slide past the curtain that separates the common room from a courtyard in back.

When I was here last, months ago, the hearth had but a single hook and spit for cooking, the flat roof was in shambles, and the two small rooms off the courtyard stank of urine and rubbish. Now a coat of whitewash makes the area gleam. Clothes dry from a line strung up on the roof between the posts of a thatched shelter, a place to sleep during the hottest nights. Beaded curtains adorn the entrances to the two rooms.

The hearth is bustling, expanded with a new brick extension presided over by Cook. Several girls kneel on a mat in a corner of the courtyard, grinding grain into flour. At a table under a cloth awning, two other young women are chopping vegetables, and it takes me a moment to recognize Amaya and Denya working together in contented cooperation. Strapped to a high chair, little Safarenwe is old enough to watch her older sister, clapping her hands and chortling whenever Amaya or Denya pauses to tickle her. How did they get here so quickly?

The back gate to the alley is open, with a young man and a young woman standing as if on guard. I recognize them as friends of Ro. A line of people wait patiently in the alley for their turn to enter. Mother sits in a sling chair, listening to a family pouring out some tale of woe. She makes a few remarks, then doles out coins as the people profusely thank her.

Seated beside Mother, Maraya appears to record the transaction in an accounts book. She then reaches out and rocks a net cradle in which Wenru lies with a remarkably bored expression on a face that should be sweet.

"Jessamy!" Mother's relieved smile is all the greeting I need, although of course it isn't all the greeting I get.

"You're safe!" Amaya runs over, flings her arms around me in a dramatic embrace, then audibly sniffs. "What is that perfume? You smell heavenly, Jes. Not sweaty, as you normally do."

"I can smell nice!"

She runs a hand down a trouser leg, fingering the high gloss of the fabric. "These are a Patron man's riding clothes, the very best grade of wool and leather. But cut for a different figure. Whose clothes are you wearing?"

The heat in my cheeks betrays me.

"I knew it," smirks Amaya.

Maraya says, "Good Goat, Jes. What were you thinking?"

Mother jumps in. "Jessamy, I told you—"

"I don't need anyone's advice!"

Behind me, the curtain sweeps up and falls. Father steps into the courtyard. In any other circumstances his trained gaze would first assess the area's dangers and potentials and the chance of ambush from the alley, but he sees nothing but her.

"Beloved," he says.

Mother's face burns with a joy as pure as sunlight. Then memory crashes down, obliterating all radiance in her face.

"Esladas."

We all hear the choked anger. The terrible disappointment that the man she loved with all her five souls had, in the end, proved so callous.

Everyone stops what they are doing. The sentries tell the people in the alley to come back in the morning, and close the gate. Polodos appears in the doorway and holds the curtain taut so no one can come through from the common room.

"I have no wish to see you," Mother says, her flat tone a harsh rebuke to the man who claimed to love her more than anything else in the world. "There is nothing you can say."

"I didn't know Lord Gargaron would act so drastically. I had it all worked out with Polodos, that he would bring money back to you. I wasn't abandoning you. I had to act quickly without Gargaron becoming suspicious."

"Is that what you tell yourself? How you excuse it? Yet you took all your male servants with you—"

"My military household! Of course I took them. But I thought of you every day!"

She presses a hand to her chest. Eases the pain out on a breath. I wish I could take that pain into myself so I wouldn't have to see the anguish on her face.

"I could have forgiven you for leaving me. We've always understood what our pledge was to each other. We always knew how hard it would be to live together. But you abandoned your own daughters, your unborn twins. And not just them. You abandoned all of the vulnerable women and children in the household. They were part of my life, but you never considered them part of yours. That is what makes it so unforgivable."

"Lord Ottonor's mismanagement of his finances and my career put us all at risk. I could not say no to Gargaron when Ottonor was dead and we had nothing but his debts."

"We could have fled Efea by ship, taken humble work, and stayed together. We could have journeyed inland and found a town to live in far from the ugly politics of the palace. But that wouldn't have been enough for you. How such a mild life would have chafed you!"

"The palace politics you speak of so contemptuously are all that prevent Efea from being conquered by a foreign army."

"Efea was already conquered by a foreign army, long before you came here. You stand on the backs of generations of people trampled by Saroese soldiers like you."

I want to break in but I don't know what to say, and anyway Mother has already gone on in the most scalding tone imaginable.

"Did you ever once think it was wrong, Esladas?"

"Don't be naïve, Kiya. War is how the world works. If it hadn't been the first Kliatemnos and Serenissima, then it would have been another Saroese fleet landing on these shores and overthrowing the corrupt Efean rulers. Our military tactics and discipline are simply superior."

"'*Our*'? I thought you considered yourself Efean now. Why do you call yourself Efean when it comes to living in this land but you don't give Efeans a share in the laws and administration the Saroese brought when they came here? Why are you always the Patron class and we the Commoners? Do you believe that the Saroese are ordained by the gods to rule over Efeans? That Efeans are somehow less worthy? That I am less worthy? That your daughters are less worthy? And even your mule son?"

Maraya stands with a hand over her mouth. Amaya presses against the table, and Denya has actually crawled underneath it as if fearful that violence will break out. I can't endure my own silence any longer.

"He just wanted to make sure everyone was healthy and safe," I cry.

She rounds so fiercely on me that I cringe. "Did you bring your father to me, Jessamy? Thinking perhaps he and I might be reconciled?"

"No. No, I didn't." I'm ashamed because of course Mother knows me too well. I *have* been clutching a fragile hope against my grieving heart that they might see each other and it might all be better. But betrayal can't be fixed with a kiss and a few coaxing words.

"No?" She's relentless. "Then how did he know I was here?"

I can't bear for Maraya to find out that Polodos is the one who told Father where they were because I don't want her to fight with him. "I mean, yes. I know things can never go back to what they were. But Father wanted to see you and I remembered how you always say it is better to face what troubles you most. That's all."

I press fingers over my mouth, afraid that Mother is going to yell at me again.

Frightened by the tension, Safarenwe begins to fret in the chair. Her movement attracts Father's eye.

Hoarsely he says, "Is that one of the twins I've heard spoken of?"

"Take Safarenwe over to him, Amaya. It is no part of Efean culture to refuse to allow a child to know its father. Not even an extra and thus disposable girl."

He winces.

All I can think of is that dark passage in Eternity Temple, the rough agony of its silence and the curdling stink of its secrets. The "extra" daughters inside.

Wan and cautious, Amaya approaches him.

"Amaya, how did you get to Saryenia so quickly? The winds were against you."

"We were transferred to a warship, a fast galley, Father." The delighted-kitten charm she used to show him has been clawed right out of her. The baby has caught the tense mood and fusses anxiously.

Father says sternly, "Let me hold her."

Amaya obeys immediately. Safarenwe lets out an indignant squawk, then lifts her dark gaze to the stranger holding her. Her lips tremble with infant concern as she leans her whole body away from his grim face.

"Safarenwe," he says, testing the name.

The baby reaches out to pat his lips. At her touch, the lines of his mouth soften. His eyes crinkle.

"Safarenwe," he repeats, seeing how the name's melody and rhythm wrap around her sweet little face and the distinct uniqueness of her presence in the world, for a name is one of the five souls that fill us. "Here is your papa, Safarenwe, home at last to meet you."

She coos and smiles.

Pressing a hand to her eyes, Mother turns away. Maraya hurries to her and tucks an arm around her waist.

"Maraya, do you have no greeting for your father?" he says, for he never takes his gaze from Mother for long.

Maraya does not release her hold on Mother as she addresses Father with her usual calm tone. "I am grateful you are whole and alive, Father. But your explanations are nothing but weak excuses. You would never be as careless with the soldiers under your command as you were with your own family."

"You left us to die in a tomb!" Amaya bursts into tears.

"I didn't know!" he shouts.

Safarenwe wails.

Mother cries, "Give her to me!"

He crosses to her and she takes the baby from him. Takes a step back so he can't touch her.

"Kiya—"

"You made your choice, Esladas. Now you will live with it. Please leave. Is Jessamy going with you?"

"No," he says, speaking before I can.

The word startles her enough that she meets his gaze without enmity. Shared understanding passes between them like heat lightning, for the years of cooperation and love have molded their minds into one instrument when it comes to their children.

"I fear for her life if she remains within the palace," he adds.

"Not for your own?"

"I am a soldier. I gave my life to Efea years ago. But I will not let them bury my daughter."

"A poor choice of words," remarks Maraya.

Polodos says, "Dearest, is it necessary to speak so harshly to your father?"

"Let her speak, Polodos, because she is not wrong," says Father. "Kiya, before I go, may I see my son?"

Mother looks at me. A flicker of shame creases her brow, smoothed out so swiftly I almost miss it. She tips her head toward the net cradle, giving me permission.

When I halt by the cradle, Wenru makes a sour face that pulls a smile to my lips.

"I'm not happy to see you either," I murmur.

Because Mother still hasn't moved or spoken, I pick him up and march to Father.

"Here is the son you've long been praying for."

My comment scratches a nerve. "I have never complained of my daughters, Jessamy."

But he is a Patron man, born and bred, for whom the siring of a son is the most distinctive mark of manhood. Pride warms his face as he takes the baby from me. A son, at last. Yet after a pause his brows wrinkle in puzzlement as he and an exceedingly disgruntled Wenru engage in a far more adult stare-off than any person would expect from a baby barely half a year old.

Ro's sister sticks her head through a gap in the curtain. She surveys our awkward stances and my flushed face with a smile tinged with malicious pleasure. "I hope I'm not interrupting anything. Polodos, I need help in here. More bread. Also, six people just came in asking for a pot of lentil stew."

All throughout, unremarked, Cook has been grilling flat

rounds of bread. Amaya hustles over and grabs the tray they are cooling on.

Father says, "My daughter does not serve strange men in a common inn—"

"I am no longer yours to command, Father! I will go about my life in my own way now." With a defiantly theatrical toss of her head and a glance toward Denya, who is still hiding under the table, Amaya vanishes behind the curtain.

"Kiya, I thought we agreed—"

"Yes, we agreed, back when you were part of my household, Esladas. You are free to leave so my household may get back to work feeding ourselves and our customers."

"I have an idea," I say before Father can go on. "Send Wenru with Father. That would be fair, would it not? Mother keeps Safarenwe, and Father keeps Wenru."

"Yes," says Mother, so quick to grab for this chance that I am surprised, despite having warned her. "It would be best for Wenru to go with Esladas."

Mother and Maraya exchange a knowing glance, and I realize that of course Mother has shared my suspicions with her other daughters.

Father holds the baby at arm's length, scrutinizing the boy's chubby little baby body for a secret deformity like Maraya's clubfoot, which Patrons consider a stain upon the flesh, a mark of the gods' disfavor. But Wenru glows with ruddy health. It is only the uncanny awareness in his gaze that curdles the natural affection a person ought to feel at the sight of him.

"How can I care for a child in my situation, without a wife to tend to my household?"

"You have a wife, Esladas. To my surprise, I feel a distinct sympathy for her situation since you have evidently forgotten your noble bride exists. By all reports she could nurse the child herself in another few months, if she can bring herself to allow mule lips to suckle from her pure Patron teats."

I gasp. Never in my life have I heard Mother belittle another person; always she taught us girls that kindness heals.

Father also recoils from her biting words. "Be angry at me, Kiya. You have that right. But it lessens you to speak so disrespectfully of a woman who has suffered terrible harm. If circumstances were different, you would shelter her and be right to do so."

Mother kisses the top of Safarenwe's head as if to comfort herself. "This is more painful even than I had imagined. Please go, Esladas."

She hands Safarenwe to Maraya and goes to the hearth, seeking refuge in work.

Cook wipes her hands on a cloth and puts an arm around Mother for a brief embrace before she grabs her tongs to flip a burning piece of flatbread. The sight of their friendship makes Father stare, for he never spoke to Cook beyond bland politeness; she belonged to the other part of the house where he never walked, a place where two women might reach beyond a world that means to divide them and discover loyalty and trust.

Father blinks rapidly. He tries to get out a word, but he cannot speak. Patron men do not weep.

I love him so much, even though he is wrong about so many things and may never know it. I draw him aside to explain about his son.

"There is magic in Efea. You know how the crow priests pull sparks from dying soldiers and place them into the spiders."

"It's a powerful gift to be allowed to serve even after death."

"Your son was stillborn."

"Stillborn? But he's here, and alive."

"I held his lifeless body in my arms in the tomb. It was much later, during the rescue, that he opened his eyes. At first I thought he must have been so weak we just thought he was dead, but now I think the magic beneath the tombs brought some other spark and self to live in his body. He's just pretending to be an infant. He can understand everything we say, can't you, Wenru?"

Belatedly, Wenru kicks his legs and smiles a toothless smile as if to say he is nothing but a harmless baby.

Father isn't really listening. His gaze has already slid away to Mother, although she keeps her back to him.

"How can I convince her to forgive me?" he asks me in a low voice. "I didn't know Gargaron meant to kill her, to imprison her in a tomb."

The forlorn words shred my heart because I don't know if I will ever see him again. Because I don't see how this can have a good ending.

Because I fear what it means for Kal and me.

I say, "You didn't want to know. If I hadn't been valuable

150

to Gargaron as an adversary, I would have been entombed with them. While you—the hero of Efea, married to the new queen, your child the heir to the throne—would sadly reflect that the family you cared for had departed Efea to make a new life." The truth has risen to the brim of me and it cascades in an unstoppable rush. If he cannot hear me, then I can never forgive him, and I want to forgive him. "You would have believed the lies Gargaron told you, Father. *And we would be dead.*"

He doesn't answer. Maybe there is no answer for him.

Instead he settles Wenru on his hip and kisses me on the brow, as he has always done. "Stay away from the palace, Jessamy. In fact, you should all leave Saryenia before Lord Gargaron returns."

Then my father walks out of the courtyard, and this time I do not go with him.

13

I keep expecting him to return, to push aside the curtain, to proclaim, "Kiya, I love you more than life itself and even more than my ambition!" and for Mother to say, "I forgive you, Esladas, for I understand you were forced into an impossible choice and did what you thought best for us, and now it will all be as it was before."

But with each breath I take in and with each breath I exhale, he does not reappear. Mother busies herself beside Cook. She makes not a single sound; she just works. I can't bear standing around so I help Denya out from under the table and offer her an encouraging smile, however false it feels.

Amaya hurries back into the courtyard. Seeing Denya's expression, she clasps her close and murmurs, "My father never hit us like yours hit you. You're free of that, my sweet. We are free."

Denya glances around the shabby courtyard. Her gaze rests longest on Cook, the only other woman of full Saroese ancestry here. As she clings to Amaya she doesn't look sure she is actually free, not surrounded by people like us.

"Are you going to leave Saryenia?" I ask Mother.

She rests her head against mine, arm around me, and her presence comforts me just enough that I can wipe my eyes.

"Polodos will keep the inn open for a few more days so nothing looks out of the ordinary but the rest of us will be leaving at dawn," Mother says. "Your father is right. We must not be here when Lord Gargaron returns to Saryenia, as he will soon."

"Where will we go?" I ask plaintively, thinking of Kal.

"We will go to the Warrens for now, to the Heart Tavern," says Mother. "I have some work to do for Inarsis."

I don't like the sound of that, but fortunately before I can say something stupid, Polodos pokes his head through the doorway.

"Doma Jessamy, we could use help in the front room. Evening is our busiest time."

All the customers are talking about the new king and how the East Saroese soldiers have been rounded up and imprisoned in warehouses in the Grain Market or on East Saroese ships that have been impounded and placed under guard in the harbor. An official enters the inn, offering to pay generous grain rations for laborers willing to work overnight and through tomorrow to reinforce weak spots in the city walls. Everyone knows an enemy army is marching toward Saryenia, that they are about two days away. The new king will not surrender, so the city must prepare for a siege.

Among themselves the Patron men whisper, "Which king shall we support? Nikonos or Kalliarkos?"

The Commoner men say nothing of kings. They take the offer of grain rations and go to work on the walls.

Late in the evening as the last two tables of customers sing songs from popular plays and drunkenly tell Amaya she is the prettiest girl in all of Saryenia, a man enters. He's dressed in worn clothes like any impoverished laborer and has the hesitant manner of a fellow looking for friends in a strange place.

He stares at Amaya for a little too long, with a gaze that is a little too intense, then takes a step toward me. "Doma Jessamy?"

"Captain Helias?" Then I realize what his presence here must mean—that Kal must have sent him with a message or even a summons—and the tray slips from my suddenly numb fingers. I'm quick; I grab it as it drops and only a single mug lands on the floor.

Amaya swoops in, batting her eyes at him while she gestures at me to go out the back; she thinks she's helping me escape an unwanted admirer. "I have not seen you here before, Domon. May I offer you a cool drink?" she says in a voice that would slay a thousand lovesick men.

He's so flustered he forgets his pretense of being a laborer and offers the polite bow that men of the highborn Patron class give as a courtesy to pretty women of their own kind. Amaya has always looked more Saroese than Efean. "Excuse me. I am here upon an errand."

His gaze shifts to me.

I shouldn't go but I know I am going to. I have to see Kal. I have to.

154

I wipe my hands and go to the back.

"Mother, I am going out."

What she sees in my face I can't know but she frowns and grasps my hands.

"This is foolishness, Jessamy. I know you are infatuated with the prince. The attention of a handsome young man who walks astride the world because all must bow before him is a heady drink. But it is poison."

"I'm going."

"Of course you are. It is just like you. I am glad you came to tell me rather than sneaking off. Take a knife."

My sisters hug me, and I grouchily say, "It's not as if I'm not coming back."

"Don't come back here. No place in the Saroese parts of the city are safe for us now." She rests gentle fingers on my cheek and gazes into my eyes, seeing what mothers see who love their children enough to let them make their own lives and their own mistakes. "You will find us in the courtyard where the Mother of All offers Her bounty to Her people. I will wait for you there, beloved daughter."

With a kiss, she releases me.

୧୭୧୭

In a delivery wagon filled with barrels I am taken to Garon Palace. At Helias's order, the Efean driver waits beside the wagon as the captain and I enter the compound.

The ruins of the palace make jagged shadows as we

pick our way past its toppled gates. Charred debris crunches beneath our feet. The festival pavilion lies like a shattered skeleton, pillars toppled.

"This way, Doma." The captain escorts me to the foot of the stairs leading up to the only private pavilion spared destruction. The others have been eaten away by flames, stairs smashed, roofs caved in, support pillars gouged with ax marks. When I climb the steps and go inside, I am surprised that although all the gold-inlaid furniture and gold-threaded carpets in the audience room are gone, the paintings of hunting and war remain untouched, as if no one had the heart to deface an artist's exquisite work.

A single lamp burns on the balcony. Its glow illuminates his face. All the sweet, easy confidence has vanished. In its place he looks grief-stricken, his eyes dark with lack of sleep, his forehead wrinkled with manifold concerns, his lips tight with the look of a man bracing himself for bad news.

The king of Efea speaks no word as I cross the empty room. I don't mean to go straight to him, to take the lamp out of his hand and set it on the floor, to pull him into my arms. But that is exactly what I do. Everything in my mind crashes into oblivion as my heart and my body embrace what they desire.

He holds me so tightly I can barely breathe. "Jes. I thought you wouldn't come."

I don't answer because I can't speak. Once words start they will not stop, and I do not want to hear what I am going to have to say.

Not yet.

He sweeps me up into his arms and carries me through the open doors into the bedchamber. The bed stands in the center, the only object left in the room. He pushes aside the draped netting. His manner is as solemn and desperate as my own, none of the laughter and wrestling and endearing awkwardness of our other times. Because the lamp has been left on the balcony, we are left in the shadow of each other, communicating by sighs, by the touch of lips and the pressure of hands.

The heart has its own speech. That is the only language and light that we need.

Yet eventually this physical conversation comes to an end. We lie in a restless silence that grows ever more tangled and uncomfortable as our sweat cools and our kisses cease. These are the hours when shadows slip free from the bodies that house them and prowl in search of satisfaction. I cannot see my own shadow. It's too dark over here where I am.

"Why is this bed still here when everything else of value was stripped from the pavilion?" Although I whisper, the sound of my voice makes me wince as if I were shouting, alerting the entire city that I'm here, where I'm not meant to be.

He shrugs, the movement shifting my head as it rests against his shoulder. "I wondered the same thing. I can only suppose it was a signal from the people of Saryenia that they respect my person enough to leave this one thing alone."

"Yours is the only pavilion that wasn't burned by the mob."

"Besides my uncle Thynos, I am the only person in Garon

Palace who hasn't been reviled in public at one time or another. Or at least not yet," he adds with a curt laugh. "I am sure there will be plenty of opportunity now."

"Do you fear the people of Saryenia will not accept your sister as queen because of all the rumors about her?" Bitterness sours my tone. *She is on her way here now to become queen and to claim my father as her husband.*

"Gossip is the least of our worries." Kal's fingers squeeze my arm. "The allied army of East Saro and Saro-Urok is about to lay siege to Saryenia. We could all still die. So Menoë must stay far away. She and the rest of the family will continue on to Maldine."

"What is in Maldine?"

"Extensive lands and a safe harbor. If Uncle Thynos has made a marriage alliance with West Saro, as we hope, then he will bring a fleet with soldiers there."

"But *you* are staying here in Saryenia."

"Yes. It is my duty and responsibility to lead the defense of the city. The king must protect his people, must he not?"

How can I possibly answer when I can hear the constriction in his voice?

His heartbeat has slowed to a lazy, exhausted pulse, but he keeps tracing circles on my skin like the spinning Rings of his agitated thoughts.

So softly I can barely hear him, he says, "This is what you wanted for me."

I sit up, pushing away. "It's not what I wanted for you!"

"No, you're right. It is the choice we both made. We cannot

158

leave Efea to the cruel mercies of Nikonos and Serenissima and their greedy allies."

"What if there is another way?" I ask.

"What other way? Let Nikonos rule? He hasn't the patience to act with wisdom and prudence. If he is king the foreigners will conquer us as soon as they can safely rid themselves of him. They'll place their own prince and a new dynasty upon the throne, probably with Serenissima's conniv-ance. Only Menoë and I can save Efea."

The memory of Eternity Temple, and the dim passageway down which a screaming Serenissima was dragged, just like so many generations of Patron girls, rises as a sickening roar in my head. I can't bear to think of how Kal watched her be car-ried away, sobbing, into a sunless tomb and did nothing to stop it, thinking it an act of justice.

"You can't save the tree if the roots are already diseased."

"What does that mean?" he asks, sounding defensive.

"No person can rule justly if the laws and customs of a land are already corrupt. For one thing, you have to immedi-ately end the custom of giving girls to the temple. Of burying women alive as oracles. You know it's wrong."

"Of course it is shameful to entomb living people. But it's the tradition we've always had. People believe Efea thrives in part because secluded holy women pray for our well-being. The priests won't alter the custom just because I ask them to."

"Does the king have no power?"

"The king has the power to command the army, the queen

controls the treasury, and the priests intercede with the gods and interpret their wishes. Maybe when the current High Priest dies I can appoint a man of my own choosing, one willing to institute small steps. And not just in the temples. General Esladas already agrees we must arm and train Efeans as well as Saroese. We can expand our troop strength quickly by allowing able men to become soldiers. I will not even be breaking with tradition but merely restoring a change first set in place by Kliatemnos the Fourth of blessed memory. That there is a precedent will make it easier to convince the royal council that such action is not only necessary to defeat the enemy but good for Efea."

His tone grows more lively as he warms to the subject of reform.

"I've been thinking a lot about this. Of course the Seon priests and the council and bureaucrats will resist but with careful maneuvering it may eventually be possible to change the law to allow all people to marry as they wish. Even perhaps to allow Commoners to own businesses in the city rather than rent licenses from Patron owners. After I have established myself I can change a few of these laws by royal proclamation. Not too many too fast, of course, but—"

"How can you bear to let a single girl or woman remain in that prison for even one more day?"

"What prison?"

"Eternity Temple!"

"It is restrictive, it's true. But it's an honor for a family to dedicate a daughter to the temple—"

"Restrictive! An honor! Did you not see what I saw inside Eternity Temple? Could you not taste the misery in the air? Didn't you hear Serenissima? What terrible things might they be doing to those caged, mistreated girls?"

"Jes! Don't blaspheme the holy priests."

"Holy? The High Priest must have colluded with Lord Gargaron to brick up my family in a tomb. They knew Mother was pregnant, that it was blasphemous to brick her up with the oracle. How can you call them holy when you have proof they aren't?"

A claw rakes at my heart, tipped in blood and fury. It opens, traps spilling one into the next as words pour out of me.

"Dead kings and dead lords like Lord Ottonor walk to their tombs, propelled by a spark the holy priests have poured into the body. What if the girls condemned to the temple aren't just raised to be buried alive as oracles and their attendants? What if some are sacrificed for the funeral rites? Their sparks forced into a dead man's body for the sake of their ugly ceremony?" The instant I speak the words, I know in my gut it's true; it's the only explanation that makes sense. "The men who do this are monsters, Kal. Monsters!"

The darkness hides him from me. All I see is his shape along the bed and how he doesn't move at all, as if he's just absorbed a killing blow.

"Good Goat," he whispers, and in his shocked tone I hear that he can't dismiss the possibility that I'm right. "If the girls dedicated to the temple are killed and perhaps even abused while alive, that would explain how Uncle Gar is able to control the High Priest. He could have forced the High Priest to entomb your pregnant mother and your sisters by threatening to reveal whatever foul misdeeds go on."

"Then it should be easy to end the tradition! Just tell the truth about it."

"You don't understand how this works. Every Patron in Efea will revile me for suggesting the Inkos priests are corrupt. Uncle Gar and my grandmother will undercut me by telling people I'm deluded and perhaps even insane. They'll block me at every turn the instant they decide I'm not their puppet. It will take years of quiet work building my own alliances before I can have a hope of managing the smallest of these changes."

My patience expires so fast it's like a flame snuffed out. "If you don't change things, Kal, then the Efeans will!"

"The Efeans? They can't rule themselves, much less Efea. If they could, my ancestors wouldn't have conquered them."

"That's what my father says. Do you also think Efeans are weak and incompetent?"

"No, that's not what I mean! But these gauzy dreams have no more substance than a dawn mist that will dissipate under the harsh light of the sun. If Efeans try to rule themselves, then the Saroese from overseas will just attack again and again until a new Saroese king takes over."

"Attack again and again? Like they already do, with your endless wars?"

"We have to defend our home."

"The home you stole!"

"You don't mean that." Despite how close we sit, we no longer touch. The cautious delicacy in his tone lights a fire of anger in my heart. "Have you been listening to Ro-emnu?"

What Kal and I just shared was so sweet that the sweetness itself is the knife that cuts me. He doesn't think of himself as the enemy, he doesn't want to be the enemy, but he can't let go of what his people took so long ago. To him it is just the natural way of things, the outcome the gods intended. I used to think that too, but I know better now.

I see the truth: he has always been my adversary on this court. And I love him.

"You know what you mean to me, Kal."

"Jes..." He shakes his head, warning me against speaking words I can't take back.

"Hear me out." How cold my voice sounds. But I have to make the break clean, because my heart is shattering. "I hate Serenissima for sacrificing her son for ambition. But even so— *even so*—you let her be imprisoned in that vile place—"

"My other choice was to kill her!"

"Why are the only two choices confining her in an unspeakable prison where girls live in darkness before they are bricked into tombs, or killing her? Why would *she* think it necessary and even acceptable to lead her son to the slaughter just to stay in power? How can Nikonos think it better to be beholden to foreigners so he can sit *on* a throne instead of next to it? Everything about this is wrong. It will always be wrong even if you institute tiny changes that, after all, are only made to benefit and solidify Saroese rule over a country your ancestors conquered. Your dynasty was founded on murder and treachery. You can never escape that."

"You *have* been listening to Ro."

"Don't act as if you are jealous! I've never—"

"Never kissed him? Kissing is the least of it. I've seen the way Ro looks at you, and now you talk and talk about the poet's justice and the poet's history and the poet's grievances, and you haven't asked me a single thing about...*me*." His voice chokes off, and he takes in a breath thick with emotion before speaking more hoarsely. "Not a single question about how I am doing now I am forced to take on the burden of king, which I never asked for, never wanted, and still don't want. But I can't refuse."

"You can refuse."

"I'm in the game now, and even if I tried to, they'd never let me leave. Surely you see that. Even you, with Ro's words so intimate on your tongue that you might as well have—" He breaks off and presses a hand over his mouth as if appalled at the words that just burst from his lips. "I didn't mean that. I'm sorry."

I grab my clothes off the bed. I can't do this. I am going to cry and I hate crying, and I hate myself.

"I beg you, Your Gracious Majesty. Protect my father. Lord Gargaron will come to see him as a threat because you trust him and your sister respects him. That is all I ask."

He catches in a breath, like I've punched him. "You're using my kingly title. You're ending it, aren't you?"

I can't get words out in answer, but it doesn't matter. He's not done stabbing me in the heart.

"It's best this way. In the palace they're already calling you 'the king's mule.' Even my own guardsmen say it when they think I'm not listening, and it makes me sick to hear it, especially after I made it clear I never want that word used. The palace ladies are sharpening their knives to go for your throat the instant you're vulnerable or alone. And I'm sure my uncle is already plotting to get back at you for saving your mother from right under his nose. I can't be with you every moment of every day and night, no matter how much I want to."

I try to say his name but it won't come.

"So it *is* better to end it now, because I could not live with myself if I knew you'd been killed because of me. If I know you're safe, I can endure the rest of it." He speaks with the knell of finality. "*Go.* That is our royal command. Leave this city and never come back."

There is nothing else to say, so I don't try to say it. I bolt from the room and stagger to the door, where I dress hastily and clumsily. It's like I am walking on all those sharpened knives as I descend the stairs. Guards in royal uniforms stand in the darkness of the ruined compound. They say nothing but I know exactly what they are thinking.

"May we go, Captain Helias?" My voice comes out in a snarl. My cheeks are hot and my hands are in fists.

"We must wait for His Gracious Majesty to depart first."

The captain draws me out of sight so I don't have to watch as the king exits the pavilion, but I hear every footfall as he walks away draped in a silence that shouts as loudly as an accusation.

When at last Helias and I make our way back through the ruined palace, he makes no attempt to engage me in conversation. His loyalty is to the king, and he must cover our tracks so no one knows His Gracious Majesty has visited a place where he is vulnerable. Kalliarkos can never be so vulnerable again, and I realize all at once that this tryst was his way of saying good-bye. He already knew it had to be over, because he wants me to survive.

My heart is so full of pain.

I walk to the wagon, with its palm-wood barrels for carrying wine and beer. I wonder if there is anything in them, a delivery yet to be made. Probably Helias recruited this wagon off the street, and of course as a Commoner the driver could not say no to a Patron officer whether or not he decides to pay the man. "Take me to the Warrens," I say.

"General Esladas told me you will be departing Saryenia in advance of the expected arrival of the enemy army."

"That's right. I hope you will defend the king with all your might, Captain. The siege will be a dangerous—"

I break off, sensing an unexpected movement as I would on the Fives court, where I have to be aware of other adversaries. Just as I turn to see who has come up behind me, a sack is pulled over my head.

I try to twist free, then kick. A shoulder rams into me. I am thrown so hard to the ground that my voice is knocked right out of my throat. I can't even cry out.

"Doma!" The Efean driver grunts, gurgles in pain, and his body thuds on the pavement.

Hands grope me with brisk efficiency, taking the knife Mother gave me and binding the coarse sackcloth against my mouth. It is all I can do to shift to breathing through my nose so as not to suffocate from sheer terror. I'm rolled onto my stomach. With a desperate surge of strength, I try to crawl out of their grasp, scraping my chin and belly. They wrench my arms behind my back and bind them. They truss my legs from knee to ankle. I'm gathered up like a sack of grain and slung onto the wagon.

My head bumps a hard edge. I smell the dregs of wine gone to vinegar. Next thing I know I am shoved headfirst into an empty barrel, crammed in with my knees up to my chest and my back pressed against wood. Through the gag I try to plead *please please* but the cloth is tied too tightly.

They hammer the lid into place.

14

The wagon's jolt forward slams my head so hard against the side of the barrel that I actually begin to whimper like a wounded animal. I can't move. *I can't move.*

Please help anyone help please.

The gag bites into the corners of my mouth. Its coarse fibers stick in my throat and I am heaving up bile but it has nowhere to go. I'm going to choke on my own vomit. Even Kal didn't grasp how quickly the people who hate me would strike. That his own captain would be complicit in an ugly palace plot. I should have known better than to think I could belong in a world in which I am nothing but trash to be carted away. I'm going to die. I'm going to die.

Terror explodes through my mind, gaining power as I fight bonds I cannot break.

Calm down. *Calm down.*

I imagine myself on a Fives court. I imagine spinning Rings, each one moving at a different speed, and how to time the rings' turning so I leap from one to the next in that gap where the two face each other open on. I run the Fives in my mind as I often did while lying in bed at night, working over and over through the mazes of Pillars and across the moving stones of Rivers. I count my breaths in and I count my breaths out and I let the counting become my entire existence.

I am not here, my body battered ceaselessly against the sides of a barrel, caught in a trap I didn't see coming. I am Spider, and I am running the trial of my life.

⟨⟨⟨⟩⟩⟩

Eventually we stop. The barrel lifts, shifts, and slams down so hard that I black out.

⟨⟨⟨⟩⟩⟩

When I surface again, I am upside down, head pressed at such an awkward angle against the bottom of the barrel that I think my neck will break. Frantic, I twist my body so my knees are braced in one place and my shoulders in another to ease the pressure. It takes every bit of concentration I have to hold this position, but during training, adversaries learn to endure long holds as they build strength. I will endure this. I will endure.

Just when I think I cannot hold any longer, the barrel is tipped onto its side and rolled down a ramp, turning over and over until I heave up convulsively against the foul-tasting cloth tied across my mouth.

By the time the barrel comes to a halt I am so dizzy that I hallucinate Serenissima being dragged into a lightless passage with the bloody corpse of her son draped as a curse over her shoulders. Women's voices murmuring inside a bricked-up tomb whisper in my memory like snakes tangling. At least oracles can move their limbs. I will die in torment, full of the poisonous, stupid dream that I could fall in love with a prince and not pay a bitter price. That he could escape the grip of generations of Patrons fighting to keep their hold on power and treasure. That he wasn't already one of them, living in the rarefied air of the palace-born, who need never see anything but what they want to see.

A crowbar scrapes and screeches. The lid pops, and the air around me changes, breathing salty and sour.

"Good Goat! What a stink!" It is the voice of Captain Neartos.

How is that possible? The surviving members of Garon Palace went north to Maldine.

Footsteps slap as a new person enters the space. A whiff of lavender touches my vomit-stained nostrils. Melding with the smell of my bile, the aroma makes me retch. Or maybe it is the sudden onset of fear. It can't be *him*. He fled north with the rest of the household.

"Lord Gargaron, here she is."

Dread fastens its teeth over my heart. How could I ever have thought I had beaten him?

170

"Ah, Jessamy. Here you are." His tone reeks of satisfaction. "Let me explain how this is going to go. If you can hear me, tap your heels against the cask."

The strength it takes me to consider refusing causes me to twitch.

"I can tell you're awake. And I know you to be an intelligent girl. So if you want to get out of this barrel, tap your heels against the cask."

I sloppily tap my heels on the barrel's side. My knees knock the wood in the other direction because I overcompensate. More bruises.

"Very good. Now, tap your heels if you will obey me, make no attempt to escape, and speak only when I give you permission."

He's taunting me. He knows it. I know it. I can't fight any more, so again I tap my heels. The pain of moving has become so familiar that it squeezes only a few more tears out, if they are tears. Maybe I am too desiccated for tears. Maybe all I have left is the last drops of a nectar gone rancid.

"Excellent." A man savoring a delicious meal might speak his approval of the food in the same tone with which he speaks to me. "I will give you a little time to think about what this means for you. Neartos, put the lid back on."

I shriek against the grimy cloth, although all that comes out is a hoarse bleat. I try to kick the lid as it is hammered into place but I have no purchase and my legs have gone numb. The cask will crush me, suffocate me.

I must calm myself. I must.

Remember the steps into cat, the first animal in the menageries. Cats wake. They stretch. They consider their surroundings. They take their time. One slow inhalation and one slower and longer exhalation at a time, I keep myself and my pain stitched together; I don't allow my five souls to scatter apart and break me into pieces.

⌖

A loud noise followed by a sharp tug alerts me.

I am dragged out of the barrel and rolled onto a floor. My legs unfold with such painful stabs in my hip joints that I start choking. The gag is untied and the sack yanked off my head.

Light from a swaying oil lamp assaults me. The floor rocks beneath me. Captain Neartos latches shut a door. I see a cheap copper basin, buckets slopping water over their brims, a sponge and a pumice stone, and a grimy-looking towel that might as well be the finest palace linen compared to what I'm wearing. There's also a big covered pot that smells of mint and chamomile, and a dead man.

His slack, sparkless face is turned toward me. It is the Efean driver, throat cut.

I shut my eyes as a shudder wracks me.

I want to beg for release but I won't. It's the last dignity I have.

"I am going to cut your bonds, Spider." Neartos's tone is conversational, not hostile, as he returns to me. "You will put the corpse into the barrel, wash yourself and your clothing thoroughly, and dress in the clean clothing provided."

The rope loosens, and all at once my hands are free.

With a grimace, I ease my shoulders forward. My numb hands turn hot, and I grit my teeth through the spasm of release. The captain cuts through the rope wrapping my legs and at last I am free. Except of course I am not free at all.

With a grunt, I push up to all fours, then clamber to my feet and attempt a stretch. Dizziness sweeps me, and the next thing I know I've fallen in a heap on the floor.

Neartos offers me a cup of mint-infused water. "Rinse out your mouth."

The slosh of liquid in my mouth makes me want to vomit all over again. But after I have rinsed and spit four times, the urge subsides and I can drink without tasting bile.

"Very good. Now, the body."

I have handled dead people before. When people died in our household Mother herself washed them so they could enter the next life clean in both flesh and souls. But this washing is unclean because they have murdered him and he will have no proper resting place, no family feast to grace his passing, no final songs. Yet what choice do I have?

It's hard to bend him; he's stiffening, as corpses do. The only dignity I can offer is to whisper prayers as I wrestle him into the barrel, hating myself for the violence of the act.

Neartos hammers the lid into place.

"I will give you privacy to bathe. Knock at the door when you are finished."

He goes out.

Every movement hurts as I undress. My clothing stinks of urine, my face is caked with dried vomit, and my hair is matted and filthy. Yet I am grateful as I sit in the basin and pour a bucket of water over my head. I stop only when I've scrubbed my skin almost raw with the pumice. Three buckets of seawater later I don't reek quite as much. The last of the mint-and-chamomile brew provides a sweeter-smelling fresh-water rinse. I can touch my hair without touching flecks and slime.

On the table sits a worn but clean keldi and vest. The vest is loose at my waist and tight in my chest, but it covers me well enough. I wash Kal's riding clothes in the filthy water.

For a while I toy with the idea of sitting in silent protest and not letting them know I've finished, but the act strikes me as futile. I rap at the door.

Neartos enters first, Lord Gargaron after, waving a ker-chief, its lavender scent so strong my eyes water. Gargaron thoughtfully brandishes the knife my mother gave me. His smile intimidates me so much I would almost rather crawl back in a barrel.

Almost.

I'm not that brave.

"Let me explain the situation to you, Jessamy. If you dis-obey, you will be put back in a barrel. Obey with courtesy, and you will be allowed the privilege of the deck."

"The deck?" Finally I understand what I've not had the wit or energy to grasp before this. "We're at sea."

He nods in acknowledgment.

His air of triumph goads me to say more. "If you'd wanted me dead, Captain Helias or Captain Neartos would have killed me already. So you want me for something else, some scheme, or simply the pleasure of a slow revenge for rescuing my mother and sisters from the tomb. Right out from under your nose."

"Is this arrogant speech meant to soothe my natural instinct to flog a recalcitrant mule?" He enjoys the way I don't back down, as long as he has the upper hand.

"No, my lord. I am simply telling the truth."

Gargaron presses the knife's tip against my lower lip. "The truth is that you belong to Garon Palace, not to yourself. Do you understand me, Jessamy?"

Hatred eats my voice.

He twists the knife's tip against my tender lip until it draws blood.

"Yes, my lord."

He turns away. "Neartos, bring her up on deck."

That my queasiness arises from the noxious reek of the hold and the terrible presence of an innocent man stuffed into a barrel becomes clear as soon as I am on deck. The air and sun clear my aching head. Wind rumbles in the sails. We're on a merchant ship with capacious holds.

Sailors stare as I make my way to the railing, testing my balance as the deck rolls and pitches. The coast of Efea lies to the ship's right-hand side, the starboard, which means we are sailing west. The land is broken by small river channels cutting through to the sea and by long stretches of beach. We tack close enough to shore that I spot people at work amid fields and orchards. Fishing boats are drawn up on the sand. I need only wait for nightfall. I can swim to shore.

As I'm contemplating this delightful prospect, Gargaron opens a door to the leftmost cabin on the afterdeck.

"Jessamy!" he calls, summoning me.

How it galls me to have to obey. Teeth gritted, I follow Captain Neartos inside.

The cabin is painted in lively colors, its walls fitted with cupboards, a built-in desk, an inset bed, and a table with four chairs fixed to the floor. A man sits at the desk with his back to me, shoulders tense. If I didn't know better, I would say the clerk has Polodos's ears.

Then I see a young woman standing to one side.

"Maraya!"

Gargaron watches my horrified reaction with the thin smile that means he is gloating. "I imagine you have questions for me, Jessamy."

Maraya gives a slight shake of the head, advising silence, but I know Gargaron better than she does. If I don't respond, he'll get angry. But I can deny him the satisfaction he craves by not betraying in tone or word the dismay that's flooding through me.

"Am I allowed to ask questions, my lord? Or will that be counted as disobedience?"

"Say what you wish. I am curious to know which questions you will ask and which you will avoid."

"I thought Captain Helias was loyal to my father."

"Helias is a highborn man with extensive palace connections. Like many officers, he both admired and resented General Esladas's success. And despised him for his...shall we say...base predilections in the matter of his family."

I had no idea Captain Helias despised me, but I'm not about to let Gargaron know I mistook his politeness for approval.

"Nikonos almost killed you," I say instead. "Why risk returning to Saryenia when it was still under his control?"

"I did not enter the city until I'd received word that Nikonos had left to pursue your father."

"So you didn't come to Saryenia to get me?"

"You? Of course not. Getting hold of you, and your sister, was serendipitous chance. As for Nikonos, battle is not the only way to secure a victory."

"Yes, secret alliances also work well. The one you have with the High Priest, for instance." By the surprised flare of Gargaron's eyelids, I see that Kal and I guessed correctly. "That's how you forced him to entomb my mother, by threatening to reveal what is really going on behind the closed gates of the Inkos temple—"

I break off as he grabs the whip.

Maraya throws her arms around me, like she means to take the blow herself.

Polodos jumps up. "My lord, it would be indecent to flog a pregnant woman!"

"Sit down!" commands Gargaron.

With breathtaking defiance, Polodos crosses to stand beside us. If this is the end, then at least we will go down together.

Neartos glances at Gargaron, but the lord shakes his head. Silence follows, and I realize Gargaron is waiting for me to speak. It takes all the courage I have to ask the next question.

"Does His Gracious Majesty know you were in the city?"

Gargaron still holds the whip aloft, but my question seems to distract him. "Of course he knows. He and I had already agreed on the strategy of sending Menoë and Princess Berenise ahead to Maldine while I secretly returned to Saryenia to negotiate with the High Priest. A good strategist keeps a plan in reserve."

"Oh, I see. If Kalliarkos and my father had failed to retake the city, then the High Priest would have found a way to kill Nikonos at your order."

"You must refer to him as Prince General Nikonos. But, yes, poisoned him. There is more than one path to the victory tower, as you certainly know, Spider."

"Did His Gracious Majesty take Queen Serenissima to Eternity Temple at your order?" I grasp at this excuse, hoping to acquit Kal of responsibility, and yet I'm ashamed of myself even as I speak the words. "He thought it would be safe to hold her there. He didn't know the truth about what the priests do to the women." I desperately hope that Kal's innocence in this, at least, is true.

He inclines his head in mocking agreement. "I kept him ignorant of such matters. As for Serenissima, I am sure she is already dead. As you would be, if I had not rescued you."

Rescued me!

My cut lip stings, but not more than my heart. This is exactly what Kal was trying to prevent when he told me to leave the city immediately. But we walked blindly into that trap, and there's no way back. I have to take all the memories and the kisses and the soft words, and I must pour them as into a ceramic vessel and seal it with wax. And then I have to figure out a way for my sister and her husband and me to escape.

"What will you do if the enemy overruns the city and kills His Gracious Majesty and my father?"

"The line remains intact through Menoë. It wasn't my idea for my nephew to stay." He waves a hand in the air in a parody of an actor's kingly gesture. "He proclaimed he would share the fate of the people he is responsible for. He even quoted noble lines from a play."

"He never told me any of these plans."

"Why would he tell you, Jessamy? It isn't as if you are going to become queen. Or perhaps Kalliarkos spoke to you about that possibility?"

My face burns. "You must know he did not."

"Of course he did not. He would no more have made that

offer to you than to an actual mule, as in the well-loved and always-popular comedy *The Emperor's Four-Legged Bride.* Have you seen the play?"

The insult spikes me straight into a red haze of anger.

Maraya's hand closes on my wrist.

In her condescending elder-sister voice she says, "Our mother refused to allow us to see it, my lord. She said it was disrespectful to think a mule would lower itself to marry a Saroese nobleman."

He sets down the whip. "Ah! I was wondering how soon I would provoke you to address me. Maraya, is it not?"

"It is, my lord."

"A fortunate chance you were still at the Least-Hill Inn. I went there after Captain Helias informed me General Esladas had broken our agreement and gone to see your mother. Unfortunately she had already left by the time I arrived with my soldiers."

I'm so relieved to hear that Mother, Amaya, and Denya escaped his foul clutches that I sag into Maraya's arms. She's shorter than me, and looks frailer, but she's always been able to hold up us younger girls.

"Your mother isn't important, not with Esladas married to Queen Menoë," he adds. "You girls are more valuable to me now. Steward Polodos is negligible but may busy himself as a clerk while he serves as a hostage whose life is dependent on your obedience."

He cranes his neck, looking past me onto the deck.

180

Sailors have hoisted the barrel out of the hold and onto the deck. They wrap it with rope, burden it with anchor stones, and roll it over the side. The sea receives it with a splash.

"In old Efea, before we Saroese came," he remarks, "it's said that any poet who told a lie was crammed into a weighted barrel and thrown into the sea. A useful custom, don't you think? Why, anyone might find themselves in a stone-anchored barrel dropped into the unforgiving sea. *Anyone*. I'm sure you understand me, Jessamy."

My dream of swimming to shore dies a swift death as I whisper a prayer for the five souls of the poor wagon driver.

"His Gracious Majesty will figure out I've gone missing," I say in my last and weakest burst of defiance.

"That's unlikely, since he thinks you went with your mother. Even if he did discover the truth, His Gracious Majesty cannot abandon his throne to charge after you as such a character would do in a play. Do not believe the fables told to make us feel better about the harsh reality of the world we live in."

"My mother—"

"Will believe you chose to stay with your father, or the king. Even if she does wish to find you, how can she possibly succeed? She is a Commoner, an uneducated woman with no connections or wealth. She can do nothing to me. You lost this trial before the start bell rang."

15

꧁~~~~꧂

"**L**ord Father, I have come according to your command." A grave-faced boy about the same age as Prince Temnos enters the cabin. He examines me and Maraya with interest. "Are you sure they are sisters? They don't look anything alike except for their eyes. The tall girl reminds me a little of the handmaiden Orchid, though."

Neartos laughs heartily. "I think not!"

"Why do you say so, Menos?" asks Lord Gargaron sharply.

"Their hands look alike."

Maraya pinches a fold of skin at my waist to keep me quiet, not that I was about to blurt out that Orchid was the name given to Amaya when she was serving in Garon Palace in disguise as Denya's handmaiden.

Gargaron is amused. "Their hands! An interesting comparison. One set so callused, dark, and rough; the other smooth, light, and soft."

The boy sighs with the lovelorn intensity of a twelve-year-old lost to the first stirrings of infatuation. Amaya certainly left a trail of flotsam in her wake.

Then he points quite rudely at Maraya. "What's wrong with her foot? It's twisted and ugly."

"It is a mark of the gods' displeasure, is it not, Maraya? The Precepts say that infants bearing such deformities must be smothered at birth to keep our lineages strong."

"In fact, my lord, no Precept says that."

"Not one? Have you read them all?" Gargaron scoffs, his tone freighted with warning.

"I have thoroughly studied the One Hundred Sages and the Ancillary Scholars. According to the forty-fourth Precept of the third branch of the curriculum, asymmetries of form appear among animals as well as people. So it is more likely people are simply like clay bowls baked in a fire. A few will shatter, while others might develop bulges or borderline cracks but still be perfectly able to hold food."

"A remarkable analogy that I reject, since I cannot equate people and bowls."

"What the Precept means is that asymmetries are accidents, not divine action, and not necessarily fatal or enfeebling. The custom of killing infants with conditions like my clubfoot is therefore ordained by humans, not by the gods."

183

"Even were that true, I wonder that your father, an obedient Saroese man, did not smother you according to custom."

"I wondered that too. When I was about the same age as Lord Menos, I asked my parents about it."

Gargaron laughs in surprise. "Did you not fear the answer?"

"Since I was alive, it meant the matter had been decided in my favor, so I could scarcely be insulted by the result, could I?"

"Go on!" cries the boy, leaning forward in rapt interest.

"I was born when my father was away on military duty. When he returned, my mother made sure to keep my legs wrapped in linen for some days and encouraged him to hold me as much as possible. Once she was sure of his affection for me, she revealed the foot."

Gargaron shakes his head. "A remarkable ruse!"

"I am grateful to have an Efean mother who followed Efean custom in this matter, that every child is a precious life to be nurtured. Indeed, the eighty-ninth Precept of the fifth branch praises the old Efean kingdom for this trait of generosity."

"You explain too much," exclaims Menos with so much excitement I can see he is greatly pleased. "Just like me."

" 'Just as I do' is more appropriate diction for a young lord," corrects Maraya, because she can't help herself any more than I can help wanting to defeat people in a trial.

A pretty young woman—Denya's replacement—enters carrying a pitcher of water and two towels folded in a basin. She assists Gargaron and his son to wash their hands as a manservant brings in a tray of food. Polodos, Maraya, and I are forced to stand in attendance, stomachs growling, while Gargaron picks through his food and drills my sister in the Precepts. Every question he asks she can answer, and twice she corrects him, not in a gloating way, of course. Polodos's willingness to remain silent, without the least attempt to prove that he is as learned as his wife—which he isn't—impresses me deeply. I have underestimated him.

"Doma Maraya knows more than my tutor," says the boy. "Can't she teach me?"

"Women do not teach men or rule men," says his father as he sips his wine.

"What of the example of Efea's queens, my lord?" Maraya interposes. "For one hundred years the many Serenissimas have effectively administered the diplomacy, merchants, and markets of Efea. The kingdom is so rich that all three of the old Saroese kingdoms covet its wealth and periodically, as now, invade to try to grab it for themselves. What need of Precepts when we see the truth in the events we are living through?"

He sets down his cup. "I am impressed despite myself by the cleverness of you girls. I never imagined Orchid was your pretty sister all along."

Maybe Maraya can control her expression. But he savors my shock with considerable gratification. "I confess I did not realize until Captain Helias recognized her when he went to the inn to fetch you, Jessamy. I am only sorry I was too late to gather her and Denya back into my net. Very well, Doma Maraya. You may assist in tutoring my son. I will monitor your progress."

Doma Maraya! I'm astounded by this courteous address.

"My sister has likely not eaten for some hours, my lord, and you can see she is pregnant." I attempt a tone of humility for Maraya's sake.

"You girls can take meals in Lord Menos's cabin."

"What of my husband, Polodos, my lord?" she asks.

"Because of the peculiar nature of your parentage, you cannot marry Steward Polodos. Neartos will keep him safe with my other clerks. If he proves useful, then I see no reason to toss him overboard in a weighted barrel."

Maraya nods at Polodos, communication passing between them in wordless signals they must have perfected in the early months of their illicit courtship, right under our father's nose. Then she blinks at me as a signal that we'll find a way to speak later.

The boy leaps up to follow her out. "What do you know about magic, Doma Maraya? I am going to the Stone Desert to study to become a priest and learn magic."

Maraya pauses to allow him to cross the threshold before her. Our gazes lock. She's remembering the ruins buried beneath the tombs in the City of the Dead, just as I am: the sparks that brought Wenru back to life, the twisting shadows, the glowing pool. The smile that tilts up her mouth brings her as close to crowing as I have ever seen her. Against all expectation, she may have just been given a door that will open onto information about these mysteries.

I'm left behind with Gargaron, who takes another sip of wine.

"And there is a fourth sister, who I never met. What became of her, Jessamy?"

"She's dead," I say in a leaden voice, although a part of me wants to rub in his face that he met Bettany and never guessed.

"And the child your mother was pregnant with?"

"Twins, my lord. A boy and a girl."

"A relief for General Esladas, I am sure, since the sages argue whether a man who cannot sire a son can call himself a man."

"If Lord Menos is destined for the priesthood, then he must not be your eldest son." I am seeing how these Rings turn, how Gargaron intends to keep control of the kingdom even as other people carry the royal titles.

"He is my third son. A dutiful and intelligent boy."

"Ah."

"Ah? Is there some wit or wisdom you wish to share with me?"

"You will have the king and queen appoint him as High Priest once he is a little older, while meanwhile you hold the current High Priest in your pocket. So the temples will remain under your control for a very long time."

Under his control. Never under Kal's.

"Very good, Jessamy. You understand me exactly. It's why you are such an exceptionally promising adversary."

Of course Gargaron's game to place his niece and nephew

187

on the throne has been rigged from the start. Why did I ever believe Kal would have a chance to make genuine reforms? Ro would tell me I was being willfully naïve, and poets always tell the truth.

⟩⟩⟩

Weeks later I am standing at the prow with the spray in my face as the sun rises. We have sailed north along the coast for day after day after day. A wide bay opens before us with a tabletop mountain rising behind it as in judgment. The choppy gray-blue of the open sea shades into a sapphire brilliance in the semicircular bay. But that is not what rivets my attention.

Maldine Harbor is filled with war galleys flying the kestrel of West Saro. They are imposing with their tiered banks of oars and their fierce bronze-sheathed battering rams visible just below the water. But are they here to invade? Or has Kal's uncle Thynos made the marriage alliance Kal told me about?

The prows of the warships have eyes that seem to follow us as our sails come down. Oared boats cast lines and tow us in.

Maldine is a town built of stone the same color as the pale rock of the bare mountainside behind it. A strip of green runs along the bay and widens where a valley with orchards and villages works a gouge in the landscape. Somewhere in this area, half a year ago, my father beat back an invasion of the East Saroese alliance. Everyone thought we had won, but of course now we know it was only a preliminary attack. Just as Gargaron has carefully laid his plans over many years, so too surely have the kings of old Saro readied their fleets and armies and their covert alliance with Nikonos.

Gargaron joins me at the railing, accompanied by his son. To my astonishment, a crow perches delicately on Menos's forearm. A tiny tube is fastened to its leg.

"Look, Spider!" says the boy in a hoarse, excited whisper. "This is the first time I've been allowed to release a messenger crow!"

He sweeps up his arm and the crow flies off, headed for the town.

"I wish I could be a crow priest," he adds. "Then I would have crows of my own."

"The High Priest must have his eyes, Menos," says Gargaron, "so you will undergo a different sort of trial."

"Will I learn the sacred magic of the priests?"

Gargaron shakes his head. "These are matters not to be spoken of outside the sanctuary of Lord Judge Inkos. Now go get the royal messenger pigeon."

"Will it really fly all the way to Saryenia, to Cousin Kal?"

"It will. You may release it as a reward for doing so well at your lessons."

The boy manages a courteous leave-taking before scampering back to the afterdeck.

"I wondered why we were sailing into a harbor filled with enemy ships," I remark. "That crow must have brought a message from Princess Berenise that all is secure. I didn't see it fly in."

"It arrived at dawn before we came in view of the harbor. Now, Jessamy, be aware that you will be on display at every moment, and always within earshot of me or Captain Neartos. Your sister and Polodos will remain on this ship under guard. The penalty will fall on them if you do not play your part."

"What exactly is my part, my lord? You could keep me on the ship with Maraya."

"But you would like that. So therefore you must accompany me and act as an obedient adversary."

"And if I act as an obedient adversary, my lord? What then?"

His thin smile is all the answer he gives me. I've learned just how far I can push him so I ask no more questions.

An honor guard awaits us at the wharf. Soldiers wearing the horned and winged fire dog of Garon Palace stand at attention. Officials garbed in gold-striped palace robes embroidered with the queen's cornucopia jostle for the right to greet Lord Gargaron.

A Garon steward approaches. "My lord! May the Sun of Justice shine upon you and your safe arrival in this haven. I'm here to escort you to the queen."

Princess Berenise and Queen Menoë hold court in the dusty garden of a palace compound that looks as if it hasn't been lived in for years. Kal's mother sits amid their ladies; when her gaze pauses on me and her eyes wrinkle up, I cannot tell if she is nearsighted or puzzled.

The garden is large and must once have been a splendid

haven in which to relax. Awnings have been strung up to provide shade. Pots with blooming flowers are set around the chairs, which are raised off the ground on a makeshift platform constructed of brick and covered with a carpet. Pellets of incense burn to purify the area. These small flourishes can't disguise that when the foreigners invaded, they trashed the palace as sacrilegiously as possible.

The lotus pond has become a scum of muddy water and dead plants. Four ancient sycamores, one at each corner of the garden, have been recently chopped down, their bare trunks a terrible scar. The back of the audience hall is two stories high and built masterfully of brick. The wall bears a magnificent relief depicting the famous arrival of Prince Kliatemnos and his sister and ships in the land of Efea at this very harbor one hundred years ago. It looks almost exactly like the mural painted in the king's audience hall in Saryenia. The relief has been defaced as high as people can reach with obscene graffiti that scrubbing hasn't quite eliminated. The highborn sit with their backs to that side of the garden wall.

"Here you are, Nephew," says Princess Berenise. "We heard from a crow priest that you were on your way. I see you brought Menos. Come up here and greet us, little one."

The boy hurries forward to get a kiss on either cheek from the old woman. Menoë also gives him a kiss, then he walks along the lower rank of chairs so the rest of the women can kiss him. If one is his mother I cannot tell, for they all smile fondly at him and give him affectionate pinches.

"You may join us, Uncle Gar," says Menoë. "We are expecting the commanders of the West Saroese fleet to arrive at any moment."

It's hard not to laugh at the way she indicates a chair set off the platform and, as such, situated below the women. But he shows no irritation as he takes a seat. His new concubine that I met on the ship bathes his hands and applies a wet towel to his face.

I've been left standing in the hot sun even though there is space under the awning. Now that we are on land again I feel how much hotter it is here than in Saryenia. The furnace blast of heat sucks the moisture right out of my eyes. Menoë's gaze touches mine, and her lips press primly together as if she is recalling an unpleasant memory. She looks deliberately away, pretending not to notice my plight. There's my thanks for rescuing her from Nikonos!

It is Kalliarkos's mother who whispers to an attendant, who whispers to a steward, who shepherds me into a patch of blessed shade. The highborn nibble from platters of dates and halved apricots as Berenise describes the long journey they took upriver, hidden belowdecks, and the grueling overland trek across the Stone Desert to reach Maldine.

A horn blows three times. A Garon steward enters. "Your Gracious Majesty. Princess Berenise. If it is your will, the honorable visitors from West Saro beg leave to enter your august presence."

"Send them in."

Menoë sits with hands folded in front of her noticeably

rounded belly. She looks robust and lovely. Being queen, and pregnant, agrees with her.

A file of resplendently robed stewards enters, each bearing a tray laden with an astonishing gift: a bowl of polished jewels, a gold cup, a pair of ivory-hilted knives, a hinged silver box, and a cedarwood chest with lid open to display nuggets of aromatic resin. It's a staggering display of wealth.

"Prince General Cissorios and Lord Admiral Dorokos."

The men and their accompanying officers look stern and competent. They wear wool trousers and calf-length wool jackets completely unsuited to the climate of Efea. All have faces flushed from the heat.

The prince general gives a flattering speech filled with meaningless phrases. When he finishes, Menoë leans sideways, looking toward the entry.

"Is my uncle Thynos not with you? I expected him and his new bride."

"We had thought the princess might prefer to go immediately to the privacy of your women's quarters rather than be assaulted by a public greeting unsuited to the delicate constitution of a lady."

"Yet here I am," remarks Menoë with a not-so-subtle edge.

"But you, Your Gracious Majesty, have been required to endure this hardship due to the absence of your esteemed and gracious brother, His Gracious Majesty King Kalliarkos. I will send for the princess at once, if I may gain your favor by doing so."

He snaps a finger to an aide, who hustles out.

The man's tiresome condescension annoys me so much that when Gargaron glances back at my shifting about and scuffing my feet, I actually roll my eyes at him as if he were one of my sisters sharing an unspoken thought. He smiles just enough to make me realize I've confided in him, who I hate. No wonder he separated me from Maraya. There isn't a single person here who will treat me as an equal, as Kal did. But I won't be humbled by Gargaron. I just remember that every time he looks at me, he has to be reminded that I defeated him by saving my family.

A phalanx of women appears at the entrance. A male steward speaks.

"Your Gracious Majesty, Princess Shenia offers greetings and begs the courtesy of being allowed to address you as elder sister."

The women all look alike, straight black hair pulled severely back without a ribbon or flourish in sight and covered by scarves whose colors range from tedious brown to exhausted gray. They look like peahens, made as drab as possible. The contrast with the bright colors, gaudy ribbons, and bold hair designs of Menoë and her court is stunning.

Curiosity coaxes Menoë's habitual arrogant sneer into the more relaxed expression of a young woman who once knew how to be happy.

"Little sister, please come forward and greet me. I am anxious to make your acquaintance." She scans the ranks of the women with a touch of puzzlement in her brow. There is nothing different in their garb or decoration except for the one girl whose skin is pale as ivory instead of an attractive golden brown. It is this freckled, brown-haired girl who comes forward. Menoë greets her with a kiss to each cheek, then indicates that another chair must be brought up to the platform where she and Berenise sit. Shenia looks toward Prince General Cissorios. His nod gives her permission to sit.

This signal allows the most exalted among the visitors to sit as well. Attendants bring around basins in which the newcomers can wash, after which drinks and platters of food are offered. I, of course, am offered nothing, not even a wet cloth to cool my face.

"Where is your new husband, my uncle Thynos?" Menoë asks Shenia.

The prince general answers for her. "He met with an Efean man who he said was a servant of yours. They intend to travel inland immediately to take charge of the garrisons in the Stone Desert, the route that leads to the fortress of Furnace Gate. Did he not pay his respects to you before he left?"

Berenise smiles with the easy sardonicism of age. "Ah, so he went with Inarsis. Thynos is a bit like the south wind from which he takes his Fives name, changeable and inconstant."

"The game of Fives!" The prince general makes a show of laughing. "Lord Thynos described this contest at great length although it is hard to picture how athletes can manage feats of agility and strength on such a small playing field. In West Saro our chief games are chariot racing, horse racing, wrestling, and archery contests."

Gargaron says, "You're in luck, Prince General. We have made plans to hold a Fives trial here in Maldine in honor of our alliance. I have my particular favorite and most obedient adversary traveling with me, who has been practicing for weeks now on the ship's rigging. Quite the boldest and most adventurous competitor I have ever watched run. Choose any man among your soldiers, and my spider will climb that wall faster than he can. I guarantee it."

As our West Saroese allies laugh in disbelief it's all I can do not to rage aloud at the thought of being ordered to perform like a trained animal. But at least now I know what Gargaron wants from me besides to keep me away from Maraya.

"How can a man climb that wall without falling?" asks the prince general.

"You have no brave man willing to risk it? What a shame." Gargaron snaps his fingers. "Spider, show them how it is done."

I'm just grateful I've been wearing Kal's riding clothes on the ship: not as supple as Fives gear but at least my knees won't get scraped up and no one will be able to look up my keldi.

"Yes, my lord."

Every gaze among the West Saroese leaps to me.

Of course I cannot help myself, even in these circumstances. The taunt slides out.

"Shall I climb up the figure of His Gracious Majesty King Kliatemnos the First, my lord, stepping atop his head? That looks to be the easiest route. But perhaps you would prefer I take a path more respectful of the dignity of the founder of the Saroese-Efean dynasty?"

"You have climbed atop enough kings recently, Spider."

Just like that, the atmosphere in the garden sharpens. Humiliation scalds me, as he means it to, especially knowing I can't talk back. The West Saroese stare, and that isn't even the worst of it. It's the snickering among the highborn Efean women, because however embarrassed I am to be mocked in this way, Gargaron is really doing it to undercut Kal.

I shouldn't care. Kal is lost to me. He's my adversary, not my lover.

And yet I do care.

As I walk over to the wall and examine the relief for the holds and pressure points by which I can create a route up to the top, a young West Saroese man hurries over. He strips out of his feathered helmet and kestrel-embroidered uniform jacket. After giving me a sharp look, he frowns at the wall.

"On my signal!" calls Gargaron.

He whistles.

16

~~~

I **fix my foot** where the foundation sticks out and
shove myself up to the main face of the wall. The hull of
the ship makes a kind of ladder because each carved plank is
delineated just enough to give purchase for me to finger-climb.
I miss my fingerless gloves and wrist wraps, which protect my
palms and capture sweat before it slicks my skin, but I don't
have such luxuries. The West Saroese man slips, drops, and
lands on his feet, but he moves right back, seeking a new way
up. I cling my way up the carved afterdeck and press my face
against the head of the steersman at the rudder. Hot stone
prickles against my cheek. If I doubt, I will fall.

Isn't that always true?

From the steersman I reach to capture the rigging and the
unfurled sail, and from there use the pressure of fingers and
toes to mount the crow's nest and thence move to the top of

the mast. My left foot slips. My shoulders tip out. A shout splits the air, and I grab for and catch the rim of the roof, dangle a moment with legs bumping a spray of carved stars, then fix my other hand beside the first, hook a foot over, and heave myself up onto the flat roof.

Up here the sun blasts me. I lie panting and also laughing under my breath as cheers and a buzz of astonishment serenade me from below. I could escape through the confusion of the half-empty compound. But he'll kill Maraya and Polodos.

So after I can breathe properly I look for a safer way down and, to my relief, find a ladder. My reward is having to return to the garden and be gawked at while the highborn eat and drink. My mouth is parched until a woman attendant appears with a cup of palm wine.

"Lady Adia sends this cleansing drink, Spider, with her compliments."

Lady Adia is Kal's mother. I lift the cup in her direction before I drink it down.

A trio of young men wearing West Saroese uniforms sidle up to me.

"How did you do that?" The speaker has a scrape on one cheek and favors his right leg, by which I recognize him as the man who contested me.

"Training. It was brave of you to try such an unfamiliar skill."

"Is there a Fives court here?" They've become fledglings eager to test their wings although they are grown men and not gangly youths.

"There is a Fives court in every city, town, and village of Efea."

Here too I see Gargaron's strategy at work. Our allies are no longer *just* thinking about politics. They want something both worthless and priceless: an entry to this game. He needs me to make it seem thrilling and also desirable, something of Efea that they won't be able to get anywhere else. After all, I am the adversary who conquered the king.

Soon afterward Neartos escorts me to a Fives stable adjoining the palace compound. The practice court hasn't been defaced and the harness room still has gear folded neatly in baskets and cedar chests.

"Spider!" One of my trainers, white-haired Darios, hails me from the stable's dining shelter. He was part of the Garon household that escaped Saryenia. He greets me with an enthusiastic slap on the shoulder but his good humor turns to a frown as he marks Neartos setting up sentries at the stable's gate. "I hope you are well."

"It's complicated."

There are six local adversaries at the table, digging into a pot of lentil stew and freshly grilled flatbread. And there is one adversary from Garon Stable here too. The highborn Saroese girl called Talon sits at the far end, alone, eating not from the common platter but from a bowl set aside only for her, exactly as she used to hold herself apart from the rest of us before. Her gaze lifts to meet mine. I'm not in the mood for her peculiar airs so I stare belligerently back until her face gets red.

200

"Spider, please eat," says Darios in a tone more gentle than I deserve.

"Where is everyone else from Garon Stable?" I ask him.

"The Commoners did not come with us, as you may recall, and Princess Berenise had already returned the fledgling Patron boys to their families before that ill-omened night when the palace was burned down."

"Now that I think about it, everyone in Garon Stable except you, Talon, and those fledglings were Efeans. Does that strike you as strange?"

"Lord Gargaron never involved himself in the stable. Lord Thynos and Tana recruited adversaries. I never thought to ask why they chose the people they did because they only chose promising ones. We assumed at first you came as part of Lord Gargaron's negotiation with your father, that the general insisted you be given a chance to train in exchange for his military services, but then we realized how good you actually are."

The instant the local adversaries discover I am General Esladas's daughter, they fall all over themselves to tell me about the battle of Maldine: how enemy ships appeared without warning one day, how the town's governor pretended to welcome them while secretly sending a message to a Stone Desert garrison under the command of Captain Esladas, how my father assembled a ragtag army with stunning speed from veterans and militia. But I can't question the Efeans among them about whether there is a local resistance, or anyone I can persuade to rescue Maraya and Polodos from the ship, because

201

Neartos sits beside me at meals and dogs my heels the rest of the time. All I'm able to find out is that every able-bodied Saroese man under the age of fifty in the Maldine region will leave with Queen Menoë's army when it departs.

For three days I train, eat, and rest under the captain's constant supervision. I'm given a tiny cubicle to sleep in, and a soldier stands guard outside.

The morning of the fourth day, our little stable, including Talon, is escorted to the Maldine Fives court. From the outside it looks exactly like every other Fives court, with circular walls and multiple entrances. The stairway down to the attiring hall is roped off. No supporters toss flower petals and ribbons at our feet. My gear is a mix of whatever I could put together from the stable, including a mask I've sewn from a scrap of brown silk. A boisterous crowd gathers, curious foreign soldiers as well as locals making a celebration of the trial, knowing the fleet and army will be leaving in two days.

Sixteen adversaries wait in the attiring hall, enough for four trials. To my surprise, the first three trials run without Talon.

Taking a break from warm-ups I approach her with my best attempt at a polite, comradely smile. "This is a big day for you. I didn't expect you to be held to the last trial, since it is your first test. What mask do you wear?"

She unfolds a mask embroidered with a stylized hawk.

"Are you originally from East Saro?" I ask, disconcerted by this reminder of the war.

Without answering, she fixes the mask over her face.

We are called into the ready cage. I'm handed the green belt, for Trees. Two adversaries I don't know are given blue and brown while Talon ties on the red belt for Traps. I can't stop staring at her hawk mask. Surely this is a clue to the mystery of who she is, and why she's being allowed to run now when she was hidden away before.

Menoë's first husband was the crown prince of East Saro, and his sister was Nikonos's bride. I remember what Menoë told me that day when I rescued her from death:

Nikonos convinced them I was nothing more than a jealous and vindictive viper who murdered both my husband and his young bride out of spite and shame.

"Spider!" The custodian's voice jars me.

I have to concentrate. I follow the custodian down a tunnel to the ladder.

The start bell rings.

I swarm up, push through the gate, and get my first look at Trees, set in a basic power configuration. No time for subtlety. Like Father on the Royal Road, I just have to punch through. So I climb, and I move well, strengthened by my time in the rigging. But just as I make the resting platform I hear the crowd roar as an adversary enters Trees behind me.

I look back and am shocked to see Talon. She is short, slender, and flat-chested; her lack of height is a disadvantage but she has less weight to haul.

I am not going to let her beat me on her first trial. I can't believe she is through Traps already. Should I race on in the opposite direction or let her chase me? Deciding on the latter, I head for Rivers. Knowing she is behind me fuels my determination.

Even so, I stumble once in Rivers and take two wrong turns in Pillars, and so I am a little shaken by the time I reach Traps. I hear her enter Pillars by the shouts of the crowd. People cry out with a harsh hawk's *skreek* for the mask she wears. I can't tell if they are cheering her on or mocking her.

The other two adversaries no longer matter; they're behind. For once I do not take the highest level through Traps to show off my flair. Pride compels me to throw in a pair of flips but I'm ashamed of my cautious performance as I climb the final resting platform overlooking Rings.

Big rings turn at different speeds in a classic configuration that forces the adversary to time them exactly right to make it through in the most direct line. This is basically the same setup as the very first Fives trial I ran, all those months ago.

My thoughts spin.

You killed Nikonos's bride too? I asked Menoë that terrible night, wondering what sort of monster I had rescued. And she replied, *No, he just thinks I did.*

Talon is ahead of me, but she jumps to the wrong ring and finds herself spun so she has to head out again, losing time. I won't make that mistake.

I leap to the first ring and work my way inward because Rings is the strength I inherited from my father: the ability to process multiple bands of information and see how they fit together. Talon was far enough ahead that her mistake sets her back but doesn't defeat her. We hit the ground at the same time for a short dash to the ladder. For an instant I'm tempted to slacken my pace and let her go up ahead of me. It's her first trial; she's done well, and I can tell by the shine in her face that she wants to win, that it means something to her that I can't even fathom. My hesitation allows her to get a step ahead of me.

I will never let anyone win if it means I have to lose.

So I leap over her, grab the ladder above her head, and surge up to the top. The victor's ribbon is nothing fancy, just a white ribbon that I snag and hold up as the crowd cheers. A few scattered voices chant, "Spider! Spider!" but more call out, "Talon! *Skreek!*"

The victory doesn't taste as sweet as usual. I don't linger on the tower.

She's still standing at the foot of the ladder with a hand on a rung, having pulled off her mask the better to catch her breath. The other two adversaries stroll toward us through Rings but for this brief interval she and I are alone.

Do I dare ask where she comes from? If she is the East Saroese princess I now realize she might be? If Menoë and Berenise have been holding her back until the exact moment they need her to show their new allies they have something that once belonged to Nikonos but escaped him?

Before I can take the leap, she heads down the ladder into the retiring hall. The other two adversaries flash me the kiss-off sign and peer with interest as her head recedes into the darkness of the undercourt.

"I have never seen a Patron woman run the Fives," says

Brown Belt, a brawny Saroese man with two rings in his ear to mark him as a former criminal allowed back into society.

"That was something, wasn't it?" agrees Blue Belt, a young Efean man who speaks Saroese as easily as I do. He grins at me but doesn't address me directly.

"Have a drink later?" asks the Saroese man, with Saroese manners.

"I surely would," I say recklessly, even though I know Gargaron will forbid it.

Captain Neartos escorts me back to the stable. He's chatty and cheerful.

"You were a bit shaky, not up to your usual standard, but that's to be expected, considering your lack of dedicated practice time. I won a tidy sum on bets with those West Saroese soldiers. They just can't believe a woman can beat a man."

"Happy to be of use."

Either my sarcasm flies over his head or he ignores it. "His lordship says to tell you he's pleased with how you are playing your part."

"What exactly is his game? Was I the lure to attract their attention so they would come to the court and see Talon for the first time?"

"You know better than to think I'll answer that. Or to think there's only one ring spinning at a time."

It's not yet midday and already scorching. I'm grateful to drink my fill at the dining shelter as Darios offers a few perfunctory critiques, although I can tell he is uneasy at Neartos's constant presence.

"I've been told Talon and I are to sail with Queen Menoë south to Saryenia," he says. "Does that mean you have different orders, Jessamy?"

"Jessamy's circumstances have changed," says Neartos.

"Captain." I don't want to beg but I don't know how else to ask. "As I have been studying the Precepts in my spare time, I had a few questions to put to Lord Menos's tutor. Perhaps as a courtesy, in reward for playing my part, I might be allowed to see that individual briefly."

He shakes his head. "If you've quenched your thirst, you may go bathe, Spider."

"Maybe send my victory ribbon to her as a token?"

"You may go bathe, Spider."

I do as I'm told. Neartos stations himself at the entry. I disrobe in the outer room and scrub myself in the bathing room until my skin starts to feel raw, then go into the inner chamber and immerse myself in the soaking pool with my head tipped back to rest against the rim. The gloom washes over me like defeat.

Soft footfalls alert me. I open my eyes. Talon ventures in with a length of linen wrapped around her from armpits to knees even though the rest of us adversaries walk around naked without giving it a thought. I always assumed she had a Patron woman's arrogance, not wishing Commoner women to see her body. Just as I'm about to congratulate her on her first Fives run, a voice from the entry startles us both.

"Why, yes, Captain, we will just go in," says Queen Menoë.

Talon flinches with acute distress and loses her grip on the linen towel. It lands at her feet, and I try not to gasp but succeed only in slapping a hand over my mouth as I flinch.

Her torso is hatched with seamed white scarring all the way down her belly, just as Menoë's is, scars of an abuse whose ferocity still has the power to rob me of words. Talon splashes clumsily down the steps as three women enter the soaking chamber.

"Here you are, Talessa," says Menoë. "I wanted you to meet Princess Shenia, for I am sure you two will be thrown together a great deal now and I, for one, recall vividly that I never had the benefit of a single friend when I lived in the palace of East Saro."

In private Princess Shenia has a bold stare and blunt manner at odds with her public modesty. "So you really *are* Princess Talessa of East Saro! Everyone thinks you are dead, murdered together with your brother, Stratios. What are those ugly marks on your body?"

Talon goes pink with shame. Of course I'm staggered by this revelation, even though I suspected it, but the rude comment so offends me that I stand up, grab the linen towel off the floor, and hand it to her.

"Excuse me, Your Gracious Majesty, we were not expecting visitors and did not dress for the occasion," I say in my best Patron accent. My nakedness disconcerts Shenia so much she stops staring at Talon and scrutinizes the floor. Lady Adia, however, gives me a long look from my head to my toes that hits like a scalding splash of boiling water.

"You may continue your soak, Spider," Menoë says with exaggerated condescension, "and indeed I wish you would."

Furious, I sink into the water. Talon has wrapped the towel around herself.

"My dear Shenia," says Menoë with a smile that skates right at the edge of mockery and yet does not quite fall over. "Perhaps you might give me and my mother a moment alone with Princess Talessa. Your ladies are outside, are they not?"

"Yes, they are watching the men practice. We are not accustomed to men racing about in front of women in so little clothing as people wear here."

"It is very hot here in Efea compared to the kingdoms of Old Saro," agrees Lady Adia placidly.

Shenia gives her a respectful bow and hurries out with a single backward glance at the blushing Talon.

"I will turn my back," says Menoë to Talon. "I apologize for any discomfort you have felt. It was not my intention to embarrass you but it is the only way I could have a private word. If you don't mind."

I start to rise but Menoë shakes her head and I finally understand.

They want a private word with *me*.

Talon climbs out of the water, the wet towel clinging to her body. I nod at her, and to my surprise, she meets my gaze and nods back at me as to a fellow adversary, then goes out.

Lady Adia looks around for a place to sit but the only benches in the soaking chamber are the ones in the pool itself.

"I can bring you a stool from the bathing chamber, my lady," I say.

"Do not bestir yourself. Are you pregnant with his child?"

I must stare like a simpleton because after a long pause she speaks more slowly and with hand gestures, as if she thinks I am deficient.

"Are. You. Pregnant. With his child?"

"Dearest Mother, you just heard her speak Saroese so you must know she understands you."

"No, my lady. I'm not pregnant."

To my absolute shock, she pats my hand with a weary smile. "I'm so glad. That way we won't have to kill the baby."

"Uh." I struggle to find an answer but all that comes out are choked fragments.

"He chose you for himself, you know. Princess Berenise and Lord Gargaron brought in attendants and concubines and all manner of attractive young women, and young men too, but it was just that he didn't want people choosing for him. He didn't trust them."

"You can scarcely blame him for that!"

"Indeed I never did. I admired him for it."

Since this is the oddest conversation I have ever had, and in circumstances that quite defy belief, I keep speaking. "Are you glad he is king, my lady?"

"My dear child, I have learned to live one day at a time. Any day my son is still alive is a day I am glad."

"May I ask you another question, my lady?"

She squints in a way that makes me think her actually nearsighted, a troubling difficulty to have in a world where people you can't trust may get close enough to knife you before you realize who they really are. "Of course."

"Dearest Mother, you don't have to answer."

"Let her ask, Menoë."

"Why doesn't Princess Talessa talk? She can't have been condemned to an ill-wisher's fate because her husband, Prince Nikonos, is still alive."

"It is easy enough to explain," Menoë jumps in. "The priests did indeed take me to the ill-wishers' temple after Prince Stratios's death."

"Because you had no child by him. But if you did kill him, why would they not take you to the Temple of Justice rather than to the ill-wishers' temple?"

"I made sure they couldn't prove I did it. At the ill-wishers' temple I was able to substitute another woman in my place by changing clothes with her. The priests do not know the difference, nor do they care. Women's tongues all look the same to them."

"You let Talon's tongue be cut out to save your own?"

"She begged me to take her from the palace and away from Nikonos—he is an abusive beast just like Stratios—and offered her tongue in place of mine as an inducement. We have hidden her at Garon Stable ever since."

"That's a good story, since she cannot speak to confirm or deny it."

"I believe it to be true," murmurs Lady Adia.

Of course you would, I think, but I'm too prudent to say so aloud.

"It's played perfectly into the brilliant plan Grandmother and I devised," Menoë goes on. "Once Nikonos is dead, Kalliarkos will marry Talessa. Then the East Saroese will feel honor-bound to ally with us and the West Saroese against Saro-Urok."

"Which is why you wanted the West Saroese to see her, but without a formal announcement, so no commitment is made, in case your plans change," I say. "But doesn't Kalliarkos also have a claim to the throne of Saro-Urok through Lady Adia?"

Menoë's prim smile is all the answer I need but she goes on anyway. "With these new alliances, we can easily defeat the current king of Saro-Urok and place Kalliarkos on that throne. Then I can rule Efea without his sanctimonious interference."

"That is indeed a comprehensive strategy," I say. I'm suddenly so nauseated that I clutch my stomach.

"You care for him, don't you?" Kal's mother says with more kindness than I expect. "I can see the news upsets you. Don't you understand, my dear child? You would not last one week as the king's mistress. In truth, I am surprised you are still alive."

The chamber seems to heave and sway around me, an

attack of dizziness. Of grief. Of savage jealousy. Leaving Kal because we disagree about the path our lives must take is a choice I can deal with. But to think of Talon and him...She is beautiful as only Patron women can be, and also really good at the Fives, a true adversary in the way he respects most, the only reason he fell in love with me....

I cannot endure it.

"Why *are* you still alive?" Menoë asks sharply.

"Because my father is smart enough to watch over me," I snap. How badly I want to yell in her face that my father went to see my mother because he still loves *her*. But if Menoë cares for him, she may protect him, and she won't if she knows the truth.

"Esladas is too much the strategist to allow anything to happen to you," she muses in a tone whose ardor I can't like. Her gaze grows puzzled. "But then why are you *here*?"

"Because I challenged Lord Gargaron and beat him."

"Ah. There are many things Uncle Gar can ignore, but not that."

"I am sorry for you," says Lady Adia as if she means it.

I grab for this tiny piece of rope. "Will you help me and my sister and her husband escape, for the sake of the love your son has shown me?"

"No. I will not interfere with Lord Gargaron's plans."

"Is that why you let them throw your son into this ugly game when you know he doesn't want to play it? Because you fear Gargaron?"

She shakes her head pityingly. "You don't fear him enough."

"Come, Mama," Menoë says. "There's no point in wasting your wise advice on her. She's too mulish to listen."

They walk to the door.

In desperate haste I rise, water dripping off me. "Will you tell my father where I am? Will you tell Kal what's become of me?"

Holding aside the curtain, Menoë looks back a final time. "I owe you one kindness for saving my life. So no, I'm not going to tell them. It's better for you that they not know."

17

I leave **Maldine in** a cage pulled by mules. At Lord Gargaron's order, they drape the cage in curtains and sew them shut. After much tugging with fingers and teeth, I rip open a gap along a seam and peer out, desperate to figure out where they are taking me and what's happened to Maraya and Polodos.

The wagon in which I am being transported follows directly behind Lord Gargaron's traveling carriage. In a way it's a relief to still be with him because I've heard he intends to personally deliver his son to the Temple of Lord Judge Inkos atop the table mountain. Surely Maraya and Polodos travel with him. If they don't, it means he has killed them. Yet as much as I frantically pry at the other corner seams, I can't get a look at the rest of the party, only his carriage and the ubiquitous Captain Neartos riding alongside.

Our route takes us around the mountain's base. We pass

abandoned villages, roofs broken and storehouses scorched, and the trampled fields where armies met. Here my father fought a foreign army. I've nothing to do in this cage but fret or think, so I think. The battle took place when Father still served Clan Tonor. Maldine, its harbor, and the surrounding region are all lands that Father's previous sponsor, Lord Ottonor, was responsible for.

It strikes me as suspicious that Garon Palace personally took over administration of Lord Ottonor's former territory. Although Father accepted Lord Gargaron's explanation that Ottonor died of ill health, I can't help but remember Mother saying that she was sure he'd been poisoned.

We hit an incline. As the beasts haul us higher, I get a view of the road below. An army marches inland, its ranks passing as in review and swelled with an unusually high number of Efean grooms and drivers. Lord Thynos rides at its head with General Inarsis beside him. If I can just shout loud enough to draw their attention to me—

Captain Neartos slaps at the bars with the flat of his sword. *"Whsst!* Don't try me, Spider."

I jerk back, but it's too late. He stops the wagon and orders a soldier to tie the seam closed, twice as strong this time.

⟣≈≈≈⟢

By the time we halt, I'm light-headed from the way the heat has built around me like uncombed cotton being stuffed piece by piece into a bag until I'm choking on it.

216

One wall of the cage is lifted away. I crawl to the tailgate, roll off, and brace myself against it as I stand, gulping in fresh air. It's hot but we have stopped in the shade of a wall so that's a mercy. By clinging to the edge of the wagon, I work my way forward. The mules have been unhitched and are being led away.

"Come along, Spider."

Neartos walks me to the stable. Inside the thick-walled building it's blessedly cooler, air circulating through slots set high in the wall. I'm given my own stall at the very end. It's actually a cage set into a stall, but I am grateful for clean straw. Neartos passes a flask of wine and three rounds of stale flatbread through the bars, then leaves. I'm so thirsty I gulp down half the wine before nausea hits. I throw it all up in a corner.

My stomach churns, but I force myself to eat a few bites of the dry bread, softening it with wine. It stays down. Day turns to night. I doze off and on, relieve myself in the corner where I vomited, and as dawn lightens darkness to gloom, I hear voices.

Without a word of greeting, Neartos escorts me outside and across the stable courtyard, back to the carriages. I look around frantically for Maraya but see only a threshold overlooking a wide stone staircase that descends into a bowl-like depression. Neartos's back is turned, so without asking permission, I go over to the top of the steps.

Below, filling the depression, lie the grounds of a temple dedicated to Lord Judge Inkos, an orderly arrangement of gardens, courtyards, barracks, a servants' village, and pavilions for the higher-ranking priests, all set around a central garden with a pond.

From this height I can't help but notice how the substructure resembles the ruins outside Akheres Oasis, where Amaya and I begged Bettany to come home, where Gargaron concealed stolen gold in his uncle's tomb and murdered innocent Efeans to keep the hiding place secret. Where I noticed how similar the ruins were to the arrangement of a Fives court: four outer quarters surrounding a round center.

A storm of comprehension blows through me, spinning my thoughts.

"If the Fives court represents the land of Efea, and the land of Efea is the Mother of All..." The circular nature of the answer is both too easy and too far-fetched. "Then the Fives court represents...the Mother of All."

"Spider! Get back here at once!" Captain Neartos calls to me from the carriages.

"You buried her beneath your dead," I whisper in Efean.

And yet she still lives.

In the servants' village a figure limps out onto a porch. My breath catches. I'm sure it is Maraya, although she's too far away to see her face. I loose the arrow of my heart toward her, willing her to look this way, and she glances up but I'm not sure she sees me.

I murmur a prayer under my breath. Am I filling my heart with false hope?

A crow startles me by landing on top of a lantern post an

arm's length from me. Below, a Patron boy using a cane taps his way up the stairs in the depression. He has a crow on either shoulder, one looking ahead and one behind, and empty sockets for his eyes.

"What is this?" says the boy.

He reaches toward me, misses, and recalibrates, just as I do when I train. This time he pats a hand up my arm.

"You smell like straw." He wrinkles his nose and sniffs. "And wine. And something sour."

"You're learning to see through their eyes," I say.

He grins, but before he can answer Neartos strides up.

"Your Holiness, pray excuse the disturbance. The mule slipped her harness."

"I see no mule, only this Efean girl," says the boy with such innocence that I want to hug him.

Neartos points down into the temple. I look that way just in time to see Lord Gargaron emerge from a pavilion, make his farewells to a black-hatted priest of Inkos, and start up the stairs.

"We must withdraw to our carriage, Your Holiness. It is time to leave."

"Where are you going?" the boy asks, then confides to me, "I've never been outside the temple except up here to the stable. I'll go when I'm older."

"Will you join the spider scouts?" I ask.

"Silence!" says Neartos.

"No, let her speak." The boy leans closer excitedly,

although he makes sure to touch my belly to gauge how close I am. "Do you know about the spiders?"

"My father was a spider scout."

"That's what I dream of doing. To see the land outside these walls."

I'm already in trouble, so I give up on obedience. "Will you learn to take the spark out of one body and place it in another?" I ask.

The crows all shift their gazes to me.

Affronted, the boy says, "You aren't allowed to know about that."

Neartos takes hold of my arm with an iron grip. "You never fail to take the leap, do you, Spider? Thank you for your patience, Your Holiness. We will take our leave now."

Steering me to the door of the traveling carriage, he indicates I must get in. Gargaron climbs in after and settles opposite me, his whip across his thighs.

"Where are my sister and her husband?" I ask.

"Out of your reach."

"Have you killed them?"

"If it weren't for her foot, I would consider taking your sister as a concubine. Her intelligence is astonishing, and she's a lovely girl."

With a false smile scalded onto my lips, I silently count to ten, and then ten more.

He smiles. "Very good, Jessamy. You are learning self-control. Good Goat! She's not a true Patron woman, despite her looks. As

220

it happens, Menos has taken an intense liking to your sister. In the outer precinct of the temple, where boys live for their first two years, they are allowed attendants. Who am I to deny him such comfort when he will afterward live a stringent and severe life in the service of the gods? Anyway, she is a brilliant tutor. I already see great improvement in his grasp of the Precepts."

"She is pregnant."

"Indeed she is, and not the first woman to be so encumbered, nor will she be the last."

"What will happen to the baby?" I demand.

"You must accept that the baby's destiny is out of your hands."

"Do you mean to have it killed?"

"I do not like this tone from you." His hands tighten on the whip.

I swallow my temper like sour wine. "What do you mean to do with me?"

"Why, Jessamy, I told you when I brought you to Garon Stable that first day what would happen if you did not pass muster." He taps the whip against my knee. "Imagine all you might have had and the glory and triumphs you could have won as an Illustrious! You have brought this on yourself."

CRUMO

We travel across the windswept plateau of the table mountain and descend its northern flank into a barren ravine. Cliffs hem us in like fortress walls. Sentinel towers rise from their heights, silhouetted by the sky, as we negotiate a guarded bottleneck. What lies beyond must be extremely valuable if it's guarded so tightly.

Stony hills devoid of vegetation are pitted with cave openings supported by pillars, the entrances to many small mineshafts. Outside the shafts, under the merciless sun, men hammer chunks of stone into smaller pieces. Most of the workers are Efean, dressed in keldis so worn they are little more than rags. Those branded with a criminal's mark on their shoulder come in all kinds, Saroese and foreigners as well as Efeans. Every one wears the gray look of people aware they are dying step-by-step.

Patron guards watch the carriage with the curiosity of people who see the same boringly cruel sights every day. Workers glance up before their overseers crack them back to work.

We pass through a dusty settlement tucked away in a side gully and enter the courtyard of an auspiciously large compound painted with bright murals as if to hide from the grit and misery outside. A man wearing an Inkos priest's garb hurries out with a coterie of fawning servants and unctuous clerks scurrying behind him.

"Your Holiness. I believe you are expecting me."

"Lord Gargaron! I had the message from a crow just a short while ago. Please, refreshments await you." He stares as I climb out of the wagon, but recovers. "This way."

The audience hall has incongruously exquisite couches, silk embroidered with delicate songbirds and windblown petals. Desperately thirsty, I wait as the lords drink.

"I am leaving a valuable object with you, Your Holiness," says Gargaron. "See that she is put to work, but do not allow her to be molested in any way. Let me make myself clear: what the king has claimed belongs to him alone."

"Like the land of Efea," I mutter, although I ought to keep my mouth shut.

"Quite so," he agrees blithely. "Who more than you is like the land of Efea, Spider?"

The thought that I am to be spared from assault makes me feel a rush of heady relief succeeded immediately by a wave of disgust and anger that I will receive a privilege not afforded to others.

Gargaron goes on. "You may beat her if she is recalcitrant. The point is, if she dies, you will have me to answer to, and you don't want that."

The priest sets down his cup as if the wine has turned to venom. "Of course not, my lord. But—"

"That is all you need to know. No matter what message you receive, or what person may arrive here, she will not leave this place unless I come personally to take her. Do you understand?"

He looks at me as he says it.

I always answer a challenge. "You want me alive to keep Kal as your puppet."

He whips me across the face.

The pain slashes so hard tears spill instantly out of my eyes, and then I realize the liquid streaming down my cheek isn't tears; it is blood. The whip has opened a gash on my right brow, a throbbing agony that doubles me over as I struggle not to cry because I will not weep in front of him.

"If you were dead, then our trial would be over and where is the challenge in that? Knowing you seek routes of escape but are trapped because your sister will be killed if you run is part of my victory. But yes, you are also a hostage. I have my own position to protect. So I am holding you in reserve."

I straighten, a hand pressed to the gash, blood leaking through my fingers and clouding my vision. "It's over between him and me. It's better this way. He said so himself."

A clot of grief chokes me, and it's hard to go on but I force the words out.

"He'll marry Princess Talessa and forget all about me."

"Ah, Jessamy. If you believe His Gracious Majesty's affections are so trifling, then you do not know him at all. I've come to see it is his good nature and sincerity that make him dangerous and unpredictable."

The fear I have felt for myself is nothing compared to the sink of terror that opens up beneath me now. "Are you going to kill him once you no longer have a use for him? Like you killed his father and grandfather? Set a child king in his place? He won't go down easily! He's smarter and tougher than you think."

"Good Goat! Do you still believe the poetical fiction that I brought about the deaths of my uncle Menos and his son? I merely took advantage of the openings their improvident deaths gave me. As for the other, do you honestly imagine a child can lead armies or rule a powerful and wealthy kingdom?"

"A general can lead an army in the name of a child. Powerful advisers can rule powerful and wealthy kingdoms on behalf of underage rulers. It's been done before."

"My one regret is that you could not see where your best advantage lies."

"Where is that?"

"Why, with me."

He picks up a covered brass bowl and takes off the lid to contemplate the unmistakable gleam of gold dust and nuggets. The sheer wealth takes my breath away.

"You and I are alike, Jessamy. We unravel the complicated patterns within the spinning Rings before others do. Working together, we could have mapped a path to the victory tower. You would have been celebrated as one of the great Illustrious of the land. But it is not to be. We must all take the long view, as you will discover, for it may be years before I return to fetch you, if I ever do."

⟨▦⟩

When Gargaron leaves in the morning the priest in charge has the guards bring me from the stall where I've been chained up overnight. He examines me as he would a tomb spider found crawling across his bed. Tomb spiders are frightening creatures, big and brown, and it's said their severed shadows haunt the dreams of any person who kills one.

"You look to be a sturdy girl, and better looking than most of your kind. If you behave, I will allow you to live quietly in the house."

"No." I'm not afraid of him. My head is in the game. Challenge accepted.

"No?" My refusal stymies him. He wrings his hands nervously.

Shivering through the night in a pile of musty straw as mules farted in neighboring stalls has cleared my mind wonderfully. Of course Mother was right. Of course Lord Ottonor didn't die of ill health. Garon Palace wanted Maldine Harbor as a staging point for their bid to take the throne. They wanted control of the isolated Inkos temple where boys are taught the arcane and precious secrets of priestly magic. They wanted these gold mines. They wanted my father under their thumb. Gargaron spun paths through these Rings long before I even knew they existed.

"I know my place, Your Holiness," I say, although the priest doesn't look soothed by my hard tone and blunt stare. "I belong in the mines with the rest of the criminals and slaves."

I still love Kal, despite everything. But I choose Ro's words and Ro's path. My place is here, in this trial, because I will find a way to defeat Gargaron and bring my people to the victory tower with me.

18

Despite my demand to work in the mines, the priest assigns me to work in the big kitchen, where all food is stored, cooked, and measured out in strict rations. The head cook is a Saroese man but his toadying Efean assistant is the one who enforces the rules with slaps and whippings.

I begin a slow sabotage as I observe the routine. I grind grain so slowly that I'm whipped. I slop soup so it spills. I burn bread on the griddle even though Mother made sure we girls all know how to cook.

Just before the other kitchen workers are ready to dislike me, I volunteer to take over for the girl who makes the water rounds in the mine. She's grateful because the guards assault her every day. The head cook does not care; working in the kitchen is a coveted job and if the girl complains, he will simply replace her. The priest is concerned only about meeting the temple's quota for gold every month.

"What's your name again?" I ask as I sling full pouches of water across my back. I'm working hard to learn names and stories, as Kal would.

"Djesa." She never once offers a welcoming grin like those I am used to from Efean girls in Saryenia. It's as if she's afraid to smile lest any scrap of happiness be torn up and stomped into bits.

"You're from Ibua, you said. How did you get here?"

"I'm one of six girls. My mother sent me north to live with her sister, who has no daughter. The boat I was traveling in was stopped and everyone on board arrested and marched here."

"For no reason."

"Why do they need a reason? They needed people, so they took us. That was a year ago."

She's too thin, like everyone here, coated with a second skin of dust, and suffering from a persistent cough. Her once-pretty sheath dress has been torn off at the knees and the extra fabric twisted around her shaved head. There are bruises on her arms. With a shy glance, she goes on.

"Is it true what they're saying, that you were the king's lover and he callously cast you out?"

Ro would tell me to give my tale the sharpest turn, but I can't name Kal as the villain. "His wicked uncle kidnapped me."

With a pitying look, she rests a hand on my arm. "The Saroese take what they want. Beware of the guards."

My wry smile surprises her. "What the king claims belongs

to the king, even here. The gods will know of their impiety if they try anything with me. But the truth is much greater than Saroese gods and rulers. I am come here on the wings of the Mother of All. Stone by stone and heart by heart, we will fight them. Be patient. Spread the word. Efea will rise."

☙⟆⟆⟆⟆☙

Days turn to weeks as my life falls into a numbing routine of delivering water to the guards and slaves. Today is no different. When the guards see me coming they smile in a peculiar way I still cannot interpret after over a month at the mines.

"Here is Lady Bountiful, the king's beautiful mistress, come to pour water into the pit of the dying."

"Someday you will be the one begging for water as you lie dying. You will receive what you have earned as the gods measure the lightness of your souls against the heaviness of your misdeeds."

I always expect to be slapped for my insolence, but as usual they instead call me a vile name, then give way to let me enter the mine.

One spits at my feet while the other sneers, "Make way for the grand procession of the King's Mule."

Two women trudge out past me into the staggering heat. Each is bent under a basket full of rock. By the lines on their faces, they might be my age or twenty years older, and that is a question I've never asked.

"Honored Ladies, will you have water?"

One mutters, "Mule." She keeps going.

The other halts. The basket slides down her back, and I catch it, stagger, and barely get it back up on her shoulders. It's heavier than I expected.

I open the seal of one of the pouches slung over my back and she opens her mouth to let me squirt liquid in. With my body hiding the action from the guards, I secretly pass a hunk of flatbread into her hands. She slips it into the band of dirty cloth wrapped around her chest, which together with her ragged keldi are the last remnants of the sheath dress she must have come here in.

"Blessings on you, Honored Lady," she murmurs.

"Efea will rise," I answer, for we speak in the language the guards do not know.

I move on. Another guard supervises the main shaft that cuts into the rock. Workers are hauling on a rope-and-pulley mechanism that brings up a platform with laden baskets. By the shaft a woman named Beswe sits cross-legged on the ground, shoulders bowed, head resting in her hands. I kneel beside her and offer from a different pouch. The supervisors think it is all water from the well but in fact it is a salty chicken broth stolen from the priest's kitchen.

"My thanks." She barely has a voice, and judging by her wheezing breaths I fear she will soon be too weak to work. Those who don't work are given no rations.

I rest beside her until a basket is swung over and given to her to haul outside. The guard gestures me onto the rope platform and whistles to the men to start pulling.

As I descend, the heat abates. Twice, the platform passes a side shaft cutting horizontally into the rock. The first is silent and dark, and it reeks of waste and sweat. People on their break sleep here, where night and day don't matter. A waft of uncomfortably hot air puffs out of the second tunnel. Echoes of hammering float like dissonant music. In the gloom of a single lantern, a man glistening with sweat stands beside a barrow filled with rocks, which he is transferring into baskets to be pulled up.

I toss him a pouch of broth, which he will transfer back to me, empty, on my way up.

He calls in soft Efean, "Stone by stone, Spider."

"Heart by heart, Menesis."

Down I go as drifts of smoky air make my eyes sting. A speck of dust gets in my eye, the one Gargaron whipped, and I forget myself and rub at it. Pain flares and I breathe through the agony like Anise taught me. Finally it fades to its usual throbbing ache.

The earth closes in around me.

A hand tugs on the rope beneath my feet. As the platform settles onto the ground, I step aside so men can load their baskets of rock. Efeans work in these depths but also Saroese men marked with a criminal's brand, most of them common murderers and thieves condemned to end their short and violent lives here. I seek through the crowd for faces that have become familiar to me, and as I pause, one of the criminals crowding around takes advantage of the dimness to grope my thigh.

I shout, "Off me!"

An overseer moves in, slashing his whip to scatter the men. "Move back! Move back! You know the rules. What the king claims belongs to the king."

Another of the branded men waves to get my attention. With his companions, he opens a path for me out of the press.

"My thanks, Selukon," I say as I come up beside him.

"You've promised us vengeance, Jessamy Tonor," Selukon says in a low voice that doesn't carry to the guards.

"We will all have vengeance." I nod at each one as I give them their ration of water.

There are seventeen men here who once, like me, belonged to Clan Tonor. They are all of Saroese ancestry, Patron-born, and they worked in the Tonor warehouses as stevedores and clerks. After I convinced them that we are allies, they told me their shocking tale.

Lord Ottonor didn't die in debt, as Gargaron claimed. Clan Tonor was growing in influence and power because Ottonor sponsored competent men whatever their birth, like my father, and so effectively managed the lands and harbor and mines he'd inherited that he had doubled his clan's wealth in a mere thirty years. But after he died and Gargaron took over, claiming that Ottonor's finances were in ruins, these humble servingmen were branded as criminals and transported here because they knew the truth.

Maybe men like Selukon look down upon Efeans, as many Saroese do, but I have persuaded him and his imprisoned brethren to join us by explaining that if we all work together, we can get out from under this common servitude.

I turn my attention to the children carrying chunks of rock out of the darkness to drop into the waiting baskets. They are as frail and bent as elders, faces filthy with dried snot and hair matted with grime, not even shaved down as is the custom with children. As each one reaches the staging ground in front of the platform, I give them broth. My heart breaks over and over as I call each by name so they will remember they are people deserving of names. Those of us in the kitchen eat twice a day, and I slip pieces of bread from my own morning meal into their grubby hands.

A boy named Anu peers at me through eyes clouded with pus. "Is it day outside? Does the sun shine?"

"It does shine," I say.

"I've forgotten what it looks like, Honored Lady."

"Do not give up hope." I don't mean to sound angry but right now anger is what holds me upright. "You will see the sun again."

I am not yet done. The final task of my thrice-daily rounds awaits me, down in the depths of a long tunnel supported at intervals by massive pillars of uncut rock. Here and there, oil lamps hang, hissing softly, but there aren't enough to chase away the wretchedness. Sound scatters around me, not talk—no one has enough air or energy to talk—but rather the sounds of mallets and chisels, of an echoing roar that halts me in my tracks.

Smoke billows into my face from one of the fires they use to crack the rock face. I cough uncontrollably. When my shudders ease, I move forward to emerge into a long open space tall enough for me to stand upright. To my horror, there's been a rockfall at the far end of the chamber. Men are desperately hammering posts from floor to ceiling to hold up the rock so the whole ceiling won't collapse and bury them all. Other workers gather around a body trapped under the fall.

A slab of rock too heavy to lift has pinned the man's leg. He is still conscious, his whimpering moans amplified by the enclosed space. As the others argue about what to do, I flash to a memory of Lord Agalar. How he devised a way to amputate a leg and sew up the gash so the victim would not bleed to death and might hope to heal with a stump.

There is no doctor at this mine.

Only here in the depths have I come to understand what Bettany saw in Agalar: a man who could save lives, not use them up.

A flake the size of my hand snaps off and thuds onto the floor next to me. My skin goes clammy cold as I sway, suddenly indecisive.

The crack of another piece of rock falling from the ceiling jolts me into action. I feel along the back wall until I find the narrow opening of an abandoned vein. The passage angles like a bent elbow, and it stinks of urine and feces. Waves of nausea sweep through me, and my belly cramps, but I push through. The tunnel dead-ends at an air vent into a neighboring mine abandoned years ago. A taste of fresher air kisses my dry lips.

Under my vest I've hidden a knife and two rock pounders,

crude implements used by the lowest of the slaves to break the big chunks of quartzite rock into smaller pieces suitable for grinding down to release their hidden flakes of gold. I hide these weapons in the vent together with scraps of leather cord knotted together to make longer lines and my prize of the night: a flask of olive oil Djesa has been filling little by little so none is missed.

It's not much. It's never much. But I have made a few trusted allies, like Menesis and Djesa and the falsely arrested Tonor men. Carefully we are hoarding supplies in abandoned shafts. I have the barest outlines of a plan, but the biggest obstacle is that we have only stone and the guards have steel.

It's searing hot as I emerge from the shaft. Panting, I pause to rest, gathering my strength. By the glare of the midday sun I realize I've been underground half the day.

I shade my eyes, searching for discarded rock pounders along the path. The gate to the priest's compound is open as a line of wagons waits to enter. There's been one supply train in and out since I arrived; they come once a month. The priest and his clerk, in company with a visiting priest and clerk sent from the temple, inventory each supply shipment together. By eavesdropping I have figured out that our priest sends exactly the mandated amount of gold each month to the Inkos temple; the excess he splits with the lord of Maldine. Once this was Ottonor. Now it is Gargaron.

An escort of guards lounges in the shade, and I slow down, too exhausted to run the gauntlet of their crude comments.

Then I see a familiar face getting down from the second wagon. At first I think I'm seeing wishful visions but instead I have underestimated my sister.

Polodos wears the uniform of Saroese servants, loose trousers and a calf-length jacket that might be fine for the climate in Old Saro but always seems too cumbersome for Efea's heat. The visiting priest calls him forward but doesn't introduce him; clerks are never important enough to be acknowledged.

The two priests will do their inventory on the portico, in the shade. I hurry to the kitchen and grab the tray being prepared with wine and a platter of food.

"Hey!" shouts the assistant as I head out. "Women aren't allowed to serve the priests!"

He chases me. In another life I would easily outdistance him, but my legs drag like they're burdened with weights. He catches me just as I reach the far end of the portico and clouts me so hard on the head that I stumble and drop the tray. Ceramic shatters. Wine splashes across the brick pavement. Warm bread slaps onto the ground, while precious dates and almonds scatter.

My knees hit the bricks, and I barely catch myself on my right hand. Pain jolts through my wrist. Yet even through the pain I can't stop myself from scooping up the nearest heap of dates and almonds and stuffing them in my mouth. I'm so hungry.

A blow slams into the back of my head again and I pitch forward. My chin strikes the ground, and then a foot smashes into my side. I lie there in a haze of agony.

236

"Stop!" cries our priest.

"Let me assist, Your Holiness," says Polodos.

"No, no, Domon," says the cook's assistant, "that is a task for the kitchen servants, not for an honored official like you. This stubborn creature tried to steal the tray."

I try to croak out a denial but my voice doesn't work.

"Do you feed the workers?" Polodos is standing an arm's length from me. "Good Goat! Her eye is badly inflamed."

"She was whipped by Lord Gargaron," says our priest, hurrying up to see what the commotion is.

"That must have been over a month ago, before he left." Polodos's tone sounds odd and fluttery. I try to focus on his face but it's blurred. "Why hasn't it healed?"

"I will deal with it later," insists our priest. "For now, move her out of the way. This is an unpleasant sight, and she smells. We must complete the inventory."

"Clerk Polodos, return to me at once," commands the visiting priest.

I don't know who grabs me but I'm dragged into the sun and left lying. My wrist really hurts now, and the sun is a punishment, but I'm too tired to move except to roll onto my back, which is a mistake because now the sun glares on my face like fury. I shove with my feet and scoot backward along the courtyard's dirt until I reach the edge of the shade and, with a final burst of energy, roll into its blessed shelter. It's peaceful here with the clerks talking as they record the inventory: goods passed from the temple to the mine and gold dust to

237

be returned to the head priest at the Inkos temple, carefully weighed.

Everything in this world is carefully weighed, stone by stone and heart by heart.

Ro's words bubble up inside me, giving me strength. This will not defeat me. I manage to sit up. By bracing myself against the nearest pillar, I'm able to stand. The guards are eating over on the far side of the courtyard. The grooms are busy watering, feeding, and brushing the mules, which are worth more than the workers because they are harder to replace.

I need to talk to Polodos. Stiff and sore, I hobble to the lavatory courtyard in back, with its limestone benches and sand buckets, hoping he will follow. Footsteps slap on the ground. A hand presses on my shoulder.

"Doma Jessamy? Maraya worked out a clever scheme for me to be assigned to come here, so I could check on you. But you are ill, and so thin."

"I need a way to poison or incapacitate the guards. Maraya will know a plant or mineral. Can she send something?"

He glances back the way we came, making sure we are alone. "What are you talking about?"

"Efea will rise. We must break these chains. But I haven't figured out how to rescue you and Maraya. Is she well, Polodos?"

"Yes, she is well treated because everyone knows Lord Menos is intended to become High Priest in time and no one wishes to offend him."

Hearing this news exhausts me with simple relief because I have had nothing to comfort me in so long. I slide down the wall to the ground as the world reels around me.

"Clerk Polodos?" asks our priest, hurrying into view. "What is going on?"

"I needed to use the lavatory, Your Holiness. This slave has collapsed at my feet. Is there no healer or sickroom here? That wound above her eye needs to be lanced and cleaned. I'm surprised she's not dead of inflammation. Is that your intention, to kill her with neglect?"

For the first time in a month, our priest is forced to take a close look at me. His mouth drops open in exaggerated alarm, and I am sure he is remembering Gargaron's threat. After a flurry of orders flies over my head, I'm carried to the stables, where the straw is a more comfortable bed than the dirt I've been sleeping on for weeks beside the outdoor hearth.

The head cook cleans out the wound and spreads a salve on it as our priest wrings his hands.

"Give her an extra ration of water and food until she recovers her strength."

"Yes, Your Holiness."

They leave. I have to see Polodos before he goes, but I'm too weak to stand, and when I push up with my right hand, a hot pain flashes up my wrist. I cry out, but there's no one to help me.

Only at dusk does Djesa appear with a tray of soup, bread, and juice. It hurts even to close my fingers around a cup.

"What's wrong?" she asks.

"I hope it's not broken. Can you get some cloth? I have to wrap it and keep weight off it. That's what Anise and Tana and Darios would say."

"Who are they?"

"My Fives trainers. I'm so hungry."

"You've been giving away your ration, haven't you? I see you hide it inside your vest. You can't feed everyone from your portion."

"But they're dying. It's so cruel."

"Efea will rise," she says, but she has fresh bruises on her arms because she had to go on water rounds in my place. She doesn't sound as if she believes it.

That night I become delirious and slip in and out, waking in sweats, shivering until I'm exhausted, then sweating again as my thoughts spin and spin. We'll wait until shift's end to pull down all the guards and pound them over and over with rocks until they're dead. We'll wait until a new supply train comes, and raid the kitchen for supplies as we flee across the Stone Desert where nothing lives. We'll die there, and crows will peck out our eyes.

It doesn't matter. Once I regain my strength we will fight. We have to, even if they kill us, even if the desert kills us. We're dying anyway. I won't let Gargaron win.

19

After some days my fever subsides and I resume my duties as water carrier. Even those days were too many for Djesa, although she does not complain. What point is there?

I'm shaky on my feet, persistently light-headed, and my wrist hurts if I put any pressure on it, but I am strangely hopeful. Maraya will come through. I'm so sure of it that I plot out a daring plan of attack, which I share with those I trust most: Djesa in the kitchen, Menesis and his cohort of laborers, Beswe and a few other trusted women, Anu among the boys, and Selukon and the other Tonor men.

"Whether we win or lose, my suffering will soon be over," Selukon confides with philosophical cheerfulness. "I just wish that I could smash a rock into Lord Gargaron's face in payment before I go. We had a decent life in Clan Tonor."

I'm no longer feverish but my brow is puffy, and I can't decide if that means the inflammation is getting better or worse, although the head cook—the closest thing the mine has to a healer—covers it with a salve every evening. I keep moving. Our hidden caches of discarded stone tools grow. I'm no longer worried about supplies for the journey; I've worked out how to deal with that.

If Maraya comes through.

She will because she's the cleverest of us girls. Because she's also one of Father's daughters, the firebird's heirs, who subsist on air and courage.

When the supply train arrives for its next scheduled visit I hang about in the shade, and I'm not surprised to see Polodos. This time I'm smarter. I go straight to the lavatory courtyard and wait in a shadowed corner amid the stink until he appears, alone, looking cautiously around.

"Jessamy?"

It's so sweet to hear my name. "Here."

He pulls a leather pouch from his sleeve. It's small enough I can hide it in my vest. "She said to tell you that under no circumstances should you touch the powder with bare skin or else you too will be poisoned. It acts quickly and will incapacitate most. Many will die. The rest you must kill. Can you kill people, Jessamy? Have you really thought about what this means?"

"If we are merciful and let them live, they'll raise the alarm and come after us and kill us before we can hope to escape. I see no other way."

"So I fear. Add extra spice to cover the taste. Make sure you burn or bury the pouch. Let all the dead look as if they have been killed by violence so no one suspects poison was involved." With a disquieting frown, he touches my forehead, just above my inflamed eye, and slips a tiny sealed pot into my hand. "She says you must use this salve on your eye."

"How is she?"

"Her position in Lord Menos's household protects her. For now we are safe, as you are not."

〇〰〰〇

I wait one day.

One long day.

In the first few days after the supply wagons come, the guards and the servants in the priest's compound eat particularly well. They are served fish from the coast, fruit that doesn't grow here because there is too little water, and imported delicacies.

Timing is everything. Workers are fed a ration of gruel at dusk but the priest, his servants, and the guards enjoy a midday meal as well. Djesa distracts the head cook as a fish soup simmers, and I pour in the powder as well as an extra dollop of spices. If anyone is caught, let it be me.

The midday meal is carried into the compound and barracks by the priest's servants. I want to carry the soup to the mine guards myself but that would break the routine. A pair of kitchen servants lug a full pot and ladle up the road with a basket of freshly cooked bread on their backs. In the back

243

of the kitchen, the cook's assistant complains that his stomach is upset and runs to the latrine. Djesa beckons to me, and we peek into the head cook's private courtyard to see him vomiting onto the stones, hands clenched at his belly.

"You know what to do," I say to her.

To my surprise, she kisses me on the cheek like a sister. Her gaze is fierce and wild. "Efea will rise," she whispers.

It's here. It's now.

I grab my bundle of filled water bottles. This time of day it is too hot to run and twice I have to pause in the shade because the heat makes me dizzy. But the weakness burns away as I climb the last slope, passing Beswe staggering under a heavy load of rocks. I nod at her, and she halts with a look of stunned fear that shifts to grim resolve.

"Back again, Mule Bountiful?" The first guard leers as I walk up. "You look so hungry these days. I'll trade you my ladle of soup for a kiss."

"It's too cursed spicy," says the other guard with a grimace. "I feel sick."

"You gulped it down too fast," replies the other guard, and I realize he's not had any.

This is our only chance. So I do it because I don't know what else to do. I shove one guard into the other and as they stumble, confused by my aggression, I push with all my might. The one who complained of feeling sick falls into the shaft, screaming. But the other guard catches himself, one leg dangling over the rim. I kick at his shoulders, trying to tip him over, but he grabs at me so I have to jump back. I stumble, off balance, and he leaps to his feet, his face red and expression murderous.

The two Efeans who work the pulley gape like comical actors.

"Efea will rise. Efea will rise!" My shouts echo down into the shaft. "Act now, while they're weak from poison!"

The men at the pulley let go of the rope. As the platform plunges, one of them grapples with the guard. But the guard is bigger, stronger, healthier, and shoves him away. As he slides his short sword free of its sheath, Beswe runs up. She lobs two rocks at him at such close range that they both hit. I tackle him and hold on to his legs as Beswe drops a big milling stone on his abdomen. The other man grabs a rock and bashes it into the guard's face over and over until he stops screaming and fighting. Somehow there is blood all over my hands.

A clamor has broken out below.

"Go to the compound and the barracks," I say to Beswe. "Take everyone, every rock, and kill them while they're down."

I climb down the rope safety ladder. The platform has crashed all the way down the shaft. The guard I pushed lies sprawled amid the debris, and two slaves have been crushed beneath the heavy baskets. Children cower as slaves and criminals struggle with the guards. The only reason the guards don't slaughter the laborers is that they are heaving and vomiting even as they fight for their lives. A group of men led by Menesis come running out of the darkness and lay into the guards with the mallets and chisels with which they work the rock.

I can barely hold myself up by clinging to the rope ladder as the last guard is slaughtered with a chisel in the eye. A haze darkens my vision, and I don't know if it is the sight of blood and violence, or my still-inflamed eye, that makes me woozy and disoriented.

Silence spills out from the miners until all I hear is their ragged breathing and the hiss of a burning lamp. There is something grotesque about the way the dead lie there with no spark. Where does a spark go when it departs the flesh, when there is no net to catch it?

Suddenly in my spinning memory I'm sealed in the oracle's tomb with my family, clutching a stillborn infant in my arms. I remember how the coffin jolted sideways, how the corpse of Lord Ottonor rolled out toward me, how his cold fingers touched my ankle. How in a panic I dropped the baby's tiny body onto that of the dead lord. Yet there was still a spark alive in the lord, a life stolen from an innocent girl to help him walk to his own tomb....

"What do we do now, Spider?" Menesis asks.

I have to focus or we won't succeed.

"Sweep the mine. Look for stragglers, for guards in hiding. Leave no one behind. We'll strip the compound of supplies and set out at once. Most important of all, don't anyone drink or touch the soup."

"Whoever goes up that ladder first is going to get a sword in his face," says one of the convicts.

"I'll go up first." I start but I'm trembling too hard and have to come back down.

The pulley has broken. Men set to work fixing it as Menesis moves up the ladder with a guard's whip and a sword slung over his back.

A voice shouts down the shaft. It's Djesa.

"Efea will rise! Can you hear me?"

"Yes! Yes!" my compatriots shout.

"It's safe. They're all dead!"

I shout, "Get wagons, supplies, everything! We have to go right away."

As the others clamber up, I sit in a daze, almost confounded that it worked. And yet we're not safe yet. We still have so far to go, a searing journey across the unforgiving Stone Desert knowing that pursuit will be on our heels all too soon.

The shadows of the dead men flicker at the edges of the lamp-light. What if their shadows swim over the ground and crawl into my body? Will I be strong enough to resist? I want to move away from all this death but I'm so tired. I didn't feel the pain in my wrist when I climbed down but it throbs so badly now that it takes all my energy just to breathe. My eye hurts every time I blink.

"Spider?" Selukon looms out of the darkness, carrying the last lit lamp.

How long have I been sitting here?

He goes on. "The mine is cleared. All the tools and weapons have been taken up."

A creak causes us both to startle, but it's Menesis, descending on the repaired pulley.

"Spider! It's time to go. Are you all right?"

"Yes." One word is all I have breath for.

We are the last ones out, leaving the bodies behind.

The women have done their work. Wagons are hitched, supplies loaded, the weakest clinging to tailgates or crammed together on the front benches beside the drivers. There's only one road out of the ravine, one path to freedom. For some reason they are waiting for me to take the lead, so even though I'm so exhausted I want only to lie down and sleep, I trudge forward.

Behind me, the wagons roll. We are on our way.

The sun is merciless, and I'm grateful when Djesa runs up and dumps an entire bucket of precious water over my head. The people around me laugh, the sound rising into the air as joy and strength. Some begin singing a song I've never heard before; its eerie melody winds a prayerful cadence around my bones.

You are the breath that sparks life in us, the earth that fashions us, the sun whose rays illuminate us, the water that nourishes us. You are the heart.

Hope burns so hard my five souls swell and strengthen. Even in our ragtag ranks we can survive the Stone Desert. We can. We will.

Then I hear a faint rumbling sound. At first I think I'm hallucinating. The sky is cloudless, as always, so it can't be thunder. It rolls on and on. Vibrations tremble through the soles of my feet.

I hold up a hand to halt the line, then walk forward past a sentinel tower, where a guard sprawls dead in the open door, an overturned soup bowl at his side. As I come around a bend in the gully I see a horrible sight ahead of me. So stunning. So unfair after everything we risked and achieved.

Wagons fly the Inkos temple banner. In long lines chained between them stride new prisoners for the mines, mostly Efeans but with a few Saroese and foreign people scattered among them. The Saroese guardsmen haven't spotted me yet. They're not expecting to meet armed and desperate people. If we rush them, take them unawares, free the captives who are with them to fight beside us...and yet that's what's odd. The prisoners don't walk like beaten, cowed people. They walk like proud soldiers.

That's when I see Ro-emnu.

He's seated beside the driver of the first wagon. He's wearing no vest, leaving his torso bare in the manner of Commoners and slaves, but he looks sturdy and well fed, glossy with health and strength. He scans the hills with a piercing gaze, as if he's already composing a poem about this sun-blasted day. At first I can't believe it's him. Surely I am dreaming. My lips form his name but I don't have enough breath to speak. Footsteps hurry up from behind as Menesis, Selukon, and Djesa join me.

"A curse on fortune," says Selukon with a cynical laugh.

"We fight," says Djesa.

"What do you say, Spider?" asks Menesis.

"Wait," I say.

Ro's gaze skims over us. He doesn't recognize me. He must think we're random workers wandering the road.

I take a step forward and with a last burst of strength open my arms wide in Spider's gesture of triumph, throwing her webs to the wind.

His eyes widen. He grabs a whip off the seat next to him, leaps from the moving wagon, and runs to me.

"Jessamy!"

"Who are you?" Menesis steps in front of me, brandishing a sword he's taken from a dead guard.

Ro slashes the whip through the air for emphasis. "This is the Lion Guard of the Efean army, come to liberate this mine."

"Too late, Honored Poet." I can't help but sound cocky even though I'm beyond exhausted and barely able to keep to my feet. "We liberated ourselves."

⟋ɰɰ৩

The Efean woman who is captain of the Lion Guard takes charge. I sink down in the closest patch of shade, grateful for a chance to rest. Ro kneels beside me and offers a flask of glorious water.

"Not all at once. You look very ill, Jessamy. You'd better travel in one of the wagons." He speaks so gently, not like the sarcastic Ro I know, and I hate his gentleness because it makes me feel vulnerable. "That cut by your eye is a fearful scar, and inflamed."

"I have salve for it. . . ." I pat around my vest with my right hand, wince at the lance of pain in my wrist. "It must have gotten lost in the fight. No matter. We're free."

He catches my elbow. "Let me see your arm."

"Are you a healer too?"

"No, just a poet." His frown worries me. "Your wrist is swollen."

"Ouch!"

"Is it broken?"

"It can't be broken! What if it doesn't heal properly and I can't run the Fives?"

"Oh, indeed, what if? I'm relieved to hear you say so. As long as you're thinking about the Fives, I know you aren't dying. Although probably even then..."

A crowd of children led by Anu swarm over to surround us. In daylight they look so skinny and abused that a towering swell of rage roars in my head. But they are smiling and giggling, damp with water they've poured over themselves, fingers gripping dates and figs and other rich food taken from the priest's supply that will probably make them sick.

"Are you a poet? That's what everyone is saying." Anu wriggles with excitement, the others jostling at his back to get a better look.

"I am a poet, sworn to speak truth."

"Why do you carry a whip? Only guards and captains carry whips."

"The whip is the goad and guard of truth. It reminds me that truth is a weapon."

"Does that mean you're a soldier too? Can we join the army? Can we fight?"

A tear runs down Ro's face as he takes in their emaciated bodies and scarred faces, but his charming smile and gracious tone don't change at all. "Yes. Those who wish can join the army. You're too young yet to carry weapons but there are many ways to serve Efea."

"The guards said she was the king's lover," adds Anu. "That's why she was sent here. Did you come for her? Are you her husband?"

For once Ro has no response. He doesn't say anything. He can't even look at me.

Anu frowns, looking scared by the poet's silence. "Are we really free?"

"Yes," I say, irritated by Ro's refusal to comfort them. "We are free, Anu. All of us."

Ro stands. "We are not free to rest. There is a long fight ahead. May I help you up, Honored Lady?"

I consider trying to get to my feet under my own power but I'm quivering with weakness, so I nod. He helps me to a wagon. In the bed, sacks are being emptied of hidden weapons as the pretend slaves arm themselves. After he props me up amid the sacks he fishes a round of bread out of a covered basket. I'm grateful he makes no comment as I struggle not to cram the whole thing into my mouth at once.

After I finish I finally ask my most pressing question.

"How is it you came here? You can't have come looking for me. No one knows I'm missing."

"Ah, well, there's a story." Yet he hesitates.

"What is it?" I demand.

He hands me a tiny strip of rolled papyrus. "I've said many

things about the Saroese, but even I am obliged to admit their calligraphy is superb."

Written in the intricate strokes of the palace trained, Princess Berenise's message to King Kalliarkos crams a great deal of information onto both sides. Menoë and Berenise will sail south with the West Saroese fleet. A regiment of Shipwright mercenaries hired for the duration of the war will march east to the Great River with Lord Thynos and descend on Saryenia from the north. The Royal Army will remain inside besieged Saryenia until these two separate groups of allies arrive. In this way the East Saro and Saro-Urok alliance, under Prince Nikonos, will be threatened on three fronts: from the sea, from the north, and from the city.

At the end of the message, in a corner of the papyrus, two words are scratched in smeared ink by an awkwardly painstaking hand.

SPYDER COT

"The message arrived in Saryenia from Maldine weeks ago with one of the royal messenger pigeons. For the king's eyes only. As you can see, this addition is a bit cryptic."

"Also misspelled."

"True, and while I first wondered if you had somehow managed to send it yourself, such a childish attempt wouldn't be like you, would it, schemer? King Kalliarkos understood the words to refer to you. *Spider caught.*"

"Oh. Of course."

"He sent a messenger upriver to his uncle Lord Thynos, asking him to inquire if you had been seen in Maldine. Thynos told Inarsis, who sent me to investigate."

"I saw Inarsis leaving Maldine in company with Thynos. Inarsis is still with the rebellion, isn't he?"

"He has always been with the rebellion."

I'm not usually this slow-witted. Thinking is as hard as dragging my feet through thigh-deep sludge. "But then...is Lord Thynos secretly part of the Efean rebellion? Of course he must be. And no one in Garon Palace knows it. Not even Kal."

A horn call lifts over us. The Efean captain rides past, spear in hand.

"Poet! We're moving out."

"Yes, Captain!"

"Is captain an Efean rank?" I ask.

He shrugs. "We're accustomed to Saroese military titles. It's an efficient system."

"Poet is a military rank?"

"I can tell you're feeling better because you're mocking me."

"Where are we going?" I ask.

"To take back what is ours."

20

I doze despite the jolting of the wagon. When I wake, the sun has shifted direction, and I'm sliding into the tailgate because we're climbing an incline. There are eight other people in the wagon. Djesa sits crammed in beside me, and she smiles with a brightness I've never seen from her before.

"The poet asked me to keep an eye on you. Is he your secret lover, the one the king sent you to the mines to keep you away from?"

"My secret lover? Did Ro tell you that?"

"He didn't have to. He's very handsome."

"I'm sure he thinks so," I reply in a raspy whisper of a voice. Then I laugh, because it's such a good story, the kind Amaya would adore. "Where are we?"

"We are in the land of Efea, among our own people,

guarded by our own soldiers. Come to take back what belongs to us."

We halt at the gates of the Inkos temple atop the table mountain, the last of the wagons to arrive. Such a frightful clamor rises from beyond the open gates that I climb out of the wagon and make my way to the top of the huge staircase. From the height I look down.

Even with their temple wardens to protect them, the priests never stood a chance. Dead people lie strewn like leaves on walkways and in courtyards, Saroese and Efean alike, marking the course of the battle. By now the surviving priests and servants are surrendering and being herded into a live-stock corral. In the training courtyard boys kneel in rows with heads bowed.

A rush of frightened energy seizes me: Where are Maraya and Polodos?

A group of wardens has been backed up against the entrance of the temple Archives, fighting a losing skirmish against the press of furious soldiers. I descend as fast as I can manage, and even that is a struggle. Fortunately the Archives are close to the main entrance because I'm wheezing as I reach the forecourt. The final rank of wardens give way, slapping hands atop heads to beg for mercy as they accept the day is lost.

I spot Ro charging ahead. Of course a poet goes straight for an Archives. Inside I discover him yanking an armful of scrolls out of reach of a soldier who is trying to set them alight.

"No! Don't burn books or scrolls," Ro shouts. "Don't burn anything!"

The smell of smoke already wafts from distant rooms as Efeans rampage through the building.

"Ro!" I call, and he turns.

"Jessamy! Go back to the wagons. It's not safe—"

"My sister is being held prisoner somewhere in the temple!"

An Efean soldier appears, a young man about the same age as the honored poet. "Hey! Ro! There's a barred door deep in the complex. Should we batter it down? The people inside claim to be innocent scholars."

"How would you know?" Ro asks him. "You don't speak Saroese."

"An honored lady is negotiating in perfect Efean."

"It has to be Maraya," I say.

The soldier leads Ro and me through a series of rooms that ends in a set of iron-reinforced doors. About ten soldiers are pressed up against them, and at first I think they are shoving, trying to open it. But when several gesture at us to keep quiet I realize they are listening with intent interest to a voice muffled by the heavy doors. The voice is declaiming in the manner of a teacher.

"We have always been told the Saroese priests brought magic from old Saro, but listen to this account, which I discovered three days ago. 'This holy metal called "winged silver" occurs in traces near the gold mines of the Stone Desert. It is rumored that this holy metal is strong enough to draw out the very spark of life from a beating heart—'"

"Maraya!" I shriek in a most undisciplined way. "Is Polodos with you?"

Silence answers me. Then, in a voice half broken by repressed tears, she says: "Yes, he's here. He's fine. Jes? Are you safe? What is Amaya's favorite mask?"

"A cat! Open the door."

"I mean no insult by this, Jes, but I need assurance from someone in charge that the scholar in here with us won't be killed. He's an elder and in poor health."

"Surely an old man won't be killed," I say with an accusatory look at Ro. "Where is the captain?"

"What need for a captain when you have a poet beside you?" Ro offers me a mocking bow and a steady look that makes me unaccountably embarrassed. Then he grins, happy to have discomfited me.

"A captain would have settled this already," I snap.

The barb digs deeper than I expected. His smile vanishes and he turns to the door. "Honored Lady, I am the poet Ro-emnu, with your permission speaking out of turn and before you have addressed me. If you shelter the head priest of this temple, I cannot offer any assurances. We have come to take back the holy temple of our Mother. That means tearing down the edifice that was erected atop her body."

"Ro-emnu! Thank goodness it's you!" She switches

to Saroese. "There is a wealth of old Archives kept in this locked chamber, including a complete history of the reign of Serenissima the Third written by the philosopher and poet Sokantes."

"The one that Serenissima the Third executed for writing rude poems about her?" Ro is so excited that he gasps like a child being given a toy.

"Yes, the very one!"

I have never heard of the philosopher and poet Sokantes.

"Also his treatise on metals, which I was just reading an excerpt from. And other material I haven't had a chance to look at. This is a treasure-house of knowledge that we can ill afford to lose to people rampaging about looting and burning."

"What? Like the Saroese did to Efean archives and records when they conquered us?"

Unlike me, Maraya takes no offense at such jabs. "In my opinion no one should ever burn archives or murder old people. Both are repositories of priceless knowledge that can't be replaced if they are carelessly or callously eradicated."

"Can we just get them out?" I demand impatiently. "Where are we going after this?"

"I will take you wherever you wish to go, Honored Lady," Ro says with a lift of the eyebrows that makes me flush and starts all the people around us guffawing because that, evidently, is Efean humor.

Maraya calls, "Do I have your assurance, Honored Poet? For myself, for my husband, Polodos, and for the old scholar?"

"I give my oath as a poet bound to the Mother of All that I will personally intercede for the safety of all three of you."

"My thanks, Honored Poet."

A bar scrapes as it is lifted away. A bolt is drawn. A latch clunks, and the door opens.

The armed people pile in, weapons ready for an ambush, and I shove my way in after them, ready to throw myself in front of Maraya if any dare strike at her. But the musty chamber looks just as Maraya suggested: an isolated storeroom with shelves, cubbyholes, windows set so high into the walls that only an adversary could climb out, and a white-haired man seated in a chair holding a cane across his lap. Maraya stands beside him with a hand on his shoulder. His hands tremble with palsy, his skin has the papery delicacy of extreme old age, and he has the distinctive nose and chin of the Kliatemnos lineage. That he's blind is obvious by his scarred-shut eyes.

"This is Warden Kallos." She ignores me as she meets Ro's gaze in the way of a person sharing a conspiratorially significant moment.

Ro whistles softly, like the name means something to him, then drops to one knee in a show of respect the old man cannot see.

"I am Ro-emnu, Domon," he says in Saroese.

"That is an Efean name," says Warden Kallos in a whispery voice. "Efeans are not allowed into any temple of Lord Judge Inkos by order of the holy priests."

"I mean no disrespect, Domon, but the temple belongs to

us now. What your ancestors took, we are taking back. I have a feeling you have a great many stories you can tell us."

"I lost my eyesight and my youth and all that came with it long ago. I have nothing to share."

"If you will accept our escort, Domon, I have something in my keeping I would like to show you. It may inspire your memory."

With attentive respect, Ro assists the old man in rising and guides him out. Polodos eyes the armed Efeans nervously, but Maraya has no fear. Her tone blends Mother's firmness, Father's bark of command, and her eldest-sister bossiness.

"These boxes must be handled with the greatest care. I will pack the loose scrolls and books into chests. In fact, if you organize yourselves into groups of four, you can help me pack."

I'm suddenly too tired to keep standing so I sit in the chair the old man vacated.

"Jes!" She grabs my shoulders. Her belly nudges me right in the face.

"You look adorable all fatly pregnant," I say, and then start coughing.

"You look awful, scarcely like yourself at all. This wound needs treatment." She brushes fingers over the scar on my brow. When I flinch because it's still tender and oozing, she frowns, then glances up at the Efeans watching us. She snaps, "Be respectful! And get moving!"

I sit in the chair as a whirlwind of activity spins around me, content just to watch her and know that she is safe. She has so much energy. Eventually Ro-emnu returns with drink and food. I'm thirsty but not hungry, but he and Maraya won't stop haranguing me until I eat.

"Was she always this stubborn?" Ro asks her in a joking way that I really dislike but am too feeble to protest.

"She's not the stubborn screamer," says Maraya as she finishes packing the last box and ties it shut with a satisfied nod. "She's more of a sullen schemer."

Ro winks at me in the most annoying fashion.

My chin comes up. "Is that where Ro's sister Coriander got the phrase? From *you*, Maraya?"

She doesn't answer. Now that she's assured I'm alive, her chief concern is the books.

The soldiers carry the boxes out to waiting wagons, where they are stacked beside expensive furniture and gold vessels. The pavilions are burning. The surviving priests and servants are being forced to carry the corpses of the dead Saroese to wagons, where they pile up like cordwood. Boys stand in ranks, stripped down to loincloths. I scan their frightened faces but I'm not sure if Lord Menos is even among them. When I spot the crow boy, looking forlorn and helpless, I can't help but pray his birds haven't been shot dead.

"What will happen to the priests?" I ask Ro as we head back into the heart of the temple. Around us the buildings are being methodically stripped of treasure, and the statues of Lord Judge Inkos dragged off their plinths and sent crashing to the ground.

262

"We negotiated an agreement with the Shipwrights."

"The same group who went with Thynos?"

"That's right. They will be paid a certain portion of all precious items from temples and estates, like gold and ivory. And they will be allowed to sell into slavery all the priests we capture."

"What about the boys?"

"We are commanded to bring all children to the council, where their fates will be determined."

"Where are we going right now?"

"Where do you think we are going? This was once our temple. For a hundred years it has been closed to us, to whom it is holy."

Amid a stream of other people we cross under an arch, into the circular, walled enclosure that lies at the heart of the compound. Djesa in her rags limps forward with an arm supporting Beswe. Menesis carries Anu as other children straggle after them. All the conversations around us cease.

The central area is nothing much to look at: a simple garden with gold chrysanthemums, white jasmine, purple betony, and red anemones set around a circular pond rimmed with stone.

In silence people walk to the edge and kneel. One by one, they dip their cupped right hands in the pool and pour a bit of water over their heads, then step back to make way for others.

Ro drops my hand. I hadn't realized he was holding it.

He paces forward, feet dragging like they are grown

heavy, and falls to both knees. Only then do I realize he is weeping. His lips move but the poet has lost his voice. He scoops up a handful of water and splashes it over his head, then braces himself on both hands as he stares into the mirror of still waters. I step up beside him. For an instant, because of the angle of the sun, I don't see my face at all, and I'm terrified, because if the person I thought I was has vanished, then surely my five souls will dissolve and I will fade with them until I do not exist at all.

But he smiles at the water, and thus his face in the water smiles at me, and there I am, my reflection swimming in the depths, half in shadow and half in light.

21

Three weeks later, after a blisteringly hot crossing of the Stone Desert, we reach the walled town of Furnace Gate and the blessed waters of the Great River. The Lion Guard remained in Maldine to garrison the harbor now that Princess Berenise, Queen Menoë, and the West Saroese have departed. They have also secured the mines, and many of the freed miners stayed to rebuild the Mother's temple. It is a much smaller group that disperses in the streets of this northernmost outpost of Efea. I say good-bye to Djesa, who is reunited with her loving aunt.

Ro, Maraya, Polodos, and I embark on a boat to take us downriver while the captured boys and the Tonor clan men follow on a separate vessel. Standing at the rope railing, under the enviable relief of an awning, I gawk at the powerful current that sweeps us along. The waters are dark and deep and the flow inexorable. I will never think of the obstacle called Rivers in the same way again.

"Why did we never travel upriver out of the delta?" I ask my sister. "Could we never afford it? Did Father not want to go?"

Maraya puts an arm around me. On the journey she has been much more affectionate than usual, fussing over me as if I can't care for myself. "We did travel upriver one time. Father had just gotten his captain's commission and a large amount of prize money. Mother wanted to celebrate the Festival of Masks in the city of Ibua so we took a family trip."

Ro stands on my other side. On the whole journey I have come to feel boxed in between them and their solicitude and their endless boring conversations about history and Archives. At least their discussions soothe my ears when I still feel so raw and confused. My head pretends to follow their lively talk but my heart lies buried and mute.

He adds, "To celebrate the Festival of Masks in Ibua is to stand where the last Protector and Custodian once ruled all Efea. People go there to remember that we once ruled ourselves. But the festival was different before the Saroese came."

"How?" Maraya asks.

"Every elder has a different opinion about that, depending on what part of Efea they come from and which traditions were passed down through their dame council. All records were destroyed by the Saroese priests at the same time as the worship of the Mother of All was banned and Efean priests executed. I personally don't believe there actually was a Festival of Masks in old Efea. All we know for sure is that Efean officials used to wear masks, so I think the Saroese made up the festival as a way to turn mask-wearing from a symbol of authority into a frivolous holiday."

"Why would officials wear masks? Isn't that like hiding their faces?" Maraya never stops probing.

"Officials wear masks to represent the authority they wield, because the office is not the person. Once the two become the same thing, people will come to believe the authority they wield is part of their own body and lineage rather than a borrowed responsibility—"

"Yes, yes, I see!" Maraya interrupts him as she would any family member, an intimacy that annoys me.

Ro nods, as easy with her as she is with him. "What do you think, Jessamy? You're awfully quiet."

I shrug, thinking of the Patrons who have blighted our lives. "Without a mask, the people who hold power may come to believe they have developed a sixth soul that elevates them above others."

"Ah. I wish I'd thought of saying it like that."

"You're welcome to it. I'm not writing any plays or making any speeches."

Instead of saying more, Ro lapses into silence.

I concentrate on my hand, squeezing and relaxing my grip on the rope railing as I strengthen the injured wrist. "It's getting better but what if it never properly heals? What if I can't compete again? What kind of life would that be?"

"People go their whole lives without competing at the

Fives," says Maraya. "Jes, do you really not remember the trip we took to Ibua?"

"No."

"You and Bettany were ten, I was eleven, and Amaya was almost nine. You and Bett started squabbling over who got to sit on Father's shoulders to see the festival barge go past. She pushed you into the water so you grabbed her ankle and dragged her in after you."

"I don't remember that."

Ro snorts. "I can imagine it, though."

I squeeze, hold, and release, wishing Maraya would stop talking, but of course she goes on.

"Father was so angry and embarrassed at the scene you two caused in public that he swatted you both very hard, right in front of all the people crowded on the bank. I started to cry because he had never hit any of us before, and Amaya started screaming because she wasn't getting attention, so he slapped us too. Mother quietly took us girls back to the hostel where we were staying. Once we were in private she told Father that no matter how his father had treated him, if he ever hit his children again she would leave him."

I think of how Father slapped me on Lord Ottonor's balcony, after Kal first talked to me, of how much his anger stung. But it wasn't just anger that drove him that day; it was fear too. He defended us as well as he could against Lord Gargaron's insults. Yet even as a general he couldn't protect me from Gargaron's revenge.

268

Maraya has slipped into her lecturing mode. "As you and Bett got older, *you* started agreeing with everything Father did and said, as if Mother had no part in the success of the household, while Bett began complaining that Mother just gave in to him and did everything the way he wanted. But actually it's just that Mother never argues in the Saroese manner, with a winner and loser. She negotiates and finds ways people can share. Ways we can live with dignity and happiness. Because we were happy then, Jes. Mother and Father were genuinely happy. That's what's so sad about it all."

I'm too choked up to answer her, so I just stare at the mesmerizing swirls and eddies of the current. Isn't this movement, which never ceases and never repeats, the essence of Rivers? Even when you are trying to stand still you are nevertheless in motion. The past clings to us as we hold tight to our regrets and our pain and to the gardens of joy we wish could bloom forever. Yet the current drags us ever forward into the future whose true face we will never see until we take the next step, where every step is a new unmasking.

⌒〰〰〰〰〰〰〰〰9

In the gray twilight just before dawn we sweep around a mighty curve in the river and come into sight of the ancient city of Ibua. Despite what I said to Maraya, I do recognize it from our long-ago visit. Temples to Seon, Inkos, and Hayiyin line the shore, asserting their power. A huge square fronts the riverside, providing a parade ground and gathering place between the temples and a royal palace whose towering fortlike walls are carved with gigantic sea-phoenix figures. Boats are tied up against stone embankments to disgorge merchandise and passengers.

But the royal enclosure and temple compound aren't what strike a resonant memory in my head. It's the conical island splitting the river that makes me stare, because I remember asking Father if we could climb to the top and him telling me it was forbidden by order of the holy priests to set foot there at all.

The island's slope is gentle on all sides, covered with a tangle of overgrown fruit trees and sprawling shrubs. Flowering vines wreath the ruins of a building at the top of the hill. I remember how Bettany and I whispered at night in the hostel when we were meant to be asleep, planning how we would swim to the island when we were grown up and be the first people in all the world to explore its secrets.

I miss her so much, even if she did push me into the river. Even if she did betray me and Amaya at Crags Fort.

But the island is no longer a forbidden landmark, now that Efeans control the city. A pontoon bridge is being built, a walkway floating atop boats and barrels to link the city to the rubble of a stone wharf on the island's bank. On the island itself, people swing machetes and axes to clear an overgrown staircase.

We tie up against an embankment alongside the square. The triple gates into the temple complex stand wide open. Inside, soldiers drill.

"We've turned the Saroese temples into army barracks," says Ro with a laugh.

"How are we supposed to find Mother in this crowded city?" I demand.

Our ship's captain commands crewmen to swing the gangplank over but a person comes running, waving an official's baton.

"You can't disembark until after the sunrise ceremony," shouts the man. "We have new orders, proclaimed last month when the Custodian was named."

"The Custodian?" I ask.

Maraya misunderstands my tone and starts explaining. "Custodian and Protector are the old Efean names for queen and king. They don't mean quite the same thing, but the principle is the same—"

She's cut off when horns blow from the palace. People flood into the square. To the beat of drums, rank upon rank of recruits march out of the temple complex. Some are clearly brand-new to soldiering because they have looks of fierce concentration as they strive to stay in step. Only the sergeants and officers at the heads of columns or the ends of lines wear uniforms, clearly taken from dead or captured soldiers because you can tell where Saroese clan badges have been picked out.

All the soldiers are Efean. I have never seen anything like it, a field of Efean faces lifted with pride and the authority of arms, and although it looks strange it also makes my heart pound with an uncanny thrill.

The wall of the palace overlooking the square includes a wide balcony. The restless crowd quiets as people carrying parasols and huge feathered fans take up stations at each corner, and a file of masked people emerges. It's too far away to make out the details of the masks but I am sure they represent all the animals from the menageries.

The morning sun clears the eastern hills. Its light spills across the balcony just as a man strides out to the railing to stand in that golden glow. He wears an ankle-length keldi and a feathered cape but no vest or jacket. Instead his chest is painted with swirls, like rings splintering apart to become swords and spears. A lion mask conceals his face but I know who it is even as the soldiers standing at attention in the square cheer him with thunderous shouts.

"Inarsis! General Inarsis! Protector Inarsis!"

He lifts a hand palm out, poised and waiting.

We are all waiting for the Custodian of the land, the representative of the Mother of All who shares Her bounty among all Her people. A wind lifts off the flowing waters to brush a ripple through the white awning that shades the palace.

She comes, a woman wearing a simple linen sheath dress, the ordinary clothing of everyday Efean women. She carries in one arm what at first glimpse I think must be a cornucopia until I realize it is a baby tucked in her strong embrace. Her cloud of black hair frames the mask of feathers she wears, shaped in the form of a butterfly.

Ro has the smug look of a man whose secrets have stayed hidden. He knew, and he never gave us even a hint.

Our mother is queen of Efea.

272

22

The royal palace and compound in Ibua is older than the king's and queen's palaces in Saryenia. According to tradition it was built by the order of Serenissima the First in the early days of her reign with her younger brother, Kliatemnos. Its rectangular courtyards and buildings with roofs curved like ships look foreign, not like the palace in Saryenia, which blends Efean and Saroese styles.

Instead of courtiers and servants, refugees crowd the courtyards and audience halls. People stand in lines to receive platters of fried millet porridge. A dame wearing an elephant mask pushed up over her white hair addresses a staggeringly ancient old woman supported on either side by young people.

"Thirty-two from your village? How many children? What craftspeople and artisans? How many recruits for the army? We need laborers as well." At her side, clerks are recording the numbers. "And you, Honored Dame, when you are recovered from the journey, will you speak with our menageries council? We are interested in whatever you recall from your childhood. You are the most precious treasure-house of all."

"That group fled from the southern coast, where the East Saroese army is pillaging and burning," Ro says over his shoulder to me. He walks beside Maraya with a hand tucked under her elbow, making sure everyone sees he is treating a Saroese-looking woman with honor and courtesy.

It isn't that she and Polodos are spit on or shoved, but people look at them as if wondering why Patrons ought to walk here at all. Yet among the refugees I see Saroese faces: a pale child seated amid darker faces plays a clapping game sung in Efean; a young Saroese soldier casually keeps order alongside two Efean comrades; and that rarest thing of all, a pregnant Saroese woman in the company of an Efean man who holds an older child who clearly belongs to them both.

When we pass into the inner courtyard I expect to be shown into the private wing where the nobility luxuriate in wealth and isolation, but this area is also crowded with refugees. Instead we make our way to a vast kitchen bigger than the compound I grew up in. An army of cooks and assistants sweats in the heat of hearth fires and griddles. Vats of porridge simmer. Wagons disgorge baskets of fruit and sacks of grain, each arrival meticulously recorded by yet more harried clerks.

Behind the main kitchen lies an herb garden. Here, at last, we find Mother seated on a reed mat nursing Safarenwe. Cook is setting out a simple, nourishing meal on a low table, helped by faces I recognize: the household women Bettany and I rescued from Akheres. It reminds me painfully of the home we once had, where we all knew who we were and did our work together.

Denya sits off by herself in the shade sewing, while Amaya stands at the far gate with her arms crossed, arguing with someone I can't see.

Her voice has always had the ability to penetrate any space she is in. "Honored Dame, the Custodian will be glad to hear petitions after she has taken a meal and fed her baby. How is it you are come to this gate? Petitions are to be brought first to the outer council so that the Honored Custodian is not overwhelmed by a thousand voices each claiming her time. No, your complaint is not important enough to disturb her!"

Ro gestures with the arm that is not assisting Maraya. "I would love to make an actress of her. Look at that posture! Imagine that beautiful voice uplifted by my magnificent words!"

"A romance devoutly to be wished," I murmur. I can't help but notice how many people are looking him over as we cross the garden, and how he struts to attract their gazes.

Mother sees us. Her expression sharpens from one of drowsy lassitude into a look of almost painful joy and relief.

"My dearest girls! We were told you'd been rescued but now I can truly believe it."

Her smile is the balm I have been craving. Maraya and I swarm forward like eager puppies and settle on either side of her on the mat so as not to jostle the vigorously nursing baby. Only now, resting against her, do I finally feel safe.

"Maraya, you are well?" she says calmly enough although her voice is hoarsened by emotion.

"I am well enough, Mother. But what really matters is that we took possession of much of the temple Archives, including treatises and tracts locked up long ago. There is a great deal for me to investigate." She rests a hand on her belly and smiles at Polodos, who waits anxiously a few steps away.

"You must sit and eat with us, Polodos. Then, if you wish some occupation in our great enterprise, you can see how badly we need clerks to keep order amid this upheaval."

"Yes, Doma. If I am allowed to participate."

"Why would it not be allowed, if you have the desire and the skill? You are my daughter's husband, after all."

"Not by law, Doma."

"Saroese law no longer rules us. Under Efean tradition two people may marry by declaring it is so in the presence of their families. Now, how is your Efean script coming?"

"It is coming well, Doma."

"You must call her 'Honored Lady,'" says Ro, in Efean.

Polodos glances at him, alert to the challenge in the poet's tone, but he's too wise to engage. "My script comes along better than my spoken Efean, Doma," he goes on in Saroese. "Reading and writing are easier for me than conversation."

An Efean boy wearing a spotless keldi hurries up to unroll a second mat beside Mother.

"Monkey!" I cry. "So all of the household *did* get here safely from Akheres."

He hunches his shoulders. "Yes, Doma," he mutters.

"Jessamy, please henceforward address people by their names instead of the insulting nicknames given to them by your father, which to my shame I did not protest vigorously enough. His is Montu-en."

I flinch at Mother's mild tone, and now I want to cry.

She touches my cheek with her free hand. "Let me look at your face, Jessamy. What a stubborn inflammation this is. I was told you were in the mines. How did you receive that injury?"

"A whip."

Her gaze meets mine in quiet fury. "Who whipped you and left you to suffer and starve?"

All my breath has left my lungs. The best I can manage is a shrug.

She nods, because she already knows who it must be.

"Mother." I don't know how to ask. The question seems stupid, but I have to know.

"Say what is in your heart, Jessamy."

"Do you come from some secret royal Efean family, living in hiding all this time?"

Her laughter makes me laugh, although I don't know why. "Not at all, although it is sweet of you to think it might be true. I grew up in a village by a marsh, fishing, weeding, and climbing palms to harvest dates. It was the most boring life imaginable." She smiles to herself, secretive and amused.

"Going to Saryenia was the greatest adventure I could imagine when I was sixteen. That's why I never looked back. Well, that and meeting your father." She grows pensive, then looks up brightly as Cook approaches. "Ah! Here is the food."

Safarenwe squirms, and Mother hands her to me to burp.

"I want something to do, Mother, a job like you gave to Polodos."

"Eat first. Ro-emnu, you may sit beside Jessamy."

"Honored Lady," he says, right hand pressed to his chest. His shining expression betrays how much he admires her.

"Jes? Maraya!" Amaya has finished dispensing with the annoying supplicant and pelts over to crush us with enthusiastic hugs. She coaxes Denya to the mat like her lover is a skittish kitten. We sit in our little family group eating our meal as if the world hasn't turned upside down around us. All we lack is Bettany criticizing anything and everything, and Father reclining at his ease amid the women he loves.

Ro touches my elbow. "Jessamy? Are you all right?"

"A speck of dirt in my eye."

Does Father suspect that Mother leads the people who intend to overthrow all he holds sacred and meaningful?

Where is Kalliarkos now? Is he eating a sumptuous meal in a pit of snakes as Gargaron gloats?

I know I shouldn't be thinking about them, and yet I can't bear to throw them into the current and allow the river to carry them away.

Yet when rebellion is stirring, a peaceful meal can last only so long. Maraya takes charge of setting up a new Archives, using an unused clerks' office as her headquarters. Amaya and I accompany Mother to a pleasure garden inside the palace, now called "the petition garden."

Mother sits patiently as people come forward with requests and disputes and demands. Watching her, I finally understand that Inarsis wasn't courting my mother because he had fallen in love with her. He was courting her fearlessness, her generosity, her intelligence, her tranquil firmness. Her skill at negotiating across a vast divide without losing her self or her temper. It's no wonder people trust her.

After a while I doze on a mat with Safarenwe curled against my chest but wake to alertness when the boys from the Inkos temple are herded in. They are frightened and dirty, and have been cowed out of their childish Patron arrogance by the long journey they undertook on foot. Three crows land on the roof. I ease away from the baby and kneel behind Mother.

"The boy with the cloth tied over his eyes was in training to become a crow priest. Allow Maraya to foster him. He knows a little about the priests' magic."

"An interesting idea. It would please Maraya."

"And be useful to us! And there in the second row? That's Lord Gargaron's son."

"Is he?" She nods in thoughtful consideration, then speaks to the assembly. "Let this be my judgment upon these children, who were given by their parents into the hands of the god Inkos and through this means delivered to us. Disperse these boys among village families. Let them be raised in those homes as sons. I will take one of the boys into my own household." She points to Menos.

"Is this how you mean to revenge yourself on Lord Gargaron?" I whisper.

"To raise his son with respect for those he despises is vengeance enough for me."

⚬〰〰〰⚬

A war council is held after the sun goes down. We enter the old temple complex in silent procession, officials wearing the masks of their offices and the rest of us masked only with hope and apprehension. After the upheavals of recent months Mother can't be comfortable with her daughters out of her sight, but we walk behind her like ordinary attendants, shown no preference. The honored poet escorts her; he's earned that right.

Soldiers stand in disciplined ranks. Only a few wear uniforms but they are an army, make no mistake. When General Inarsis appears they tap fists to chests and shout "Efea will rise!" When Mother in her butterfly mask steps forward, they drop to one knee.

Statues of gods and rulers overlook this forecourt, but now their heads are concealed by cloth. Only Hayiyin, Mistress of the Sea, still shows her face, her granite shoulders newly wreathed in necklaces of fresh flowers.

In the garden where the High Priest of Seon once took his ease, a bent and aged dame wearing a wasp mask calls the council to order. Inarsis and Mother sit side by side on fancy chairs molded for highborn Saroese. Ro recites a poem in which he describes seeing his reflection in the face of the Mother of All. He's beautiful when he declaims, a vessel for the truth. Like me, he's most alive when he's in motion. There's no stillness in him, and maybe that's one of the reasons I get to feeling exhausted when around him.

Administrators report on the readiness of recruits, the availability and manufacture of weapons, and an inventory of supplies. Scouts and hunters give accounts of regions in the north still not under the complete control of the new government, followed by a long and contentious discussion over whether to send soldiers in to defeat the garrisons or to seal off these towns until they can be mopped up later. Different factions argue vociferously about what strategy to take in the south. I'm dismayed by how much disagreement there is, although Inarsis takes it in stride.

Efean refugees from Saryenia describe how the East Saroese army has set up a siege that rings the city on the landward side while their fleet blockades the harbor.

"Has there been starvation?" It is the first time Mother has spoken.

"The royal palace took control of the Grain Market. Strict rationing has been implemented throughout the city. People say the king eats only two meals of porridge every day."

I press a hand to my heart because it suddenly hurts. Of course that is what Kal would do.

"How did you get out?" Inarsis asks.

"General Esladas approached the dames in the Warrens. He wanted to get information to his allies and thought Efeans would have an easier time slipping through the lines. We thought the risk worth it, especially when the dames told us privately that we could serve the cause of Efea by delivering his messages to you, Honored Protector, instead of to his allies. Here they are."

"So the Saroese inside the city still do not know of our uprising, that we control most of the north," Inarsis muses. He accepts a pouch of waxed oilcloth. Inside are sheets of papyrus. "This is a detailed map of the disposition of East Saroese and Saro-Urok forces and fleets around the city. And this..." He frowns at a small note tucked inside the map. "Some kind of cipher."

"Let me see." Mother reads it, brow wrinkling, then glances at me.

"What is it?" I ask nervously.

"A personal request from King Kalliarkos to Lord Thynos, asking him to send word on whether you have been found. It's written in the cipher your father taught me."

"So his uncle Gargaron cannot read it, should he get hold of it," I mutter. "May I see it?"

Smoothing it out over my leg, I stare at the skilled lines of Kal's precise and elegant writing. Then I see what upset Mother: a second message appended below the king's, in which Father personally requests news of members of his family, that he may know they are alive. I should burn it. I should. But when a horn blares an alert and an officer appears to announce the arrival of a messenger from the south, I roll it up and slip it beneath the scarf covering my hair.

A travel-worn individual strides into view with a pair of saddlebags slapping her back.

"Mis!" I leap to my feet, shaken by the sight of a person I feared might be dead.

She nods at me, even flashes me the kiss-off gesture, but she doesn't reply because she is a soldier on duty. When she reaches the front she drops to one knee.

"I bring word from General Thynos. The Garon Palace militia and their West Saroese allies have left their beachhead on the Reed Shore and are marching toward Saryenia. General Thynos says we must move immediately to take advantage of the forthcoming clash between the two Saroese armies."

Her words send the assembly into a buzz as Inarsis calls for a fast strike force to depart in the morning with the main army to follow a day behind.

I volunteer to escort Mis to her billet. "So you're a soldier now," I say as we walk hand in hand like we've never been apart.

"I said I was going to fight for Efea. What happened to you? I heard a song as I was riding into Ibua about how a tomb spider led Efeans out of the underground prison in which they'd been buried."

"Ro," I mutter, but also I'm a little flattered.

"What it really sounds like is that something terrible happened that you barely survived, and I'd believe it. You look awful."

"Thank you!"

She punches me on the shoulder, and we embrace and cry a little.

"What about Dusty?" I ask as we go on.

She sighs. "The most boring story of all. He just wants to be friends because he's infatuated with someone else. Tell me what happened to you."

Speaking lightens me because she doesn't judge or fuss or give advice. She just listens. Yet when our path twists into the narrow, dark passages of the part of the temple dedicated to Lord Judge Inkos, I shudder.

"What's wrong?"

"It reminds me of the mines. And of Eternity Temple."

She puts an arm around me and hurries me along to the servants' compound at the far end of the complex from where we entered. At the stables she checks in with a captain in charge of the courier riders and, upon being released from duty for the night, guides me to a courtyard surrounded by storehouses and workshops. Wagons with broken axles are being fixed, and armor, weapons, and harnesses repaired.

"Hey! Dusty!" She waves at a man standing in the open door of a storehouse. He's wearing a patch over his mutilated eye.

"Glad you're back." He gives Mis a brotherly hug that makes her roll her eyes at me over his shoulder. The greeting he gives me is more muted and less welcoming, as if he isn't sure he can trust me.

"You look better than when I last saw you," I mutter, and when he taps his ear I repeat it in a louder voice.

"You look worse," he answers with a pained gaze.

"I like how everyone points that out."

Mis chuckles. "Because we love you. Over here, Jes. I want to show you something."

I don't see them at first because it's night. Instead odd flashes of what I think is lamplight draw my attention to hulking forms lined up in a row along a shadowed wall.·

It is a full squadron of twelve spiders. Wisps of spark-light chase through the curves of brass bodies.

"Good Goat," I murmur.

"You see why I brought you here."

"They're not set in proper resting configuration." I walk down the row, touching each one to feel the buzz of its spark. "The forelegs are supposed to be raised, so the scout can mount easily into the carapace. And they've not been oiled and polished. Father used to talk about how much time the scouts spent making sure spider joints didn't get clogged with sand. Who is in charge of this squad?"

"It isn't as if we have any sergeants or captains from the Royal Army to train us."

The last spider in line rests in shadow, but when I place my hand on its dented carapace I recognize it at once: years ago my father patrolled in this spider.

"Mis, where were these spiders captured? And how? They

were stationed at Crags Fort." I'm stricken by a memory of Sergeant Oras as he tried to apologize for an insult to my mother that he later regretted. "These are the spiders from my father's old unit. The sergeant in charge there remembered me."

She grips my elbow, watching me carefully. "I'm glad to see you, never think otherwise, Jes, but I have to ask. Are you here only because you escaped the mine and are stuck with us for now?"

"Do you mean do I wish I was back with the Royal Army? With my father?" I don't add, *With Kal?*

"I didn't want to say it so bluntly. But yes, do you?"

I don't take my gaze from hers. "No, I don't. I was intending to leave Saryenia with my mother when Lord Gargaron kidnapped me."

She releases me with an apologetic smile. "I'm sorry but I had to ask. I don't know what happened to these particular spider scouts, but if you think we've taken control of the north by politely asking Saroese garrisons to trot off home, then you don't understand how a rebellion works. Can you truly fight for Efea, Jes? Do you understand what that means?"

Is Oras dead? The thought raises a pang in my heart. But what happened to the scouts who once controlled these spiders is beyond any effort of mine to sway the outcome.

"I do understand, Mis. We did what we had to at the mines. Anyway, a captured spider squad offers an astonishing opportunity."

"To use in battle?"

"That, yes. But there was a crow priest assigned to Crags Fort. Do you know if the scouts' gear has been kept with the spiders?"

"I'm not the one to ask—"

"Here's Dagger!" Dusty says enthusiastically.

A small, muscular woman jogs up to us. She nods at Dusty in the way older siblings nod at pesky young ones they've been assigned to mind. "Good to see you back, Mis," she says with more warmth. "Did you bring me a recruit?"

"I know you!" I say. "I ran against you at the Royal Fives Court."

"So you did! You're Spider, aren't you?" She gestures a kiss-off as a sign of respect.

I flash the gesture back with a grin. "You joined the rebellion?"

"Yes, and for my pains I've been assigned as temporary sergeant of these spiders even though I have no idea what I'm doing."

"You're an excellent sergeant," says Dusty, gazing at her with the same longing look he used to cast at Amaya. Mis elbows me before I can make a sardonic remark about his taste for unobtainable women.

"Is there any chance you have some insight into the spiders?" Dagger asks, ignoring him. "Wasn't your father a spider scout once?"

"He was, and I do, but first I need to know if there is any gear that came with the spiders."

"Yes. It's all been cataloged and stored. I'll show you. You can't believe what a strict accounting system the Honored Custodian has instituted."

"I can believe it."

In the storeroom behind where the spider unit sleeps there are shelves built into the wall with odds and ends stacked beside a papyrus scroll. I push items aside as Dagger talks behind me.

"We've been allowed to use the blankets and cooking utensils and knives and weapons but some of what they carried is just...odd."

There it is, shoved into the back: a worn leather pouch incised with crow feathers and decorated with dangling strings of glass beads, polished stones, and slender bones that I abruptly realize are finger bones.

"We'd have thrown it in the trash," Dagger says hastily, "but the clerks said we have to keep everything together until there's time to sort it out."

I pick it up, and whatever I expect, it feels like ordinary leather, no bolt of lightning or sizzle of arcane power. I don't quite have enough courage to look inside an object not meant for me.

"This belonged to a crow priest. I need to take it to the Archivists."

◌◌◌

Our family garden is dark when I return, only a single lamp burning, everyone asleep except Mother, who hurries over the moment I enter.

"I couldn't rest until you came back. Maraya and I were talking—"

"Is she still awake?"

Maraya is lying on her side on a mat as Polodos kneels behind her. He's rubbing her back as they whisper to each other. Such bold displays of affection are quite un-Saroese, but no one takes note of them among Efeans. When I hand her the leather pouch her eyes widen.

"Is this what I think it is?" she gasps.

"Yes."

"Where did you get this, Jessamy?" Mother asks. "In a time of disorder people can't be allowed to just take what they want, especially not my children. That will lead to precisely the same unfair hoarding and stealing that Saroese law allowed."

"I'm not hiding that I took it. Polodos can record where it's gone."

Maraya breaks in. "Mother, we all know the priests have used magic to help kings and queens hold on to their power. But they can't keep their knowledge hidden from me. I will discover how they transfer sparks from one body to another. I will find out how a blinded child can learn to see through the eyes of crows, which must have something to do with binding the shadow or the self of a crow to a person."

"Perhaps you could do it with any animal," I mutter. "I mean, transfer something of their power to a person."

She flashes an approving smile at me, then turns back to Mother. "So you see, the contents of this bag will be invaluable to my investigation, and possibly more important to Efea's freedom than any of us can predict."

Of course Maraya always gets her way.

"Very well. Polodos, make sure the transfer is noted."

"And another thing," I add. "Maraya has started looking through administrative accounts from the Inkos temple Archives and the records from the mines that relate to Lord Ottonor's management of Maldine. We don't think Ottonor died in debt as Lord Gargaron claimed."

"Yes, I already have a significant list of Clan Tonor's wealth and holdings," says Maraya.

"I'm proud of you girls. What happened to Lord Ottonor was a crime, even if no one believed me at the time." Mother takes my arm. "Now, Jessamy, sit down. I am going to properly wash out that terrible gash."

It doesn't hurt as much as I fear as she probes the scar. I remember how gently and thoroughly she would clean out Father's wounds when they festered. It's strange to think that by healing him she made him ready to go out and risk his life again and again. That every time he went to war he helped our Saroese masters keep their grip upon our lives.

"I'm going to train the spider scouts. They don't have anyone who knows how to properly maintain and use them, and I know the basics."

Perhaps it is my still-inflamed gash that makes her frown. "I won't bother to try to dissuade you because it never worked before. You'll need Inarsis's permission first. But why that task, Jessamy?"

"Do you think this is about Father?"

"It will always be partly about him, for you. Do you understand that?"

"I'm not going back, I promise you. Amaya and Maraya have their skills, and I have mine. To win, we're going to need all the weapons we can get."

23

⟨⟨⟨⟨⟩⟩⟩⟩

I **sleep heavily and** long. When I finally yawn
my way into the garden at midmorning I find it empty
except for Denya. She's sitting in the shade, embroidering
masks and looking as peaceful as I've seen her.

"Jessamy! You surprised me."

"Where is everyone?"

"They went to the petition garden. I should go along, I
know. My mother always said it is best to accept things the way
they are, but I feel so uncomfortable and out of place."

"Do you wish you were back living in your father's household, or married to a Saroese captain?"

Her gaze drops to the fabric she's holding. In neat, delicate
stitches a circle of lotus blooms frames a scene of struggling war-
riors, and when I look more closely I realize they are all women.

"No, I don't," she says softly. "I'm glad I'm here, even if

it seems strange. It's a better life than the one I had. But is it wrong of me to wish Amaya and I could just have a little market stall and sell the crafts we make and live a quiet life?"

"I don't think it's wrong."

A thought occurs to her, and she covers a smile with a hand as if she's amused and doesn't want me to guess. "The poet was here looking for you. He said to meet him at the lion gate at midday if you want to find out what happened to the oracle."

"The oracle! That's what he said?"

She blushes as if I've criticized her, for even a slightly raised voice causes her to cringe. A rush of affection from an undiscovered territory of my heart floods me. I kiss her on the cheek as I would a sister.

"Thank you, Denya. I'm glad you've found a home with us."

⊙๏๏๏๏๏๏๏๏9

By the lion gate that leads into the High Priest's compound within the temple complex, three young men wait beside an empty sedan chair.

"Are you waiting for Ro-emnu?" I ask.

"We're helping him out today." They introduce themselves. "You're Spider, aren't you? He talks about you a lot."

A woman's flirtatious laughter catches my attention. Ro stands at the gate teasing the guard on duty, a young woman with a height and build similar to mine although she is a lot freer with her smiles and in the way she caresses his arm. She sees me and gives him a long, lingering kiss on the mouth.

"He doesn't talk about her as much as he does about you," offers one of the young men helpfully.

If I retort that I don't care how much he talks about her, it will sound as if I do, so I say, "Are we going soon?"

Instead of answering they hammer me with questions. "How did you plan and lead the mine revolt?" "Was the Inkos temple really built on top of a temple dedicated to the Mother of All?" "Are you so good at the Fives because you are the guardian of all that which is buried and thus have been granted the Mother's favor?" "What do you think of Ro's song about you?"

Their enthusiastic curiosity is a bit overwhelming and thus I'm relieved when a soldier wearing a Lion Guard badge appears and beckons to Ro, who waves to us. As I follow the sedan chair under the gate the attractive guard flashes me the kiss-off sign in challenge, and I'm so delighted that I send it right back with more zeal than I intended. But as we walk into a garden once reserved for the holiest of Saroese priests, I realize it's not any competition over Ro that rouses me. Love isn't a victor's ribbon to be snatched away from another adversary. It's the chance that maybe someday I can go back to the Fives that makes me respond this way.

If the Fives survive the war.

General Inarsis awaits us beneath an arbor. The old scholar whom Maraya protected in the temple sits in a sling chair padded with extra pillows, a cup cradled in his hands. The two men have been drinking together.

"Here is the poet Ro-Emnu, who brought you across the

Stone Desert. He will show you to your new home. May you bide there in peace, Domon."

"My thanks, General."

As Ro's friends respectfully help the elder into the sedan chair and cushion him with pillows, I sidle over to the general. Even though he has made himself Protector of all Efea, king by another name, he waits for me to speak first.

"General Inarsis—"

"Honored Protector," corrects Ro.

"Honored Protector and General, you should assign me to the spider scouts."

Inarsis lifts an eyebrow. "Should I? Is all the acclaim going to your head?"

"I'm probably the only person in this city who has actual experience as a spider scout."

"I don't think you're officer material, Spider."

"I don't want to be an officer or even a soldier, just a trainer. At the stable where I first learned the Fives, all adversaries had to train fledglings as a part of their own training, so I have some experience." I close my hand into a fist, feeling the strain even that movement still causes my injured wrist. "I need a job to do while we fight this war."

"*This war* is not going to be over quickly. I daresay it will never be over, not as long as foreigners covet our land and our wealth."

"Which is why you need to incorporate the spiders into the new army. I can train recruits in the basics of operating them."

Ro crosses his arms. "I thought you were going to stay

with your mother. Hasn't she suffered enough wondering what happened to you?"

"Honored Poet, let it go," says General Inarsis in a mild voice. He turns his keen gaze on me. "Why should I trust you, Spider? When we last parted you were determined to set Lord Kalliarkos on the throne."

"Yes, to my regret I was. I see now that I was mistaken."

"Mistaken in your loyalties?" He watches me closely.

"Not in the way you mean. I was mistaken in believing that the change Efea needs can come about through them."

He reflects before answering, while I fidget.

"Very well. Report at dawn tomorrow to your new unit."

"Thank you, Honored Protector. Can I get Missenshe transferred to the spider scouts? I think people with experience as adversaries might be fastest at getting the coordinated movements necessary to operate the spiders effectively. I can train them as we march south."

"You think an untrained spider squadron should march south with the strike force?"

"I do. Spiders aren't just strong and deadly. They're a disguise too. The Saroese won't guess it's us."

"You never stop spinning the Rings in your head, do you?"

"Never."

A subtle smile transforms his harsh expression. "I'm glad to hear it. Honored Poet, you are dismissed to take this elder where he needs to go."

Ro opens his mouth to say something to me, realizes that I

have not in fact spoken directly to him yet, and closes it. Inarsis chuckles.

With a smirk, I say, "Yes, I'm coming with you, Honored Poet."

I walk behind the sedan chair, its curtains drawn, as Ro and his three friends carry it out of the temple, across the square, and through the streets of Ibua. Once away from the Saroese-built district along the river, the city turns into a maze of confusing lanes that double back on each other or dead-end in fragrant gardens. The only familiar structures I see are fountains crowned with the animals of the menageries, just like in the Warrens of Saryenia.

We enter one of the typical outdoor Efean taverns, although at this time of day it's almost empty, with only two napping cats and a child sweeping. Past the kitchen a narrow passageway cuts between high walls and opens into a garden. Here a house built in the Efean style stands in the shade of a massive tamarisk tree.

An old woman sits on a bench, face turned to the sky. It takes me a moment to recognize her as the oracle my family was entombed with. Fresh air and sunshine have brought color to her cheeks. She looks more relaxed although she twists her hands over and over in her lap as if it is a nervous habit picked up during her decades of imprisonment inside Eternity Temple. As our feet crunch up she turns to watch us arrive, and it's clear she recognizes Ro with a mixture of relief and disdain.

"Have you not troubled me enough with your questions? I've told you everything I know five times over. Also, the new cook makes the lentil stew too spicy, and that nice boy who drew up water and sang in such a sweet voice left to join the army. I was not aware you people were allowed to join the army."

They set down the sedan chair. The three friends hurry back the way we came, eager to get a drink at the empty tavern.

Ro walks over to the bench. "We have brought you a gift, Princess Selene. Something you lost long ago."

Princess Selene. I shape the name but can't find a place to fit it in the history I know about the generations of Kliatemnoses, Serenissimas, and all their relations.

Parting the curtains, the old scholar leans forward to take in a breath of the perfumed air. "What garden is this, poet?" the old man asks.

The oracle stares at his aged face for so long that a bird flits down from a tree to peck at the platter of fruit sitting on the bench beside her.

"Kallos?" Her voice trembles on the name, and I remember how, in the tomb, she mistook Kalliarkos for someone she knew. She grasps her cane and rises. The bird flies away in a blur of wings. "Is it truly you, my beloved Kallos?"

"Who is that?" He turns his head to seek her direction by the sound of her voice.

I take his hand and help him out of the sedan chair. He doesn't even ask who I am or why I am assisting him. There's a light in his face that's painful to see, where a feather of hope collides with an ancient wall of grief. She stares, sways, and makes no protest as Ro tucks a strong hand under her arm.

As the old man and I approach, she speaks in a trembling voice. "They told me they'd killed you."

He stops, hearing her words clearly now, and extends a hand. "Selene. Is it truly you? Have the gods answered my prayers even after all this time?"

Ro nods toward the bench, and I seat the old man there. For an instant I think the oracle will collapse from sheer emotion, but Ro eases her down beside the man she lost so long ago. Then the poet takes my hand and draws me down the path after his friends. I glance back to see her touch the old man's scarred face, and yet her expression is not one of horror but of unlooked-for joy, as radiant as the sun rising after its long darkness.

I wipe tears from my cheeks. Ro doesn't let go of my hand and I'm so overcome that I don't even want to shake it off.

"They are the last survivors of the previous family battle over the throne, which took place two generations ago," he says as we keep walking. "How spiteful, to separate two innocent lovers for more than fifty years."

"You wrote about those events in your play, didn't you? But I've never heard their names. I didn't even know they existed."

"The official histories buried the story. Instead we were all taught that after the tragic early deaths of her father and uncle, Serenissima the Third became queen, the benevolent ruler who showered generosity upon all. But that's not what happened. I've heard the whole story now from someone who lived through it. The throne was intended for Serenissima's younger brother, Kallos, but she wanted it for herself. She killed her father and an uncle because they stood in her way. And then she married her other uncle, who took the name Kliatemnos the Third, and made him her puppet."

Much as Gargaron and maybe even Menoë intend Kalliarkos to be a puppet, I think as Ro goes on.

"At first she claimed to be ruling as regent for Kallos, because he was still a child. She had him raised in isolation, far from the court, together with his young cousin, Princess Selene, who was the only child of the murdered uncle. She and Kallos always knew their situation was precarious, that they lived on Serenissima the Third's sufferance. They only had each other to trust, and they fell in love."

"That's so heartbreaking," I murmur.

"Heartbreak is the wine of poets," he murmurs, flashing a look at me from his handsome eyes. "As I contemplate every day you refuse me."

To my annoyance, I blush but I don't look away, because I won't back down. "Then what happened?"

"When Selene gave birth, Serenissima killed the baby and imprisoned them in different temples."

"Why didn't she kill them too? She'd already murdered her father, her uncle, and the baby."

"They don't know. Since I've still found no private records from that time, we may never know."

We have reached the passage that leads out of the hidden garden and its secrets. Ro halts under the shade of a massive sycamore.

"Jessamy. I'm glad you left the palace. The royal air may smell of nectar but it's nothing but poison. We'll drive out the Saroese—"

"All of them? Even Denya and Cook?"

"'Cook'? She has a name. You should use it."

"You're right, I should," I mutter, shamefaced since I can't help but wonder if Father ever knew that Cook's name is Yenia. "But that doesn't change my question."

"Foreigners settled in Efea before the Saroese arrived. Including some Saroese. But they came to become part of Efea, like a guest who decides to marry one of your cousins. So I don't care about the ordinary people who live and work here now. We can make our peace with many of them. But not with the palace and the temples, their rulers and their gods. Never with that."

I think of Queen Serenissima, who let her son, Temnos, be killed and then was herself dragged through a gate into darkness. Of Selene, who lived so many long years trapped inside a crushing prison. Of my father and Kal, each threatened by Gargaron.

"Never with that," I echo.

He rests his hands on my shoulders quite boldly.

"I'm glad you came home to us. This is where you belong."

He smells of orange blossom, like he's rubbed petals onto his skin in anticipation of this delicate moment. His lips part as he leans in, leaving a pause to allow me to speak, to refuse. But I don't speak. I don't refuse. My heart, so long bricked up, has started to crack the seams of its prison. He's here, and he's fine, and he's so brilliantly alive.

"Jessamy," he whispers.

His mouth brushes mine, warm and urgent. I sink into his embrace without shame. There's no one to judge us. Nothing to hold us back.

Nothing except the memory of Kal's face in shadow as he said he could not live with himself if he knew I'd been killed because of him. He broke it off because he thought forcing me to go would keep me safe. And when he discovered he was wrong, he sent people to look for me because he is trapped in a besieged city. I'm the one who didn't want to face the truth about putting him on the throne. He knew better, and I didn't listen.

I take a step back, out from under Ro's hands. "I'm not ready."

By the stunned look on his face, I might as well have slapped him.

"You still believe you're in love with him!"

"Is kissing me really about me? Or is it about who you are, and who Kal is? And which one of you wins?"

"You can't see past your misguided adulation of your Patron father. Much less Lord Kalliarkos, the golden prince."

"You like Kal."

A wry smile softens his face with a rare sweetness. "I do rather like Kal, don't I? He's so hard to dislike. So good-looking. So sure of his place in the world. So pleasant to people, because he can't imagine what it's like to be treated as rubbish. He listens, and he tries to do better, and people praise him for it. It infuriates me. And yet I still like him. How annoying is that?"

His words pry a smile out of me. "I like you better when you're not so sure of yourself."

"How much better do you like me?" His seductive poet's voice shivers through me. "You want to be with me, Jessamy. Admit it."

"I can imagine being with you, yes. Then I remember your one hundred other girlfriends and I think I'm not so enamored of being one hundred and one."

"Ouch."

"Am I the only one who hasn't immediately succumbed to your charm? Is that what this is about? Because you did win the trial between you and Kal. I chose Efea."

"That's not what this is about."

"Then what am I compared to all the other girls you flirt with and kiss?"

He puffs out a breath of air, momentarily stymied, then puts on one of those dazzling smiles that draw people to him as we are all drawn to heat when it is coldest.

"When the threads that bind a heart to the past are severed and the old ways scattered to the four winds, how do you raise a new world, a new land, a new life? You gather the bones and from them weave a new garment: its warp is the words and memories passed down from the last of the elders, and its weft is the courage and determination of those raised in the wilderness. From this fusion a spark kindles to become the light that will guide you home. You can be that light, Jessamy. You're the fiercest self I have ever met, as bold as lightning. How can my poet's heart resist?"

At dusk Mother takes us girls to the island.

"You were out with the honored poet for some time today," says Mother as we cross the square, dressed like any humble family, unremarkable except for the fact that we have escorts on every side and people dropping to one knee as they recognize her.

"That probing question wasn't very subtle, Mother." Amaya elbows me with a violent dig into my ribs that makes me jump. "Did you K-I-S-S him, Jes? Are you going to get married? How many children do you hope to have?"

"Ow! Stop it, you beast!"

"Ha ha. You're so funny when you're flustered."

"I am not flustered! Just getting ready to grind your pretty face into the dirt."

"Could you two stop arguing like children?" Maraya glares with her best eldest-sister superiority. "It's so embarrassing."

"Girls. Hush. We are entering a sacred place."

In respectful silence we walk across the rocking pontoon bridge.

"There is so much we will never be able to recover," Mother says as we climb newly cleared stairs. The lamp she holds is unlit because there is just enough light to see. The entire hill is covered with structures, concealed beneath vegetation that has grown here untouched for five generations. "We'll clear away what we can. And rebuild with what is still here."

At the top she leads us up a final set of stairs to a platform carved with the signs used to identify the obstacles of the Fives court. Lanterns wink along the river, bobbing on boats, shining amid the lanes of Ibua. Stark bluffs mark the edge of the desert lying beyond the floodplain.   ·

Mother gathers us close: me, Maraya, Amaya, and little Safarenwe tucked in a sling against her hip. Our escort has remained at the base of the stairs, allowing us to climb alone, just she and her four girls pretending to be an ordinary family even though nothing will ever be the same for us again.

"Ibua the heart," Mother says. "This is where we begin."

"Ba ba ba," says Safarenwe, clapping her hands.

"Where Efea began?" Amaya asks. "Right here? On this island?"

Maraya says, "I just today read in the Archival material that scholars claim—"

"Maraya!" Amaya and I interrupt her at the same time, in the same voice.

Mother pats us each on the arm, but she is smiling. "This is where *we* begin. We can't remake the past that is lost. But with the threads of that past we can weave the cloth of our future."

"Do you still love him, Mother?" I ask, because I can't help but ask.

"Of course a part of me still loves him. But I can no longer trust him. We tried so hard, yet the well was already poisoned. Isn't that the cruelest thing of all?"

"Like Kal and me." Although I think I've whispered the words so only I can hear, Mother puts a comforting arm around my shoulders.

We stand for a long time as the stars come out and the wind curls around our bodies. The river streams below like years and memories pouring away toward the sea in an unstoppable rush.

"What will happen to Efea if we lose?" Amaya says. "Father is the best general in the world and, as Jes has reminded us more than once, the army he commands is better trained and better armed. The king and queen have all Efea's wealth at their disposal while we have to keep count of each chicken and jar of olive oil to feed thousands of people who have fled their homes. And besides all that, there are foreign invaders here too."

I grasp her hand. "This trial isn't over yet. We have the advantage of knowing how many spinning rings are in place, whereas they don't know we're in the game."

"Do you really think we can win?" She asks not because she's frail and frightened but because she's clear-eyed and brave.

"What matters is that we fight for Efea," says Mother. "That we have taken our stand at long last. Here. Now."

24

The fast-moving Falcon Guard is assigned to be the strike force sent ahead to support General Thynos while the rest of the army lumbers several days behind. The plan is that after the Saroese armies fight, the Efean rebellion must be in position to mop up the weakened winners. It's all a matter of timing.

I convince Inarsis to allow the spiders to lead the way as the Falcon Guard marches out of Ibua on streets lined by a crowd eager to cheer us on. As our heavy brass bodies pound down the great avenue that leads out of the city, people step back in fear, as they always had to do before. The spiders once used to keep the population in order; mere months ago they stomped through the Ribbon Market to arrest Ro and sweep up whatever Commoners the Patrons wished to arrest. But this time when people see our faces they step forward with courage and excitement because now the spiders march for Efea.

The other scouts don't have the hang of smooth walking yet so I am at the front, setting a pace they can follow.

"Spider! Spider!" the people cry. They sing Ro's new song, which is a little too mawkish for my taste, not his best work. *Hasten after the tomb spider! Do not be afraid. You will see the sun again if you follow where she leads.*

Their shining faces and exuberant cheers lift my heart into the heavens, and as we march toward the coming battle I am sure the Mother of All smiles upon Her children.

◖◍◗

By the time we reach the secret forward encampment on a hill west of Saryenia eight days later, I have the eleven spider scout recruits marching like real soldiers. They can move forward and backward and sideways, and they can climb pretty well, although they're still getting used to coordinating the forelegs and back legs as weapons. They'll be fine as long as we don't come up against trained spider scouts or Father's firebird veterans.

Guides sent by Lord Thynos hurry us forward through territory crawling with enemy soldiers. At first I don't understand where we are going because the hill we're aiming for is too steep and rugged even for spiders to climb. Our escorts steer us single file through dense vegetation. It conceals a narrow cleft that cuts through the hill's slope like a canyon. Two of the scouts don't pull their forelegs in tightly enough and get wedged in. The easiest thing for me to do would be to switch places with them and extricate their spiders myself, but instead I laboriously direct them until they have worked themselves free. Finally we move on, into the hill.

The cleft opens into a crater, a huge bowl that takes up most of the interior. Inside, shielded by cliff walls, lies a perfectly lovely village tucked amid a vineyard. But I don't see a single Efean villager, only Shipwright mercenaries and Efean soldiers busy amid the village's boardwalks, storehouses, and central Fives court. There is even a company of Saroese soldiers wearing sea-phoenix tabards who are somehow part of the revolt. Observers stand atop the crater amid a concealing grove of trees.

Because she has the most military experience, Mis was promoted over Dagger to become the sergeant in charge of our spider scouts, and I invite myself along as she leaves the squad and climbs a switchback path up the steep interior cliff. We are accompanied by Captain Mahu of the Falcon Guard, a lean man about my father's age who requires his soldiers to pace through the menageries with us every morning and every night.

"Captain Mahu and Sergeant Missenshe reporting from Ibua," Mis says to a sentry, who waves us forward.

Thynos and his companions watch us approach. The Shipwright officers are a varied crew, women and men of disparate complexions and features like they were plucked out of various countries and thrown together, which, given the tradition of the Shipwrights, I'm sure they were. They all wear their hair in a version of the distinctive triple braids the Shipwrights are famous for. I wonder if Bettany has started braiding her hair in their fashion, if she likes their blunt manners and infamous equality of status.

When he ran the Fives under the name Southwind, Thynos wore his hair clubbed back in the style of old Saro, but it's shaved short now. He has a fresh scar on his neck, and a new tightness to his eyes.

"Sergeant Missenshe, good to see you back. Well done on your promotion. Captain Mahu, what news from Ibua?" In all the months I've known him I've never heard him speak anything but the highborn Saroese of his birth, yet he speaks Efean with creditable fluency.

"The army is on its way," Mahu says.

"I didn't know we'd captured spiders." He looks at me. "Or Spider. So you were a prisoner in the north, just as my nephew feared."

"Yes, my lord."

"No need for such titles here," he says graciously, and with a stab of a smile adds, "You may address me as General."

"General Thynos, I thought you were allied with the West Saroese and thus with Garon Palace. If you do not mind my saying so, I am a trifle confused by your situation."

"By my loyalties, is that what you are asking?"

"Jes," warns Mis.

"Yes, your loyalties."

He nods. I don't take the gesture as a sign of amiability. A lifetime of getting his way means he never has to be acquiescent. "The kingdom of West Saro is suffering from a famine. They desperately need an alliance with Efea for our wheat. They are not particular about which king they seal a pact with, whether Nikonos, Kalliarkos...or Inarsis."

"It is the Efean queen who supervises trade and diplomacy."

"The rulers of old Saro don't see women in that way. At the moment we don't have time to quarrel with them about that."

"Do your Shipwright allies know they aren't fighting for Garon Palace?"

"Of course they know. The new Efean government is paying them, not Garon."

"But Lord Gargaron and Princess Berenise don't know. You're betraying your own kinfolk."

"I like to think of it as choosing new kin, but you're welcome to call it whatever you wish. Have you chosen a side, Spider?"

"I know where I belong. Aren't you worried about what will happen to your sister, Lady Adia? To Kalliarkos and Menoë? Your very own nephew and niece?"

"I'm sorry for it, because I care for them, but their fates were sealed when they were born into a game in which people kill to gain and keep power. Neither you nor I can change the fact of their lineage, and neither can they, no matter how much poor Kal tried to make a different life for himself. Even I can't step out of it, and I have no claim to any throne."

"What about your new bride, Princess Shenia? Isn't she part of the game too?"

"None of your business, Spider. Why are you here on the front lines, anyway?"

"Because you need me to see the openings you're going to miss." I'm so angry about his dismissal of "poor Kal" that I flash him the kiss-off sign.

He answers with a look that could kill from a hundred paces, then gestures the sign back to me, because no adversary can resist. "Take a look at Saryenia under siege, Spider. Let me know what I'm missing."

From up here the world seems mostly water, shining in the afternoon sun. The East Saroese fleet waits out on the sea while a few of its war galleys patrol Mist Lake, drawing a ring around the city. Although I can't see such detail, I'm guessing the city's twin harbors have chains run across them to block enemy ships from sailing in, but those same chains prevent our own ships from sailing out.

Wedged between lake and sea, the fields and orchards of the villages surrounding the city appear to have been infested with locusts: the swarming mass of the allied East Saroese and Saro-Urok armies. They've filled in the canal outside the walls so they can pull catapults up within range of the population inside. A command camp flies both hawk and peacock banners as well as the gold sea-phoenix banner that shows Nikonos is alive and determined to be king even if it means destroying the city he would rule over. He's set up on the west side of the city because there are four gates on this side as opposed to a single gate on the less vulnerable eastern wall.

With the gates shut tight, it's hard to see inside the city, but that's not where the action is right now. The enemy army is on the move. Horses hitched to catapults are dragging them away from the walls as units re-form into a position facing *west*. Haze rims the western horizon, and a restless vibration stirs on the edge of my hearing like the rumble of drums.

"That haze is the dust kicked up by an approaching army," I say.

"Very good, Spider."

"It must be Garon Palace and their West Saroese allies. Do they know you're here?"

"Of course they know. We're sending them reports. They just don't know that I am actually fighting for the Efeans."

"Why isn't the enemy using this hill for reconnaissance?"

"They are. We've set up a decoy post over the crest of the hill, to our left. The soldiers wearing the sea-phoenix tabards are working for us but Nikonos thinks they're loyal to him."

"So you are supplying both Nikonos and Gargaron with information."

"Yes. Some of it is false, and all of it tells them only what we want them to know."

"And neither army suspects?"

"How can they suspect when none of them believe Efeans are capable of rebellion? Much less that a highborn man like me would throw in his lot with a people they look down on?" He cocks his head to one side and, crossing his arms, smiles cuttingly. "So far you haven't told me anything I haven't already anticipated, Spider. You need to do better."

Then he nods at Mahu, person to person, a gesture between equals, and Mahu nods back. "Sergeant Missenshe, you and Trooper Spider may retire to the camp. Nothing will happen until morning."

"And then what will happen?" I ask, because I need to know and also I'm annoyed that Thynos beat me in even this trifling contest.

"A battle."

"What if the East Saroese and Nikonos defeat the Garon alliance?"

"Who wins tomorrow doesn't matter. What matters is that the winner of their conflict be so weakened by the battle that it leaves us as the only healthy adversary on the court."

꧁∞꧂

Before dawn I climb on foot with the other observers to our hidden overlook on the rim of the crater. As the sun rises the armies begin moving ponderously into place. The army of the old Saro alliance under the command of Nikonos is huge, but they are caught between the smaller Garon alliance and the city walls. Therefore they have to keep two front lines intact. A mass of pikemen and archers face Saryenia's walls in case of a sortie from the gates. The other line, the bulk of Nikonos's infantry and cavalry, confronts the approaching Garon and West Saroese forces.

The Shipwrights have tubes that they say aren't magic, but when I hold one up to my eye I exclaim and almost drop it, for my vision leaps a vast distance. Through the tube I see the faces of men so closely I can identify their features, but when I lower the tube they appear as tiny, indistinct figures.

"Is a bird trapped inside, that we can see through its eyes like a crow priest?"

"No. It uses a glass lens to magnify." Thynos has his own tube, which he uses to keep track of the enemy movements.

When I raise it a second time to my eye, the shift in perspective doesn't shock me. I search for and find Prince Nikonos at the center of the East Saroese command company. He wears the gold-and-purple tabard of the king of Efea although he's not yet put on his helmet.

"Let me see," says Mis.

"How much longer must we wait?" I ask Thynos as she peers through it.

"Once the two armies have settled into position on the field they'll blow horns, shout insults, and move units around behind the main lines. That's how every battle in the Oyia campaign started."

"Is that where you met Inarsis?"

He smiles to himself like a man in love and abruptly several pieces of his and Inarsis's story make sense to me. However, he doesn't answer my question. "The Garon alliance is

315

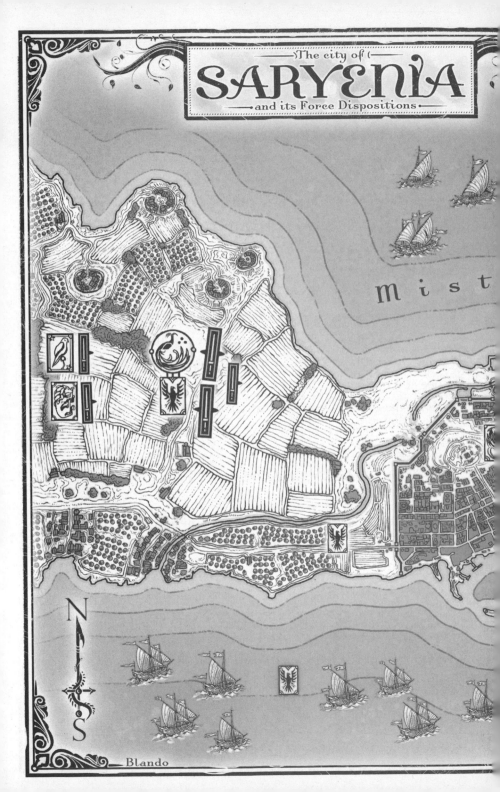

The city of
SARYENIA
and its Force Dispositions

mist

N

S

Blando

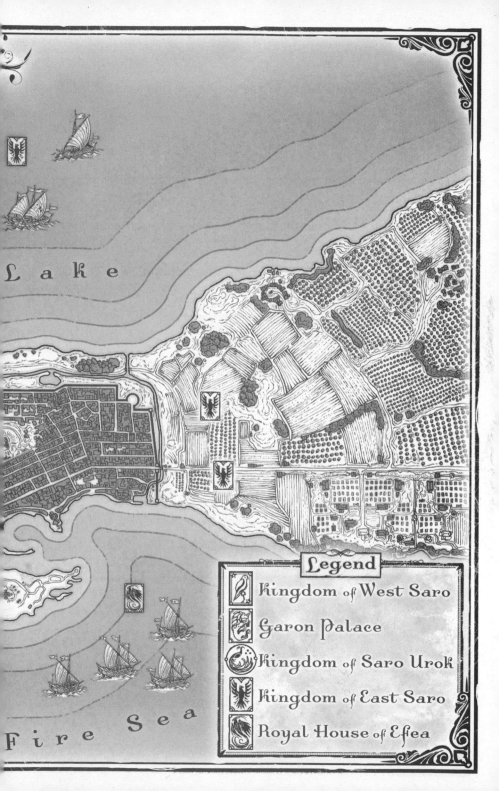

Lake

Fire Sea

Legend

Kingdom of West Saro

Garon Palace

Kingdom of Saro Urok

Kingdom of East Saro

Royal House of Effea

grossly outnumbered. I can't figure out what General Esladas means to do from inside the walls."

"What's that?" Mis points toward the city.

A flight of birds rises from the walls of Saryenia, followed by a second flight and then a third, as if every songbird and pigeon inside the city has been released at the same time.

Horns blare from the Garon alliance. A thunderous crash of drums arises as its army starts lumbering toward the East Saroese line. The East Saroese wave banners and, with cheers, push forward to meet them.

"What are they doing?" Thynos cries. "It's too soon! Without support, Garon will be crushed."

The Shipwright officers surrounding him look alarmed by this reckless act.

"The birds are a signal," I say as I look back toward Saryenia. "My father must be communicating with Lord Gargaron by crow priests and messenger pigeons."

All four western gates swing open without a horn call or a drumroll of warning. Horsemen pour out, but the East Saroese have prepared for an attack from the city by deploying companies of pikemen in the line facing the city. Horses won't charge a solid line of pikes.

Thynos says to his companions, "If the East Saroese rout them, we don't want to get caught in the slaughter afterward. Prepare to retreat."

"Wait," I say. "My father must have a plan."

The cavalry units sweep a wide circle across the fields, not yet closing with the enemy line. They leave space for the second wave to emerge from the city: spider scouts. The heavy spiders stump forward, picking up speed as they cross the empty ground toward the enemy. A first volley of arrows loosed from the East Saroese line bounces harmlessly off their carapaces. There's something exhilarating about watching experienced spider scouts gain speed and cohesion as they turn into a headlong charge and crash into the front line of pikemen.

The sudden carnage of spider blades sweeping through the enemy does not prepare me for what comes next.

The horsemen converge, taking arrow-shot along their flank as they gallop at the East Saroese line at an angle. The force with which the cavalry charge hits shatters the already damaged East Saro line. And they keep going, deep, like a spearhead plunging into a body.

"Good Goat!" Tube held to an eye, Thynos follows the track of the charge. "Does he have a death wish?"

That's when I see a person wearing a feathered lion helmet and a gold-and-purple tabard that's exactly the same as the one Nikonos wears riding in the midst of the cavalry. He's part of a wedge that's cutting into the East Saroese center, protected by a screen of riders on every side. I snatch the tube out of Mis's hands and put it to my own eye.

Of course it is Kal. Who else could it be?

Now I see Father's plan. On the western, outer side of their formation, East Saroese troops face the main Garon army, and the two armies engage amid a clamor of drums and horns and the screaming of men and horses. Meanwhile, from Saryenia, Kal and his cavalry are charging straight for the banners of the command company.

Nikonos is caught with nowhere to run.

But the clash of battle isn't what scares me.

What scares me is that the charge from the city is a suicide run. Spiders are getting swarmed, and horses are getting their legs cut out from under them. Kal's company is taking casualty after casualty and yet even so its momentum is unstoppable as it punches in and starts smashing down banners. The whirlpool of battle spins the two kings to face each other. Nikonos casts a lance at Kal, and Kal ducks aside, then throws a rope. The loop flies over Nikonos's helmet and settles around his shoulders.

Kal reins his horse into a hard turn that drags Nikonos from the saddle.

Around Kal, his officers also turn to create a new wedge, one that will take them back to Saryenia's gates. They cut across the havoc, opening a path.

Kalliarkos drags his rival, who runs at first, trying to twist out of the rope that's now settled around his torso and pinned his arms to his side. Men try to cut Nikonos free but are struck down by the soldiers surrounding Kal. The moment Kal breaks out of the mass of fighting, he urges his horse into a gallop, and of course Nikonos can't keep his feet. The man who murdered his brother and young nephew tumbles over the ground like a sack of rubbish.

It's horrific, and yet my free hand is in a fist and I want to shout aloud in triumph because it's so satisfying.

People crowd the walls of Saryenia. We can hear their cheers even from this distance. Infantry wearing the bright tabards of Father's firebird veterans sorties from the gates, streams of men joining to push a fresh attack.

Thrown into utter confusion by the capture of the man they are here to support, the army of old Saro pulls into a turtle to protect itself.

Kal makes a wide sweeping turn with the limp body bumping behind him and comes to a halt halfway between the walls and the enemy. He raises his sword for all to see: the triumphant model of a Saroese ruler displaying the corpse of his defeated rival.

His surviving companions form up around him, facing the enemy as if daring it to charge. But the bold strike has done its work.

The East Saroese soldiers raise their shields above their heads as a sign of surrender. From within the enemy command company a white flag is raised on a pole.

The battle is over.

Watching Kal embrace the brutal tradition of his forebears is like ripping out a piece of my heart.

Beside me, Thynos stands stunned. "That was the worst possible outcome. We can't fight the Garon alliance now. We have to abandon this position and retreat at once. We must warn the Efean army and get them to turn around so they do not march into this disaster. We can take a defensive position in the far north—"

"No."

They all stare at me.

"No," I repeat.

As I find the anchor that binds my five souls to the land, the whirl of confusion in my mind slows. There are so many Rings turning at different speeds, and I can see them all.

Inarsis's strategy was based on the expectation that the two Saroese factions would do so much damage fighting each other that the victor would be weak afterward, not strong. But Garon has no losses and a complete victory.

Even if the Efeans immediately surrendered and begged the pardon of the new king and queen, the chief officials of the Efean rebellion would be captured and sentenced to death in the mines. Kal and my father wouldn't be able to stop it even if they wanted to. All across Efea there would be a series of executions to set an example and restore order. And everything would go back to being what it was.

But so far the Saroese don't know how widespread the Efean revolt is. Until they figure it out, we have that advantage.

As for Gargaron himself, I now know how to defeat him.

That leaves Kal, heir to two thrones.

I still love him, and I do still trust him, but maybe there is no way out of the pit of vipers where he's fallen; maybe he's already been stung. Maybe there can be only tears and loss, just as everyone has kept telling him and me all along.

Amaya loves tragic stories of heartbreak and doomed lovers. But I don't.

I like to win.

"We need a bold strike of our own," I say to my disbelieving audience.

Thynos slaps me on the head just as he would at Garon Stable. "That's impossible. General Esladas's firebird veterans and the Royal Army will cut us to ribbons on the battlefield. Add the West Saroese troops to his command, and it doesn't matter that we outnumber them both in bodies and in righteousness, because we have too many inexperienced recruits with not enough weapons."

"That's why we can't meet them on the battlefield. Our path to victory is a matter of narrow openings, perfect timing, and a daring piece of risk-taking."

"We're at war, not on a Fives court."

"A Fives court is exactly where we need to confront our adversaries."

He shakes his head impatiently, not understanding and waving a dismissive hand, but I keep going. I can tell the Shipwrights are curious. Maybe their interest is only that of people watching a wagon careening toward a wreck, but I have their attention.

"The Garon alliance hasn't yet realized you are working for the Efean rebellion," I say to Thynos. "Meanwhile no one trusts the East Saroese, not even as prisoners. I can't imagine anyone trusts the West Saroese either, considering they were part of the old Saro alliance just a few months ago."

"True enough. What's your point?"

"Convince the royal council to allow *you* to accompany the East Saroese prisoners to the harbor west of here where the Garon alliance landed. You can argue they must be transferred onto ships to go home there instead of in Saryenia's harbor. Insist that the West Saroese army accompany you to guard the prisoners. The West Saroese will trust you because you're married to a West Saroese princess, and Gargaron believes you fight for the Garon alliance."

"I see. Get both foreign armies away from Saryenia."

"That's right. Get those soldiers out of the way. You and the Shipwrights have to meet up with the Garon alliance now as if that's what you always intended to do. Mis can carry our message to General Inarsis outlining the new plan. We have a brief opening to take control of the city while Lord Gargaron and the monarchs don't yet know how extensive the Efean rebellion is. We need a single, audacious blow that they won't see coming."

"How can that be managed?" he scoffs. "The royal family is in possession of Saryenia and the palaces. They are protected by the Royal Army under the command of the brilliant and ruthless General Esladas."

"Aren't we fortunate, then, that I can negotiate with the general?"

25

With a scarf wrapped around my face to conceal everything except my eyes, I clank my spider past fields and orchards and several deserted Efean villages before I come back into sight of the city walls. To the west, the East Saro army is kneeling, weapons thrown to the ground. They number in so many thousands, so packed together, that the fields they've trampled in their maneuvers lie invisible beneath them. From ground level I can't even see the Garon and West Saro banners that must be flying west of them.

The King's Gate to the city is open, guarded by ranks of soldiers. They cheer as I stamp into view, thinking I am one of the courageous spiders who had a hand in the stunning triumph over Nikonos.

I call out, hoping they will mistake my perfect Saroese and low voice for a Patron man's since they can't see my face and body.

"Where is the army assembling? What happened to the king?"

"The king and queen mean to make a victory procession down the Avenue of Triumphs. Victory to you and yours, brave spider!"

What a pang the praise twists through my heart.

I take the long path around the base of the King's Hill past the Temple of Justice and reach an intersection with the Avenue of Triumphs right where it starts up its steepest incline. From here I can see up the avenue to the golden sea-phoenix gate of the king's palace. Its stone wings unfold as if it is about to take flight across the city, reborn from the foam of the waves.

So many people line the avenue that I fear to push forward, afraid I might crush a child. I can't help but notice that most of the people out celebrating are Saroese, not Efeans. This is a victory for Patrons, not for Commoners.

"Spider! Spider!" The onlookers call my Fives name not knowing it is really mine. They make way to let me through to the street, throwing flowers just as they would at the Fives court. I decide it makes sense to wait here for my father.

Triumphal horns announce the swinging open of the palace gates. Even given how long it took me to cross the countryside to get here, I'm still amazed a royal procession has been assembled in such haste. First march the proud horse guards, the king's personal cavalry. Their splendid gold uniforms hang tattered and bloody. Some are wounded, with an arm in a sling or a leg wrapped in a stained bandage. They have deliberately left gaps in their ranks in tribute to the men who have fallen earlier today. Half their number is missing. It's a grisly toll, and yet they shine.

This is the world my father loved and taught his girls to love. I can't help it: my heart swells as they pass, seeing what he saw in these stalwart soldiers who nobly sacrifice their lives to protect the land they love. Many of the soldiers salute me with their whips.

Next come the royal heralds carrying the white sea-phoenix banners. The fanfare from their curved trumpets announces the royal carriage.

The cheers grow deafening. Flowers pelt the avenue.

King Kalliarkos sits alone in the royal carriage. Like all the processional carriages, it's open, not enclosed, and shaded by a silk awning. He stares straight ahead, still wearing his field armor and gold-and-purple royal tabard and carrying his feathered lion helmet under one arm. He does not wave or smile. His stiff expression might as well be that of a statue despite the clamor of people calling his name over and over. He stares as into a chasm of horror that only he can see, all traces of easy lighthearted grace erased from his features.

The ecstatic cheers quiet abruptly as the carriage rolls on and the crowd sees what's behind it.

In a grotesque imitation of a funeral procession, Nikonos's corpse is tied to the royal carriage and is being dragged down the Avenue of Triumphs to the City of the Dead.

It's so shocking, so impious, but death has always been

the price we pay for our victories. I don't mourn Nikonos. But I am horribly afraid for Kal. What if the nectar of power is starting to taste sweet to him?

Yet I must stick to the path I've chosen through these Rings. If I want to reach the victory tower I have to take the risk that I'm right about him, that he's not completely lost.

As the next carriage rolls into view, this one escorted by firebird veterans, people recover their breath and cheer with renewed enthusiasm. There sits Father, looking as stern as ever, wearing polished leather armor and holding a gold-studded general's whip but in no other way adorned with highborn spoils.

I think of Mother weeping tears of joy to see him honored with a general's rank, on the last day our family was still together.

I think of what it means that Kalliarkos has placed him in the next carriage, ahead of the lords who ought to take precedence.

This is the opening I was hoping for, and I take it.

I swing in behind Father's carriage. Of course he notices the movement. His gaze fixes on the dent that shows mine to be the spider he patrolled in for so many years. He's had weeks stuck inside a besieged city to inventory his army and get news from the desert frontier via messenger pigeon. It's possible he knows this squad went missing.

He taps his whip twice against the side of the carriage. An adjutant runs up, then darts forward to the infantry honor guard. The infantry adjust their marching order from four abreast to eight abreast so they fill up the avenue, making it a tiny bit harder for me to charge through and attack the king, if that is my goal. Father reaches under the bench and pulls out his sheathed short sword, which he sets on the cushion beside him.

The king's carriage halts at the wide intersection where the processional way meets the Avenue of the Soldier. The slope of the land and the height of my spider give me a good view as a pair of closed carriages rolls up the Avenue of the Soldier from one of the western gates. Attendants wearing the gray of palace stewards swarm the forward carriage. When the door opens, a frail Princess Berenise is assisted into the royal carriage, where Kal greets her gravely. After her grandmother is settled, Menoë steps out, needing help to negotiate the steps because of her pregnancy. Her hair is braided into a beribboned fan studded with jeweled flowers. Her exquisite features appear serene as she acknowledges the crowd's cheers by raising a golden fan.

She sees Nikonos.

She walks over and kicks the corpse in the face.

Kal's eyes widen, and he flinches so minutely that most people wouldn't notice. Nor would they notice how he takes in a breath and uses the air to straighten his back and lift his chin to a posture of grim rigidity. Extending a hand, he assists his sister into the rulers' carriage beside him.

I almost miss Lord Gargaron's arrival. I don't see which carriage he came from, but he goes straight to Father with a thin smile that might as well be a dagger. He considers the sword Father has set on the cushion, then takes it upon himself to set it back under the bench out of easy reach. Father does not react as Gargaron seats himself opposite, just as if he too is a victorious general sharing in the day's great triumph.

And of course, he is.

We descend amid the crowd's adulation to the Square of the Moon and the Sun, and we cross it to reach Eternity Temple. The reason for dragging Nikonos's corpse to the City of the Dead escapes me until Kal gives an order to halt the carriage inside the arched tunnel.

He stands and calls out in a tone that sounds reckless, and thus quite unlike him, as if he's thrown prudence and consideration to the winds. "Let the High Priest of Lord Judge Inkos present himself before us. Do not delay."

Menoë tugs on her brother's arm, clearly angry with him. He ignores her and waits.

Gargaron shakes his head impatiently and says to my father, "Good Goat. This is unseemly. Go tell the boy we need to move on."

"He is king, my lord, and can make his own decisions," Father says with a defiance that amazes me.

"Can he? Whose tactics just won that battle for us?"

"Mine, my lord. But it was his choice to lead the charge, rather than have me do it."

"Foolhardy and rash! I knew the rank would be too great a strain on his weak character."

"Quite the contrary, my lord. He strives to be a better man

and a good king. During the siege he insisted on riding out every morning among the populace. He made sure rations were fairly distributed, even refusing to eat more than what any common citizen could expect for a daily meal—"

"Is that what you call a good king?" Gargaron raps his whip on the carriage door. "Enough! Do as I say, General!"

Father glances back at my spider, then climbs down. As he walks forward to the king, Gargaron sits unprotected in front of me.

I could slice his head off with my fore blade. He wouldn't know what hit him.

And I'd be captured and executed on the spot, and not even Father or Kal could save me. My goal is to safeguard the Efean rebellion, not to satisfy my personal anger.

This is why people who leap into the obvious openings in Rings don't succeed.

I have to bide my time.

Father reaches the royal carriage. Because I can see over everyone's head I get a full view of Menoë when she greets him after so many months apart: she smiles effusively, her expression like an open bloom. They look each other in the eye as two people might who have been intimate as equals. Color heightens in her cheek as he nods at her in polite greeting before addressing the king.

What Father says to Kal I cannot hear. What the king answers I cannot hear either, of course, but Father stiffens as if the king has rebuked him.

The gate into the inner temple swings open. The High Priest arrives. Every gaze follows him as he goes straight to Gargaron rather than to the king.

"Your Holiness." Kal raises his voice so everyone must hear and witness, so the High Priest must stop in his tracks and turn. "Twelve times in the last three months, during the siege of Saryenia, we have come here to Eternity Gate to speak to our cousin Serenissima, who we placed in your care. Twelve times we have been refused entrance. Today we will not move from this place until we speak to her. If we must, we will command our honor guard to search the premises."

The High Priest sways, caught on a wave of fear. "Lord Gargaron! Can you not counsel sense into your nephew?"

"Am I not king?" Kal cries, breaking out of his formal speech. "Do I not rule Efea? Menoë, is there some other claimant I'm not aware of?"

When she rests a hand on her pregnant belly, I am shocked even though Princess Berenise once told me that my father's son by Menoë would be the next king of Efea.

Kal lifts his chin. Anger spills from him like poison. "Ah, I see. Well, I have some time before I'm no longer useful to you. So hear me clearly, Your Holiness. Bring Serenissima out or I will enter. Or else confess to me that she is dead, as I suspect she is."

"Your Gracious Majesty..." The High Priest glances around as if seeking an escape route, then remembers that he is the most powerful priest in the land and has the support of Lord Gargaron. With pompous outrage he gathers himself up.

"I don't know what it is you want from me that you dare speak to the gods' most holy representative in this disrespectful way."

Of course Kal is too smart to accuse the High Priest in public of colluding with Gargaron to kill Serenissima. But even I don't expect what comes next.

"I want them all released."

"All of whom released, Your Gracious Majesty?"

"Every girl and woman currently residing in Eternity Temple must be released, now, into the custody of Queen Menoë."

Released. At first I am sure I have misheard him.

Kal has already gone on. "To show these innocent women the proper respect due to their dedication to the gods, the blessed and benevolent queen will take them into the queen's palace as attendants, where they may serve Efea with equal honor."

"I will?" says Menoë.

"Of course you will." Kal's corrosive tone bleeds into the air. "It's a big palace. You can put Mama in charge of seeing they are all peaceably settled. You can give their number a flattering name, the Queen's Most Honored Guard of Maidens or some such."

"You can't do this," says the High Priest in a trembling voice.

Lord Gargaron does not move, only watches, and that worries me, but not more than Kal's caustic tone and reckless demeanor as he plunges on.

"I. Am. King. You wouldn't want to have the highborn

clans hear how for all these years the daughters they dedicated to a chaste and holy life in the temple have in fact been foully mistreated and even killed. Would you?"

An offended silence greets this accusation. Soldiers look at one another in shock. Officials whisper, and a few even hiss to hear the temple profaned with such a charge.

As if pressed past endurance, Princess Berenise finally speaks. "You may congratulate yourself for what you believe is a daring reform, Grandson, although I assure you that Saryenia's populace won't see it the same way you do. But have it your way. Take your uncle Gargaron to make sure that the women have all been released. He won't see anything that will shock him."

"Good Goat," mutters Gargaron to himself, subtle shades of discomfort written through his frown as he hears the threat in the princess's words. Yet he is required to act obediently to the wishes of a woman who outranks him.

Kalliarkos and Gargaron proceed inside with the fearful High Priest and several of the honor guard, including, I note, Captain Helias. My betrayer.

Surrounded by enemies, I have to tread carefully, spider and all.

I shift my right fore blade just enough to draw my father's attention. After a polite interval he withdraws from the royal carriage and returns to stand by the back wheels of his. With hands clasped behind his back, not looking at me, he says, "Identify yourself, Soldier."

"Father," I say.

He raises a hand to forestall further words, then pretends the gesture was merely to scratch his ear. "Abandon this spider elsewhere in the city. Go to our old home and await me. Let no one see you. I'll clear a path."

He waves aside the infantry troop behind me, giving me enough room to clank back out onto the square. I don't dare look back, not until I reach the far edge of the square. Only then do I halt and swivel around to wait, because I have to see if Kal really did it.

After some time a strange procession emerges from Eternity Temple. First comes a group of priest-wardens moving with the faltering walk of people sure they are about to be punished for what they are doing. They are followed by a double line of highborn Saroese girls and women of all ages, on foot, well over one hundred. Drab scarves cover their hair. Most are hiding their faces behind those same scarves, but some of the younger girls stare in delight at the new wonders unveiled this day, because they're not yet resigned to the darkness.

Crowds have a temperament, and I can taste the way the people celebrating in the square swing wildly between joyous gaiety and a hungry anger left over from the weeks of enduring a siege. The anxious women and confused priest-wardens hang like bait before the agitated crowd.

"Shame! Shame!" a man shouts from the crowd. "Who has forced these holy women out of their sanctuary? Ill fortune upon us!"

More voices take up the call. "Go back! Go back inside lest the gods punish us for impiety!"

The crowd presses forward menacingly. The terrified wardens flee, abandoning their charges. But this is my responsibility too, because I set Kal on this path, and I won't show less courage than he has.

I stump over. People scatter from my path. I ignore the frightened looks of the temple women as I place myself at their head and brandish my forelegs to keep the crowd at a distance. To my surprise, a troop of infantry trots out from the tunnel to take up a loose perimeter around the procession in support, as if Kal just realized what a whirlwind he has unleashed. At a deadly slow pace I and the nervous soldiers accompany the procession all the way beneath the hot sun from the City of the Dead to the queen's palace.

It's a long walk for people who have been trapped inside walls their whole lives but I can't bear to leave them to make the journey alone. The first time we stop so they can rest, a small girl sidles forward to take advantage of the cooling shade the spider's shadow casts. Her skin is so pale, as if in all her days the sun has never touched her. And after that, each time we halt they cluster as close as they can, perhaps convinced I am a talisman who will lead them to a brighter place. Some of the braver ones even touch the spider's metal legs.

Only after they have all filed past the gates into the dubious safety of the queen's palace do I leave.

I hide the spider in an overgrown section of the Queen's

Garden. From there it's a quick walk on familiar side streets to the neighborhood where a lowborn man struggling to maintain a captain's position could afford to live in a measure of peace with his most peculiar family. The compound gates are locked, but I know how to sneak in over the roof.

At first I think the compound is abandoned because the front rooms where we lived are empty, but signs of life stir in the kitchen courtyard with its cistern, hearth, and grain storehouse up on stilts. An Efean woman emerges from the interior to stir the embers of the griddle into life.

She's followed out by a second woman, who begins kneading dough for bread. "You'd think he'd have sent warning he was coming. I wanted to go to the walls, see those cursed Saroese surrender and get their throats cut for the misery they've put us through."

"Which Saroese?" asks the woman at the griddle as she coaxes sparks into flames. "The foreigners look no different from our own, do they? Efea will rise."

"Hush, Tenefre. Not when he's in the house."

A third woman appears, yawning, with Wenru in a sling at her hip and a barely toddling child clinging to her hand. She glances toward the closed gates that lead into the private family courtyard. "Usually he comes to see Wenru right away. Should I knock on the gate and offer to bring the baby in to him?"

"No! You know he doesn't like to be disturbed. He'll come when he's ready, Santhay."

The wet nurse sits in a chair, shifts Wenru to her lap, and

kisses the toddler on the head. The child wobbles off in the direction of a gull come to search for crumbs, and the startled bird flutters away over my head. The women don't even look up, but Wenru follows the bird's flight with longing.

"Mmm. I'm so hungry I could eat a crocodile." Santhay taps Wenru on the nose with a generous smile, her voice lilting into a singsong. "Or a fat baby. I could eat a fat baby!"

He blinks, all solemn eyes and resigned boredom.

She sighs. "You are the most unnaturally quiet child."

He ventures, awkwardly, "Baba. Baba."

To laugh would be to give myself away and anyway, as false as his baby talk sounds, I have to admire him for trying. I creep around the roof, leaving them behind.

Father is standing alone in the family courtyard where once everything he cherished most could be found. The space lies empty, inhabited only by birds and lizards. He's wearing the ordinary clothes of a common laborer. The sight sparks old memories, for when I was little this was how he always dressed. He was easier then, more relaxed, before he gained a captain's rank and had to maintain a captain's dignity.

I drop down from the roof. He turns.

"Jessamy!"

He strides across the gap and crushes me to him so tightly I can't speak.

"Father," I wheeze.

He sets me back and frowns with such anger that it isn't until he touches the scar above my eye that I realize it isn't me he's angry at. "Where have you been? Was the king correct? He received a strange message—'spyder cot'—written in the margin of Princess Berenise's letter from Maldine. He was sure it referred to you."

"Yes. Lord Gargaron kidnapped me and sent me to the mines."

"The mines!" He rubs his forehead, then closes the hand into a fist. "And here I have sat, stuck like a bird in a cage while my daughter—"

"I am safe, Father. But you need to know that Captain Helias betrayed me to Gargaron. He betrayed the trust both you and Kal have shown him."

"Helias." He doesn't look surprised. "Highborn men like him resent my success. That explains why I was moved out of the palace to quarters in the Royal Barracks. There's been talk lately among the court officials about how lowborn men should no longer be allowed to become officers, that only high-born men are fit for leadership."

"Isn't that what you left Saro-Urok to escape?"

"In Efea, the poets sang, a man can be anything. Even a poor baker's son like myself. Do you know why our Royal Army has time and again defeated larger enemy forces? Because our soldiers rise if they show promise. To change that is to corrupt the heart of Efea."

"That's what I came here to talk to you about."

I glance toward the gate because I do not want Wenru's attendants to barge in unexpectedly and find me here, but the gate is barred from the inside, as if Father wants peace to consider the life he threw away.

"It's true. Efea *is* in danger, but we have a chance to save ourselves. I need your help. I have to meet the king in secret. Tomorrow."

"Surely by now you comprehend why you have to stay away from the palace. Anyway, there's nowhere His Gracious Majesty can secretly meet you. He can't come to this compound because people know I come here. He is surrounded day and night by officials, servants, and soldiers. And now, of course, by his family. His affianced bride will be arriving soon."

"Talon!" Now I understand.

"What?"

"Princess Talessa must have sent the message in Princess Berenise's missive, although I can't fathom why she would do such a thing. The words were spelled wrong because she only started learning her letters while training at Garon Stable. Did you know they're hiding that she is an ill-wisher? That her tongue was cut out to spare Menoë?"

"Yes, Lady Menoë told me when we discussed … her scars. How do you know about the words being spelled wrong?"

I can't tell him, but I already see the next opening of these Rings. "I assure you, Father, I will never go back to the palace of a Saroese king. Convince Kal to announce a victory game to be held tomorrow. An all-comers Fives trial at the City Fives Court to honor the citizens' courage in outlasting the siege. He can come masked, and we can speak secretly."

"I won't agree to anything until you explain how you escaped the mines. Did the king's agents rescue you, as he hoped?" Again he touches the scar.

"I led a revolt in the mines where Gargaron was keeping me. My comrades and I were then aided by Efeans, and we went on to rescue Maraya and Polodos."

"Maraya? He had Maraya too?"

"Yes. But he doesn't have us now. We have joined the rebellion."

"The poet's words we see written on walls? Of course we've been cut off from our usual sources of news but a few messenger pigeons have flown in from garrisons in the north with reports they are being attacked and overrun by outlaws and criminals. There was even a report that outlying temples have been turned into stables in a most impious manner...."

"That's not true! The temples are being restored to the Mother of All."

He stares. "Have you something to say on this subject, Jessamy? Are you saying these are not isolated incidents but part of a broader action?"

For one breath I hesitate, gathering my courage for the risk I must take if I want my plan to work. Can I trust my father not to give us up? Does he mourn what he lost enough to choose his family over his ambition this time?

"The Efean rebellion has taken over the north."

"And you've come to warn me. What do you know?"

"You're not listening. I am part of the rebellion. So are

Amaya and Maraya. So is Mother. In fact, Mother is one of its leaders. She is its queen."

He takes an agitated turn around the courtyard before returning to stand in front of me. "Kiya? What can you mean by saying this?"

"All of our wars have to do with the Saroese still fighting over their broken empire. If Efea must keep fighting, she should do so for herself, not for others. So here is your choice, Father. You can fight for Efea, or you can fight for the Saroese who conquered Efea one hundred years ago. If the Efean revolt loses, Lord Gargaron will hunt Mother down and he will kill her. This time you can't pretend otherwise. You can't look the other way. Is that what you want? For Efea to be watered by her blood?"

"Did she send you?"

"No."

"Ah." He looks away, regret a shadow that will haunt him for the rest of his life.

"You can make this choice not because there is a reward in it for you, but because you know it is right. Do you hear what I'm saying?"

He stares at me for so long, too incredulous to reply, that I finally reach for his hand. He shakes me off.

"You want me to betray the king and queen and join the rebellion."

"I am asking you to fight for Efea. Not for Efea's conquerors. Fight for your daughters, and for your strange new son.

Fight for the woman you love because you were afraid to fight for her when she needed it most. Don't abandon us this time, Father." I wipe away tears and say the words we never used in our house. "I love you."

"Jessamy..." He is powerfully affected, almost too choked to speak, but before he can go on we are interrupted by a hammering on the closed gate between this courtyard and the kitchen yard.

"General Esladas! Open up at once." The voice belongs to Captain Neartos.

26

I immediately clamber up the trellis and swing onto the roof. When I glance down Father is watching me with a look caught between amazement and pride. Then he waves at me to retreat, to get out. But of course I disobey. As he unbars the gate I roll up against the kitchen trellis so it hides me. In the kitchen yard Santhay has set Wenru in a leather cradle and taken her own child into her arms protectively. Lord Gargaron stands beside the cradle, looking down at Wenru with distaste.

He glances at the three women and says sharply, "Go inside and do not come out until you are called."

They flee, so frightened that none bother to pick up Wenru, poor little mite.

Father walks into view. "My lord, this is an unexpected visit."

"Indeed I am sure it must be, you keeping this compound

as your secret hideaway. Does Her Gracious Majesty know you have taken a new Commoner concubine?"

"I have taken no concubine or lover, my lord. I hired Santhay as a wet nurse for my son." He picks up Wenru, who clutches his vest with little baby fists in a gesture so precious that for an instant I wonder if I have dreamed all my other interactions with him. But the baby stares with such rancor at Gargaron that I could almost cheer, because I think I have finally figured out who Wenru is.

"What a sour, dark little face that baby has. You confound me by acknowledging him so openly!"

Father's next words genuinely shock me for their open provocation of a man he would have obeyed blindly a year ago.

"Doma Kiya gave birth to twins in Lord Ottonor's tomb. You knew she was pregnant and yet you and the High Priest entombed her anyway. That's blasphemy."

"A charge you will never be able to prove. The priests are furious at having their authority flouted by a callow boy who has allowed power and a single victory on the field to go to his head. Much like the daughter you threw at him."

"My lord, I forbade her from talking to him. Alas that my strictures went unheeded."

"I would feel more sympathy for you, General, if Jessamy did not remind me so much of you. Ah, Captain Neartos."

The captain walks up to the other side of the cradle. "I searched every room. The house is empty, my lord."

"Is there something you are looking for, my lord?" I can't

see Father's face, only the perfect military posture of his back and the powerful muscles of his bare arms.

"There is something I am looking for that has escaped me, but it's hard to imagine how it could have crawled so far without help. Never mind. I am here to give you your next assignment, General. We have received an increasing number of messages from the north of criminals and outlaws disrupting garrisons and temples, stealing grain and gold, and making a nuisance of themselves. Now that Nikonos is dead, you will take the Royal Army and restore order in the northern provinces. Kill the rank-and-file rebels but bring the ringleaders here for trial and public execution. Is that clear, General?"

"Yes, my lord."

Crushed behind the trellis, I exhale my hate into the tiles.

"Now, the war council awaits our presence. There's a carriage waiting outside."

With badly concealed reluctance, Father settles Wenru in the cradle, hesitates without looking up on the roof as if to remind me to stay hidden, and at last strides out.

Gargaron and Neartos exchange words in such low voices that I can't hear, a longer conversation than I expect, and one that I'm sure contains vital information if my plan is to work. At length, tapping his whip against his thigh, Gargaron departs. Neartos goes into the kitchen. Soon after the women hurry out into the courtyard. A carriage rumbles away, easy to hear now that I'm listening for it. After a while Santhay goes back into the kitchen and returns outdoors with a lightened expression.

"They're gone, thank the Mother. What were they looking for?"

I scrape out of my hiding place and drop into the courtyard, immediately scooping up Wenru. Kicking, he squawks in outrage. At once the three of them surround me.

"Who are you and what do you think you're doing?" demands Santhay.

"I'm General Esladas's daughter. I want to see my brother, just for a moment, if you don't mind." I can't quite bring myself to cradle Wenru in my arms, so I hold him by the armpits as I hurry into the family courtyard.

"What did they say?" I demand as soon as we are alone.

When he sticks out his lower lip in petty defiance, I pinch his thigh.

He wails, and I pinch him again, so he stops. Santhay appears at the gate and I wave her away with a false smile as I pretend to soothe him.

"There was only one other person in the tomb with us. Lord Ottonor had a living spark placed in his body so he could walk to his final resting place. I'm sure I heard scratching later, like someone desperately trying to claw their way out of the coffin. It terrified me. So maybe that spark hadn't quite faded when the coffin got tipped over and his corpse fell onto my stillborn brother's body."

His stubborn stare challenges me, as if to say I can't get him to talk no matter what I threaten, but I sense a quiver of curiosity.

"Here's what I think happened: The spark and Ottonor's frightened, trapped self leaped into the baby's flesh, but the stolen spark was by then too weak to jolt the dead baby's heart. Later, beneath the City of the Dead, we were flooded by a tide of sparks, and the baby woke, quite to our shock."

His eyelids flare.

"A strong second spark could have fused the baby's heart and shadow with Ottonor's self and the weakened first spark. Thus, Wenru was born. Is your self that of Lord Ottonor?"

He stuffs a chubby fist in his mouth and glares at me.

"I understand why you fear to confide in me. No one cares about the part of you that was once Lord Ottonor. All they see is a mule. But what if I told you I can get you revenge on the man who murdered you?"

After a long, considering pause, he removes his hand from his mouth. The eerie voice that emerges has the soft tone of a baby's, not yet hardened by years and lies.

"Can you truly?"

"With your cooperation, yes. Or things can just go on as before, and you can hope General Esladas isn't murdered by his palace rivals, leaving you an orphan with no protection."

The threat convinces him. "Gargaron told Captain Neartos that in three days the Royal Army will march north to put down the rebellion. He wants them to wait to leave Saryenia until the West and East Saroese armies are well away from the city with Lord Thynos. Then he told the captain to kill Esladas after the rebellion is put down, or at any time if Neartos feels the general's loyalty is wavering, and name himself as the general in command."

"Go on," I say grimly.

"He said Kalliarkos has become incorrigible and unmanageable. That if Queen Menoë doesn't give birth to a boy, there are foreign princes available who can become king consort to an Efean queen."

"Can you get word of this to my father?"

"You want me to speak to him, when he has no idea what I am, and then pray he doesn't kill me because he thinks I'm a monster? Do you think it's been easy, knowing I must hide myself?"

"But I told him about you at the inn." Yet I'm not sure he was really listening because he could think only about Mother. "I don't know how long the war council will go on, although obviously Gargaron has already decided the outcome. But I need Father to get this message immediately. What if he can't come back here tonight?"

"Steward Haredas comes by every evening to check on me."

"Of course! I'll write a note in cipher that you can give him. Do you promise you'll pass on the message? Will you swear on the gods?"

"I swear on the holy names of Seon and Inkos and Hayiyin that I will cooperate with you if you can promise me revenge on Gargaron. And anyway…"

He sighs a baby sigh. His lower lip trembles.

A thread of sympathy vibrates in my heart. "What?"

"I'm afraid to grow up in this body. I have a better chance with Esladas to support me. As he did with you and his other daughters. We all noticed his loyalty, even if most people couldn't approve of it."

The words offer an odd sort of comfort.

"All right, then. It must be hard to have to pretend to be something you're not. Truce?"

He has such a solemn baby face that I want to laugh but manage not to.

"Truce."

⌇

It's midafternoon by the time I make my way past Scorpion Fountain to Anise's stable, where I first learned the Fives. I slip inside to find Anise lounging with her household in the shade of a porch, napping in the heat of the day. I stand by the gate until they see me.

Anise strides over. She's a big woman, but it's her unsmiling expression that intimidates most as she looms over me. "Jessamy."

"Honored Lady."

"Given everything I've heard about you recently, I'd say your presence creates an unacceptable risk to my household. Why are you here?"

"General Thynos told me to come to you if I needed assistance."

"Ah." She indicates that I may accompany her to the

porch. After I have greeted everyone, a child brings me a cup of refreshing sugarcane juice spiced with ginger.

"He said you can get a message to General Inarsis, that you run a network of couriers and messenger pigeons that the rebels have been using for months now. Is that true?"

"Yes."

"I had no idea!"

Anise does not laugh, but everyone else does, and one whistles the tune to "The General's Valiant Daughter."

Anise shushes them and says, "We heard the Efean army has been forced to retreat and that our situation is dire. What information do you have for Inarsis?"

"He needs to be warned that the Royal Army is being sent to pacify the north. I plan to personally deliver a more detailed version of my plan to him but I can't do that until I've spoken to the king. And also... could I please stay here tonight? I have nowhere else to go."

They leave me sitting alone while they discuss the issue in the Efean manner, letting everyone give an opinion before they come to a conclusion. In the end they let me stay because I'm part of the rebellion, but I can tell they're skeptical that speaking to the king will solve anything.

That night, after Anise unfolds a cot for me on the porch, I gesture toward the court's pillars and posts.

"How did the Fives court come to be? Is the game Efean or Saroese?"

"How can we know, who weren't alive in those days?" Her face gleams in lamplight as she contemplates all we have lost.

"I have seen so many astonishing things in the last few months." I tell her about the buried complex underneath the tombs in the City of the Dead. I tell her about the ruins in Akheres and the architecture of the Inkos temple in Maldine. I tell her about the island at the heart of Ibua with the Fives symbols carved into the stone of its top platform, and how the victory tower in some villages is actually a well. "I don't think it belongs to one or the other. What if, after the Saroese conquered Efea, they and their priests buried the Mother of All by turning Her worship into a game? What if we Efeans embraced and influenced the Fives because it is built on Her bones and heart, and it was a way to remember Her?"

"That would make the Fives a little like you, Jessamy. Both your father's blood and your mother's five souls have made you what you are."

⟨∭⟩

The next day I join a stream of adversaries crowding down the stairs to the attiring hall of the City Fives Court. I'm wearing ordinary Fives gear, pretending to be a fledgling. My face is concealed behind a butterfly mask that I decorated myself although Amaya would be appalled at its slapdash design. The bell rings as I'm descending. Above, the doors shut.

I'm so nervous I'm bouncing on my toes. What if he doesn't

352

come? What if he's changed? What if he's already courting brave, beautiful Talon and doesn't care that I'm here?

"First trial!" cries a ready cage custodian.

That's when I spot him. He's wearing Fives gear scuffed at the knees and elbows from steady practice, and an undyed linen mask.

As I approach he turns and sees me. It's like a bolt goes through him.

He grabs my hand, lifts my palm to his lips, and kisses it, his mouth a fire against my skin. Seen through the holes in the mask, his eyes have a feverish intensity.

"Is it true?" he whispers harshly. "Did my uncle kidnap you?"

"Yes. With the help of Captain Helias."

"Snake." His voice is rough. "You shouldn't have come back."

"Which trial are you in?"

He glances at his token. "Seventh."

"I'm third. I'll wait for you in the retiring room afterward."

"No."

"Why did you come here today if you don't want to hear what I have to say?"

"To tell you to stay away from me. Now, and always." He lets go of my hand and takes a step back. "The one thing that keeps me going is knowing you'll survive."

But I follow him. I take hold of his arm and lean in close. "You have to listen to me. We can carve a new path."

Again he shakes me off. "You can't save me, Jes. I'm not the person you want me to be. All my life it's been so easy not to see what I didn't want to see. I thought I was fighting for Efea but I've just been the puppet my uncle and my grandmother needed to foment their own ambitious plans. I thought I would be so brave, killing Nikonos, but all it means is they have everything they want: the throne, the gold, all of it. And Menoë's son to replace me, if I cause too much trouble."

"You're not a puppet. You've taken action. You freed the women from the temple!"

"Yes, aren't I a hero?" The self-loathing in his voice is so sharp that I flinch. "Don't condescend to me like they do. You tried to tell me and I ignored you. At least look me in the eye and remind me that I forced my cousin to enter a prison where she knew she would be murdered. Because it was easy for me to tell myself she was lying. It was convenient to throw her in that dark place, and maybe even to hope I would not have to preside over her execution."

I look him in the eye. "You did do that. And even though I hate her for all the terrible things she did, you were still wrong."

He whispers. I can barely hear him above the buzz of the crowded hall. "I freed them because it is shameful to continue that horrible custom, but mostly I did it because I couldn't bear what you would think of me if I didn't stop it."

"But you did stop it. And you acted responsibly during the siege. You treated all the citizens of Efea fairly." When he doesn't answer or look at me, I go on. "I know my father meant to lead the charge against Nikonos. Why did you go instead of him?"

"Because they couldn't order me not to." There's an edge to his laugh.

"That's not an answer."

Shadows weight his gaze. He looks so weary.

"Maybe because I hoped to die in a blaze of glory. Then I could be the tragic and noble king, cut short too soon. The honored poet Ro-emnu could write a play about me. Wouldn't that be for the best?"

He pauses, and I want to shake him to tell him it would be the worst thing that had ever happened to me. Instead I wait, sensing he has more to say. That his deepest fears are about to spill out.

"How long until I agree to just one small vile act because I'm afraid they'll kill me if I don't go along with them? Before I start repainting things that are wrong and start calling them right because slow rot is how we keep ourselves alive? In the end I will become the monster they want me to be."

I take his hand in mine and hold on so tight. I have to keep him from sinking until he can climb out of this pit himself.

"Listen to me—"

"Stop it!"

He steps away so precipitously that he bumps hard into another adversary. Jostled, the stranger drops a token marked with the number three.

"Three! Third trial!" cries the ready cage custodian.

I set my foot over the fallen token, then snatch the one Kal is holding and flip it so it lands behind the adversary, who's scrambling to find the one lost. The moment the competitor's back is turned I pick up the one on the floor and press it into Kal's hand.

"Third trial," I say, and trot over to the ready cage.

He doesn't hesitate. That's good.

I'm handed the brown belt for Pillars. Kal gets the red belt for Traps. He'll start one obstacle away from me. That's good.

I barely notice the other two adversaries because I can't take my eyes off the way his hands are clenched, the way his gaze darts to me and away and back again. He bounces on his toes not with excitement but because he's stretched so taut he's near to breaking. The friendly, confident, cheerful Kal I knew has vanished into this maelstrom.

The start bell rings. I swarm up the ladder into the maze of Pillars.

It's hard to concentrate because I keep seeing the way he held his body; I keep hearing the snap in his voice. If you soak a decent person in poison for long enough, will it seep through their skin, rot out their bones, and dissolve their heart until it is nothing but a sac of venom?

A cheer startles me. One of the other adversaries has made a daring move. I must focus. I climb out of Pillars just as I hear the entry bell ring. I'm sure it's him behind me.

This configuration of Rivers emphasizes balance and it's

not hard for me to get across a series of swinging beams. But when I hit Trees I struggle with the first part of the obstacle: a simple finger climb sets my wrist to throbbing. By the time I reach the resting platform I'm almost crying from the pain. I've reinjured it, or maybe it never healed properly. Maybe the wounds we have sustained will never fully heal.

Rubbing my wrist, I glance around to get my bearings. The adversary wearing the blue belt moves effectively through Traps, but I can't see the green belt. I'm puzzled about where Kal has gotten to when abruptly he swarms up to the platform to loom over me. He's breathing hard and there's something almost cruel about the energy of his stance as he stares me down.

"You refuse to understand," he says curtly. "It was too late the day I was born."

Leaping across the opposite platform, the green-belted adversary jumps into Rings. Kal pushes past me and descends into this final obstacle as well. They are both already that far ahead of me. I scramble down and run for Traps, but not because I care about winning. I can't win with this wrist anyway. I have to catch up before he leaves the undercourt.

From the high beam in Traps I watch as the two adversaries spin their way in toward the center. I've never seen Kal work Rings like this. Reckless despair propels him through the best trial of his life. He doesn't care if he hurts himself; he takes chances that are impetuous and bold, and he lands every mark. He's splendid. The crowd loves him.

I was sure he wouldn't get this far or that, if he did, he

would give up on victory and fake a fall, as I once did. I was sure he wouldn't unmask for fear of drawing attention to me. Instead he puts on a burst of speed and beats Green Belt to the tower. He scrambles up, grabs the victor's ribbon, and pulls off his mask. He's not smiling but he shines, because this trial he has won.

It takes several breaths for people to recognize him. For the ordinary laughter and cheers to turn to shouts of acclaim as the spectators leap to their feet in a rush of emotion. He is the handsome young People's King, the one who suffered the siege beside them, who ran a Novice trial as if he's one of them, asking for no special favors. He defeated the enemy in one precipitous stroke.

What if he could fight back against the palace? Defeat all the people who mean to use him? What if he could become the People's King in truth and usher in a golden age of peace and harmony?

I crush the thought even as it tries to bloom. That is my father's dream, and it can't be mine. Even King Kalliarkos with the best will in the world can't create a Saroese-ruled Efea that truly includes me and mine. He's right: it was too late the day he was born.

So I will destroy his victory even as I tell myself I'm saving him.

I scramble down from Traps as he descends the tower. I'm so far behind I'm the last one down the ladder into the undercourt. It's dim in the windowless chamber belowground.

Attendants hand out cups and take belts; trainers and stewards collect their adversaries, handing them towels or changes of clothes. For a heart-stabbing interval I think he's already gone, that he didn't wait.... Then I notice there's a ring of attendants and adversaries pretending not to look into the dimmest corner of the retiring court.

Despite his warning he has chosen to wait for me, leaning against a wall as he taps a foot impatiently against the floor. As I walk up he straightens. He pulls me against him, drags off my mask, and kisses me.

This is no soft feather of a kiss. He's triumphant and angry and desperate. I hold him so tight. It's not his anger I fear; it's his despair. All I want is to gift him the courage to believe in himself. To believe there can be a way out for him.

When he shifts his grip on me, sliding a hand from my elbow to my wrist, pain flares and I gasp. At once he breaks off.

"You're hurt. Of course. That's the only reason I could have beaten you." For the first time he sees the scar at my eye. "Good Goat."

More gently than I expect, given his mood, he brushes the scar at my eye, then probes the wrist. My grimace makes him curse under his breath.

"My uncle did this to you, didn't he?" His gaze cuts to my heart. "This is why there's no path for us. I can't protect you, even if I keep you at my side day and night as I wish I could. There are too many of them and only one of me. And you would hate that life anyway. It's not the one you're meant to live. So I will try to be a good king, even if they murder me for it. But you have to leave Saryenia, Jes. You have to leave. And don't ever come back."

I tug him to a halt before he can walk away.

"I'm not giving up on you. Do you trust me?"

"Yes," he says without hesitation.

I take the leap although I don't know how he will react. It's a long way to fall.

"The Efean rebellion must win."

"So there *is* a rebellion. A real one, not just a loudmouthed poet singing the words he thinks will get a girl's attention."

"Ro is the voice. He's not the heart. The rebellion is real. Efea will rise. She is rising now."

For a frozen moment I await his reply. I hold my breath. Has his transformation into a monster already begun, or is there still a chance?

"Even if I agree, how can an untrained and disorganized rabble of villagers and craftsmen defeat professional soldiers?"

I press a hand over my mouth to stifle a gasp of relief, collect myself, then reply, "Ally with the Efeans, Kal, and they will protect you."

"You're asking me to betray my family. My whole life."

"No. I'm asking you to fight for Efea. Not for me—I don't mean it like that. You can't do it for me. You have to believe it's the right thing for everyone who lives here." I press a hand to his chest. His heart pulses beneath my palm. "If the Efeans win, you won't be king. You'll be free."

He rests a hand over mine. "Oh, Jes. I'll never be free. Not as long as I live."

He breaks off, gaze flashing past me. With the same decisive speed he used in the trial, he presses me against the wall behind him, making his body into a shield.

But it's too late. The armed men pushing their way through the adversaries and attendants in the retiring hall have seen us. Lord Gargaron has arrived.

27

Your **Gracious Majesty, did** you really think I would not have you followed?" says Gargaron. He's flanked to his left by Captain Helias and to his right by Captain Neartos. "Or that I wouldn't recognize my most promising adversary on the court, even masked and injured as she is? How did you do it, Jessamy? How did you escape the mines?"

I know better than to say anything that might reveal how much of the north the Efean rebellion now controls, so I flash him the kiss-off sign instead. And I look him right in the eye when I do it.

He flushes, whip twitching in his hand, but Kal is in the way. Captain Helias calls me a very rude epithet although I'm too angry to be shamed by words. Captain Neartos smiles, as if my defiance is what he expected.

Kal commands, "Captain Helias, give me your sword."

Gargaron sighs as a parent does when a child has pettily disobeyed for the hundredth time. "Kalliarkos, it is time to return to the palace. Surely you have done enough for now."

"Just what is it you think I have done enough of, Uncle?"

"Why, you have courted the loyalty of lowborn Patrons rather than strengthening the ties that bind Garon Palace to our noble brethren like Helias, whose support we need most. Men like General Esladas and his lowborn firebirds never can see where their best interests lie. Such people will always wallow back into the mud where they feel most comfortable."

Gargaron looks at me, awaiting an imprudent response, but I am in the game. This is trivial, meant to distract me. Instead I carefully check out the retiring hall to confirm my avenues of escape. There are two ways out, and the main staircase is heavily guarded by soldiers wearing Garon livery.

Realizing I don't intend to answer, Gargaron turns back to Kal.

"This painted mask of righteousness you have assumed is nothing but show, Kalliarkos. You have angered the priestly establishment. I assure you, the royal family and the temples work together, not in opposition."

"Yes, I think we know how you have worked with the priests, Uncle Gar."

I nudge Kal's leg as a warning. To my relief he presses a hand to my arm to reassure me. He's not going to do anything stupid like announcing Gargaron's blasphemous crime to an unwilling audience trapped in the retiring hall who might be killed for hearing it.

These Rings are still turning. I step up beside him and make a show of giving Kal a boastful kiss, as if I'm the kind of person who likes to rub my victories into the face of my adversaries. And because I am, Gargaron will believe in it.

Kal is surprised but he doesn't push me away. Lips by his ear, I whisper, "If you believe the Efean rebellion is the right and just path for Efea, then in five days' time hold a victory game in the Royal Fives Court. Require all the noble clans to be in attendance. Let a rumor spread that you're doing it to reintroduce me as your favorite."

He presses a finger to my palm, then touches his forehead against mine and kisses my lips a final time.

Pulling away, I say to Gargaron, "You haven't won this trial yet, my lord. You claimed a victory when in fact we are still racing through Rings. I have a new stable I'm training in, one where you can't touch me. I will win the favor of the crowd, and they will exalt me and give me whatever I want. Even the king."

"Helias, kill her."

I'm fast enough that I don't need an opening but Kal kicks his uncle in the groin anyway. As Gargaron doubles over with a satisfying screech of pain I dart toward the exit, then cut back immediately. Helias chases me; at first he doesn't see me double back because he's so sure I'm headed for the stairs that are my only path outside. Instead I race for the ladder back onto the court and I climb.

Behind I hear Kal speak in his most royal tone. "Lord Gargaron, do you really think we came unattended? The Royal Army is loyal to the king of Efea, and they are here with us."

At the top of the ladder I glance back into the cavernous hall. Among those dressed as attendants, many converge on Kal to protect him. I recognize firebird veteran faces among them.

Helias spots me on the ladder and races after, shoving aside anyone who gets in his way. I pop up onto the Fives court.

The fourth trial is still under way. No one has reached Rings so the crowd's attention remains focused elsewhere as I roll under the scaffolding of the victory tower. There's a trapdoor here that leads into the machinery. We all know it's here. An adversary who descends into the hidden area of the undercourt where the mechanisms turn will be banned forever.

Forever.

But I am running the most consequential Fives trial of my life. I will give up my future as an adversary if I must, so Efea can win.

I hook the latch with my uninjured hand and drag the trapdoor open just as Helias appears on the court. A roil of heat rushes up out of the opening, drenched in the stench of hot oil and rancid sweat.

Seeing me, Helias draws his sword. I slide down the ladder, letting the trapdoor flip shut over my head. It's dark and hot down here. A single glass-caged flame burns on the other side of the giant horizontal escapement that keeps the Rings spinning on the court. A steady *clap clap clap* sets the time by which workers push the main wheel that turns the well-oiled gears. Timing is everything. During a trial the Rings cannot falter, nor their rhythm skip, slow, or speed up. I listen, gauging the speed of the giant escapement.

Feet scuff on the rungs behind me. Helias jumps the last distance and lands with a thump. His sword tastes of death as it slashes past my head in a wild cut.

Clap clap.

I leap backward into a gap that opens as a metal bar swings past and fades into shadow. "You'll never be the soldier my father is. You don't have it in you."

It's a cheap insult but he bites. Insecure adversaries always do.

A gear clicks. The metal arm swings back just as he steps forward to strike me. It slams him sideways, into the teeth of a gear. He screams. Just in time I duck, the arm swiping over my hair like the hand of death. I roll sideways out of the way. He gets dragged into the next circle of gears with a shriek of such agony that it shocks tears from my eyes.

The scream cuts off. The machinery grinds to a squealing halt. Men begin shouting. I crawl through the frozen mechanism to its other side and crouch beneath a wheel's shadow as the engineers on duty unlock the door. The captain has started screaming again. An engineer grabs the glass lantern and starts around the escapement, leaving a momentary gap at the exit. I dart into the warren of the undercourt's passages, running past winches and capstans and ropes, the undergirding of the obstacles we race through. I can tell which quarter of the court I'm under by the arrangement of its walls, posts, and pulleys. Sweat pours off me from the heat. Fortunately it's easy to hide beneath folded nets and stacks of beams neatly placed along walls for another day's trial. Bells are ringing. The crowd roars.

An unlocked door allows me to sneak into the attiring hall, which is in chaos, everyone talking. I steal a cat mask. Behind this disguise I whisper that a highborn conspiracy is trying to eliminate the new king because he is too popular among the lowborn and the Commoners. By the time the lord engineer in charge calls off the games for the day, the entire attiring hall is buzzing with the rumor I've started. I ascend the steps amid the others and slide into the masses of spectators streaming out of the huge building. Everyone is chattering. As I push through the crowd I drop my rumor every few steps. Words are weapons too, as the honored poet would love to remind me. Even small ripples spread.

The crowds give me cover as I walk downhill from the City Fives Court into the Queen's Garden that lies at the foot of the Queen's Hill. In the day and a half since the raising of the siege, people have had better things to do than walk through the overgrown sections of the public garden. The spider sits crouched where I left it amid a screen of bushes. The shield hinges open smoothly but I taste the problem before I even climb in.

The spark that powers the spider has finally faded. The metal creature is dead, useless to me or to anyone.

I had thought to walk out of the city disguised as a spider scout so I could personally speak to Inarsis about how the new information I've learned can be used in the plan. And maybe I would also have had a chance to infiltrate the Royal Army on its first day of march and personally warn my father about the plot to kill him rather than leave it up to a note. But now, leaning against my spider's metal carapace in the humid shade, I consider my options and the Rings I have already set spinning.

The East and West Saroese armies have left Saryenia, although the West Saroese will come back in about ten days. Mis and the other spiders have delivered my first message to Inarsis, and Anise can get further messages out to him and to Maraya, who will understand and even anticipate what I need to make this reckless undertaking work.

So maybe the sparkless spider is the excuse I need to stay in the city for the next five days, close to Kal, even though I can't see him or influence him. It's probably a bad idea, and yet in a way I'm glad of it.

But when I return to Anise's stable she tells me I can't stay there, that's she arranged a different place for me to sleep. I'm allowed to practice on the Fives court until an Efean man appears at dusk to take me away. The trowel of the masons' guild is inked on his shoulder.

"Are we acquainted, Honored Sir?" I ask.

"You're that spider who rescued the women from the

tombs. I was one of the masons who assisted you that day. My name's Dedu. Come along."

"Where are we going? To the Heart Tavern?"

"No. That's where the dame council and the Honored Custodian preside. I'm taking you to where the war council meets."

"A war council meets in Saryenia?"

He gives me a side-eyed look. "Do you think we haven't been preparing for this day for many years, Spider? Anyway, you've been to the Jasmine Inn before."

I remember the compound where we met Thynos and Inarsis after the masons led us out of the buried ruins beneath the City of the Dead. Somehow it seems appropriate that I will end up there, where beneath a trellis of night-blooming jasmine I almost kissed Kal for the first time.

We stride along less traveled side streets to the East Harbor District, whose boisterous taverns and boardinghouses are frequented by stevedores and dockworkers. Like the markets, it's one of the places in the city where Saroese and Efean mix. In some crews the men work side by side as sailors do out on the perilous sea. I have vague memories of coming down here when I was little but those expeditions ended the day Father gained a captain's rank.

There's a festive air in the city tonight. Singing and laughter float on the breeze. Beer and wine flow freely. Maybe it's my imagination but it seems there are more Efeans in the streets than there were yesterday.

A group of Saroese laborers jostle past us, talking in loud

voices. "Not only did the king win the trial today but he foiled a plot to depose him." "I heard he threw a traitorous body-guard into the undercourt to be crushed to death."

They all laugh like it's the funniest thing in the world but Helias's screams echo in my mind. Did I actually hear his bones break as the gears crushed him? A memory of the battle on the Royal Road flashes: blood on the pavement, a man's guts spilling out while his eyes were still open, one of my fore-legs crashing down on a prone body.

I stagger. Dedu grabs my arm and hauls me through a gate. When I begin to retch he hurries me to a latrine but I don't have anything in my stomach to heave up. After a while the nausea subsides. I bury the ugly images beneath a mask of calm and take a deep breath, centering my focus.

"Are you well?" Dedu asks more gently than I expect.

"Yes. Thank you, Honored Sir."

He leads me through a crowded courtyard of revelers and into a shadow-washed space behind it. The scent of jasmine floods me with the physical memory of Kal hooking his little finger around mine, a gesture of such intimacy that I have to stop and catch my breath again. But that's not the only thing that takes me aback.

In a dim garden, people are pacing through menageries. Beyond them rises an open-air dining hall, its roof raised on brick pillars. Six people are seated at a round table with a lamp set in the middle. Light softens their features, which is a good thing because none are smiling.

I'm so startled to see Inarsis that I put on a burst of speed, but am yanked to a halt by Dedu before I can charge in. The Honored Protector looks over and recognizes me. But he's an Efean man, so I have to speak first, and of course I make a hash of it.

"General, what you doing here already?"

"I came into Saryenia with the vanguard." He doesn't invite me to sit. To his left sits an elderly Efean man and to his right an honored dame. The other three people at the table are Saroese. "Honored Dames and Sirs, this is Spider. She is General Esladas's daughter."

The first to speak is a Saroese man with a military bearing, a firebird badge, and a vaguely familiar face. "The general's daughter and I have met."

I make a polite reply in Saroese as I frantically try to remember him.

He takes pity on me. "I am Sergeant Leukos. You helped me negotiate for oil and naphtha during the retreat from Port Selene. Do you not recall it?"

"Oh. Of course! Are you here..." It's hard to speak. What if I hear the answer I dread? "...on behalf of my father?"

"Yes."

I sway, catching myself on one of the pillars. Relief hits me like weakness.

"He gathered his trusted firebird veterans and explained the situation to us. We voted to join him. The sergeants of the Firebird Guard elected me to act as our representative in negotiations because your father can't risk coming here himself."

I blink back tears, too choked up to do anything but nod in gratitude.

Next to him sits a haughty young man wearing the sun insignia of a priest who serves Seon, the Sun of Justice. I'm afraid to ask him any questions, and a holy Saroese priest doesn't feel the need to speak to such as me.

But the Saroese woman has leaned forward to study me with lively interest. She is expensively dressed and carries herself with the effortless confidence of a person who has lived all her life with the expectation of wealth and privilege. Yet in the lineaments of her face I see she resembles Amaya in having skin a little too dark and hair a little too curly for a Patron woman. She smiles.

"So you are Doma Jessamy. My cousin Lady Petreia wrote to me about meeting you at Port Selene, with your father. I am Clan Petros's representative here in Saryenia."

"Clan Petros owns a merchant fleet," I say, recalling how Father arranged for ships to transport the wounded out of Port Selene.

She nods at Inarsis. "We look forward to being given the monopoly on shipping grain to West Saro for the next five years. Do we not, General Inarsis? Honored Dame?"

"Indeed. Now if you will excuse me, Honored Dames and Sirs, I must briefly speak with Spider."

He beckons me to a corner bench. We sit beneath the stars.

"Aren't you putting yourself at risk to enter the city while we still could lose? Did you even get Mis's message?"

"I did get it. But unless Lord Gargaron or one of Princess Berenise's stewards sees me, I don't fear being recognized. To most Saroese I'm not the infamous king-killer. I'm just another Commoner man." His smile cuts with a wry humor. "It's an impressive plan, Spider. But it needs some additional elements that you haven't considered. Which is why I entered the city early, despite the risk."

"I have new information for you too. But can you trust the Saroese you're negotiating with?"

"The firebird veterans are loyal to the commander they trust, and we have made a particularly generous offer to Clan Petros, which they can't benefit from unless we win."

"A monopoly on shipping grain to West Saro?"

"Yes. And ownership of half of Princess Berenise's merchant fleet."

I whistle. "That will make them the most powerful shipping clan in Efea. And if you're looking for Saroese who have skills we need and reason to be angry with the royal clan, then I suggest we speak to Lord Perikos, the Fives administrator. His son was killed for his spark to keep Prince Temnos alive. But I don't understand why you have a priest here. Why would you even negotiate with those men?"

"There are Efeans who worship Seon and Hayiyin. Who are we to forbid them a sanctuary, as was done to our ancestors? There is no reason the temples of Seon and Hayiyin cannot bide quietly beside the rebuilt temples of the Mother of All."

"Is it not an insult to the Mother?"

"If their belief is sincere, then why is it an insult?"

"Because the Saroese tore down our temples and built their own on top of them. Our people had no choice but to worship Saroese gods."

"Shall we do the same in return? Is that how we should wield power? We cannot speak only with the tongue of vengefulness. We must also speak with the tongue of righteousness. Anyway, no one survives a trial like this without compromise. We benefit if we can convince some among the Saroese priestly establishment to support us. The young priest in question is of lowborn Patron stock, fiercely devoted to the ideal of justice, and well aware that his efforts for reform will always be blocked by his highborn superiors. We have offered to name him as High Priest, if we win."

"When we win."

"You never lack confidence, Spider. But can you trust Kalliarkos? Can you really, honestly trust him? Your plan relies on the cooperation of a young man who will lose everything *when* we win."

28

*I*narsis instructs me to stay in seclusion
at the Jasmine Inn until we find out what choice the king
has made, but of course I don't. After I finish morning training, a girl at the inn helps me use cosmetics to paint my face,
and I get my hair braided in a village style of old-fashioned
knots. The result is spectacular: When I go down to look at
the Clan Petros merchant ships being secured at the wharfs, a
pair of Garon stewards escorted by soldiers emerge unexpectedly from a warehouse right in front of me. But they glance at
my hair and walk past without recognition.

Moments later I hear the shout of a royal herald proclaim-
ing from horseback that the king and queen have called for a
five-day citywide festival that will culminate in victory games
to honor their ascension to the throne. I actually have to turn

aside and hide my face because I don't know whether to shout with triumph or weep with relief.

Kal has done as I asked.

The citizens of Saryenia throng the streets in a celebratory mood. Plays run twice a day in the Lantern District, and night performances are lit by oil donated at the order of the new king and queen. Rations are still in effect because regular shipments from the interior aren't yet restored, but people wait in orderly lines at the Grain Market, confident they will get a share at a fair price. Efean workmen toil day and night to spruce up the awnings and balconies of the Royal Fives Court so they will be fitting for the highborn audience, since everyone is talking about how all the highborn clans must be in attendance lest they be seen as disloyal to the new regime.

On the third day of the festival, amid ribbons being waved for good fortune, I watch from the walls as part of the Royal Army marches out under the command of the much-lauded General Esladas to put down the rumored skirmishes in the north. The hero of the Eastern Reach and Maldine will sort out any unpleasantness, say the people around me, and yet they're also happy that his firebird veterans have stayed behind to protect the city just in case there's trouble. They don't realize the rebellion is already here, that day by day more Efeans filter in through the gates in groups. It's so easy for Commoners to arrive pushing carts filled with produce, hauling oysters and fish, in work gangs to repair roofs and walls damaged by the East Saroese catapults during the months-long siege. The ill-equipped Efean army meant to meet a battered enemy in battle has hidden its weapons and flooded the city.

The night before the trial I'm restless, so I walk the Avenue of Triumphs. At the base of the steep incline up to the king's palace I pause. From high on the hill drift the sounds of revelry.

Our success rests on my gamble that Kal will do what is right for Efea, that he sees the justice in our cause. That he wants out and knows this is the only way. And if I'm honest, it rests in part on my belief that he still cares for me.

What if I'm wrong? What if he can't do it and means to betray me as Father once betrayed Mother? Yet it isn't the wine of power and the glitter of ambition that might weaken his resolve. It's the enormity of what I'm asking of him, a repudiation of his entire life up to now, turning his back on his own family. What if he can't go through with it? What if all I've done is walk the Efean rebellion into a trap? Will I be able to tell before it's too late?

I won't know until the trial. That's the gamble we're taking.

For the first time since I've returned to Saryenia I make my way to the eight-spouted spider fountain at the heart of the Warrens. Heart Tavern is crowded but eerily silent. People watch me without offering a single greeting although a couple of women touch their wrapped or braided heads with expressions I am sure show envy for my elaborate knots. By the oval terrace I enter the inner passages. At every turn I am inspected and allowed to pass by armed Efeans.

One soldier about my age can't stop glancing at me so I finally acknowledge him.

"Honored Cousin?"

He whispers, "I love your hair. My grandmother used to wear hers like that."

I flash him a kiss-off gesture, and he chuckles and flashes it back. Between one breath and the next a sharp and solid sense of comradeship soaks me like an unlooked-for cloudburst. We share a destiny. We are together, all of us.

A modest curtain separates the last passageway from a bowl-shaped courtyard surrounded by high walls and a circular terrace of seats: the heart of the Warrens. Beneath a mural depicting the Mother of All the seats are crowded with dames and elders and so many people that I'm dizzied at the energy pouring off them amid the flare of lamps. For an instant I think some of them have taken on the faces of animals and then I realize the officials are wearing masks.

I take a quick step sideways into an alcove to catch my breath and almost trip over a boy. He's sleeping on a blanket on the ground. Three crows roost, one on his leg, one on his hip, and one on his thin shoulder. A cloth binds his sightless eyes.

"Jes?" A shape rises beyond him.

"Polodos! Is Maraya here?"

"Yes, and I don't thank you for insisting she walk into such danger in her condition. But she was certain your message said for her to come to the city."

"If we fail, every part of Efea will be dangerous for her."

I step out to see what the dazzle of lamplight obscured from me. Seated upon boxy stools inlaid with faience, the Honored Protector and the Honored Custodian face the dame council and an assembly of elders and officials: Inarsis in his lion mask, Mother the butterfly in all its graceful colors, with ribbons stirring in the soft night breeze. The honored poet stands between them, holding a braided whip against his chest. Of course he isn't wearing a mask, since it would conceal his handsome features, and Ro never passes up a chance to be the center of attention. He is the voice of the Mother of All.

The tiered aisles are lined with soldiers on guard, some wearing spider scout gear. I recognize Dagger's silhouette, lean and honed. A tall woman at the top of the stairs turns as I step forward to get a better look.

"Jes," she whispers, but she doesn't step out of line; this isn't the place or time for hugs.

"Mis? What are you doing here?"

"We had to sneak the general back into the city."

"But Inarsis is already here...."

That's when I see him. He's wearing the same humble spider scout's gear as the others but he walks with the pride of a man who has nothing left to prove except that he can be trusted to protect the ones he loves. Among so many Efeans he stands out with his golden-brown complexion and stocky build laced with muscle from years of soldiering. His tightly clipped hair sticks straight up as if he's just pulled a dusty desert scarf off it, one that would conceal his features. There's a streak of dirt on his right cheek that he's not had time or water to wash off.

The silence in the courtyard and the judgment of the Efeans settles into my bones.

Even the city beyond seems to have fallen away, as if nothing exists except the man who kneels and sets his sword on the ground. Inarsis nods regally in acknowledgment but Mother sits as still and stares as straight ahead as the figures painted on the wall.

He does not address himself to her but rather to Ro-emnu. His Efean is heavily accented by his Saroese birth but he knows the language even if he rarely spoke it at home.

"I ask for nothing except their honored permission to fight for Efea."

Tears run down my face.

Even yet he does not look at Mother, makes no plea to her, asks for nothing in exchange. Perhaps he's playing the long game, ever the strategist. Or maybe he really is fighting for Efea because it is the right thing rather than what he needs to do to get her back.

The Honored Protector picks up the sword and returns it hilt first, trusting Father not to stab him on the spot. "You are welcome among us. Our war council will begin."

Dismissed as if he is a mere adjutant, Father retreats from the center and stands amid the Efean captains, hands clasped behind his back at parade rest. On the other side, three clerks are keeping an account of the proceedings, scribbling away, and I am not surprised to see Maraya among them. There's a dab of ink on her nose, and she's squinting at the page with prim satisfaction as she writes. I'm not sure if it is Father's presence, Mother's coldness, the general atmosphere, or my brilliant plan that pleases her.

Inarsis pulls his mask back to sit atop his head but Mother keeps her face hidden, her back ramrod straight.

"Let the four Challengers who will run this trial come forward," says Inarsis.

Ro looks up at me so quickly I realize he must have noticed me come in. I offer him a nod as I descend, and his wry smile answers me, as if he guesses at the words I've not said and the choice I've made.

Dagger kneels next to me and gives me a friendly kiss-off. Pythias, an Efean man who ran for Garon Stable, is the third adversary; he nods a greeting. The fourth adversary surprises me: he is the stocky older Saroese man who protested my victory in my first Challenger trial, angrily accusing me of cheating. Yet here he stands in the heart of the rebellion, for what reason I cannot know except that someone whom Inarsis trusts vouched for him. But it makes sense. Adversaries meet as equals whether they are Saroese or Efean.

"You know your part," Inarsis goes on. "Now disperse to your respective stables so there can be no chance that in the morning you are seen to arrive in company with the others."

Mother says to me, "Please wait, Spider."

Obediently I retreat to the alcove where Polodos is seated

381

on a bench, peeking out at the proceedings as the boy sleeps. I sit beside him.

"Why aren't you clerking?"

"My Efean isn't good enough yet. I can't record that fast."

Mis slides back into the alcove. We embrace.

"Take care, Mis. Be safe tomorrow. Are the spiders ready?"

"Your father has taken over command of our unit. I must say, he's a harder taskmaster even than you." Before she goes back out she adds, "I brought your Fives gear. Your sister has it."

When the council is over, Father departs with the spider scouts, not once speaking to Mother. As Maraya enters the alcove she is huffing from climbing the stairs. We hug, although her huge belly gets in our way.

"I'm ready," she says. "But I have to tell you, Jes. What I found in the crow priest's gear that you brought me...and what I've learned from Sandos...it's astounding."

"Sandos? Oh, the crow priest. I'm surprised you trust him with our secrets."

"He's a boy who had his eyes burned out because he performed well in a blindfolded test of agility. It's remarkable what a little kindness and my perfect Saroese diction will do to draw out a vulnerable child. He was so young when he was dedicated to the temple that all he remembers is he had an older sister who cried the day the priests took him away."

"Where is Gargaron's son?"

"My exceptional scholarly skills were no match for Amaya's allure. He stayed in Ibua with her and Denya. Anyway

Mother didn't want Menos here. Menos knows who he is. He would try to escape."

"So he's being held as a hostage."

"Of course he is a hostage. Efea has been held hostage for a hundred years."

Ro slips inside the alcove and shamelessly smiles at me. Why am I blushing? I look away as Mother arrives, draws the curtain, and pulls off her mask without preamble.

"Jessamy, is your father's presence here your idea? Inarsis did not have the courtesy to warn me in advance. I feel I am being worked around, and I don't like it."

Sandos coughs in his sleep, and at once Mother says to me, "Shhh!" as if I were the one talking in a loud voice.

"Doma, will you have something to drink?" Polodos asks her.

"You're on edge, Mother," says Maraya. "Please sit down."

"Efea needs Father's help now that the original plan didn't go as expected," I say.

She looks away with a frown, and I can see her collect and set aside her anger, just as she's always done over the years. After a pause she takes my hand.

"My dear Jessamy, you must take care tomorrow. I objected to your part in this, but I was outvoted. In case of trouble I have specifically asked Ro-emnu to get you safely out of Saryenia, as he did before."

"Mother! I'm not ten anymore. I'm the one who led the revolt at the mine! And most of this plan is my idea!"

That's when I see in my mother's face the months of endurance, the shock and the misery, and the way fear has made her irritable. She lost the life she built over twenty years, the life she gave everything to. It's no wonder she's willing to place herself at the forefront. Her Efea is gone. What's left for her is a future she hopes to shape through the lives of others.

"I love you, Mother," I say.

She embraces me for the longest time, then sets me back and examines me searchingly. "Who did your hair? It's an old-fashioned village style, a little complicated and showy. It suits you."

I'm slightly taller than her now. When did that happen?

"You must live, my daughter. That is all I ask when I pray to the Mother of All: that my children, and the land of my birth, can live the lives that should be rightfully theirs."

29

The Royal Fives Court is built of marble and hung with painted silk tapestries depicting famous adversaries of old, Saroese and Efean alike. A Fives court is the only place in Saryenia where Patrons celebrate Commoners who have dared and won. A buzz of lively and nervous chatter rises from inside the walls. I make my way along the servants' lane of the outer court amid a group of Efeans carrying baskets of grapes and figs for the kitchens. The highborn crowd must be fed the sweetest and freshest of delicacies. Spiders patrol the exterior, two crouched motionless by each of the main gates.

I glimpse latecomers in the arrival yard scurrying out of their expensive carriages. Highborn women with hair done up in the most outrageous ribbons and bows take comically mincing steps toward the gates, followed by their impatient lords.

Sons follow in order of age, oldest at the front and youngest trotting at the rear. Not a single family has more than two daughters.

The gates will be closed when the king and queen make their entrance. Everyone must be in their seats or be locked out, the worst possible fate for people wanting to claw their way into the favor of the new royal clan.

As an adversary I descend through a different gate, one crowned by carvings that depict each animal of the menageries and guarded by men wearing the badge of the firebirds. No onlookers crowd the adversary's gate today to cheer our entrance, because the highborn are intent on making their presence known inside. But despite their absence, the stairs have been strewn with blossoms of jasmine. Kal has arranged for this offering, I'm sure of it. As our feet crush the blooms their rich scent envelops us.

Two Garon stewards by the entrance mark my spider mask and my gear of ordinary brown, but they don't try to stop me. We're still on the court, Gargaron and I. He thinks he's an obstacle or two ahead, and that's exactly what I want him to think.

The attiring hall is unusually crowded. If this many adversaries ran we would be at the court for three days. But of course they aren't all adversaries. Few speak; the atmosphere is one of tense expectation.

As I push my way toward the ready cage a man says my name.

"Spider."

Lord Perikos stands by a locked door that leads into the undercourt and its secret mechanisms. He nods at me, but I hesitate before I go over to him. Adversaries are never allowed to speak to any of the Fives administrators or engineers.

"What did General Inarsis say to convince you to join our cause?" I ask.

He answers in a somber voice. "It was the king who persuaded me. Of course he mentioned my son, but that's not all we discussed. Some years ago my wife and I dedicated a daughter to Eternity Temple. When the holy priestesses were expelled from the temple we went at once to the queen's palace to find her, but she wasn't there. We were told she was given the honor of accompanying the oracle to the tomb of Clan Tonor. King Kalliarkos revealed to me that she could not have been among the oracle's attendants. The priests did not even have the decency and courage to admit that she is dead, and that they killed her."

"I'm sorry." The heat of his sadness fuels my resolve. I wonder if it was her spark that walked Lord Ottonor to his tomb, if the vitality of the nameless girl lives on in Wenru. "I thank you for what you have done for us today."

"I have done as the king requested. You'll see some familiar patterns, Spider. May fortune be with you."

He retreats into the undercourt. Through the briefly opened door I glimpse a passage and beyond it a dim underhall packed with people.

A fanfare announces the arrival of the royal households. No boisterous cheers greet the king and queen, because the highborn are above such enthusiastic displays. Even Father tempered his behavior after he was raised to the rank of captain and stopped socializing with the companions of his early days. I see now that Mother, wanting him to be happy, went along with his efforts to turn our family into a mimicry of a highborn Patron household.

"First trial!" shouts the custodian at the ready cage.

It's time for the last obstacle in the fight for Efea.

I'm ready.

I'm not surprised when I am given the same belt I received the other time I raced at the Royal Fives Court: the brown belt, for Pillars. Like the flowers strewn at the entrance, like Perikos waiting to reassure me, I feel Kal's hand in this. He's sending me signals, telling me that I can trust him.

I have no choice but to trust him now.

I follow my custodian up a ladder into the dim passageway that leads to the start gate. From above only a thin skin of conversation buzzes. It seems awfully muted. Do the highborn Patrons suspect? Have the lords come armed, as they would normally never do on the Fives court? What if I'm wrong? What if Kal intends to betray us? Will I be captured and killed? Will the rebellion die here, put to rest for another hundred years?

Or what if Kal doesn't have the strength I believe he does? What if he simply doesn't have the courage to go through with it? But that's what Gargaron would say, the man who never believed his royal nephew had the toughness to succeed.

I won't follow Gargaron's lead. I'll know when I see Kal with my own eyes.

We halt beneath the closed hatch, where I rub chalk on my hands and shoes. The gate-custodian and my custodian nod at each other. They are conspirators too, although they are Saroese.

"Why do this, when you know what the outcome will be?" I ask them.

The gate-custodian shrugs. "I work for Clan Rikos. I do what Lord Perikos tells me. I trust him to take care of his retainers."

The other custodian says, "My beloved daughter fell in love with a mule like you. When I shut her in her room to keep her away from him she ran away. We didn't see her for five years and my wife stopped speaking to me because of it. Then she came back with her partner and their two children, the sweetest little babies you ever saw, our first grandchildren. I still wish she'd accepted a decent Patron suitor, but since she didn't it would be better if her and her love could get married like respectable people."

A shout of excitement heralds the canvas's being pulled back, unveiling today's configuration. After the siege and the uncertainty of the last months, even highborn Patrons willingly break into the customary song that begins the Fives. The words convey such a different meaning to me now.

Shadows fall where pillars stand.
Traps spill sparks like grains of sand.
Seen atop the trees, you're known.
Rivers flow to seas and home.
Rings around them, rings inside,
The tower at the heart abides.

Deep in the undercourt the start bell rings. The hatch opens. Sunlight spills down over me, and on its rays of brightness I climb.

The tiers of seating ripple with color as ribbons tied to the awnings flutter in the breeze. From here I can't get a good look at the royal balcony but that's not my first concern. A quick scan reveals soldiers stationed at all the entrance arches. They're standing at parade rest like people expecting no trouble, just an ordinary day of duty. Most wear the colors of the Firebird Guard, but soldiers wearing the sea-phoenix tabards of the palace surround the royal balcony. They will become a problem, but that obstacle is not mine to solve.

Rope stairs lead up to a maze negotiated off the ground on a series of narrow beams. It's a clever design: the need to balance diverts a certain amount of concentration from figuring out the correct route. I've been on a maze rigged like this one so recently that my body remembers the course it took. At one turning when I step to the right instead of the left an odd reluctance checks me; this way leads to a dead end. I'm so sure I know this route that I let go of thinking and let memory guide me without a single wrong turn.

My bell is first to ring for a second obstacle as I head into Traps.

I've seen this exact entry into Traps before: a choice between ropes and beams running hip high above the ground and a set of ascending horizontal bars that lead up to a faster, and highly dangerous, route. Pythias is still in this obstacle, doggedly clambering upside down along a tipping bridge at the lower level. He's right where an adversary named Sandstorm was, the only other time I ran a trial in the Royal Fives Court.

That's when I realize what Perikos was telling me. Kal must have ordered him to re-create the course from the Maldine victory games, a course that favors my skills. I once swore never to run a rigged court again, but today the Fives obstacles aren't the real trial, and anyway the court of Efea has been rigged for a long time; it's just I couldn't see it before.

Of all the chances I must take this is the big one. I test the brace and binding on my wrist. It's not hurting yet. So I leap, grasp the horizontal bar, swing up to catch the next-higher bar with my knees, and fly backward to release and catch the highest bar, which swings me up onto the most dangerous and thus shortest path, beams and ropes so high that if you fall, you can die.

I should go slowly. I should.

But the crowd has gotten excited at last. They need to recognize me.

Extending my arms wide, I play the crowd, my gesture a boast that they must look at me. That they should know who I am.

I don't look toward the royal balcony. Not yet.

Instead I spin my web of tricks across the ropes and beams and bars and traps, my somersaults and leaps, my tucks and flips, so high off the ground that if I fall then it will all be over for me, no coming back from such a disaster. This is our day. If we don't fly, we *will* fall.

The crowd is roaring by the time I reach the resting platform for Traps.

"The general's valiant daughter!"

"Spider! Spider!"

Only then do I pause to catch my breath. Only then when they are thrilled by my daring do I turn to face the royal balcony, where a king and a queen sit side by side beneath an awning. Gold silk sways up and down like the breath of the land trying to tug free from the stakes that moor it. Beside the royal sea-phoenix banner flies the banner of the horned and winged fire dog, marking the ascendency of Clan Garon, no longer languishing on a lesser balcony off to one side.

Lord Gargaron stares at me from where he sits next to Queen Menoë. Although I can't really see his expression, the way he's holding a cup like he wants to throw it at me reveals everything I need to know. If there is anything he hates, it is defiance.

My gaze slides to the king. He is dressed all in gold, and a gold diadem circles his brow like a ribbon of sunlight.

When I turn his way he stands, and thus every person in the Fives court except his sister and his grandmother must stand. That is his tribute to me, the only tribute I need.

The crowd erupts into a frenzy of astonished and outraged speculation. Everyone thinks today's story is about forbidden love between a reckless adversary and a headstrong young king. It's the best distraction of all. No one is watching as the entry gates that lead out of the tiers are closed.

His sister tugs impatiently on his arm, and he relents and sits.

I clamber down, chalk my sweating hands, and enter Trees. When I ran that very first trial, in this configuration the entry was a high horizontal bar the adversary had to leap to grab, but now it's a simple ladder. I am certain Kalliarkos told Lord Perikos to change it because of my wrist. The climbing within these posts and shafts relies more on skill than hand strength but it doesn't matter. I'm not halfway through before my wrist is throbbing. I struggle. Atop a set of posts I pause to breathe down the worst of the pain, and Dagger comes up beside me.

"Can you make it through with that injury?" she asks. "You have to win. You're the only one who can be sure."

"I'll make it," I say through teeth gritted from pain. "But it might take me a while."

She flashes me a kiss-off sign and leaps away.

She's so clean and strong as she climbs. We can all be strong, each in our own way, if we are not lashed into submission. The crowd salutes her skill with a cheer, and yet by the time I grind my way through the last of Trees, struggling through pain, they are cheering me even louder because they can see I am injured but unwilling to give up.

By now the other three adversaries have all reached Rings. My wrist just didn't hold up, and the truth is they are all more experienced Challengers than I and would likely have beaten me anyway.

But I have to keep going. When I drop into Rivers it's easy to recall the pattern of which stones will shift, like Father's loyalty to his family when he was offered the sum of his ambition, and which will hold firm, like Mother's love for her children. Yet as I cross in haste I hear the crowd's noise start to falter into confusion. No shout of triumph greets a victor although there should be one by now. When I pull myself up onto the final resting platform, my entry point to Rings, I see why.

Dagger has reached the victory tower but she stands beside it, not climbing. Just then the older Saroese man dashes up, and he too halts at the base of the ladder.

I leap into the spinning Rings. I already know its pattern because I've been this way before. As I throw in twists and tucks for flair, the loudest sound in the court is the scuff and slap of my feet and hands. I've gone beyond pain; blood thunders in my ears, and my wrist pulsates with agony. The crowd has gone silent in furious disapproval, withholding their approbation. In any other circumstances it would destroy the career of a promising adversary. But I pay no attention. I swing down onto the ground to see all three adversaries standing at the base of the tower.

Waiting for the tomb spider, the herald of death.

"It's up to you now," says Dagger.

"Don't signal unless you're certain he's with us," adds the Saroese man.

"Efea is in your hands," says Pythias.

They step away from the ladder to let me through. In tears I climb as the crowd begins to jeer and scream. What words they shout I will not hear for they are ugly. They think the new king has cheated to let his lover win.

It takes all my concentration to climb one-handed to the top. There flies the ribbon, purple silk embroidered with gold thread. In my rush I grab it with the wrong hand, and the pain that stabs through my flesh doubles me over. But I straighten.

The king is standing. Gaze fixed on me, he taps his chest twice with an open hand to show he has fulfilled his orders. Then he touches a forefinger to his lips and holds it out to me.

The crowd has gone wild with anger at this perversion of the sacred rules of the Fives.

Lord Gargaron is both enraged and gloating, thinking I've overstepped, that Kal's attentions have made me overconfident, that I've missed my mark and begun my fall.

But he is the one whose arrogance has led him to this cliff's edge.

I pull my mask from my face.

And I shout, "Efea will rise!"

30

Below, the other three adversaries join me, our voices together amplifying the words.

"Efea will rise! *Efea will rise!*"

That is the signal for my father's loyal Firebird Guard to bar the gates from the outside and trap the highborn Patrons inside the Fives court. That is the signal for the hatches and trapdoors of every mechanism in the undercourt to open.

That is the signal for the Efean soldiers who entered the undercourt as workmen to climb into the light.

An arrow skitters across the victor's platform and skids off. A second clatters through the scaffolding. It takes me that long to realize someone is shooting at me. I swing around to see a crossbowman on a balcony taking aim. At me.

I throw myself behind one of the big scaffolding beams. A bolt slams into its other side.

Shouting and screams break out on the seating terraces as Efean soldiers swarm up from the court, climbing into the tiers. People race for the exits but the Firebird Guard controls the gates and aisles with its intimidating shield walls and spears. Their job is merely to hold so no one can get out or come in. It's the Efeans who take charge.

Each highborn clan has guards; it's how they display their importance. Those who kneel and surrender are allowed to live but the guards who draw their swords and fight are cut down as the Efeans wade in with fierce resolve and a supple and disciplined fighting style honed by the menageries.

Two more arrows flash past me from different directions, one hissing so close to my face I can taste its iron. A bolt from the first archer scrapes my left thigh and slides away across the planks. Across the distance he cranks back the crossbow, lowering his sights on me yet again. Then he's hit from behind by a sword thrust, so intent on harming me that he failed to notice Efean soldiers storming the balcony.

A shout from below: "Spider! Get down!"

I flop down, face against the platform, as more arrows whistle over, where my head just was. One stabs into the plank next to my shoulder, quivering from the force of its impact. A thin rail of blood leaks through ripped cloth on my thigh but my pulse is pounding so hard I don't feel any pain except in my wrist. Up here I'm a target and yet if I try to climb down the ladder while they're still fighting I'll be even more exposed. I have to hang on.

Pockets of resistance drop back toward the royal balcony,

hoping to join up with the sea-phoenix soldiers who have frantically set up a perimeter around the royal household. But Efean squads swarm the retreating Saroese guardsmen time and again. Each clash of swords and spears leaves broken bodies bleeding out onto stone, some Saroese and some Efean.

The royal balcony has become an island of shocked calm isolated amid the chaos. My scan of the terraces reveals how comprehensively we have ambushed them, how many people kneel with hands on heads, shaking as they beg for mercy. Parents clutch children to their breasts. Women strip themselves of jewels and gold braid to throw at the feet of their assailants in the wild hope that all the rebels want is loot. From up here I see a few Efean soldiers grab a ring or necklace for themselves but most kick the baubles aside to officers who are collecting the valuables into bags. Trust Mother to have made the demand that everything be accounted for so she can disburse it fairly later.

All through the seating terraces that have come under the complete control of the Efeans, the Saroese are driven into lines and roped up like criminals.

After a bit, when no more arrows fly past, I risk rising to my knees, then to my feet. I turn toward the royal balcony. The king has not budged from his throne. He sits rigidly as he watches the end of his world. A last few knots of loyal guardsmen trying to fight their way to the royal balcony are overwhelmed and slaughtered.

The women and children and unarmed officials of the Garon household have been pressed back under the balcony's awning, protected by a last circle of sea-phoenix and fire dog soldiers standing three deep. A captain daringly tugs on the king's arm, trying to get him to move back so he won't be so exposed, but he shakes him off. He doesn't budge. A single well-aimed arrow could kill him.

A noise grinds on the floor of the court, and it seems every gaze fixes there. Four big platforms are winched up through the open trapdoors. Normally they would hold a change of equipment for Rings. But today brass carapaces gleam as spiders emerge into the sunlight.

The king stands, in defiance or in welcome. A great shout arises from the Patrons, because for one moment they believe the spiders have come to rescue them.

The spiders scuttle up the tiers in a terrifying display of flashing limbs. I'm sure that the spider scout leading the way is Father, risking himself at the forefront as always. They slam to a halt as they crash over the railing onto the royal balcony. There they loom above the royal guards, their bladed forelegs held ready to slash through the massed line. But they wait.

Menoë bravely tries to go forward to stand beside her brother but Lady Adia holds her back. In a show of courage I wasn't sure he possessed, Lord Gargaron walks from the group hiding in the back and right up to the exposed throne. He speaks sharply to the king. Kal raises a hand to gesture Gargaron away. Briefly Kal's gaze drifts to where I stand atop the tower but there's no relief or lightness in his posture. How can there be?

Thousands of highborn Saroese have been taken prisoner and hundreds killed, and he had a hand in it, even though none of them know that he's complicit in their defeat. That's part of the plan: That they believe he, too, has been taken by surprise, betrayed by his lover.

Out of the mass of Efean soldiers the Honored Protector in his lion mask pushes forward. Beneath the sheltering shadow of a spider he faces the royal Saroese. Astoundingly, no one in the Garon household appears to recognize Inarsis in his mask and armor.

The honored poet at his side speaks. His actor's voice carries easily to all the tiers. He speaks Saroese as well as those seated there do, because we must learn the language of the conqueror while they can remain ignorant of ours.

"There has come this day when truth will bloom and Efea will rise. You are done, you who have walked on our bones and nourished yourselves on our blood for so many generations. I counseled that we kill you all. But *she* who is rightful Custodian of the land desires mercy, so she makes this offer: Let the heads of your highborn clans make a formal surrender in your own Temple of Justice under the gaze of your god Seon. These clan heads alone will be held responsible. Do this, and your households will be allowed to embark on ships waiting in the harbor, which will take you to the lands of old Saro whence you came."

Gargaron actually laughs. "Do you mean to cleanse every person of Saroese ancestry from Efea? Most of us were born here, just like you."

"That is Efea's offer to the highborn clans," says the honored poet. "Take it, and most of you will live. Refuse it, and you will surely die."

400

Menoë yanks free of her mother's restraining arm and comes forward to Kal. The girth of her pregnancy gives her the weight of authority.

"Esladas will turn the Royal Army home to come to our rescue. Our West Saroese allies will return." She looks ready to spit in Ro's face although she wisely restrains herself as she turns to her brother. "Let them have their way for now so no one else dies. I counsel surrender because it will be temporary. These Commoners will rue the day they dared to defy us."

The king has gone as ashy pale as if all the blood has been drained from his body, but he refuses to look away. In fact I think he is staring at Ro as if a crawling suspicion is worming its way through him, as if he is wondering if I have played these Rings against him, if it was Ro all along I favored. If I will actually stab him in the back as I did once before on this very Fives court.

Again he looks up at me, where I still stand atop the victory tower. I can make no gesture. I can shout no words of encouragement. There can be no hint that he's in on it.

In the end it is his decision alone, and he knows it.

The legacy of the first Kliatemnos and Serenissima is one betrayal after the next, their descendants steeped in an ugly history. Even though his cause is just, King Kalliarkos is a betrayer too. He knows it as he speaks the words that spell the end of the royal dynasty he was meant to inherit.

"So say we, Queen Menoë and King Kalliarkos. Seeking the path of mercy rather than blood, we surrender into the custody of the gods' judgment."

31

As we leave the Fives court for the Temple of
Justice I still clutch the victor's ribbon. I walk with the
other three adversaries alongside columns of Efean soldiers.
Marching in disciplined ranks, they escort the royal household
and the head of each highborn clan to Seon's temple. The firebird veterans remain behind in the Royal Fives Court to stand
guard over the thousands of highborn Saroese captives. The
Honored Protector, still hidden by his mask and armor, leads
the procession down the King's Hill in a silence that contrasts
with the turmoil unfurling throughout the city.

Threads of smoke rise from within Saryenia's walls and
I don't know if it is the Saroese or Efeans who have set the
fires. The city rumbles with noise and confusion. Even so, our
prisoners, surrounded by a tight wall of Efean troops, might as
well be in a cage. Four spiders clank along, two on either side.

The only courtesy shown is toward Princess Berenise, who is carried in a litter because of her age. Even Menoë in the fullness of her pregnancy is forced to walk in the heat and the dust, the sun blasting down on her. She's leaning heavily on Kal. His face looks dead.

Numbness has turned my heart to stone as we reach the wide staircase that leads up to the portico of the Temple of Justice. We are welcomed by a colossal statue of Seon with his stern Saroese face and his neck wreathed with flowers in the Efean manner. The hall of the Sun of Justice admits Saroese and Efeans alike even if the laws favor Patrons. Father has always preferred Seon's worship to that of Inkos although he was not a man who prayed beyond what was socially required.

By now ordinary city dwellers have crept to the edges of the square that fronts Seon's temple. There are far more Efeans than Saroese in this growing crowd. However fast news travels, not everyone in the city yet knows what is going on. And why would they? We haven't won yet. There are still Rings turning that we have to leap through to reach the victory tower.

The Honored Protector halts at the base of the temple steps. The four spiders thump up the stairs to its portico, where they halt on either side of the monumental entrance. Each one is accompanied by a squad of firebird veterans detached from the main unit that remained behind to guard the Royal Fives Court with the rest of the spiders. I'm sure they're here because Father never fully trusts anyone except men he has himself trained.

Although I'm separated from Kal by only a few ranks of

403

soldiers, he never looks around, only straight ahead and up the stairs, awaiting the arrival of the High Priest. For the last many years, the Inkos priest Lord Gargaron blackmailed has presided as High Priest over all the temples of Efea. But it is not a man dressed in the red robe and black hat of Inkos who emerges.

Instead a woman wearing a simple linen sheath gown walks out and halts at the top of the stairs. A butterfly mask fashioned from blue, yellow, and red feathers conceals her face but her bare black arms and her hair reveal to the prisoners what manner of person this is who has usurped the priests' territory. Despite their helplessness the men of the royal household and the captured heads of clans murmur angrily. By Patron custom, for a woman to preside over a temple is blasphemy. That she is a Commoner of course makes it worse.

"What mockery is this with which you defile our holy temple?" calls Gargaron.

"Silence!" shouts Ro.

The Honored Protector starts up the stairs. Ro murmurs into Kal's ear like a sage steward giving advice to a beleaguered lord in a play. Ro's part is crucial, because he has only these few moments to persuade Kal to take the biggest chance of all.

Kal says something short to Ro and, still supporting his sister, climbs the stairs in the wake of the Honored Protector. Lord Gargaron, the heads of the many highborn clans, and the Garon Palace men come next. At the back the ladies of the royal household hold hands as they follow their menfolk. Most are weeping, but nevertheless they keep their chins high. Lady

Adia has fallen to the rear amid the stewards and officials, not one person extending a hand to aid her. Something about the way her body sways and her chin dips down alerts me. I shove through the ranks and dart up just as she begins to collapse with the passive invisibility of people who are drowning.

I grasp her arm in time to stop her from hitting the ground. Only then, seeing my hands on her, do the nearest stewards yank her away and hastily convey her forward out of my reach. One spits at me.

The Efean soldiers at my back break their silence, muttering furiously, but I wave them back. This is not the place. We must let the performance continue to its end.

We enter the temple, a square hall lined with pillars. A statue of four-faced Seon rises at the center, looking in every direction for, as the sages teach, justice shines in every direction. Two stone goats kneel, one by each of the god's legs, according to an ancient custom by which the good, unblemished goat is given to the god as a sacrifice that atones for the misdeeds of the people while the other goat is expelled as an outcast into the wilderness.

"This is a farce." Gargaron strides past Princess Berenise and steps in front of his niece and nephew to command the stage. "Only the High Priest can judge the royal clan and the highborn lords."

"I am the High Priest," says a yellow-robed young man sitting in the seat of judgment, which is placed at Seon's feet between the two goats. He is the man I met at the Jasmine

Inn, the one who was promised this job, whose name I never learned. He is flanked by nervous priest-wardens armed with swords and spears festooned with the colored ribbons of the holy temples. The old High Priest, stripped of his hat, cowers amid a huddle of frightened colleagues off to one side.

The young priest of Seon looks down his nose at Gargaron with searing contempt. "I and my pure-hearted confederates will restore the worship at the temples so its judgments are not bought by gifts and favors. You, Lord Gargaron, stand chief among those who have bribed the very priests who claim to be the holy servants of the gods but instead have been corrupted by greed and lust."

Gargaron gestures toward the masked Protector and Custodian, who still have not spoken. "I see you have found Efean puppets whose strings you can pull. Who has masterminded this plan? Surely not you, a mere youth?"

The High Priest ignores him. "The trial of Garon Palace begins now. You are accused of bribery, perjury, theft, and murder."

With her distinctive rolling walk, Maraya approaches the High Priest, scrolls piled in her arms. She is accompanied by other clerks, each of whom carries additional documents. Gargaron's stunned expression gratifies me for only a moment, because like me he is a decisive person.

"You should have been smothered at birth," he snarls. "Your father was weak to allow you to live, much less to breed another like yourself."

He leaps forward and, taking her completely by surprise,

sweeps the scrolls out of her arms, then slaps her across the face. As she stumbles back, he shoves her viciously to the ground. She hits hard, with a cry of pain.

I push forward, trying to reach her.

But of course Father did not stay in his spider, not knowing how quickly the situation might change inside the temple hall. In dusty scout's gear he shoves roughly through the ranks faster than I can. Just as Gargaron is about to kick Maraya in the belly, Father grabs him by the shoulder of his silk jacket and flings him to one side with so much force that the lord slams into the blemished goat with a smack that makes everyone wince.

"You will not harm my daughters ever again."

By now I've broken through and rush up as Father kneels beside Maraya.

He tips her face so he can look into her eyes. "Can you speak, Maraya?"

"Yes, just shaken up." She clings to him, and he lifts her, sets her on her feet, and indicates that I should let her lean on me.

"So it was you all along, General Esladas." Breathing hard, one hand pressed to his side, Gargaron glares with the enraged satisfaction of a man who has finally figured it out. "Your ambition could not be content with the command of the Royal Army. Now you have turned against your rightful masters and fomented this overthrow. How clever of you to use Commoners as your figureheads to get them on your side. They're easily led, as you must know from years of experience."

"You don't understand what is going on at all." When

Father drops the *my lord* from his answer I know beyond all doubt that he has chosen Efea.

"Of course I understand." Gargaron gestures toward Mother. "You can crown yourself king and call a Commoner woman your queen, but you will never be royal."

"This can't be true, Esladas. I'm your wife, not her." Menoë presses a hand to her chest.

Father has kept his gaze fixed on Gargaron, but when Menoë speaks he glances toward her. It's not regret, precisely, that shadows his face, but disquiet that he has caused pain where he intended none.

That glance is all it takes. That one moment of distraction. Gargaron moves, grabbing a sword out of the hand of one of the priest-wardens.

"Father, behind you!"

Father thinks I'm warning him about a threat to Mother, and he looks the wrong way. He looks toward the woman he has loved from the first day he set foot in Efea. I release Maraya and jump forward, but it's too late.

Gargaron's blade enters Father from the back, thrust so hard the point comes out through his belly, a wink of bloody metal that's withdrawn as quickly as I glimpsed it.

Maybe I mistook a flash of light for a blade. It can't really have happened.

Father staggers a step, then collapses. Blood pumps out of the wound.

Gargaron lifts the sword to point at the heavens. "Cut off

the head, and the body will die. Now. All of you, kneel before your rightful king and queen and I will forgive this trespass. This one time. But do it quickly because my patience and my mercy have worn thin."

In the horrible silence, I throw myself down beside Father. Maraya cradles his head in her hands as he just did to her. The royal household, the highborn clan heads, and the disgraced priests kneel before Kalliarkos and Menoë, bowing their heads. But all the other people gathered in the temple—and they are many—stay on their feet.

The Honored Protector pulls off his mask and draws his sword.

"Good Goat! Inarsis! Whom do you pretend to be in this festival mask?" Gargaron demands with a laugh.

"I am the king of Efea," says Inarsis without the slightest flicker of doubt, "and this man was my general, who served me."

Gargaron shakes his head. "After all that Princess Berenise did for you, this is how you repay us? Today will not end well for you, Inarsis."

"I have killed Saroese kings. Don't think I don't know how to kill a lord."

Inarsis is a man who has trained long and hard for victory. After a short, sharp exchange he neatly disarms Gargaron, slapping his sword aside by sheer force. He backhands Gargaron across the face so hard he stumbles, then punches him in the jaw with the hilt of his sword. Forcing the lord to his knees, Inarsis lays the edge of his blade against Gargaron's throat and looks to Mother.

"What is your wish, Honored Custodian?"

Father breathes hoarsely as he fights to stay conscious. His blood leaks over my fingers in steady, sluggish pumps.

I want to scream for Inarsis to stab Gargaron again and again in the gut so he can feel this pain too.

Mother has still not removed her mask. As much as Gargaron has done to me, his offense against her outweighs all else.

In a hoarse voice she says, "Don't kill him. Let the trial proceed. Let the evidence be presented. Then judgment will be passed in the sight of their own gods and their own laws."

Only then does she walk to us and, with a hand pressed to her side like she too has been stabbed, kneel at Father's side.

His eyes track her. His lips shape, "Beloved," but he can't get enough air to speak. He raises a hand to touch her yet hesitates, not sure if she will accept it. Instead he pulls the hand to his chest, fist to heart, in the theatrical gesture of a person heart-stricken by a hopeless love.

She takes off her mask and presses his palm to her cheek.

"Maraya!" I've slammed into the worst of dead ends but a desperate opening winks into view. "Do you have the crow priest's bag? Please tell me you have it."

Of course she understands me instantly.

"Yes, I have it with me. But I don't know if I can.... I only read about the transfer and discussed it with the boy, because he's helped with it twice."

410

"You have to try." My voice is ragged as I fight back sobs. "It's what he would want."

He can hear us. He whispers, "Let me serve, even after death."

"There's no spider."

"There is!" I say. "There is one waiting for him. We just have to get him there before..."

I can't say the word. Instead I look around, the hall a blur of confusing light and movement, so many people ablaze with the spark that is life.

Menoë has collapsed into Kal's arms; she's not weeping and she hasn't fainted but she looks as if the world has given way beneath her, and it has. Kal's gaze snags on mine. I shake my head. He can't help us, not for this.

The curtain of the litter is being held open by an attendant so Princess Berenise can see. She's not looking at me because I was never anything to her except a tool she could use to get Kal to do what she wanted. She's looking at Gargaron.

"Ro! I need Princess Berenise's litter. Now."

Of course Kal's gaze flashes to Ro, then back to me. Of course Ro leaps to obey, paying no attention to Kal.

The princess's attendants refuse to move.

Kal orders, "Let them take the litter."

Only then do the princess's attendants assist her to get out. Firebird soldiers carry the litter to us. I rip down one of the curtains. We slide the cloth under Father and lift him onto the cushioned platform. Even jostled as he is, which must

411

be agony, he makes not one sound, but his hand tightens on Mother's fingers until tears start up from her eyes. She grits her teeth and lets him hold on as she stays by his side.

We walk in procession, leaving as we came, only there are fewer of us now: the baker's youngest son and the woman he loves and two of his daughters, attended by some of the trusted veterans he led in war.

When we reach the Queen's Garden I lead us to the overgrown thicket. The dented spider sits where I left it, dappled by sunlight beneath the foliage. We set down the litter, but Father's hand has gone limp. His whole body is slack. At first I think he's stopped breathing, that he's dead, that it's too late. But then Mother bends close to him, trembling as she brushes her mouth to his as in a kiss.

"He's still alive." She exhales her breath into him, as if her will can make it so. "Do it now, Maraya."

With remarkable composure, Maraya says, "Hold his arms and legs."

I do as she asks but I watch my mother's face as Maraya casts the netting over our dying father, cracks his breastbone, and cuts out his heart. Mother ignores the grisly surgery. She looks only at his face as his eyes flutter open from the shock, and he sees her so close, just as it used to be, and he smiles.

32

Father's spark leaps from the netting into the brass of the sleeping spider. The metal flares as brightly as if the sun has plunged from the heavens to inhabit it, and we all cover our eyes.

The glow fades. When I lower my hand the spider gleams with traces like the ghosts of heat lightning chasing shadows through its metal skin. Maraya's hands are bloody yet she wears a look of peace. She neatly tucks the lifeless heart back into the red gaping wound in Father's chest as she might put away a tool. After she rolls up the net and stuffs it into the bag, her gaze flashes up to meet mine with grief-stricken eyes. It scares me a little that she dared to try it, that she holds a terrifying capability in her hands, but then she smiles her comforting eldest-sister smile and I remember that after all she is Maraya, not a Saroese priest with the power of life and death over the land.

Mother cups her hands around Father's face, now emptied of the spark that fuses the five souls together. His shadow is cut into patches by the heavy vegetation around us. Unbidden and unasked, the soldiers who served with him speak of his deeds, stories I haven't heard, for he never boasted of his exploits. All he is to me is my father, who flew to Efea nourished by air and courage, who fell in love with a girl he met in the market, and who did his best.

When the witnesses fall silent, Mother sits back on her heels and wipes a smear of his blood onto richly embroidered silk.

"This palace curtain will be a fitting shroud, for he let ambition goad him into forgetting those he cherished most and yet in the end he turned aside to walk the righteous path."

"A shroud?" I murmur. "Will he not be interred in a tomb?"

"He fought for Efea, so he will receive an Efean funeral."

When the Saroese soldiers murmur discontentedly she rises to face them. All fall silent before her grief. We roll his body up in the bloody curtain and lay it on the cushions of the litter. Men of his Firebird Guard become his bearers and we his entourage. When I step away to climb up into the spider, Mother catches my arm. Her grasp is harsher than usual as she fights to keep a composed face.

"Please stay beside me, Jessamy. Another can be found."

So another person takes the levers of Father's spider to lead the procession as we head back to the Temple of Justice.

As we come out of the Queen's Garden near the walls of

414

the Lantern District we meet a seething crowd of Saroese who have set up a barrier to close off their residential neighborhood. They fall silent and let us pass, confused by our purpose and intimidated by the clanking spider. The gates of the Lantern District are guarded by Efean soldiers. They stare belligerently at our numbers, and one of their sergeants approaches us.

Even in shock Mother retains her wits. When she pulls on her butterfly mask, the sergeant touches hand to heart and lets us pass.

As we cross the lower slope of the King's Hill back toward the temple, uniformed men wearing the firebird tabard come pelting down in squads from the King's Hill above. They line the street and pound swords against shields in tribute to their commander. More spiders swing in before and behind us as we cross the Avenue of Triumphs, and so the Honored Custodian returns to the Temple of Justice as might any Saroese queen attended by a martial honor guard in a land imperiled by war.

She leans heavily on me as we ascend the steps and enter the temple hall. As strong as she is, without Maraya and me on either side of her holding her up, she would fall.

We move forward down the center aisle. I'm so numb that at first I don't realize Kal keeps looking at me, trying to get a response. I shake my head just once but he must already know by the way Mother can't even stand on her own.

When we reach the Honored Protector, Inarsis indicates that Mother should sit. I help her onto a stool and kneel, leaning against her for fear she may topple over. Yet despite everything she sits with back straight, like the queen she is.

The proceedings do not falter to accommodate our entrance. It is Saroese custom that once a trial begins it must end with a decision.

A Saroese priest finishes reading out loud from the extensive list of evidence that Maraya, Polodos, and their assistants have compiled from various documents.

"Documents may be altered or forged." Gargaron stands at the railing, in the place allotted to the accused.

"For the eleventh time, my lord, you have not been given leave to speak," says the High Priest in the tone of a man who knows his words will be ignored yet again.

"Since I reject your authority, I do not require your permission. As I said, there is no evidence that can be proven to be authentic."

"If I may, Your Holiness," says Maraya to the High Priest, and he nods with relief at seeing she has returned to take over the prosecution. She beckons to a group of men waiting off to one side. "We also bring witnesses. I will start with seventeen servants of Clan Tonor who worked as stevedores and clerks in the Tonor warehouses in the Grain Market."

"These men are criminals!" cries Gargaron the moment Selukon steps forward, a criminal's brand cut starkly onto his face. "Their testimony is thereby tainted, as it is recorded in the twelfth Precept of—"

"Silence!" Mother breaks in. Her body is rigid, her jaw

clenched. "Let the testimony of these witnesses continue without interruption."

"According to the law," Gargaron continues as if she hasn't spoken, "the testimony of a criminal is worth only half that of an unblemished man."

Maraya has an answer to everything. "Unless the criminal in question brings to the court a case that he has been unjustly accused of a crime by a person who intends to profit from the accusation. Garon Palace profited from the death and disgrace of Lord Ottonor and Clan Tonor. Please, Domon Selukon, tell us the story of how you and these other men were illegally arrested and forced into slavery in the mines."

"This is outrageous! For a woman who is also a mule to pretend to conduct herself in the place of an honorable priest—"

"Enough!" Mother braces herself to rise. But I tighten my grip on her and whisper, "Let Maraya handle it."

No spear can pierce Maraya's calm. She already knows she has him. If it were me up there, I would flash him the kiss-off gesture, but that's not Maraya's style.

"Lord Gargaron's protests are his last desperate attempts to obstruct justice, Your Holiness. If we may proceed with the testimony—"

"I protest!" cries Gargaron. "As the head of Garon Palace, my voice must be heard—"

"Cut out his tongue, for he is an ill-wisher in truth," says Mother.

Her words fall like naphtha, seemingly innocent as they first splash over us. Even Gargaron falters and blinks in surprise at the cold ferocity of her tone.

This time when she rises, I sit back. Days ago I chose not to kill him because I knew vengeance was not mine to dole out. I will not get in Mother's way.

"Since he refuses to respect the sanctity of his own laws, cut out his tongue. Then he cannot interrupt but can still communicate if you have questions for him, Your Holiness, because he can write."

Inarsis signals, and six Efean soldiers swarm forward and throw Gargaron down. Kal doesn't move. He doesn't speak, although many of the Garon Palace women shriek. The Saroese lords in attendance burst out in vociferously indignant cries although they dare not try to scuffle. Their voices die when a knife glints in the hand of Inarsis himself.

"Do you want to do it, Kiya?" he asks in Efean.

"My hand is not steady enough today," she murmurs. Her fingers open and close convulsively, and I jump up to put an arm around her as Inarsis himself kneels by the lord pinned to the floor.

Gargaron spits. "This is—! You can't—!"

Soldiers grab his lips and hold his mouth open, and for all he struggles he cannot escape them. Mother's gaze on him does not waver but I have to look away. The agony of others gives me no satisfaction, not even his. Yet his helpless, gargled cries make me wonder if the women fated to become ill-wishers struggled as their tongues were cut out or if they had already accepted the inevitable. If they knew no one would save them. Does Taberta still live, and can we find her and bring her back to a peaceful home where she is respected? And where has Talon gone, for she does not bide among the nobles of Garon Palace? I pray she has escaped to a better life.

When Inarsis sits back with a bloody mass of flesh in his hand, Mother says, "Burn it."

She walks over to stand above Gargaron as he whimpers in pain. I have never seen her expression so pitiless as this.

"So will your lies burn, Lord Gargaron. Had you left my family alone, none of this would have happened. I promise you will have the leisure to consider this irony for a long time."

She steps back to allow the soldiers to haul him up.

"Let the trial proceed."

The Clan Tonor laborers testify, speaking of how they were kidnapped and abused. Gargaron slumps on his knees against the railing, blood dribbling out of his mouth. The highborn stand in terrified silence, even the slightest fearful sob stifled at once by the whispers and nudges of others. They fear us now, as they never did before.

Finally it is time for the testimony of Lord Ottonor himself, a record of how his prosperous clan was cheated and disgraced so Garon Palace could take their holdings for itself. A few nervous giggles erupt as Polodos carries Wenru forward, but every whisper of puzzled amusement vanishes when the baby starts to talk. As a stream of comprehensive knowledge

419

pours from an infant's lips, even the disgraced priests and the heads of noble clans look chastened. The dishonest theft of another clan's wealth is bad enough, but it pales compared to the fact that the former High Priest allowed a pregnant Efean woman to be blasphemously entombed with an oracle. I am not sure whether the Saroese listening are more appalled that Mother was pregnant or that a Commoner was allowed to defile that most holy of Patron sanctuaries, its tombs.

Their consternation makes no difference to me. We have walked Lord Gargaron into the Temple of Justice and implicated him under his own laws. No matter what else happens, he is condemned as a criminal in the court of Seon, the Sun of Justice, and his crimes written into the official record.

When Wenru finishes, the young High Priest rises.

"The punishment for Gargaron's crimes is death, exile, or the mines. So also must the heads of households be judged and sentenced. According to our agreement and in respect of custom, the choice of penalty will be left to the palace."

He looks at Inarsis, thinking this is men's business, but it is Mother who speaks, because that is the Efean way.

"Gargaron will be given the punishment he has earned. As for the others, this is my judgment. For the highborn clans, exile. From each highborn clan the head of household will be given to the Shipwrights. If your clans wish to ransom you, they may apply to the Shipwrights. Additionally from each highborn clan one child of the house will be held as hostage in Efea and raised among our people."

She surveys the men who stand before her, all too cowed to speak.

"For the ordinary Saroese who refuse to live where we now rule, exile. Those who do not fear us are welcome to remain and call themselves Efean. That is my judgment. There now only remains the question of the royal palace and what will become of the surviving members of the royal family."

Ro brings forward a cup of juice and she drinks. All clan heads and Garon women and officials are pushed back, leaving Gargaron and the last three descendants of the first Kliatemnos and Serenissima: Berenise, Menoë, and Kalliarkos alone before the god.

Both women have been given stools to sit on but Kal has remained standing throughout the trial. He's fixed his hands behind his back as at parade rest but there is nothing relaxed or withdrawn about his aspect. He watches everything; he hears every word; he sees all reactions.

Mother turns first to Princess Berenise. "To you, Honored Dame, I offer the respect due to the elderly. To you, I offer exile."

Princess Berenise has the inhospitable eyes of a woman who has survived all the reversals and hairbreadth escapes of the ugliest Fives trial there is. She does not deign to reply but a flicker of cunning animates her haughty face.

"To you, Lady Menoë—"

"I am queen and you may address me as Your Gracious Majesty, although in truth no Commoner ought to be speaking to me at all."

Her words are like flies to be swatted away.

"To you, Lady Menoë, I offer the respect due to a pregnant woman, even though I did not receive such respect myself. To you, I offer exile."

"Does it bother you that I carry his son? The son you could not give him?"

Wenru catches my eye and gives a sour frown.

Mother says nothing.

Her dignified silence goads Menoë on. "My son will return to take back the throne that is rightfully his!"

"Given Esladas's history, I think it more likely you will give birth to a daughter. A precious gift she will be to you, for I cannot find it in me to begrudge any person a safe delivery and a healthy child. I hope you will cherish her as she deserves, because daughters are the life of the land."

"Menoë," says Princess Berenise like the lash of a whip. "Remember who you are."

Menoë releases a long and shuddering breath, trembling as she retreats to her grandmother. Berenise clasps her hand in comfort, and when Kal's gaze flashes to them I see that these two women—the grandmother and the granddaughter—have always shared a connection that he was adjunct to. They love him but not enough to protect him.

"But all this comes upon one condition." Mother faces the only person left who has not received the hammer of judgment. She too has her part to play in my plan. "I have this to say to Lord Kalliarkos. You placed yourself on the throne of

Kliatemnos the First. You accepted the mantle of your ancestors' legacy."

"I did." He stares not at me, not at his family, and not
even at Mother but rather at the massive statue of the god. His
cheeks are pale, and his eyes bear the strain of the choices he
has made, but he does not waver as Mother goes on.

"I have been told that, according to the custom of old Saro,
in times of trouble and wickedness when the gods are angry
and the people wish to repent of their misdeeds, two goats are
brought before Seon, the Sun of Justice. They are examined,
and the blemished goat is sent into exile, into the wilderness,
but the unblemished goat, the good goat, is accepted by the
gods as a worthy sacrifice." She gestures to the statue of Seon,
which illustrates her story.

The Honored Custodian inclines her head, so stern and
somber that I scarcely recognize her as my loving mother at
all. When she looks at me, to make sure I mean her to proceed,
I nod. There is only one way out of these Rings that will give
me the victory I desire most.

"To you, Lord Kalliarkos, I offer the chance to stand in
the place of your people and accept on their behalf the punishment for their crimes. To you I offer death, this one death, to
set the seal on the end of your family's rule."

Before Kal can reply, a commotion stirs within the huddle
of palace women. Lady Adia stumbles forward and throws
herself at Mother's feet.

"I pray you, spare him. Please do not condemn my only

son. He is just a boy. Just a puppet in the hands of his grandmother and uncle. Let the mercy of the blessed Hayiyin stay your hand and commute death to exile. Let him come with us. I promise you he will never set foot in Efea again."

Kal gently raises his mother to her feet. He sets his jaw against the despair of knowing he is the cause of an anguish that will never heal.

He too could get down on his knees and beg for mercy. But he won't. For one thing Kal is no coward. For another he is too proud. For the last, he knows what Ro has passed on to him. The final spin in my intricate plan is that death is the only way for Kal to become free.

So he hands his mother back to attendants, who bundle her away, and he turns to face the judgment of the Efeans. His gaze flicks to mine and away. We can't afford to give anything away, but there is a darkness in his eyes that troubles me. There is a grim resonance to his speech that makes me fear I have read these Rings wrong, that the obstacle I've so carefully negotiated is about to spin out of my control.

"I accept this burden, my death in exchange for the safe passage of my people into exile."

33

Every official procession in the city of Saryenia begins at the King's Hill and descends along the Avenue of Triumphs to the Square of the Moon and the Sun. Our path is no different although everything has changed.

First clank our squad of spiders, their thudding steps and huge metal bodies a barrier to any unexpected attacks. After them marches a cohort of the Lion Guard, tawny ribbons tied to their leather armor and beads adorning their braided and knotted hair. They sing, for our voices announce our arrival, not Saroese trumpets and drums.

We will fight for Efea, and win!

The Efeans who line the avenue join in the song. Here and there Saroese faces peep anxiously over the walls of barricaded compounds but other Saroese stand amid the Efeans as if they have already accepted the change of rulership. For many, of course, the king and queen are merely words that have little to do with the daily round of their lives.

The song fades to silence as the royal carriage rolls into view. Both the king's and the queen's seats are empty. The carriage itself is festooned in the manner of a funeral wagon although the corpse of the royal family who walks behind the carriage is not dead.

It is a measure of the respect Kalliarkos earned in the siege that no one cheers or hisses as he walks. Silence is both the curse and the honor offered to the last of the Saroese kings of Efea. Behind him, hands and feet shackled by silken rope, trudges a single shrouded funeral attendant, who must be prodded forward at intervals by soldiers with spears.

Only after these two have passed do voices rise again into a roar of singing and acclamation as the Honored Protector and Custodian pass, wearing their masks and accompanied by the honored poet. After them walk the officials in their animal masks, the High Priest with a modest retinue, and carriages bearing the dames and elders of the new council.

I walk beside the litter in which lies my father, carried by firebird soldiers, and another litter bearing Maraya, who by now is too exhausted to walk. Tucked at her side, Wenru wears an almost comical frown as he studies the triumphant Efean faces and, with a pursing of his baby lips, examines his own brown arm and considers his change of fortune.

We are followed by the rumbling tramp of many footsteps and the lamentations of the Saroese prisoners, for they too are part of the procession. Escorted by the Firebird Guard, the highborn clans are departing to the West Harbor. But we're not going that way, not yet.

In the center of the Square of the Moon and the Sun stands a great scaffold. Onto this pyre the litter and Father's body are placed, and oil is poured over them. Inarsis lights a torch and Mother places it beside Father's body. We retreat as the flames catch and leap. To my surprise a number of people hurry forward with shroud-wrapped bodies and place them on the pyre before the fire mounts so high that no one can come close. And they begin singing:

You are the breath that sparks life in us, the earth that fashions us, the sun whose rays illuminate us, the water that nourishes us. You are the heart to which we return.

I am beyond tears. I tug on Mother's arm. "What is this? I've heard it before."

"It is the Efean way to release departing souls back into the land to be reshaped and reborn. The Saroese priests banned our custom because they considered it savage and blasphemous, as if entombing women against their will is a badge of civilization."

Her gaze moves inexorably to the forbidding wall of Eternity Temple.

"Are you sure of this, Kiya?" Inarsis asks softly. "Death might be a mercy."

"I find I am not merciful enough to grant death to the man who willfully and maliciously destroyed my family and the lives of so many others."

Our company is fewer in number now. The spiders stand

guard over the pyre while the Lion Guard escorts our group through the now-empty Eternity Temple and into the City of the Dead. How silent the tombs lie, no worshippers bringing offerings of food and flowers, no priests sweeping the walkways. Embers and fragments of burning cloth rain down upon the tombs, blown by the wind. Kal does not look at me or at anyone, only at the royal tomb rising atop the central hill. Even among the dead the Saroese insist that rank be respected.

The royal tomb has been broken open. The oracle and her attendants who were placed inside with Kliatemnos and his innocent son months ago have been released, but a narrow gap remains, enough space to admit a single attendant shrouded with cloth over his head.

The shroud is pulled off and Lord Gargaron finally realizes what his fate is to be.

He twists and turns but cannot escape their grip as guards shove him into the tomb and hold him back with spears. He bawls out sounds like the braying of an animal, but there is no recourse against mortar and brick as the masons close up the gap.

Mother does not once look away. She holds his gaze with hers as she speaks.

"You mistook quiet joy and a calm smile for weakness. This is my answer to you."

I twitch, wanting to gesture the kiss-off sign because I know he is looking and I know he is helpless to look away, but Mother grasps my hand and I let her have her victory. I would have just killed him and been done with it, and I see now that all along I have not understood Mother quite as well as I thought I did.

When the tomb is bricked up, and the last King Kliatemnos given his final attendant, Mother looks at Kal. He nods, face a mask of determination.

I break away, meaning to run to him, but he extends a hand, palm out, to halt me. He holds his head in the posture of the king who, sitting in procession, must be seen as beyond ordinary concerns because he is himself the repository of power, the gods-anointed sovereign who wields life and death.

"Come no closer," he says to me in a cold voice. "This is my journey. Mine alone."

"But Kal—"

"Jessamy. Return to me at once." No one disobeys Mother when she uses that tone, not even me.

She gestures for me to get in the wagon. "This is his journey. None of us, not even you, can walk this path beside him."

At the harbor the prisoners wait in long lines to board ships that will deliver them to one of the ports of old Saro. They have the clothes on their backs and their lives. The Garon household has become but one clan amid many. Stripped of their royal titles they must await their turn.

Mother takes pity and allows Kalliarkos a final farewell with his mother, but when Lady Adia collapses as he breaks out of her embrace for a final time, I am not sure we have shown her a kindness.

"You don't have to do this, Kal," Menoë says. "It doesn't all fall on your shoulders. Beg for mercy."

"No. One of us must stand as the goat who goes in place of the rest. I accept the burden. I never wanted this, and now I will be free of the scheming and fighting you and Grandmother are sure to start up all over again. Let me go."

When Menoë begins to sob I see she does care for him and always has, however strangely she may have shown it.

Only Princess Berenise makes a good-bye without tears, allowing her grandson to kiss her aged hand as if he is a supplicant.

"Come along, Menoë," she says, withdrawing her hand from Kal's fingers and moving them toward the ship on which they'll sail. "We are done here. Tell your mother to stop weeping. She is not too old to have another son, if she marries again soon. As you must, once you are delivered of this child. I have some prospects in mind."

Only when they have embarked does the last Saroese king of Efea make his way to the pier where a separate harbor barge is moored. He's accompanied by eight Efean soldiers to row the barge, and the honored poet. Before Mother or Inarsis can stop me, I jump on too, because there is a darkness in Kal's eyes that terrifies me.

Ro grasps my elbow. "Jessamy, you coming along isn't part of the plan."

I shake him off, turn to Kal, and whisper the words I dare not say aloud lest anyone but the three of us hear.

430

"Ro was supposed to explain it to you. I thought it all through. You said yourself that only death will free you. So you have to be *seen* to die in order to be free to live. That's the plan."

"That's your plan. Our agreement was that I would betray my people, my family, and my own mother for the cause of Efean freedom. Even if it is right to do it, and it is, it's still treachery. Because even now"—he gestures toward the many Saroese lining the railings of ships to watch this final act in the play, in which the anguished lover makes her farewell to the doomed prince—"even now they think I am the noble, unblemished hero who willingly and honorably goes to my death to protect them, when it was I who sold them out."

"I will write a play that will make the tragic tale of King Kalliarkos famous throughout the Three Seas," murmurs Ro so softly I can't tell if he is mocking Kal or praising him.

Kal's gaze rests on Ro for a little too long, his eyes narrowing with a hint of suspicion. Then he shakes his head impatiently, and that's the worst part of all: that he is willing to undergo this not knowing if Ro has kept his side of the bargain between us.

"All these fine words don't matter. I could have fought you, Jes. I could have told my uncle and grandmother the truth. But I didn't. I betrayed all the Saroese people. That is why this burden falls on me."

On the barge lies a barrel, wrapped in chains, with one end open and its lid propped against its side. *A useful custom,*

Gargaron once said when he threatened my sister and me with execution by this means.

We reach the breakwater at the harbor's entrance. Smoke billows up from the direction of Eternity Temple, flames leaping in jagged bursts off the pyre. The first of the ships cast their lines, and their rowers pull them out into the channel past our slow-moving barge. And it's true: the Saroese crowded on the decks call out prayers and blessings upon the king they believe accepted death so they would not be slaughtered.

He stands staring straight ahead.

Ro says, "All those here today will pass this place and remember how the Saroese invasion ended."

Kal looks at me.

I whisper, "Meet me in the ruins of Garon Palace. Do you promise me? Do you?"

With a gesture he cuts me off, as if he can't bear to hear my voice. His sketch of a regretful smile makes my heart break, and then he takes in a deep breath and lets it out. He drops to his knees and crawls into the empty barrel.

Ro hammers on the lid.

I can't move. I can't speak. I can't even cry. I have made my gamble and now I fear I have lost. I thought through every spin of the plan except this one: that Kal has a heart, and his heart is broken.

As we reach the edge of the channel Ro, with a spasm of strength and a grimace, shoves the barrel off the barge. It hits with a massive splash. Weighted with so many chains, it plunges like stone, a shadow sinking away from light and air and life. The ripples smooth out and the wind teases waves over the water until it's as if he were never here at all.

A great shout arises from the ships and the shore. All I can do is stare at the water but of course no head breaks the surface. I cover my face with my hands.

"Turn around," says Ro curtly to the men at the oars. "Move fast."

I can't breathe. I can't think. White ashes from the still-burning pyre drift down over me, stinging my neck and bare arms.

Ro takes hold of my shoulders and shifts me to face the shore. "Jessamy, his fate is out of our hands now."

"He's supposed to kick out the lid. He's supposed to swim to shore."

"That's his choice, not ours. We have a different task. Efea's future is ours to build."

⟨ഇ⟩

When all the highborn Saroese have sailed out of the harbor, a great celebration overtakes the city, except for the barricaded neighborhoods, which are guarded but left untouched. They'll give way in time. Numbers are against them, and in the end, as Mother says, they will leave or they will remain.

I slip away from the festivities and no one stops me.

In the ruins of Garon Palace I make my way through the rubble to the pavilion where Kal once lived. The remains of a small tray of tea and cakes have been disturbed by wind and

433

mice: a trail of crumbs, a leaf floating in the cloudy tea. During the siege did he come here for a moment's peace from the intrigues of the palace? Did he think of me?

I sit on the balcony overlooking the once-beautiful garden all afternoon, and all night, and all the next day, but he never shows up.

34

*J*es. You need to get up."

Amaya is poking and prodding me and I don't have the energy to swat at her.

"You've scarcely moved for ten days. You can't just lie there forever."

"Leave me alone."

She grabs my ankles and hauls me off the narrow bed I have claimed for my own. I hit the ground with a thump that rattles me. Once the ache subsides I decide the floor suits me just fine. I cover my eyes with an arm so I don't have to look at her worried face.

"Jes!"

My silence encourages her to finally leave. It's so blessedly quiet in this tiny servants' storeroom at the heart of the queen's palace. It takes as much effort as I can muster just to breathe in the fragrance of lotus blossoms drifting in from the central garden. I'd rather live anywhere else but Mother says that while the city is still so volatile we girls can't just wander around freely as if nothing has happened, as if we aren't her daughters.

I would laugh at the irony but that would take too much effort.

"I have given up," proclaims Amaya off in the distance, thankfully out of my sight.

"Please, Honored Lady, please tell me that you will take the part of the Benevolent Serenissima when my play opens after things have settled down."

"She's the villain! People will throw rotten fruit at me!"

"Yes. In tribute to your skill. If you can make them hate you, that means they love you. Will you think about it, Honored Lady?"

"Your eyes are so beautiful, Honored Sir. How can I resist?"

"With less sarcasm and eyelash fluttering?"

Amaya laughs. "She's in there. The only reason she eats is that Mother herself, with everything she has to do, personally comes in twice a day to force her to eat a bowl of porridge."

Rude footsteps disturb my peaceful hideaway. By throwing my other arm over my eyes I hope to doubly protect my gaze, but without a word my unwanted intruder hauls me up and carries me out into the terrible bright sun.

"Leave me alone."

"Honored Lady, it is good to see you too. With the

permission of the Honored Custodian, you and I are going to take a trip to the harbor."

I should kick him but I just don't care, and anyway there is a weight like a stone crushing my chest that makes it impossible to struggle.

We move from sun into shade. Slitting open my eyes, I see we have entered a long colonnade that links the central garden to the private living quarters. Workers are busy whitewashing over a long mural that depicts the glorious arrival of the Saroese. They glance curiously at us as we pass, nodding at Ro as if they know him. At the far end of the colonnade, by the doors that lead inside, two women have begun sketching out the features of a new mural to be painted in. The main image depicts the procession of Protector and Custodian and all the officials and professions and clans as they approach the Mother of All, who lives at the heart of Efea. Along the bottom third of the wall a third artist is sketching in the outlines of smaller tales: women building a rudimentary Fives court, an Efean soldier killing a Saroese king on a foreign battlefield, a ship arriving in the harbor with a young man of Saroese features standing at its rail as a newcomer to an old land.

"Ro," I whisper.

He sets me down.

For a while I stand there watching as, against a background of sea and sky, the artist marks in the blossoms and lamps of the night market and a young Efean woman standing beside baskets of persimmons.

My legs feel so heavy. They begin to wilt, and I begin to sag. But when Ro puts an arm around me, ready to pick me up, a burst of energy allows me to shake him off.

"I can walk."

"I'm relieved to hear it since my arms are already aching. You're not small, you know." When I don't answer this pointless attempt at humor, he relents. "This way."

We pass an audience chamber where the Honored Custodian is receiving a delegation from the West Saroese army. Prince General Cissorios and Lord Admiral Dorokos look a little disgruntled, probably because they have to negotiate with a woman when they were expecting a man. Thynos is whispering in their ears, no doubt explaining the proper protocol they must observe if they want the treaty and the grain they so badly need.

I'm relieved Mother is busy; it means I don't have to answer any questions.

I have nothing to say.

Ro guides me through another massive hall. Here clerks are inventorying the contents of the palace, a tedious task ripe for exploitation and theft that I am glad I do not need to concern myself with, although Mother has decided it is vital. Several of the clerks recognize Ro and call greetings to him.

"When will your play open, Honored Poet?"

"Too early to know yet, Honored Lady. The theaters will reopen when the council of dames and elders decides it is fitting."

"Soon, I hope." They let him go and immediately begin whispering among themselves as they glance our way.

"Do you ever get bored of the attention?" I ask as we escape into a courtyard where a delivery wagon awaits us.

"I know that is not a real question, so I won't answer it."

I don't ask for his help but he hoists me up anyway to the driver's bench, and climbs up beside me. Six young men are seated in the back of the wagon with oars, a puzzle that briefly nags at me before I subside into apathy. Since I don't speak to them they don't speak to me, nor do they pretend they are there for an innocent reason as we make our way out the palace gate.

"They're going to open the City Fives Court and the Royal Fives Court too, once things settle down." Ro glances at me.

Since I don't see the point in shrugging I wait for him to go on.

"I thought you might be interested. Some people, including me, have argued we ought to tear down the Fives courts. The game is what the Saroese made out of our holiest beliefs after they buried our temples beneath their gods and their dead. It's an insult. But others argue with equal force that the game is how Efeans kept the Mother's temple alive at the heart of every community. That it is a valued tradition that is part of Efea now. In the end, the council voted to leave things as they are and let the people decide if they want to keep attending the Fives."

I'm grateful that he finally stops speaking because it means he stops looking at me, wondering if I'm going to express an opinion, and I don't have the energy to have opinions. In silence we drive down to the sea.

We come at last to the Square of the Moon and the Sun, which has become an obstacle course made of heaps of stone. People are dismantling Eternity Temple, a task that even to contemplate exhausts me. Already the gate and tunnel have been torn open. We remain in sunlight as we pass from the city of the living onto the peninsula. Activity swarms here too, the beginnings of an excavation that will uncover the ruins beneath.

"It will take years, but that's all right. We don't call it the City of the Dead anymore. We call it 'the buried heart.' Soon light will warm it again." Ro is radiant, all sun and glamour.

"What about Gargaron?" I shade my eyes as I look toward the royal tombs at the top of the hill.

"The Honored Custodian counsels one major decision at a time. For now the agreement is to dismantle the highborn clan tombs but leave the common tombs out of respect for those of Saroese ancestry who intend to stay, and to leave the royal tomb intact as a reminder of the past."

We roll on around the rim of West Harbor to the lighthouse and its dock, where a big harbor rowboat, the kind that may help tow a ship to its berth, is tied up. His friends jump out of the wagon and ready the oars.

I finally understand where he's taking me.

"No."

"Just this one thing and then I will leave you alone unless you yourself request my presence."

"Do you promise?"

"Yes. A poet's promise."

His friends remain mercifully silent as we row into the channel and out just a little more, drifting toward shore. Abruptly Ro pushes me over the gunwale. I hit, go under, and sink into the depths. I could open my mouth and fill up with water. I could let the sea take me and this weight in my chest would go away forever.

But then I'm flailing, desperate to get air. I fight to the surface to see Ro laughing at me and his friends trying not to because they, at least, are decent people.

"What was that for?"

He strips off his vest and dives in, so sleek and assured.

Surfacing, he says, "You have to see this for yourself."

He dives under again, fishtailing down with powerful kicks. I don't want to go but I have to. I see that now. I fill my lungs with air and go under, kicking and stroking hard as I follow him, pressure streaming against my face. The water is a little murky but not too deep away from the dredged channel. There is debris on the seafloor: planks, broken pots, a building stone.

A barrel wrapped in chains.

It's too deep for me to reach but not too deep to let me see that one end has been pried or kicked open, the lid lying on the bottom. A school of fish swims out of the barrel. There's nothing inside.

My lungs are burning. I claw for the surface and barely get my nose above water before my mouth gasps open and I swallow a mouthful of salt water. Retching, I flounder, then spit the worst of the nasty taste out and tread water.

Ro's dark head breaches next to me. Water streams down his face.

"It really was set up so he could kick it open," he says. "Just in case you doubted me."

"But he never came to meet me." I watch his face. "Do you know where he is?"

"Poet's truth, Jessamy. I don't know. I saw him for the last time the same as you. He made me promise not to ask or to interfere. I wondered what he would choose, and I still wonder."

"Why?"

"Because he told me he thought it would be better for you if he died."

"He doesn't get to make that choice on my behalf!"

I swim back to the boat and let his friends help me onboard. The sun overhead blinds me so I have to blink constantly. When we get to shore I refuse a ride. At first I drip with each step like grief leaking from my flesh, but by the time I reach the queen's palace my short keldi and vest have dried. I feel so salt crusted and slimy that I decide to bathe.

As I'm washing, Amaya comes into the bathing courtyard with a folded sheath dress.

"Thank the gods. You really reeked, Jes, even if Mother is too kind to say so. I'm surprised Ro didn't choke. Where is he?"

"I don't know."

She considers this statement and, to my disappointment,

does not make a witty and annoying retort. "The clothing is for you."

After I dress in the soft, clean linen, she sits me in the shade and works through my hair until it is presentable.

"Let's go to the Ribbon Market. It's close by."

"Is it open?"

"Of course it is open. Commerce never ceases."

"Where is Maraya?"

She gives me a look of surprise.

"What was that for?" I demand.

"It's just the first time you've shown interest in anyone in ten days. We'll go see her before the market."

"What about my dirty clothes?"

"You can wash them later."

"I thought you would have an army of laundresses and seamstresses at your beck and call."

"Mother has gotten so particular about how we behave. She's worse than Father ever was...." She gulps, breaks off, and hugs me. We stand unmoving and I am so grateful for her presence. The seawall in my heart is starting to crack.

"It hurts so much," I whisper.

"I know. Just take it one obstacle at a time."

I push her away, wiping my eyes. "When did you start using Fives comparisons?"

"I use the language I must to get through to you. You really scared us, Jes."

She takes my hand and leads me to an airy room crammed

with writing desks. Maraya is seated amid a squad of busy clerks, all copying. The crow boy stands at a table where his birds hop amid scrolls held flat; I think he's practicing reading through their eyes.

When Maraya sees me she gets up and waddles over before I can reach her, and she too crushes me against her or tries to, given her belly.

"Are you ever going to have that baby?"

"I'm glad to see you up and about, Jes." She kisses my cheek.

"We are going to the Ribbon Market," adds Amaya in her chirpiest voice, the one that irritates me most.

"What are you doing here?" I ask Maraya.

"I'm having all the most important documents we took from the Inkos temple copied. Then no one can lose or hide them."

"I thought you would be studying to take the Archives exam."

"Maybe." She leans against me and whispers, "But I'm thinking we must create our own Archives. Think of it. The magic the priests kept hidden is now ours to study and learn. Because I have to wonder how much of it was stolen from what our ancestors already knew."

"If you want it, it's yours to uncover. I think it's horrible."

She sees me hesitate and sets me at arm's length. "What is it?"

"Is there any way... I could see Father's spider?"

She and Amaya exchange frowning glances. "So many scouts left the army that they've had to start with fresh recruits. All the spiders are in training with the army."

I smile sadly. "That's all right. It's where he would have wanted to be."

She gives me a tender sisterly embrace and sends me and Amaya on our way.

Not many customers browse the Ribbon Market although the merchandise of masks and ribbons hasn't changed. Amaya tugs me impatiently along the stairs and aisles, not pausing to shop, for which I am thankful. Even so I am surprised when we halt by a stall and find Denya sitting on a pillow. She is embroidering on silk next to an Efean woman with a vaguely familiar face who embroiders as well, pausing now and again to give Denya pointers.

Amaya gives Denya a kiss, and Denya gives me a shy smile.

"How goes business, Honored Lady?" Amaya asks the Efean woman.

"Not many sales but more people are coming by to look over our product, what with the new year coming up. Denya's work is very good. She's the most adept pupil I've ever had. I thank you for bringing her to me for instruction."

Amaya glows. I wonder if she will take up Ro's offer. She has the gift for the stage, and no one to forbid it as improper for girls like us.

The embroiderer goes on. "I hear at the new year there will be a mask procession down to the harbor, as some say was the tradition in the old days to welcome in the new moon and the rising sun. That will be good for business!" Her gaze flicks to me. A curl of disdain darkens her face, but she smooths it away as she smiles at Amaya again. Then I realize she is the woman who spit to insult me, that day so long ago when Kal followed me to the Ribbon Market to ask me where I trained for the Fives. I guess some things haven't changed.

A weight shifts in my heart.

He isn't dead. He kicked out of the barrel. He chose to live.

"I can manage, knowing that," I say aloud, and Amaya gives me a quizzical look. "He has to find his own way when for all his life he was told what path was ordained for him."

She takes my hand and studies me for the longest time, until I start shifting from foot to foot uncomfortably. "Let's go buy some pancakes," she says. "There's a stall here that sells them wrapped around a paste of chopped almonds, dates, and cinnamon."

"That's the best kind!"

I'm so hungry I eat four and then I feel sick, but it's the most wonderful feeling I've had in days. It's ordinary.

That evening I join the others for a household gathering in the private garden, the one time during the day when Mother can relax. She sits on a couch with Safarenwe in her lap. To my surprise Wenru is there too. He clutches the side of the couch, determined to stand.

"What are you doing here?" I lean over to stick my face next to his.

He gives me a side-eye so monstrously outraged that we girls all laugh, and Safarenwe joins in by clapping her hands.

"I hate you," he whispers in his strange little voice.

"I hate you too," I whisper back, and he gurgles like a little laugh.

446

"Let him be," says Mother in her mildest tone. "We are responsible for him. He's content with his wet nurse, and I've made my peace with his unexpected arrangement of souls."

I settle at Mother's feet as the household trades stories of their day, just as we used to in the old days: calm voices, laughter, affection. Maraya asks Polodos for his opinion of the meaning of an old Saroese word she's never come across before. Amaya reads aloud lines from a comedy Ro-emnu is writing for her.

"It's just a small role to start, only thirty lines as the maid-servant," she says. "I need to get experience before I become the leading actress of the Lantern District."

"That will be your second play," remarks Maraya without looking up from the papyrus she is squinting at in lamplight.

In a low voice, I say, "I'm going to start training at Anise's stable again."

"Of course, Jessamy. That's a lovely idea." Mother can't hide the relief in her tone. "I'll just go with you in the morning to sort everything out. I'm afraid I'll have to insist that you are accompanied by trusted individuals, for a while anyway. They'll stay out of your way."

"Mother!"

But that night, for the first time since Father's death and Kal's staged execution, I sleep through to morning and have no bad dreams.

35

Two months later I run in the first trials of the new year, held in the City Fives Court in front of a packed audience with both the Protector and the Custodian in attendance. I run as Spider, wearing ordinary brown.

The crowd is enlivened by the presence of the first graduating class of new recruits for the Efean army, and they cheer me lustily as I win my Challenger round.

I wave my victor's ribbon from the tower, reflecting that I need to up my game. Adversary training has been disrupted by the war, the siege, the number of Challengers and Illustrious who have left the country or joined the army, and people's need to work at regular jobs because there is less money to be won. But once things settle into their usual routine the competition will ramp up again.

I have to be ready.

In the undercourt there's no royal nectar on offer. Instead we are given hibiscus juice because it is in season. I'm so thirsty I drink two cups. The adversaries I defeated linger, and when I nod at them, they invite me to join them in the Lantern District that evening for a drink.

I consider sneaking out but instead I tell Mother that I'm going, and I accept an escort of two guards dressed like regular people even though no one will be fooled. The Lantern District is alive with a festive crowd. It doesn't look so much different from before except that there are a lot fewer people of Saroese ancestry. The ones who haven't left seem just as happy to get drunk and celebrate as they ever did. There are new soldiers too, with their shaved short hair and the way they trawl in groups of four and six.

"Hey! Spider!" My old friends Gira and Shorty charge out of a tavern catering to adversaries and drag me in to hoots and cheers of welcome. "Look what we found!"

"Spider! Spider!" The tavern-goers bang fists and cups on the table until my ears hurt.

About ten drinks appear at our table.

"How drunk do you want to get?" Gira chortles.

I slide drinks to my guards, who politely take them aside and sit where they can keep an eye on me without having to listen to every word we say. Gira and Shorty kindly do not mention them.

"Where's Mis?" Gira asks.

"She went into the army."

"No, really?"

"Really. Where are you two training now?"

"Up at the old Royal Stable. It's been renamed Southwind Stable, and Lord Thynos—"

Shorty elbows her. "It's just 'honored sir' now. We don't have to use those titles anymore."

"Anyway, he's decided to become head trainer of his own stable. Said he was feeling too old to compete. Shorty is apprenticing with him as a trainer. You know, we could use a strong Challenger like you, Jes. That was a good run today."

"Your right wrist is weak, though," says Shorty. "Did you injure it?"

Before I can answer, a commotion stirs at the tavern gate. Cursed if the poet doesn't make an entrance as onto a stage, flanked by admiring girls and stalwart companions. He's wearing a formal keldi that reaches his ankles but spoils the elegant effect by letting his vest gape open.

"A song!" people cry. "Give us a song, Honored Poet!"

He jumps up on top of a table and strikes a pose. His gaze arrows to me and he grins, knowing I know he must have seen me and followed me in here. I slap a hand over my face as he begins singing "The General's Valiant Daughter." The whole tavern joins in on the chorus. But I'm an adversary. Reputation is one of the Trees I must climb.

So I stand and I wait it out, and when he finishes I open my arms with a flourish, a spider casting thread to the winds, and accept their acclamation. If I'm honest with myself, I have to admit that I like it.

After the clamor dies down he comes over and, in the proper way, waits for me to greet him.

"How's the play coming?"

"Which one? I'm a busy man, very productive."

"The comedy for Amaya."

He leans closer, lips a breath away from my ear. "I could write a play for you, Jessamy. One we can rehearse in private."

I shouldn't, but I laugh anyway. "Your persistence is extraordinary, and it's even growing on me. But I'm not…" The words I mean to say won't come out.

"You're not ready?" he finishes for me with a wry smile.

For weeks now I've allowed training to carry me from one day into the next. The Fives gives me focus. It keeps me moving. But it also means I don't have to stop and examine my own heart.

I let out a sharp breath. "I haven't let go of him yet, Ro. That's my truth."

"I'll buy you a drink anyway."

"Actually, you and your friends can help me with these. I'm quite popular, you know."

As he is waving his entourage over, I spot a face I recognize at the gate.

"I'll be back," I say over my shoulder as I weave through the crowd rather more slowly than I intend because people keep gesturing the kiss-off sign and I have to respond in kind. But I finally get close enough to call.

"Dusty!"

He turns. "Jes! I was looking for you. Word on the street said a spider came in here."

I hug him as I would a cousin and step back to examine his clothes. Instead of the usual keldi and vest he's wearing linen trousers and a jacket cut in a soldier's style. The scuff marks on the fabric have a familiar pattern. "Where have you been? By the wear on your clothes it looks like you've been training in a spider."

"I have. Mis sent me to find you."

"How is she?"

"No longer a temporary sergeant. She's been officially commissioned as a sergeant in the spider scouts."

"That doesn't surprise me. You're serving as a scout as well?"

"You mean even missing one eye and half-deaf in one ear? We lost almost all of the Saroese spider scouts. However many recruits signed up for training in the regular army, they didn't get so many volunteers for the desert posting. I'm doing all right. Will you come?"

I take my leave of Gira, Shorty, and Ro and his admirers, and I can't help but notice how the young women effusively claim to be devastated that I'm leaving. I flash him the kiss-off sign as I go, and he blows me a kiss back.

Dusty has a brisk walk and a way of turning his head to catch sounds on his impaired side.

"You look good, Dusty. Tell me about training."

It's a long walk across town to the East Gate. My two guards keep well back, and I'm not sure Dusty even notices them. He regales me with stories of rising at dawn and drilling

452

all day and dropping exhausted onto a cot at dusk, for two months without a break. Of how half the recruits dropped out or transferred because they couldn't get the hang of the spiders or found the eerie presence of the spark too disturbing.

"We finished up with a ten-day march, got assigned into squads and our sergeants commissioned, and now we are headed out because if any place needs guarding it's the Eastern Reaches and the desert crossing."

"You sound content, Dusty."

"I thought I was going to die when I was captured at Crags Fort. I wanted to die after what they did to me. But now I am a soldier in Efea's army, and they're dead or crawled home in defeat. So I can live with that for now. Here we are."

I thought maybe we were going all the way to the army camps outside town, but then I remember they were trashed by the enemy during the siege. Instead he shows me into a run-down boardinghouse of the kind common in this cheap part of town. This is the kind of place where Father first lived when he arrived in Saryenia as a young man.

Despite the late hour people are bustling around, stuffing gear into canvas bags and polishing short swords and oiling harnesses. They're a mix of men and women, mostly Efean but with a few Saroese and a random foreigner sprinkled among them. It's so odd to see soldiers walking around so casually who look so much like me. It might take me a while to get used to it but I like the thought that I will.

"Jes! Just in time." Mis strides up.

I thump her as hard as I can on the shoulder. "Excuse me, Sergeant. I'm sorry I'm late, Sergeant. Whatever did you do to deserve this, Sergeant?"

"Performed too well, so I'm told. It's my adversary reflexes." She grins. "They had to elevate a few people to official command ranks, even me."

"You're not nearly bossy enough yet. I could get you lessons with Maraya."

"We're being posted to the desert forts for six months, so I'm sure I'll get better at it. But listen, Jes..." She scratches her forehead and gets a funny look on her face, like I've caught a disease and no one has had the courage to tell me yet. "I didn't mean to be party to keeping this from you, but—"

That's when I see Father's spider, with its distinctive dent. It's drawn up in proper resting configuration beside a gate that opens onto an inner courtyard where more spiders squat in the shadows. Traceries of light flash and fade on the brass surfaces like hope and pain. So much anger floods me that I start shaking.

"So that's why my family has all been so cagey when I ask about the spiders. They made it seem like you were already gone off to the desert. They didn't want me to know the new scouts were training right here. They hid it from me!"

That's when I see him.

He's standing in the deeper shadow cast by the looming spider, and his back is to me, but of course I would recognize those shoulders anywhere.

Someone calls, "Sergeant Kallos!"

He turns into the illumination of the courtyard lamps.

My legs give out. It happens so fast Mis and Dusty can't catch me, and I don't even feel the transition. First I'm standing. Then I'm sitting on the ground and my tailbone is throbbing and someone's strong arm is pulling me up.

"Jes?"

I open my mouth. Close it. Words flee like shadows at midday.

"You fainted."

I touch his face. He's real. The same lips. The same eyes except for bruising around the right. He studies me with the familiar wrinkle of concern on his brow.

"I thought you were going to yell at me," he adds.

"I will. I just need to catch my breath."

He helps me up. Mis opens a door into a cramped barracks room where a couple of Efean soldiers are stretched out on their cots. They look up as we come in.

"You need us to leave, Sergeant?" says one with a laugh, then subsides as the other kicks him.

I think Kal is going to let me sit on one of the cots but he's headed for an inner room that's slightly wider than its narrow bed, with just enough extra space to stow a storage chest at one end. In this bare closet I sink onto the bed while he lights a lamp. My souls are so jumbled that I can't make sense of what I'm seeing.

"Not the reunion I was imagining," he says, gesturing to the mudbrick walls and the mudbrick floor and the curtain for a door. There's not even a side table with a basin and pitcher for washing. They must all wash together, in the trough outside.

He's wearing a keldi and vest. His kit is packed away except for his spider scout gear, folded neatly on the bed. They're marching out in the morning.

"You don't have to do this," I say.

He folds his hands behind his back at parade rest, feet braced apart. "I do have to do this. I was never trained to do anything else. I have to earn my own way now."

"How is it you've already made sergeant, then?"

His grin peeps out. He's honestly embarrassed. "I couldn't disguise that I had experience as a spider scout and as a commander."

"Don't they know who you really are?"

"Kallos is a good name to hide behind, as Ro taught me. The truth is so unbelievable it's easier for people to accept the lie. It's helped that Mis and Dusty have had my back since the first day, said they knew me when we were fledglings training together."

"Someone punched you. Have you been fighting? Usually you have the knack of settling fights before they start."

"In the first week of training I got into a few fights to prove I have the right to be here, because I'm Saroese. Sometimes a fistfight is the only way to settle things."

I study him. Like the sea-phoenix, he rose as if out of his own ashes from the waters, but I wonder how much of the boy I love was burned away and how much remains. "That bruise on your face is recent. Is that from a training accident or are you still having to prove you belong here?"

He looks away, deciding whether to keep something from me.

"You'd better tell me, or I'm going to give you a second black eye."

"This fight was different. It was over my spider."

"Your spider?"

"One of the recruits insulted the memory of General Esladas."

I press a hand to my chest, feeling my heart pound. "You have my father's spider, don't you?"

"If that seems strange to you, so be it, but I just feel it helps me be a better soldier."

At first I'm too choked to speak as I realize that I'm here with Father's spider at last. "Can I ... can we ... ?"

"Of course."

He picks up the lamp and, as if it is the most ordinary act in the world, takes my hand. It is so remarkably easy and comfortable to walk beside him back out through the barracks and the courtyard to the gate. In the inner courtyard spiders sit motionless and inert but for the restless lightning that gives them a form of life.

I'm drawn to Father's spider as to his presence, even though it is a creature of brass and courage and not a man. I rest my forehead against the curve of its metal carapace and imagine I feel his ambitious heart and his solid strength that he passed on to me.

"I miss you," I whisper. Out of the depths of its spark-lit

metal I think I hear his voice as down a vast distance, and even though it can never be a substitute for him, I know he will always be with me in my five souls. That has to be good enough.

I wipe my eyes and look at Kal. He's watching me with a wary expression, poised like he will retreat if he must but is otherwise determined to stick it out.

"So you chose to live." It comes out more harshly than I intend.

His gaze dips to the ground, then comes back to me. "No. I chose to die. I was too exhausted to fight. I wanted to be the good goat in truth, because I betrayed them. I think I did die. That's what betrayal is, isn't it? A kind of death."

"Kal!" I take a step toward him but he raises a hand to forestall me.

"Let me tell it. I wanted to have the courage to die, so I kicked out the lid and let the water rush in. I drowned. It was so peaceful just to give in to how much I hated myself."

I shut my eyes because it's so distressing to hear him speak calmly of what I feared most. His hand touches mine and I clutch it like I can drag him out of drowning in despair, out of death, out of the end of the world he knew.

He says, "I think I died. But I wasn't dead. I can't explain it, but it's as if I was given a second chance at life."

At first I just hold on to him because I don't know what to say to him or how to describe the churning confusion inside me: a bone-deep relief that he's alive and an embarrassing amount of anger that he made the choice to die when he knew

I was waiting for him. I have to let that go, to let him be who he is…and even as I think it, a months-old memory wells up.

"I can explain it," I say, my voice rough with all the emotion I'm trying to hold in. "Do you remember that day in the desert when you were commanding the spider scouts, when you were knocked to the ground by an enemy soldier? Everyone thought you'd been killed."

"Yes." His gaze grows distant. "It's when I saw you again for the first time. I thought I was dreaming that you'd kissed me."

"I did kiss you, in a manner of speaking. You weren't breathing, so I breathed air back into you. It's something my mother taught us girls. But the crow priest thought you were dead so he poured the spark of the dying enemy into you too. Which means you've had a second spark all this time."

"That would explain it." He presses a hand against his spider, like he's listening to a whisper of a voice, then flashes a wry grin. "But I guess that means I'm back to just one spark now."

"How can you joke about it? And why *didn't* you meet me at Garon Palace afterward? Why did you let me wonder for all this time? I was so miserable. First my father died and then you, and I didn't see any reason to ever get out of my bed again."

He removes his hand from the spider and rests it against my cheek. We stare at each other as he considers his words.

"You rescued me when I thought I couldn't fight, you forced me to look at what I didn't want to see, and I cherish you for it. But I had to do this on my own terms, with no expectation of success or reward. I have to make my own way, when for all my life the path was smoothed for me. In the desert I'll have no one to rely on but myself and my comrades."

I clasp his hand in mine. "Is this what you truly want? To be a soldier?"

"For always? I don't know. It's what I can do right now. Meanwhile you'll keep climbing the Fives ladder until it kills you, or you'll get so injured that you can't continue, or you won't reach as far as you hope, or you'll retire in glory as an Illustrious. I don't know. When one of those things happens you'll have to decide what comes next, and that will be your desert to walk when you get there. I guess what I'm asking is, do you think you might want to be here when I get back?"

When I get back.

I'm not sure I've ever heard a sweeter promise.

"Yes! I have no idea why you would think otherwise!"

He exhales in relief, and his gaze sharpens intensely as he leans forward. "I'm counting on parading around the Lantern District with you when I'm on leave, and having all of Saryenia be jealous that you chose a humble spider scout to wear your victor's ribbons."

"Are you?"

"Oh, I am."

"Well, then." I put my arms around him, but just before our lips touch I stiffen.

"Jes?"

"I can't do it, Kal. I can't kiss you right here next to my father's spider."

He laughs, and it's like a fragment of the shadow of the old, genial, carefree Kal has found its way back to him. Tucking an arm tightly around me, he draws me toward the gate.

"If we're very quiet, I have that tiny little room where we can be alone." To my surprise he switches to speaking in Efean with a heavy Saroese accent. "Is that good enough for you, Honored Lady?"

I bump my shoulder against his. "I guess I'll have to let you know afterward."

⌒⫙⫙⫙⊘

At dawn I stand at the gate as the spiders clank out on the first stage of a long journey to their desert posting. To watch them go feels familiar in so many bittersweet ways. Their discipline of march is no different from memories of my father's time in the spider scouts except these soldiers call out to one another in Efean instead of Saroese.

Six months is a long time to be apart, I reflect as I walk back to the palace amid the early-morning traffic of wagons heaped with baskets of produce, cut flowers, and fish still glistening from the water. The promise of reunion makes it bearable.

My escorts are rubbing their eyes and stretching.

"I feel I should apologize to you for having to stand guard all night outside the boardinghouse." My face heats as I speak, thinking of how narrow Kal's bed was and how it didn't matter, but it seems rude to ignore the situation.

They laugh. They're both older men, the age of Inarsis,

and probably they served with him back in the day. "Never apologize for that, Honored Niece. We all deserve joy."

When we reach the palace, they're dismissed to get much-needed rest.

I am delighted to discover Inarsis and Mother in an early-morning conference over hot bread and cool hibiscus juice in Mother's private garden. As I approach, Safarenwe toddles over to me with arms outstretched and a smile on her face, tipping toward a fall just as I catch her and swing her into my arms. Her chortling laughter brightens the world. Wenru is seated on a mat where he is reading in the most unbabylike way imaginable. He glances up, sees me, sighs as if he hoped to see someone better, and goes back to his book.

I pause at a polite distance, not wanting to interrupt them without permission, but Mother waves me forward. She wears a sling at her side in which Maraya and Polodos's adorable tiny newborn child sleeps, her first grandchild, the next link in the chain that pulls us ever onward down the river of life.

"How surprising to find you here, Honored Protector," I say, settling Safarenwe comfortably on my hip. "This couldn't have anything to do with where I spent last night, could it?"

They look at each other, sharing a thought, and I wonder how I could ever have thought there was anything romantic between them. Their bond reminds me of the one I have with my sisters, with Mis, with other adversaries: the solidarity of people with the same obstacles to face down.

I don't attempt to hide my anger. "You both knew where he was, and you didn't tell me."

Safarenwe frowns, lower lip trembling.

"Don't frighten your sister." Mother offers me a cup of juice and a place beside her on her couch. As I sit, shifting Safarenwe to my lap, Mother goes on. "Kalliarkos turned his back on things most people would not have the courage, strength, or will to let go of. For one thing, we weren't sure he could manage it. For another, he had to make a place under the same conditions everyone else did, so we respected his request that he be left to manage it alone."

"Except for Mis and Dusty. Did you arrange with them to join the scouts so they could keep an eye on him?"

"No, but it worked out well to have them there," says Inarsis. "By the way, I have a proposition for you, Spider."

"It wouldn't have anything to do with this new stable being set up, would it? Run by Thynos?"

"It's nothing to do with me, of course," says Inarsis, and Mother snorts indelicately. He smiles wryly. "With all the palace and clan stables dissolved, people will be forming up new consortiums. Thynos intends to be among the most competitive and lucrative."

"My thanks, Honored Protector. But I already have a stable I call home."

After I've eaten I change into my Fives gear and walk back across town, to the Warrens. The path to Scorpion Fountain is so familiar that my feet walk themselves there as I daydream about Kal. The moment I come in the gate Anise spots me.

"There you are, Spider. I thought you might be late after too much celebrating last night. You missed the morning menageries. Don't do it again."

"Yes, Honored Lady. I won't." Not for the next six months, anyway.

"As it happens, after yesterday's trials we have a flock of new fledglings eager to test their wings. Since you need to warm up anyway, you can lead them in their first menageries. Afterward I'll push you through some strengthening exercises. Your Trees was awful yesterday. You only won because the competition wasn't up to standard."

"Yes, Honored Lady." But I feel good. Anise is gentle only with the ones she doesn't think will amount to much.

I saunter out onto the exercise yard and place myself in front of the fledglings, none of whom can stand at attention, much less in proper columns and rows. There are a few young people of Saroese ancestry including, to my amazement, a girl, since before now Saroese women have never been allowed by their families to compete. She's fidgeting with anxious expectation beside a bored-looking youth, who I'm guessing is a brother she strong-armed into accompanying her.

"You're Spider," says a brawny young Efean woman at the front, trying not to grin with excitement. "They say you're going to become an Illustrious."

"That's right. I am."

Their eyes open wide.

"One of you might too. If you want it, if you work hard enough. There's no secret to winning. Act boldly when you need to, and be cautious when you must."

I gesture toward the Fives court, which is the land of Efea, the temple of the Mother of All. Yet it is also simply a Fives court, a creation grown from the circumstances in which we have lived. With a smile I turn back to them, who are all squirming with enthusiasm for this new endeavor they've undertaken, not knowing where it will lead or how it will end. I flash them the kiss-off sign, and they practically jump out of their skins with eagerness to go, to try, to succeed.

"Above all else, do not fear to climb the victory tower."

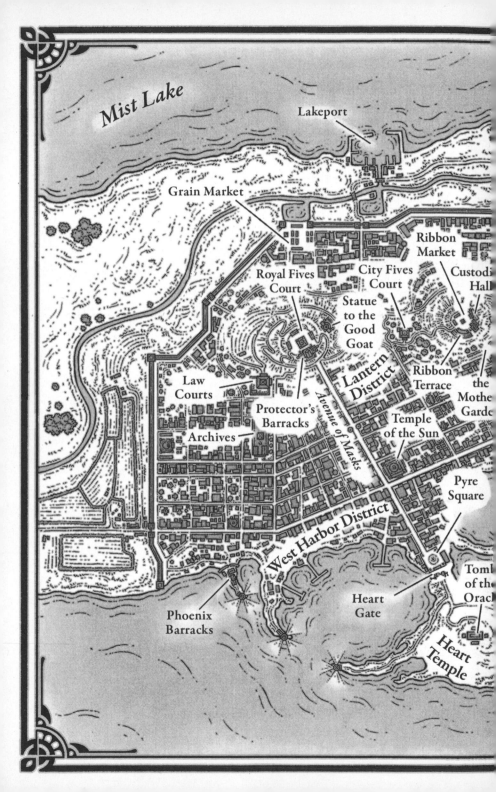

Warrens

Scorpion
Fountain

House of
Wenru

Avenue of the Soldier

East Harbor District

Temple of
the Sea

Saryenwe
on the Sea

Fire Sea

ACKNOWLEDGMENTS

Special thanks to Aliette de Bodard for pulling me back from the brink. As always I am unutterably grateful for my ace crop of beta readers: Nafiza Azad, Andrea Chandler, Justina Ireland, Malinda Lo, and Dani McKenzie. My journey into YA began with early encouragement from Matt de la Peña, Gene Yuen Lang, and Faye Bi, who told me I could and should try writing a YA novel.

The fantastic team at Little, Brown Books for Young Readers has guided me through this, my first YA trilogy, with expertise, patience, and professionalism: Kheryn Callender, Jenny Choy, Saraceia Fennell, Elisabeth Ferrari, Karina Granda, Allegra Green, Jane Lee, Annie McDonnell, Liza Patinkin, Jessica Shoffel, Erika Schwartz, Victoria Stapleton, and Danielle Yadao. Many other people at LBYR worked on the books without directly interacting with me, and I want to offer an extra thanks to them. Finally, warmest thanks to the most excellent Andrea Spooner, who took a chance on me because she believed I could figure out how to write YA, and to my entirely fabulous editor Deirdre Jones, who has been through every line of this trilogy possibly more times than I have—and believe me, I've been through it many, many, many times as she cracked that whip and kept us all on schedule.

For more information on *Buried Heart* and the Fives or Kate's other series, or to sign up for her newsletter, the author invites you to visit her website at KateElliott.com or her Facebook page, or you can follow her on Twitter @KateElliottSFF.